Praise for
ELIZABETH PETERS

"This author never fails to entertain."
Cleveland Plain Dealer

"No one is better at juggling torches while
dancing on a high wire than Elizabeth Peters."
Chicago Tribune

"If bestsellerdom were based on merit and
displayed ability, Elizabeth Peters would
be one of the most popular and famous
adventure authors in America."
Baltimore Sun

"Peters's many fans can count on her
for romantic mysteries full of
action and suspense."
Publishers Weekly

"[Peters] keeps the reader
coming back for more."
San Francisco Chronicle

Books by Elizabeth Peters

HE SHALL THUNDER IN THE SKY
THE FALCON AT THE PORTAL
THE APE WHO GUARDS THE BALANCE
SEEING A LARGE CAT • THE HIPPOPOTAMUS POOL
NIGHT TRAIN TO MEMPHIS
THE SNAKE, THE CROCODILE AND THE DOG
THE LAST CAMEL DIED AT NOON
NAKED ONCE MORE • THE DEEDS OF THE DISTURBER
TROJAN GOLD • LION IN THE VALLEY
THE MUMMY CASE • DIE FOR LOVE
SILHOUETTE IN SCARLET
THE COPENHAGEN CONNECTION
THE CURSE OF THE PHARAOHS
THE LOVE TALKER • SUMMER OF THE DRAGON
STREET OF THE FIVE MOONS
DEVIL MAY CARE • LEGEND IN GREEN VELVET
CROCODILE ON THE SANDBANK
THE MURDERS OF RICHARD III
BORROWER OF THE NIGHT • THE SEVENTH SINNER
THE NIGHT OF FOUR HUNDRED RABBITS
THE DEAD SEA CIPHER • THE CAMELOT CAPER
THE JACKAL'S HEAD

And in Hardcover

LORD OF THE SILENT

ELIZABETH PETERS

Die for Love

AVON BOOKS

An Imprint of HarperCollinsPublishers

This is a work of fiction. Names, characters, places, and incidents are products of the author's imagination or are used fictitiously and are not to be construed as real. Any resemblance to actual events, locales, organizations, or persons, living or dead, is entirely coincidental.

AVON BOOKS
An Imprint of HarperCollins*Publishers*
10 East 53rd Street
New York, New York 10022-5299

First Avon Books paperback printing: January 2002

Avon Trademark Reg. U.S. Pat. Off. and in Other Countries, Marca Registrada, Hecho en U.S.A.
HarperCollins ® is a registered trademark of HarperCollins Publishers Inc.

Printed in the U.S.A.

10 9 8 7 6 5 4 3 2 1

To Louise and Jim
and their four-footed friends

Chapter 1

"When Blaze awoke she found herself lying on a silken soft surface amid the seductive scent of strange perfumes. A cool night breeze—the air of the desert, exotic and amorous—stroked her naked flesh. Naked? A soft cry escaped her voluptuous lips as she realized the truth. Where were her clothes? What unknown hands had stripped them from her helpless body? Where was she?

"Lamps carved of alabaster gave enough light to answer the last question. Overhead a silken canopy shielded her from the night sky, a patch of which, glittering with stars, was visible through the open flap of the tent. Scarcely had she realized this when the stars were blotted out by a dark form. Stooping, he entered the tent, and Blaze's white hands fluttered, trying in vain to conceal her softness. It was the Arab who had stared at her so boldly in the bazaar. Intense blue eyes studied her over the folds of the kaffiyeh that hid the lower part of his face. 'You are no Arab,' Blaze gasped. 'I know those eyes—you are—you are—'

1

" 'Your husband.' The kaffiyeh fell away; it was indeed the face of Lance, Earl of Deptford, his chiseled lips curved in a mocking smile. 'Come to claim the rights you have so long denied me, my love. The disguise disturbs you? Off with it, then.' And he flung the robe aside.

"Blaze's eyes moved from the bronzed chest, seamed with the white scars of a hundred duels, to the narrow waist and flat, muscled abdomen, down to . . ."

Jacqueline's eyes bulged. "My God," she said aloud. "It's *The Lusful Turk*."

"It is?"

Jacqueline looked up from the pages of *Slave of Lust*. The stewardess stood beside her, trying to read over her shoulder. Obligingly she held the book up so the girl could see better.

The young woman's eyes lit up. "It's the new Valerie Vanderbilt! I haven't read that one yet. But I just love her books, don't you?"

Jacqueline inspected the cover of the paperback. Blaze ("the streak of silver in the midnight blackness of her flowing locks had given her her name") reclined on silken coverlets, her softness discreetly veiled by the broad bronzed body of the Earl of Deptford. The title and the name of the author were printed in brilliant scarlet letters.

"Valerie Vanderbilt," Jacqueline repeated. "I must admit this is the first of her books I have read."

"She's divine." The stewardess sighed voluptuously. "They say she's really a countess or something, but she doesn't use her title because her noble family has disowned her on account of she's had so many love affairs. This one is about a Turk?"

"You misunderstood my reference," said Jacqueline. She glanced at the cart, with its rows of bottles and glasses, whose progress along the aisle of the plane had been interrupted by the stewardess's literary interests. "Are you by any chance selling drinks? I'll have Scotch. No. I'll have a double."

It was an unseemly hour for alcohol—barely eight A.M.—but as the airlines had learned to their profit, some passengers resorted to liquor in an effort to dull their fear of flying. Jacqueline was not afraid of flying. What she wanted to dull were her critical faculties.

Her reminder of duties unfulfilled was reinforced by a chorus of requests from nervous customers nearby. Murmuring an apology, the attendant filled Jacqueline's order. When she gave Jacqueline the glass, a pair of miniature bottles, and a small package of petrified peanuts, Jacqueline said, "You can have this when I'm finished, if you like."

"Really? Oh, that's really nice! But you won't finish it before we get to New York."

"Oh yes, I will."

"Well, that is really nice of you. Books are so expensive. I read four or five of them a week, and that really adds up, even though my friends and I exchange when we—"

A wild-eyed businessman in the seat ahead leaned out into the aisle, waving a five-dollar bill and babbling incoherently.

"Yes, sir, right away." With a smile at Jacqueline, the girl moved on.

Jacqueline refreshed herself copiously but decided she still wasn't prepared to return to the perfumed canopied tent. I should have ordered three drinks, she thought. At least I can be sure of getting the attendant's services from now on. Four or five of these books a week? If all the examples of the genre resembled *Slave of Lust,* it was a wonder the hard-core readers could talk at all, much less frame a coherent English sentence.

She turned her gaze to the window. There was nothing to be seen except an undulating blanket of gray cloud. It had been raining when she left Nebraska. It had rained in Nebraska every day for the past two weeks. The farmers were tearing their hair and the local papers carried dire predictions of crop failures— rotting corn, mildewed hay—higher prices, and general despair. Jacqueline had lived in Nebraska for three years, and in her experience the farmers were always complaining and food prices were always going up. It was either too hot or too cold, too wet or too dry. She had no great opinion of Nebraska or the agricultural community, and in this particular spring she had had far too much rain to suit her. It was one of the factors that had prompted her passionate outcry the previous Sunday, as she stood at the window of her apartment watching raindrops pelt the puddles on the balcony.

"I've got to get out of this backwater before I lose my mind!"

"Backwater is not inappropriate," her friend replied, putting his stockinged feet on a hassock and reaching for his glass.

"Where do you want to go?"

"A city." Jacqueline gestured dramatically at the window. Beyond the red brick college buildings, empty fields stretched endlessly to the horizon. "Any city. Preferably one where it isn't raining."

"Cairo would seem to be your best bet. Or Rome."

"I can't afford to go to Europe."

Her companion, Professor James Whittier, head of the English Department at Coldwater College, watched her with a faintly malicious smile. Her tall, upright figure was as slim as that of a woman half her age—not that James had ever been officially informed of that number, but since she had two adult children he knew she must be over forty. Her thick auburn hair had not a touch of gray, and James, who was well acquainted with Jacqueline's hair and with the products women use to conceal that particular sign of aging, would have sworn she employed none of them. She was wearing a hostess gown in glowing peacock colors, green shading to aquamarine, azure and cobalt, with which he was equally well acquainted, and the relative age of this garment, coupled with her last statement, roused his curiosity.

"I thought you were going abroad this summer."

"So did I."

"What happened?"

Jacqueline swung around to face him and glowered at him over the tops of her glasses. The fact that she made no effort to restore them to their proper place on the bridge of her nose was a bad sign. Jacqueline's glasses were a barometer of her feelings. Slippage indicated strong emotion, often of a negative variety.

"None of your business, James. You're the nosiest

man I've ever met! Do you know what your students call you?"

"I know what the female students call me," James said, passing a complacent hand over his waving white locks and smiling his famous crooked smile.

"Don't waste that crooked smile on me," Jacqueline snapped. "Mr. Buttinsky. . . . No, I think my favorite is Granny Jimmy."

"Granny, is it? Come here and let me show you—"

"I'm not in the mood."

"Hmmm." James decided this was not the time to remind Jacqueline of the nicknames the students had invented for her. She thought of herself as a detached, ironic observer of life. The fact was that she was just as inquisitive as James and even more inclined to interfere in other people's business, when she felt her advice and assistance would improve matters—and she almost always felt they would. However, she believed wholeheartedly in her self-image and would have been outraged at any suggestion that it was inaccurate.

It would also be inadvisable, James knew, to ask any more questions about Jacqueline's change of plan for the summer. She must have had financial reverses. He wouldn't get anything out of her; she was maddeningly tight-lipped about her personal affairs. Almost unfeminine, James thought resentfully. He'd have to find out some other way.

"We could go to New Orleans for a few days," he suggested. "Or San Francisco."

"It always rains in San Francisco. I'm going to New York."

"I?"

"I."

"So it's come to this," James mourned. "The first crack in the wall of love. The first wilted flower in the bouquet. The first . . ."

Additional metaphors failed him. He picked up his glass and drank.

Jacqueline sat down in the chair opposite his, nudged his feet off the hassock, and put her own in their place. "The first sour grape in the fruit salad of togetherness."

James knew he was not the first man in Jacqueline's life; he wasn't even sure he was the only man in her life. Their affair had been conducted with the discretion demanded by the university, whose midwestern trustees still had a pathetic faith in the traditions of a vanished era. Ostensibly he and Jacqueline were co-authoring a textbook. The briefcase James carried whenever he went to her apartment brought nudges and knowing grins from his colleagues and pointed comments from the students, who were less inhibited. But those who laughed would have been surprised to learn that the briefcase actually contained three chapters of a textbook. Sometimes he and Jacqueline even worked on it.

Yet the relationship had gotten into a rut, and James knew it. He sat in the same chair he had occupied for the past fourteen Sundays, in stocking feet and shirt sleeves, with the Sunday papers strewn around and the breakfast dishes still on the table. Presently they would wash the dishes, and then go out to dinner at the Old Redde Barn. All the pleasures of marriage without the attendant inconveniences. James liked the arrangement. Apparently Jacqueline didn't.

She began sorting through a stack of clippings and papers. "I'm going to a writers' conference," she announced.

"Business deduction?"

"Naturally."

"But you aren't a writer."

Jacqueline indicated the briefcase. "We're writing a textbook, aren't we?"

"Slowly," James said. "Very slowly."

"Anyway, I am a librarian. Library, books, writers. . . . Even the fascists at Internal Revenue can follow that connection."

James grinned. Jacqueline's feud with the local IRS office was a campus legend. Once she had tried to deduct her new television set on the grounds that her professional duties required her to watch writers being interviewed on the *Today* show.

"What conference are you attending?" he asked diplomatically.

Jacqueline flourished a newspaper clipping. "The Historical Romance Writers of the World. It's the only one I could find. The ABA meetings were last month, and the ALA is meeting in Birmingham. I wouldn't be caught dead in Birmingham."

"The Historical Romance Writers," James repeated. "Ah. I see. . . . Have you read any historical romances lately?"

"Not lately, no. I loved them when I was young. *The Prisoner of Zenda, Gone with the Wind, Forever Amber.*"

"Ah. *Forever Amber.*"

"It's not a bad book," Jacqueline said.

"No."

"What's the matter?" Jacqueline looked at him suspiciously. "You're smirking, James. I know that smirk."

"I'm not sure the IRS will buy it, that's all. University libraries don't stock many novels. Especially romantic novels."

"Then I'll have to write one," Jacqueline said. "Actually, that's not a bad idea. Someone told me they are selling very well these days."

"Oh, they are. They certainly are. . . . Well, that sounds like an excellent idea. Let's see; two weeks in New York, back here by the Fourth of July; you should have a manuscript finished before Labor Day."

"Your classroom wit is wasted on me," Jacqueline said coldly. "I'm well aware of the fact that writing a book is not the easy job laymen believe it is. But with all due modesty . . ."

"I'm sure you could do it." James studied her for a moment, then nodded. "Yes, you could. When are you leaving?"

He drove her to Omaha. On the way they chatted about college business and the weather, but Jacqueline was not deceived by James's amiability. He was still smarting over her refusal to let him accompany her. Just like a man, she told herself. Their egos were so fragile, they took everything personally.

James made no reference to his hurt feelings, but demonstrated them by driving so slowly Jacqueline began to fear she would miss her plane. When she remonstrated, he said cheerfully, "Oh, there's plenty of time," and indeed they reached the gate several seconds before the loudspeaker announced the last call for Flight 576. "Told you we'd make it," James said. "Have a good time. Here's a little farewell present."

Jacqueline took the wrapped parcel. "Books? How nice, James."

"You said you hadn't read any historical romances lately. These are two of the hottest sellers—or so I'm told." Chastely James shook her hand. He smiled. It was a broad, evil smile, as overpowering as that of the Cheshire cat. The lower half of his face was swallowed up by it.

And that is how Jacqueline Kirby, assistant head librarian of Coldwater College, B.A., M.A., scholar and self-confessed intellectual snob, found herself in possession of two volumes entitled *Slave of Lust* and *Crimson Bloom of Love*.

Contrary to popular opinion, librarians are not prim, unworldly spinsters, isolated from the modern world; nor are university librarians unacquainted with what is loosely termed popular culture. If you prick them they bleed, if you drop in on them unexpectedly you may find them engrossed in a soap opera or a copy of *Playgirl*. It was pure accident that Jacqueline was unfamiliar with the publishing industry's latest and hottest fad. "I don't buy books in supermarkets," she had been heard to say. "I buy grapefruit and toilet paper in supermarkets." In fact, she bought very few books. A librarian doesn't have to buy books, in supermarkets or elsewhere. Books are the one commodity of which librarians have more than enough.

Assisted by libations of spiritous liquids, Jacqueline

read on, in growing fascination, unaware of the landscape opening up below as the clouds gradually dissipated or of the wistful glances of the flight attendant who passed from time to time, lusting after *Slave of Lust*. The girl was not far away when Jacqueline closed the cover of *Crimson Bloom of Love*. Catching the hopeful gaze fixed upon her, she smiled, and the stewardess hastened to her side.

"Can I get you anything, ma'am?"

Jacqueline considered the offer. "I guess I can survive without more Scotch. Sit down a minute, if you have the time."

"Oh, I couldn't sit down. We're landing in half an hour."

"I've finished *Slave of Lust*. And this one as well. Would you like them?"

"Oh, thank you. Are you sure you don't—"

"No, I don't," Jacqueline said decidedly.

"I haven't read this one either." The attendant gloated over *Crimson Bloom of Love*. "Valerie Fitzgerald—she's good, but not as good as Valerie Vanderbilt. Of course Valerie Valentine is my all-time favorite. Don't you love her?"

"I don't know her," Jacqueline said, dazed by a superfluity of Valeries.

"Oh, you're in for a treat. She's the greatest. She's going to be guest of honor at the conference. I want to go, so bad, but I've got to work. Maybe I can sneak into Manhattan for one session."

"I'm going," Jacqueline said.

"You are? Lucky you. Oh, but—I didn't think—are you an author? What name do you write under?"

"I haven't had anything published yet," Jacqueline said. "I'm planning to call myself Valerie von Hentzau."

"That's a good name."

"I thought so."

"You look like an author," the young woman assured her. "I mean, you look like you could be glamorous if you—I mean—"

"I write for an older readership," Jacqueline said seriously, as the girl blushed and stammered. "Some of us still remember the love affairs of bygone days; it is my aim and my ambition to recreate those moments for those who are now too decrepit to engage in them."

There was no sensible answer to this, and Jacqueline received none; with a doubtful smile the stewardess retreated, clutching her books to her breast. Jacqueline settled back and reached for her purse. From its cavernous depths she took a copy of *Love in the Ruins,* hoping its astringent style would cleanse her palate of a surfeit of lust. Yet there was an anticipatory gleam in her eye as she heard the pilot announce their imminent landing. The conference promised to be a source of utter delight. She could hardly wait.

As the airport bus jostled through the thickening traffic toward the city, Jacqueline looked out the window with fond nostalgia. It had been three years since she left the East Coast for the pastoral charm of America's heartland. There had been good and sufficient reasons for her decision—a chance to succeed the amiably senile head librarian at Coldwater (who was still hanging in there, in defiance of all predictions); the high cost of food and housing in the eastern United States; and the proximity of Jacqueline's children, now adult and theoretically independent, but inclined to inquire too often and too solicitously into dear old mum's habits, finances, love life and refrigerator. They visited, almost always accompanied by members of the opposite sex, and Jacqueline had begun to detect ominous portents of future grandmotherhood. When they materialized, as they surely would in time, she planned to be a thousand miles away. She had no violent objection to the state itself or to babies in general; nevertheless, distance seemed a sensible precaution, and it would have been too flagrantly insulting if she waited until the condition was actually upon her before running away. Now, however, she felt she was returning to her spiritual home.

The bus disgorged most of its passengers at Grand Central Station. Drawing a breath compounded equally of satisfaction and carbon monoxide, Jacqueline lifted her suitcase and began walking. It was almost noon, and she knew the futility of trying to get a cab at that hour. Besides, her hotel was at Fifty-third, only a fifteen-minute walk.

By the time she reached Fifth, she had fallen back into the old city-dweller's stride—weaving expertly through breaks in the crowd, darting across streets against the light whenever traffic halted. Needless to say, this skill necessitates total concentration, and is one way of distinguishing the Manhattanites from the tourists. The latter, buffeted and bewildered, gravitate toward the store fronts, where they are shielded on one side at least from the madding crowds. Jacqueline was tempted by the display windows, especially those of the bookstores; Coldwater's single shopping mall contained no comparable charms. But she resisted. She had barely time to check in and change before attending the opening event of the conference—a formal luncheon at which the "mystery guest of honor" would be introduced.

She had not been able to get a room at the Harrison Hotel, where the conference was being held, but hers was right across the street. Furthermore, it offered a "vacation special" rate at a price considerably less than was usual. The room was standard American motel in decor and arrangement: two "king-sized" beds, shabby wall-to-wall carpeting, and a bedside lamp immovably fixed in a spot that rendered reading in bed an exercise in eyestrain. The view from the thirty-fifth floor took in the greenery of Central Park and the spires of the skyscrapers bordering it. The park left Jacqueline unmoved; she was surfeited with trees; but she spared a few moments to gloat over the tall buildings and the wonders they contained— wonders of which she had been long deprived. Saks and Altman's and Lord and Taylor—not that she could afford to buy clothes at those establishments, or at any of the delightful specialty shops on Park and Lexington, but even window-shopping would be a pleasure after the cut-rate boutiques of Coldwater Mall. The museums—the Guggenheim, the Cloisters, the Metropolitan—the Met's new Egyptian galleries were open, as well as the American Wing, and there was an exhibit at the Costume Institute she wanted to see. But man cannot live on museums alone, and Jacqueline's tastes were eclectic. She would have to consult friends in the city about the new places, nightclubs and cafés and bistros, for fashions in those fields change rapidly and she knew her old hangouts would probably have disappeared. Even that charming gay bar on Seventy-ninth, where she had had so many friends . . .

With a sigh she turned from the window and began unpacking. Halfway through *Slave of Lust* she had begun to suspect that her clothes weren't going to suit the mood of the conference. There wasn't a ruffle or a diaphanous blouse in her suitcase—nor in her closet at home, for that matter. She would have to see what she could do about the problem later; for the moment, a tailored linen suit must suffice. She left the top two buttons of her blouse unfastened, arranged her hair in romantic coils and clusters, and picked up her purse.

The last act wasn't as easy as it sounds. Though Jacqueline asserted that her purses were no bigger than the ones some women carried, they were undoubtedly bigger than the ones most women carried. They tended to bulge oddly, and no one, including Jacqueline, was ever entirely certain what was inside them. The student body at C.C. had regarded Jacqueline's purses with superstitious awe since the day of the graduation exercises, when she had produced an umbrella, a raincoat, and a pair of rainboots from her bag. This would not have been so surprising in itself, but for the fact that the weather forecast had promised clear skies with no chance of precipitation. The ceremonies were outside, and when the clouds opened up, Jacqueline was the only participant who wasn't drenched.

Aside from its other advantages, the purse could serve as a defensive weapon or a form of battering ram if circumstances required. Jacqueline used it in the latter capacity when she emerged from the hotel into a crowd that filled the sidewalk. Traffic on Sixth Avenue was backed up for blocks, and the noise level was even higher than usual for Manhattan at midday.

The light at the corner turned green as Jacqueline reached that point, and the frustrated drivers increased the volume of their complaints. Horns blared, voices rose in passionate invective. A taxi nudged the bumper of the car ahead; the driver of the latter vehicle, an elderly woman with lovely white hair, put a distorted face out the window and commented forcibly. Her words were inaudible to Jacqueline, but apparently not to the taxi driver, who replied in kind, and in Spanish. Jacqueline made a mental note of several words she had not heard before. The driver was blessed with a voice of penetrating shrillness.

The problem seemed to be the cross street. The intersection was blocked by two vehicles of distinctly unusual appearance. Both were open convertibles, of a vintage no longer commonly seen on American highways. Both were pink—bright shocking pink.

Jacqueline could see only the hood of the second car, but she had a good view of the first and its occupants. The driver was obviously a native New Yorker; unperturbed by the complaints hurled at him, he stared straight ahead, bored and detached. The passengers were not so blasé. One of the women was visible only as a mop of brassy yellow hair; she had slumped down as far as she could go without actually kneeling on the floor. The other woman was a redhead, of indeterminate age and remarkable plainness. Embarrassment, or sunburn, had turned her face a strange shade of red that clashed horribly with her pink bonnet, pink gown, and pink gloves.

The third person in the car . . . Jacqueline stood on tiptoe so she could see better. At that moment the young man rose, displaying his attire in its full glory: a white shirt open to the navel, with billowing sleeves; tight black trousers; a red satin cummerbund; and a black cape, lined in scarlet. Its sable and red folds flapped as he raised both arms and saluted the audience, which returned his greeting with a decidedly ambiguous howl. Some spectators laughed, some scowled, and all the taxi drivers swore. A voice somewhere in the area of Jacqueline's left elbow let out a gasp and a comment that included the word "hunk."

Jacqueline looked down. When she wore heels she was almost five feet ten inches tall; the girl who had sighed was a good six inches shorter. Catching Jacqueline's eye, she giggled and shrugged.

"Who is he?" Jacqueline mouthed.

"Who knows? He's gorgeous, though. Must be one of those writers." She gestured at the hotel on the opposite corner.

"Of course," said Jacqueline, enlightened and enraptured. "Rudolph Rassendyll, Zorro, Edmond Dantes . . . Romance isn't dead after all."

"Huh?"

"Definitely a hunk," Jacqueline said.

Sunlight glistened on the mat of black hair displayed by the youth's open shirt. The convertible jerked forward. He sat down, more suddenly than he had intended. He was smiling broadly.

Jacqueline decided she had better get moving too. If the occupants of the pink automobiles were the guests of honor at the luncheon, that affair would probably not start on time, but she wanted to get a good seat. She crossed Sixth Avenue without difficulty—nothing vehicular was moving—but before entering the hotel she paused for another look at the procession. It had now edged forward far enough for her to see the second car in line. It was an antique Cadillac convertible, complete with tail fins, and in impeccable condition. Its owner, who probably belonged to the austere and select group of classic car collectors, would have been appalled at its present appearance. It had been decorated like a float in a Thanksgiving parade—or rather, a Valentine's Day parade. From grille to tail fins the vehicle was draped with white cotton lace. A gilded cupid had replaced the original hood ornament. To the side door someone had affixed an insignia, like a coat of arms: paired golden hearts surmounted by a crown and flanked by more gilded cupids.

There were three people in the backseat. One was a balding middle-aged man. His face was as bland and disinterested as those of the drivers. The second was a gray-haired woman who looked like a suburban housewife. The third . . .

Beauty is, to a great extent, in the eye of the beholder and defined by personal taste. True beauty is rarer than diamonds and more remarkable. Few of the famous lovelies of stage and screen deserve that accolade; makeup, lighting, and, above all, the hypnotic hyperbole of press agents and publicity firms, create a false image that has nothing to do with beauty itself.

The girl in the pink convertible was beautiful. Sitting between the two older people, she looked like a rose in a row of zucchini. She had it all—the bone structure, the coloring, the perfect skin and sculptured features. The hair tumbling over her shoulders and clustering in soft curls around her face was not yellow or blond or fair, but pure red-gold; its strands shone like the finest silk threads. Her face was heart-shaped, curving delicately from rounded cheeks to a small pointed chin. She was wearing a low-cut blouse or dress—Jacqueline could see only the upper part of her body—of pure white, with a soft frill that framed a slender throat, and bared arms as perfect as those of a Greek statue of Aphrodite. But her beauty was not classical; the rose-petal cheeks and rounded curves were more reminiscent of the painted beauties of Boucher and Fragonard.

The parade moved forward another foot. The cries of the onlookers rose to a decibel level ordinarily achieved only by certain punk-rock groups. A red-faced policeman hurled himself into the fray and was swallowed up by the cabdrivers, who had abandoned their vehicles and were advancing on the convertibles. Reluctantly, Jacqueline tore herself away.

A list of scheduled activities posted in the lobby of the hotel directed her to the mezzanine, where registration for the Historical Romance Writers' Conference was taking place. Here Jacqueline found a cloudburst of pink and white, lace and paper hearts, and a few gilt cupids. Across from the registration table, which was draped in pink crepe paper and manned by three hard-eyed females in pink pinafores, was a row of publishers' display booths, with such names as Wax Candle Romances, Long-Ago Love, and Moonlight Love Romance. Moonlight apparently specialized in Valeries; Jacqueline saw several copies of *Slave of Lust* and a pile of books bearing the name the stewardess had mentioned as her favorite—Valerie Valentine.

As she stood admiring the decor, Jacqueline was accosted by a mustachioed man in a three-piece suit who inquired, "You looking for an agent, honey? I represent . . ."

Jacqueline took his card. After all, one never knew.

Another booth, some distance from those of the publishers, had the rickety homemade look of a display at a high school craft fair. Ruffles of pink and white crepe paper framed a tottery arch with a banner on which someone had laboriously and ineptly printed the name of the organization. It appeared to read, "Walentine Lowers of America." Jacqueline wondered which of the teenage girls gathered around the booth was the calligrapher. They appeared to be a fairly representative sampling of their age group; some were slim and pretty, some were chubby and homely, and most had braces or acne or both.

Jacqueline advanced on the registration table, receipt in hand. "Fans?" she inquired, indicating the Walentine Lowers.

One of the secretaries glanced up from the checks she was sorting. Jacqueline's dignified appearance seemed to impress her, for she said apologetically, "I assure you, they aren't representative of our readers. If my advice had been followed, they wouldn't be here.

They should have been made to buy tickets, like everyone else."

Her more kindly colleague said, "Most of them don't have the money. You know what Mrs. Foster said about fans: Keep them out, but keep them around. Yes, miss? Are you an author or a publisher?"

Jacqueline reflected. Presumably the alternative category was "fan" or "miscellaneous." Neither appealed to her. "Author," she said, and was presented with a blank name tag, a program, and a sheaf of tickets, one for each of the events of the conference. Taking a pen from her purse, she printed her name on the tag: J. KIRBY; and stuck the tag to the pocket of her suit. It was shaped like a heart, and was bright red.

The decorations of the automobiles and the mezzanine should have prepared her for the ballroom, where the luncheon was to be held, but Jacqueline was momentarily taken aback. Standing in the doorway, she stared appreciatively. It wasn't so much the hearts and the paper lace and the tinsel cupids; she had gotten used to them. It was the balloons—hundreds of helium-filled balloons, pink, red, white, and a few purple, clinging in clusters to every conceivable point of attachment and floating free like miniature flying saucers. Jacqueline batted a pink balloon out of her path and went in.

Most of the seats were filled—not surprising, since it was almost twelve-thirty, and the luncheon was scheduled to begin at noon. At the far end of the room, on a platform decked in red velvet and (of course) pink paper hearts, was the table reserved for the speakers and the mystery guest. There was not an empty chair at the nearby tables, but Jacqueline spotted one chair occupied only by a mink jacket and a purse. Stopping behind it, she nudged the occupant of the neighboring chair.

"Excuse me. I believe this is my place."

As she had suspected, the implication that the seat was reserved had been a bluff. Faced by effrontery even greater than her own, the owner of the mink jacket gave in with no more than a glare and a muttered "Well, really!" Jacqueline returned the glare. The woman wore an author's red name tag pinned to a décolletage exposing shoulders that should have been concealed from public scrutiny. Her dress was chiffon, printed with huge red roses on a pink background. Her features reminded Jacqueline of a vulgar midwestern adage that refers to the back end of a horse.

Jacqueline slipped into the vacated chair, put her purse under the table and her feet on the purse, and opened her program. Her perusal of that document was interrupted by a timid voice inquiring, "Do you know if smoking is allowed?"

Jacqueline turned to contemplate the speaker, who was seated on her left. The girl looked no more than eighteen. Soft brown hair framed a round, ingenuous face. Her snub nose was liberally freckled and her horn-rimmed glasses magnified a pair of gentle blue eyes. Her dress matched her eyes; it had long sleeves and a modest boat neckline. Jacqueline, an avid collector of mail-order catalogs, had seen the same garment advertised. The text assured the prospective purchaser that she would look "every inch the lady." In this case at least the claim was correct.

"I don't see any signs forbidding it," Jacqueline said.

"But there aren't any ashtrays."

There were also no waiters within hailing distance. Jacqueline retrieved her purse from the floor. After fumbling for a while she produced a tarnished brass box and removed the lid. "You can use this."

"Oh, but—"

"It's meant to be used as an ashtray." Jacqueline sighed. "I still carry it, even though I've quit smoking."

"Oh. I was about to offer you—"

"Thanks." Jacqueline grabbed for the cigarettes. "I quit smoking once a month," she admitted.

Her new friend scrutinized her name tag. "I'm afraid I haven't read any of your books. Oh, but you probably use a pseudonym."

"No." Jacqueline inhaled blissfully. "I'm not a writer."

"But your tag—"

"I lied."

"Oh!"

"You wouldn't lie, would you?" The girl's tag was also red. Her name was Susan Moberley. "I haven't read any of your books either," Jacqueline said. "Unless you are Valerie Vanderbilt."

"I wish I were. She's a big name. I'm just a beginner. My first book is coming out this fall."

"I'll be sure to look for it. What's the title?"

"I was going to call it *This Blessed Plot*. It's set in England during the reign of Richard the Second, so I got the title from—"

"I know the speech."

"Oh. Anyhow, my editor decided it wasn't a very good title. She wants to call it *Dark Night of Loving*."

"I see."

Her noncommittal tone brought a blush to Sue's freckled cheeks. "It isn't that kind of book," she said defensively.

"How many rape scenes?"

"Two. But they aren't really—"

"Got any sodomy?" Jacqueline asked. "Incest? Sado-masochistic orgies, whips, chains, dismemberment?"

Sue's face was scarlet, matching the balloon that had dropped onto the table. Jacqueline took pity on her. "You must be very poor," she said in a kindly voice.

"I don't know why you think—"

"What do you do for a living, Susan Moberley?"

"I teach school. Sixth grade."

"It figures. Where are you from? Iowa, Kansas?"

"A little town in Nebraska. You've never heard of it."

"I wouldn't bet on that," Jacqueline said morosely.

"You Easterners always assume people from my part of the U.S. are hicks. We're just as familiar with—"

"Sodomy, incest, and whips. No doubt you are. But you seem to be possessed of a reasonable degree of taste and intelligence. Doesn't the image of woman as willing victim featured in books of this kind disturb you?"

Before Sue could reply, the lady in mink, who had been eavesdropping, exclaimed vehemently, "Now I do agree with you wholeheartedly. I never allow my heroines to be exploited. They are independent, sexually liberated women who control their own destinies."

An animated discussion followed. All the authors at the table agreed with the speaker in principle and in practice. Their heroines were all independent and sexually liberated. They admitted, however, that lesser writers sometimes fell into this trap.

Jacqueline was not sufficiently familiar with the genre to be certain that the speakers were lying, but she caught strong echoes of "methinks she doth protest too much." Becoming bored with the conversation, she stopped listening and amused herself by batting at the balloons, which were sinking slowly toward the tables as the helium leaked out of them.

"I'm starved," Sue muttered. "When do you suppose we're going to eat?"

"God knows." Jacqueline reached in her purse. "Would you like half my candy bar?"

As they munched, Jacqueline added, "I suppose the guest of honor has been held up. There was a massive traffic jam outside when I came in. The center of it appeared to be a pair of pink convertibles."

The woman in mink chuckled maliciously. "That's typical of Hattie. She probably forgot to get permission from the police to stop traffic for her stupid procession."

"She wouldn't forget," said another woman across the table from Jacqueline. "She asked, and they turned her down. Naturally. So she went right ahead without permission. Naturally."

"Hattie? Who is she?" Jacqueline asked.

"You don't know Hattie? My dear, you are really out of your milieu. She organized this conference. She's head of the Historical Romance Writers of the World."

"Good gracious me," Jacqueline said humbly. "I didn't realize. Is that all she does for a living—organize conferences?"

Her informant cackled like one of the witches in
Macbeth. "Hattie Foster is an agent, dearie. *The* agent.
All the top writers in the field are in her stable—
Vanderbilt and Valentine and Victor von Damm—all of
them. That gives her a monopoly."

"Really?" Jacqueline's curiosity was genuine. The un-
dercurrents of nonacademic publishing were unknown to
her, and she was interested in almost everything.

"Think about it, dearie. Not one of the big names—
all of them. If a publisher wants to make money in this
market, he has to deal with Hattie, and she drives a
hard bargain. That means she can pick and choose
among the new writers. Most of 'em would kill to have
her handle their work. Stupid jerks."

The speaker's name tag was pink. It was not difficult
to deduce that this category included agents; the bitter-
ness in the woman's voice was heartfelt and personal.
The lady in mink, who had shown signs of perturbation
during the agent's tirade, exclaimed, with a nervous tit-
ter, "All the big names, Pat? All of them?"

"What? Oh—oh, no. Not all." The agent got her face
under control. "Uh—ladies, you all know the famous
Rosalind Roman, I'm sure. My client."

"Dear Pat . . . Hattie isn't the only agent who counts,
ladies."

There was an uncomfortable pause. Then everyone
started talking at once. Under the noise Sue said, out of
the corner of her mouth, "Bet Rosalind is one who'd
kill to get in Hattie's stable."

An outburst of trumpets sounded, ending in a dying
groan as someone switched off the tape too soon. A
velvet drapery behind the platform lifted, and in

marched the gray-haired woman Jacqueline had seen riding with the beautiful young girl. A ragged and somewhat ironic cheer greeted her. Perhaps the guests were cheering the imminent arrival of food as much as they were welcoming the head of the Historical Romance Writers.

She looked like everyone's Aunt Hattie—beaming smile, twinkling eyeglasses, and a massive motherly shelf of a bosom. Wisps of hair escaped from her untidy gray bun. In a cooing Virginia accent she welcomed the guests, hoped they weren't dyin' of starvation, laughed merrily at her own wit, and introduced the guests of honor, who emerged one by one from behind the velvet drapery and took their places as Hattie eulogized them. The hairy-chested hero in the black cape was Victor von Damm. He was followed by Emerald Fitzroy, author of *Love Blooms at Twilight*—the redhead—and then by Valerie Vanderbilt. Jacqueline would not have expected the author of *Slave of Lust* to be shy, but evidently Valerie was; her brassy wig still hid her face as she scuttled to take the chair Victor held for her.

A breathless pause followed, broken only by the growling of empty stomachs. "And now the moment you've all been waiting for," Hattie cried. "Our mystery guest. Can you guess who she is? Can you believe our luck, girls? Here she is—the Queen of Love in person—the most popular, most beautiful, most talented writer of historical romances in the whole big world—Valerie Valentine!"

The moment Jacqueline had been waiting for was the arrival of something to eat, but not all the guests were as cynical. A storm of applause greeted the appearance of the beautiful young girl with the rosy-gold hair. Exquisite in white organdy, she glided to the platform on the arm of a tall, impossibly handsome man wearing white tie and tails. He bowed her into her thronelike chair, next to Hattie's, and took his place beside her.

Hattie reached for the microphone, but her comments were drowned out by the rush of dozens of waiters. They were already late and they wanted to get the tedious job over and done with. Food was slammed down on the tables, wine sloshed into glasses, and Hattie sank back into her chair.

The food was ladies' luncheon classic—chicken à la king, one cold roll per guest, limp lettuce with bottled French dressing. The dessert was the pièce de résistance—heart-shaped tarts with four glazed strawberries peering coyly out from under a coating of plastic whipped cream. Then the waiters stormed the tables with carafes of tea and coffee, and the guests, sated if not satisfied, turned their attention from food to intellectual sustenance.

"Who's the man with Valerie . . . my God," Jacqueline said piously. "How can you tell them apart?"

"Valerie Vanderbilt's fans call her VV," Sue said. "Valentine uses her last name. That's her lover, the Earl of Devonshire."

"The Earl of Devonshire is eighty-four and has been happily married for sixty years to the Queen's first cousin."

"Really?"

"I haven't the faintest idea," Jacqueline said. "But

I'll bet my last buck that creature has not the slightest
connection with the British aristocracy."

"Maybe he's the Earl of Devonbrook. Something
like that."

"My God," Jacqueline repeated.

"I guess it is rather awful, isn't it?"

"Awful?" Jacqueline fished a limp purple balloon
out of her coffee. "I haven't enjoyed anything so much
in years."

The post-luncheon speeches were mercifully short; as
Hattie merrily admitted, they were running a wee bitty
behind schedule. She had only a few tiny things to
say. . . .

Cliché piled upon cliché, culled in the main from the
romantic poets. "Who knows better than we that love
conquers all?" cooed Hattie.

Jacqueline was very bored. Not quite sotto voce, she
remarked, "Oh, what a plague is love."

"All for love," Hattie proclaimed. "And a little for
the bottle," Jacqueline added. "That's from an obscure
poet named Charles Dibdon. He said it all. . . ."

"Sssh," the lady in mink hissed angrily. Sue giggled.

Jacqueline needed no encouragement. Hattie's,
"Love is heaven and heaven is love," inspired, "Love is
like the measles; we kent have it bad but onst and the
later in life we have it the tuffer it goes with us." "All
the world loves a lover," Hattie insisted, and Jacqueline
shook her head as she scraped up the crumbs on her
plate. "Not me. Comfort me with apples and stay me
with almost anything—for I am sick of love. Sick and
tired."

"You must be an English teacher," Susan said, as Hattie sat down amid a spatter of applause.

"Librarian." Jacqueline spoke absently; as the meal progressed she had been increasingly distracted by the peculiar behavior of Valerie Vanderbilt. Though the latter sat hunched over with her face practically in her plate, she occasionally glanced up when she forked food into her mouth, and the features thus displayed struck Jacqueline as familiar. She ran down a mental list of well-known personalities and half-forgotten acquaintances until suddenly the connection clicked into place. But surely it was not possible. . . . As if tickled by a tendril of ESP, VV looked in Jacqueline's direction. The expression of utter panic that distorted her face convinced Jacqueline she was right.

The waiters began grabbing plates and glasses off the tables and the guests of honor retired. VV bolted for the velvet drapery, but her hope of a quick exit was foiled by Hattie, whose stout form blocked the doorway. Jacqueline said, "See you," to Sue, and took off in pursuit.

VV saw her coming and attempted to elude her. Jacqueline cut the writer off and backed her into a corner.

"Jean. How long has it been? I'd know you anywhere, you gorgeous creature!"

"You're mistaken," VV mumbled, from under her wig. "My name isn't—"

"Jean Frascatti, class of . . . Well, never mind; I'm no more eager to remember the year than you. Is it still Frascatti, or have you—"

"Sssh! Don't say my name!"

It would, in fact, have taken a keen eye to spot the familiar features, now twenty years older, under the thick mask of makeup. Jean's complexion was several shades lighter than Jacqueline remembered, and her bright-red lipstick outlined a mouth that was not the same shape as her own. But they had been friends once, and although Jean had changed her appearance she had not changed the mannerisms that define an individual more unmistakably than physical features.

"Never mind," Jacqueline said. "If that's the way you want it. . . . It was nice seeing you."

"Wait." A clawed hand clutched at her sleeve. "Oh God, of all the people to run into. . . . What are you doing here?"

"I'm apt to turn up almost anywhere," Jacqueline said, unoffended. "What are *you* doing here? Are you really—"

"Yes. Why deny it?" It was a cry of anguish.

"No reason I can think of. I gather no one knows your real name."

"No one must know it." Jean's voice broke. "You promise? You won't tell?"

"Not if you don't want me to."

"Swear. Swear by—by Van Johnson."

Jacqueline laughed spontaneously. "I'd forgotten that."

"You had a terrible crush on him."

"The snows of yesteryear. . . . Ah, well. I swear by Van Johnson. I suppose, the circumstances being what they are—though I'll be damned if I know what they are—you won't want me to approach you again."

"No. Yes. Wait a minute."

Jacqueline waited. After a moment Valerie-Jean said, "If I tell you to leave me alone, you will. Won't you?"

"Certainly."

"But I'd like to talk to you. Oh God, do I need to talk."

"Fine."

"But not here. I have to be at some horrible lecture."

"Anywhere you say."

"After the lecture. I'll meet you— Oh God!" With a shriek she turned and fled, tottering on heels too high for her.

Jacqueline turned to see what had occasioned such consternation. It wouldn't take much; Jean had been terrified of beetles, boys, bats, and a hundred other things.

Bearing down on her was a woman wearing a shabby tweed suit. She was a formidable figure— heavy-set and sturdy, with strong features and traces of a mustache—but the ballpoint pen she brandished did not seem terrifying enough to have sent Jean into precipitate retreat. Then Jacqueline reconsidered. The bag hanging from the woman's shoulder was as large as her own, and she was taking a notebook out of it. "Journalist" might have been inscribed across her forehead.

"Which Valerie are you?" the mustached lady demanded, poising the pen.

"None as yet. If I do write a novel, I intend to call myself Valerie von Hentzau."

"Not bad." The woman bared her teeth. "Then your tag—"

"I lied."

"Right."

Jacqueline studied the other's tag. For almost the first time that day she recognized a name. "D. Duberstein. Are you Dubretta? The columnist?"

"That's one of the things they call me." Dubretta's keen black eyes shifted, searching. "Wasn't that Valerie Vanderbilt you were talking to?"

"I'm a great fan of hers," Jacqueline murmured.

"Oh yeah? Funny. From the look on her face I figured you were accusing her of something criminal."

"She seems rather shy."

"She's hiding something. I can tell. I wonder . . ."

Jacqueline moved with her, blocking her path. "I'm a fan of yours, too," she said. "I read your column."

"How often?"

"About once in a blue moon."

"That's what I figured." The other woman laughed, loudly and appreciatively. "You sound too intelligent to fall for tripe like mine."

"I remember one case you covered," Jacqueline said. "A couple of years ago. Sexual harassment in the mayor's office."

"Oh, that. Almost got me fired. My readers prefer scandal about famous people."

"It was an excellent series." Jean should be safe by now; Jacqueline's motives were almost entirely sincere when she went on, "It should have been nominated for a Pulitzer."

Dubretta's features had not been designed to display the softer emotions, and years of a notoriously cynical profession had hardened them even more, but the look she gave Jacqueline struck the latter as rather touching.

Pride, gratification, and appreciation lifted the corners of her mouth in a fleeting smile before she said gruffly, "Which of the lectures are you attending?"

"The one on promotion. It promises to be the most entertaining."

"Right again." They fell into step together. After a moment Dubretta asked, "What are you doing here? Off the record; I'm just curious."

Jacqueline knew the "off the record" assurance was meaningless, but she also knew she was too obscure to rate a mention in Dubretta's column. Unfortunately. The column was considered scandalous and lowbrow in staid Coldwater, whose academic denizens read it greedily on the sly. It would have delighted Jacqueline to appear in it.

"I'm a librarian," she explained. "I wanted to come to New York, and I needed a business deduction."

They followed the last of the luncheon guests out of the room. "I've got to powder my nose," Jacqueline said. "Perhaps we'll meet again one day, when all this is over."

Dubretta grinned. "I'll save you a seat."

"You're wasting your time, Dubretta. I will never betray Valerie Vanderbilt. Wild horses couldn't drag the truth from me."

She and Dubretta parted with expressions of mutual esteem.

Jacqueline was in fact powdering her nose when she realized that among the faces reflected with hers one seemed to be staring at her—or rather, at her mirrored image. This was not another ghost from the past; the face was young enough to be a daughter, or even a granddaughter (Jacqueline winced) of the class of . . . She tried not to think about the date.

The girl would not have made a prepossessing granddaughter. A thick coating of foundation failed to conceal past scars and present eruptions, and heavy eyeshadow, inexpertly applied, made her look as if she had been punched in the nose. The tiny eyes, plump cheeks, and blobby nose completed the resemblance to a homicidal pig Jacqueline had once known, Hammerhead Jones by name. Mr. Jones had reduced Hammerhead to chops the previous February, with the enthusiastic approval of his friends and neighbors.

Jacqueline turned from the mirror to find herself nose to nose with this apparition. She stepped to one side. The girl stepped to one side. She was a big girl, as tall as Jacqueline and considerably wider. The dress she wore did nothing to minimize her bulk, though it was beautifully made and looked expensive. Yards of pink dotted swiss swung from a ruffled yoke, with puffed sleeves as big as balloons.

"Yes?" Jacqueline inquired.

"I want to talk to you."

"Do I know you?"

"I'm Laurie Schellhammer."

"What a coincidence," Jacqueline said, thinking of Hammerhead.

"Huh?"

"Never mind." The girl's tag was white. "If you're a fan, you have the wrong person. I'm not a Valerie."

"I know that." Laurie looked scornful. "I'm Laurie Schellhammer, president of the Valentine Lovers of America. I know all the big writers."

"What do you want from me, Laurie Schellhammer?"

"Are you a new writer?"

"No."

Laurie made a grab for her as Jacqueline tried to get past her. "Listen, I don't know you, so I figure you must be new in the business. I want to warn you. Stay away from that woman. She'll try to get you to tell her things. She's trying to smear all the writers. Especially Valentine."

"What woman?"

"Duberstein." Laurie spat the word as if it tasted rancid. "She's a bitch. A cheap, dirty bitch. Didn't you read what she wrote about Valentine yesterday? God, it was such a cheap shot—"

"I get the idea," Jacqueline said. Reaching in her purse, she handed Laurie a tissue. "Here. You're drooling."

Automatically Laurie applied the tissue to the trickle of saliva running down her chin. "God, I hate that woman. You stay away from her. She'll crucify you. She's trying to crucify Valentine. Well, I won't let her get away with it. I'll stop her. I won't let her. . . ."

Jacqueline made her escape, leaving Laurie muttering and dribbling.

The lecture room was filled, but Dubretta saw Jacqueline and beckoned her to the seat she had saved.

"Isn't this fun?" she inquired sardonically.

"I'm enjoying myself."

"Then you must have a weakness for weirdos."

"I do—if you mean people with unorthodox opinions about obscure subjects. They're much more interesting than so-called normal people."

"I'll point out some of the nuttier types, if you like."

"That would be nice. I can't imagine why you're being so sweet to little old unimportant me."

"Can't you?" They exchanged smiles, then Dubretta sobered. "To tell you the truth, it's relaxing to talk to an innocent bystander—someone who has no ax to grind, and a measurable IQ."

"Pour it on, Dubretta. I love flattery." But Jacqueline sensed that there was a degree of sincerity in the columnist's statement. Praise of a writer's favorite work is the surest way to her heart, and proof of superior intelligence.

Speakers and guests began to take their places on the platform. True to her promise, Dubretta identified the more important of them. The white-haired octogenarian who supported her wobbling steps with a cane was Rosemary Radley, author of *Sweet Sensuous Sixteen*. A shambling hulk of a man with the frontal development and long arms of a gibbon was Amber Graustark, author of the seventeen-volume De Toqueville saga, which traced that fictitious and doom-laden family from medieval England to nineteenth-century Mexico.

"Amber?" Jacqueline repeated.

"Several of the top romance writers are men." Dubretta added cynically, "This is one of the few professions in which the male sex is at a disadvantage. The readership is ninety-eight percent female, and publishers think they prefer books written by women."

"What about him?" Jacqueline indicated the hairy-chested hunk.

"Von Damm? He's one of Hattie's brighter ideas." Dubretta's voice was grudging. "She figured a handsome, sexy male would go over well, and she was right. His real name is Joe Kirby. . . . Hey—you two aren't related, are you?"

"No. Believe it or not."

"I never believe anybody without an affidavit, and sometimes not then." Dubretta made a note in her book. "Joe's an out-of-work actor Hattie set up to play the part. His so-called books are ghostwritten by various bored housewives from Brooklyn."

She didn't bother to lower her voice, and several of the women in the row ahead turned to stare at her. One of them said, in a well-bred Bostonian voice, "I beg your pardon, miss, but you are mistaken. Victor knows a woman's heart as few men can; he writes every word of his wonderful books."

Dubretta's face split in a wide, froglike grin. She said to Jacqueline, "Get the picture?"

"I'm beginning to," Jacqueline said, fascinated.

Hattie bustled onto the platform and took her place behind the podium. The buzz of conversation died. Dubretta fumbled in her pocket. "What the hell did I do with my cigarettes?"

Her search dislodged a flutter of miscellaneous items—crumpled tissues, business cards, coupons for coffee and soap, and a pink, heart-shaped name tag. Jacqueline bent to help her recover the objects. As she was about to restore them to their owner, she glanced at the name tag. It was not, as she had supposed, a forgotten extra. Across its width someone had scrawled a message.

"Stop it, you dirty bitch, or you'll be sorry."

The accompanying sketch was as badly done as the

lettering on the Valentine Lovers sign. It might have been meant to represent a cross. Jacqueline didn't think so.

Chapter 2

Hattie had begun her introductory remarks. Jacqueline poked Debretta and hissed, "Is this a joke, or what?"

Dubretta glanced at the pink paper heart. An expression of mild vexation crossed her face. "Damn that kid. How did she. . . . Never mind, I'll explain later."

Jacqueline found the seminar even more entertaining than she had expected. She had supposed the speakers would be publicity agents, editors, and publishers. Instead the audience heard from a fashion photographer, a hairdresser, the representative of a famous line of cosmetics, and a dress designer. A dazzled girl from the audience was selected as guinea pig, upon whom these experts went to work. By the time they finished she was unrecognizable. Mascaraed, bewigged, and draped in gold lamé, she resembled a wax mannequin. In case there was any doubt as to the purpose of the demonstration, Hattie spelled it out: "You must look the part, my dears—romance, *toujours* romance. Now don't you-all look at me, because it's just hopeless for old Aunt Hattie, darlings; so you do what I say, not what I do. And if everything else fails, well, here's Mr. Johnson, who photographs all the famous beauties, to tell you how to make your pictures lovelier still."

Mr. Johnson discussed lighting, makeup, and—in desperate cases—air-brushing. "They want to see your eyes, darlings. Look straight at the camera—'I love you, camera!' "

Except for an occasional snicker, Dubretta paid little attention to the speeches; she took copious notes but her eyes moved constantly, from the audience to the guests seated on the platform. These included the wretched Valerie Vanderbilt, whose flowing locks had been tugged down over most of her face. The moment the seminar ended, Dubretta jumped to her feet. As Valerie-Jean scuttled toward the door, Jacqueline caught Dubretta's arm. "What about that threatening message?"

Dubretta tried to free herself. Jacqueline hung on. With a shrug and a grin, Dubretta accepted defeat. "Oh, that. The kid is the president of Valentine's fan club. She's seventeen, and crazy as a loon; thinks I'm trying to destroy her idol. She keeps slipping me these weird notes."

"I've met Laurie," Jacqueline said slowly. "Are you out to destroy her idol?"

"Iconoclasm is my job—and," Dubretta added, with a malevolent smile, "my pleasure. If I could get anything on Valentine, you're damned right I'd destroy her. Come on; I'll introduce you to Joe."

She started for the platform, where a group of admirers had converged on Joe, AKA Victor von Damm. The author was alternately kissing hands and signing autographs.

Jacqueline was about to follow when the well-bred lady from Boston addressed her. "Forgive me, my dear, but are you a friend of that woman?"

"Dubretta? I met her today."

"Then I may speak candidly. You don't want to know her. She is unprincipled and unscrupulous—no fit associate for a lady."

"Do you really think so?"

"You heard what she said about Victor." The soft wrinkled face twisted, suddenly and terribly, into a Medusa mask. "That was a vicious lie. You mustn't believe her. The only thing a creature like that understands is hatred. She should be silenced—forcibly, if necessary."

Jacqueline did not reply. After a moment the other woman's distorted face relaxed. She smiled gently at Jacqueline.

"I only speak out of concern for you, my dear."

"How nice of you. Aren't you going to meet Mr. von Damm? He seems to be signing autographs."

"Oh, dear no, I wouldn't think of such a thing." A blush tarnished the wrinkled cheeks. "I think it's frightfully rude to intrude on people to whom one has not been introduced."

"Some of them expect and enjoy that sort of intrusion."

"Possibly. But not Victor—not that shy, sensitive man. Can you see how uncomfortable he is?"

Jacqueline couldn't. In her opinion the mechanical

perfection of Victor's performance stemmed not from shyness but from boredom, and when Dubretta extracted him from the group of fans he looked relieved.

Accustomed as she was to male loveliness in all its youthful variations, Jacqueline felt a faint but localized flutter when Victor von Damm stood face to face with her. He loomed over her—not only because he was several inches taller, but because he knew how to loom. He probably practiced it daily, along with hand-kissing, smiling, and smoldering looks. Resentment rendered her more than usually acerbic; when he reached for her hand she fought his attempt to raise it to his lips. A modified variety of arm-wrestling ensued. Jacqueline won, but only because Victor was distracted by Dubretta's introduction.

"Joe Kirby, Jacqueline Kirby. Are you two related?"

"Dubretta will have her little joke," said Victor. His voice was a mellow baritone. He gave Jacqueline a smoldering look. "Would that I could claim a relationship, beautiful lady."

"Come off it, Joe, she's not a fan," Dubretta said. "She's a friend of VV's."

"A mere acquaintance," Jacqueline said. "I dote on her books. I felt I had to tell her so."

"Name one of her books," Dubretta said skeptically.

"*Slave of Lust*. I especially like the part where Blaze saves Lance from being emasculated by the order of the *Emiress* of Ballahooly. She wants him for her plaything—the *Emiress* does—and the only way she can get him into the harem is by—"

"Jesus," Dubretta said prayerfully. "That does it. I'm off in pursuit of other victims. See you later."

She trotted away, notebook in hand. "Is Dubretta a friend of yours?" Victor asked warily.

"A mere acquaintance," Jacqueline repeated. "I don't think I want to be a friend of hers. I'd rather not be in the way when someone takes a pot shot at her."

"She is not universally popular," Victor said. Absently he scratched the hair on his chest. "Sorry," he said, catching Jacqueline's eye.

"I expect it itches," Jacqueline said sympathetically. "The glue."

The affected smile left Victor's face. "How did you know?"

"The top left corner is coming unpeeled. Besides, you are singularly hairless except in that one area. I'll bet it takes you months to grow a beard."

"Damn," said Victor, covering the offending spot with his smooth brown hand.

"It's been nice meeting you, Mr. von Damm," Jacqueline said, turning away.

"Don't go."

"You must have other duties," Jacqueline said. "Hattie seems to be looking for you—"

"Why do you suppose I'm clinging to you?" Victor said, with refreshing candor. "Let's get out of here. I'll tell Hattie you wanted to interview me, or something. Are you a writer?"

His arm around her shoulders, he led her toward the door. "I'm a librarian," Jacqueline said, a trifle breathlessly.

"I was going to be a librarian once," Victor said mournfully.

"What happened?"

"My damned rotten handsome face, that's what happened. It's a curse. A visiting talent scout picked me for a small part in a film. The film bombed. And there I was in Hollywood, lost in the shuffle, without so much as bus fare home."

"So you are an actor," Jacqueline said.

Victor came to a halt. Still holding Jacqueline in the curve of his arm, he said, "What am I doing? What is it with you? Hypnotism? Does everyone tell you things they shouldn't tell anyone?"

"It's my curse," Jacqueline said irritably. "I don't encourage confidences." (She really believed this.) "In fact, I have better things to do with my time than listen to people bleat about their problems. Joe—Victor—I don't care what your real name is, and if you tell me your books are really written by a team of trained orangutans, I'll just shrug. Now, if you'll excuse me, I want a drink."

A slow and wholly engaging smile transformed Victor von Damm into Joe Kirby, unemployed actor. If he had been seductive before, he was now virtually irresistible. Unwillingly, Jacqueline returned his smile.

"You really are a beautiful lady," Joe said. His natural voice was several tones higher than Victor's.

"Don't give me that. I'm too old and cynical." But she let him take her arm.

"You are beautiful, compared to that bunch of hags I associate with. Everything about them is artificial, from their painted faces to their names."

"The theater is all artifice," Jacqueline pointed out. "If you despise that, you've chosen the wrong profession."

"I agree. Is it hard to get into library school?"

"You're joking."

Joe emitted a groan as heartfelt as any Victor von Damm might have uttered. "I wish I weren't. I'd like to chuck this whole stinking business. A nice quiet grad school, someplace in Alaska—or Utah—"

"Why don't you?"

They reached the lobby. Joe had forgotten his assumed persona. The black cloak hung limp and pathetic from his stooped shoulders. He shuffled when he walked. "I can't. I can't even tell you. . . . Hey. Did Dubretta say you were a friend of VV's?"

"She said it. I denied it."

"Yeah, but . . . Tell you what," Joe said slowly. "You talk to VV. There's one unhappy lady, you know? Tell her I . . . Talk to her. Come on, I'll buy you that drink."

"I'm afraid I can't." His mention of Jean reminded Jacqueline that she was supposed to meet her former schoolmate. They hadn't had time to arrange a rendezvous, and Jean didn't know where Jacqueline was staying; the most sensible course was to remain in the lobby until Jean could find her. Which Jean would probably not do unless Jacqueline was alone. She was about to dismiss Victor-Joe when she heard a voice she knew, raised in poignant protest.

"But that's way too much. I can't afford a hundred and ten dollars a night! You said it would only be—"

The desk clerk interrupted Sue's protest. He spoke in a discreet murmur, but Jacqueline caught a few words. ". . . economy rate limited . . . reservation misplaced . . . nothing I can do."

Sue's chin wobbled. A single crystalline tear materialized at the corner of her eye and slid gently down the curve of her smooth cheek.

"Look at that tear," said Joe softly. "Like a diamond. It didn't even plow a track through her makeup. Who is she?"

"Who wants to know, Joe or Victor von Damm?"

"Me," said Joe, staring. "I noticed her at the luncheon. She was sitting at a table near the platform. Stood out like a rose in a garden full of weeds. Or a kitten surrounded by stray cats. . . . What's the matter?"

"I," said Jacqueline, "was sitting next to her."

"Were you?" Joe's voice was abstracted. "Damn it, she's crying. And that bastard of a clerk—"

Weeping women were no novelty to the hotel clerk. He turned away with a shrug. Joe took an impulsive step forward.

To her horror, Jacqueline heard her own voice say, "Sue, if you need a place to stay . . ."

The transformation in the girl's face, from wistful disappointment to smiling, dimpled happiness, completed Joe's bemusement. Jacqueline did not introduce him and he made no attempt to attract Sue's attention. Silent and staring, he stood a few paces off until Sue had gone.

"Damn," Jacqueline said. "I hate myself. What makes me do these things?"

"I don't know," Joe said. "But it was a damned dirty trick. I was just about to—"

"That was probably one of the reasons," Jacqueline said drily.

"Hey, what do you mean? My intentions were strictly honorable. That girl's no swinging city type;

she's . . . She looks . . . She's probably from Utah—or Alaska . . . ." He sighed. "So why did you come to the rescue? It couldn't have been kindness."

"Certainly not. I—uh—I'm on a budget. My room rent is the same whether one or two people occupy the room; she'll pay half, save me some money."

Joe wasn't really interested. "I'd better make sure she gets across the street okay," he said.

"Even if she's from Utah or Alaska, she's smart enough to cross a street by herself."

"Yes, but—listen to that racket outside. There's some kind of a riot or something. I'll see you later, Miss—um—"

"Kirby," Jacqueline shouted. "Kirby. You ought to remember that name."

The black cape billowed dramatically as Joe ran after Sue. To Jacqueline's disappointment, it did not get caught in the revolving door.

Cursing her incurable tendency to interfere in other people's business, she took up a position next to one of the gilded pillars adorning the lobby. She didn't have to wait long. Jean had been trying to attract her attention. A blond wig bobbed up and down behind the plate-glass window of the gift shop, between a rack of paperback books and a shelf of folded T-shirts. As soon as Jacqueline acknowledged she had seen it, it disappeared.

Jean was in the farthest corner of the gift shop, crouched behind a counter of souvenirs. She started convulsively when Jacqueline tapped her shoulder.

"You need a drink," Jacqueline said. "Or something."

"Not here."

"Where then?"

"Anyplace but here." Jean wrung her hands.

"My hotel is across the street."

"Your room?"

"No. I've just acquired a roommate. She's probably there now. Oh, for heaven's sake, this is ridiculous. We'll go to the bar at my hotel. Come on."

She took Jean in a firm grip and marched her toward the door. Jean revived a trifle in Jacqueline's protective shadow; but when they emerged from the hotel, Jacqueline realized that Joe's reference to a riot had had some foundation in fact. At first she thought Hattie had instigated another parade. However, the barricade to traffic was not vehicular. Bodies blocked the sidewalk and spilled out into the street. Signs were being brandished; and as Jacqueline listened, the outcry resolved itself into a ragged chant: "We hate rape. We hate rape. We hate the Romance piglets, 'cause they love rape."

"It doesn't scan," Jacqueline said. "But the sentiment has a certain merit."

Being several inches shorter than Jacqueline and considerably more distracted, Jean was still in the dark as to the nature of the demonstration. Jacqueline helpfully read a few of the signs for her benefit. "Down with Lust." "Down with Valentine, rape and sexism." "Romance writers are traitors to women." "Ah— there's a sign that says, 'Valeries, go home.' I expect that includes you."

Jean realized what was happening. "Oh God," she cried. "I've got to get out of here. Oh God, oh God."

"They can't even see you," Jacqueline said. She stood on tiptoe. "For goodness' sake. Look—isn't that Betsy Markham?"

Torn between the terror behind, where Dubretta lurked and fellow romance writers swarmed, and the confusion ahead, Jean was paralyzed by this last catastrophe. The woman Jacqueline had indicated was indeed their old schoolmate. Tall and rangy, she had cropped graying hair and a bony, rather attractive face. Either she had heard Jacqueline's voice, which was not noted for its dulcet, ladylike quality, or she was alerted by the sixth sense developed by radicals when they are the object of intense scrutiny. Betsy looked straight at Jacqueline, grinned, waved, and brought her sign down on the head of a policeman who was attempting to escort her out of the middle of the street. Hers was the sign that read, "Valeries, go home."

Betsy and the policeman vanished in a maelstrom of struggling forms. Jacqueline led her gibbering friend away.

Jean didn't come out of her stupor until they had seated themselves in a booth in the semi-darkened bar. After the waiter had brought their drinks, Jacqueline said, "Now. What's this all about?"

Jean snatched up her gin and tonic and drank deeply. Then she said in a fading voice, "You wouldn't have to ask if you had read any of my books."

"I have. *Slave of Lust*. I read it this morning on the plane."

"*Slave of . . .*" Jean shuddered. "Oh, my God."

"It was wonderfully bad," Jacqueline said enthusiastically. "Magnificently, sensationally terrible. Aside from that, about half of it was plagiarized, especially the descriptions of male anatomy. You don't suppose I would ever forget *The Lustful Turk,* do you?"

Jean's reaction to this was a wry smile. Pushing the wig away from her face, she drank again, and then said, more calmly, "Nobody but you would know it. You and half a dozen dim specialists in Victorian pornography."

"And you assumed none of the above, including me, would read your book?"

"I didn't care if you did." Alcohol, or the relief of confession, had restored Jean's courage. "I didn't violate copyright or anything; that book's been out of print for a hundred years. Who's gonna sue me?"

"Not me, dear. That little volume enlivened my junior year. Did you ever get your master's?"

Designed to be harmless and reassuring, the question had the opposite effect. Jean's eyes took on a hunted look. "Doctorate," she whispered.

"Congratulations."

"I'm an assistant professor."

Jacqueline did not repeat her congratulations; Jean's tone seemed to demand commiseration instead.

"This year," Jean went on, like the Delphic oracle pronouncing the fall of Athens, "I am being considered for tenure."

"Oh?" Then Jacqueline understood. "Oh."

"Uh-huh." Jean nodded. "If they ever find out I'm— you know—"

Thanks to her occupation on the fringes of academe, Jacqueline was able to follow the oblique references and the even more obscure reasoning. She translated.

"If your colleagues learned you were writing soft-porn novels, you wouldn't get tenure. Jean, do you really believe that? This is not 1850, or even 1950."

"Not get tenure? I'd lose my job! You know how the system works; after a certain number of years you either get promoted or you move on. I'm almost—well, you know how old I am. What do you think it's like, looking for a job at my age—competing with all those smart-aleck kids fresh out of grad school?"

Jacqueline was not wholly convinced. However, she was well acquainted with the unstable and treacherous nature of the paths that lead to security in the academic world. Competition was cutthroat; there were dozens of well-qualified candidates for every position, and a seemingly unimportant factor could tip the scales. More important, Jean believed in the danger, and nothing anyone could say would convince her she was wrong.

Jacqueline tried another argument. "So what if you lose your job? You must be making a lot of money out of your books."

"I do," Jean said sadly. "I do."

"Then cry all the way to the bank. Who cares what a lot of stodgy academics think?"

"I care."

"Oh."

"I love teaching. I love the atmosphere—the quiet, the respect. . . . Oh, you wouldn't understand. You were always a rebel."

"Me?" Jacqueline was indignant. "I'm the most conventional—"

Jean giggled. "Like the time you got all those black football players from Washington Park to sit in the front row when Professor Hoffmeyer lectured on inherited racial traits?"

Jacqueline brushed this aside. "Your problem is that you're ashamed of your books. You're projecting your contempt onto your colleagues, rightly or wrongly. If you hate writing so much, why don't you stop doing it?"

"I can't."

"Why not, for God's sake?"

"Well . . ." Jean blinked rapidly. "I make a lot of money; one becomes accustomed to a certain standard of living. . . ."

"What do you spend the money on? Clothes?"

Jean flushed and pawed nervously at her wig. "This outfit? You know I don't dress like this unless I have to. I mean—"

"What do you spend it on?"

"Oh—things. I buy a lot of books. . . ."

"Why am I doing this?" Jacqueline demanded rhetorically. "I must be crazy. Not half an hour ago I told Victor von Damm that confidences bore me, and here I sit—"

"Victor? What did he tell you?"

"Nothing. I managed to get him off my back before . . . Well," Jacqueline admitted, "there was another distraction. I wonder how Sue is making out. . . . Dear me. That *was* a Freudian slip. What was I saying?"

"Victor."

"Joe."

"He told you that was his name?"

"Not exactly. Someone else told me. He told me he wants to be a librarian."

"Poor Joe," Jean murmured.

"He also said you were one unhappy lady. He intimated that you two shared some hideous secret. That I should talk to you. That shocking disclosures would follow. But—" Jacqueline raised a magisterial hand. "But I don't want to hear them. I have no wish to share in the childish yearnings of two jerks who don't seem to realize they are in the catbird seat riding the gravy train up the ladder of success. What ails you people, anyway? Don't answer that."

She slid toward the edge of the seat. Jean reached for her.

"Please, Jake—"

"Tacky," Jacqueline said with a sneer. "If you think I can be softened by antique and unsuitable nicknames . . ." But she stopped sliding.

A brief silence followed. Jean said, "I read about that case in Rome. There was an article in some magazine."

It would have been hypocritical to ask, "What case?" The affair had received considerable coverage, since the protagonists had included a scholar as well known to the lay public as he was to the academic world; and Lieutenant di Cavallo of the Carabinieri had not been averse to publicity. A reminiscent smile curved Jacqueline's lips. Capri—the tiny hotel near the ruins of Tiberius' palace, the private beach they had found. . . . Lost in fond memories, she missed Jean's next comment and had to ask her to repeat it.

"And there was another time, in England—something about the society to restore the good name of King John—"

"Richard. How did you hear about that?"

"I was at a party once, with Nigel Strangways, the historian. We were exchanging 'Do you knows' and he—"

"What did he say about me?" Jacqueline's eyes narrowed.

Jean hesitated long enough to convince Jacqueline that some editing of Strangways' comments seemed expedient. "There was a murder, or attempted murder, and you were responsible for solving it. He said you were a—a remarkable woman."

"Hmmmm," said Jacqueline.

"Did you solve the case?"

"Yes," said Jacqueline.

"Then you know about things like that."

"Things like what? Your brain is decaying, Jean; how did you ever get an academic job?"

Jean ignored this. Her face was intent. "Crime," she said. "Blackmail is a crime, isn't it?"

"Is someone blackmailing you?"

Faced with a direct question, Jean backed off. In avoiding Jacqueline's gaze, her eyes were caught and held by some person or object behind the latter. With a bleat of terror she got out of the booth and disappeared into the shadows.

Jacqueline expected to see Dubretta, and did not know whether to be relieved or not when she recognized the lanky form of her other erstwhile classmate. Seeing her, Betsy waved and came toward her.

"I thought I'd find you boozing it up," she said, taking the place Jean had left.

"Don't give me that. You weren't looking for me. Why aren't you in jail?"

Betsy ran her fingers through her graying locks. "So okay, I was looking for gin. Waiter! Jail? My dear, I haven't been in the slammer since '78. One learns certain techniques. . . . Yes, waiter, I'll have gin on the rocks. Tanqueray."

"I guess I've been in the boonies too long," Jacqueline said. "I thought if a person hit a cop on the head—"

"I didn't hit him hard." Betsy dismissed this tedious problem and gave Jacqueline an affectionate smile. "How long has it been, Jake? You look marvelous. And who was that who flashed out just now? She looked familiar."

"Nigh on twenty years," Jacqueline said. "What are you—"

"She was dressed like one of those love-story bitches. How come you're snuggling up to them?"

"How come you're so hostile toward them?"

Betsy grinned. "What is this, Questions and Answers? Okay, if you don't want to tell me, you don't have to. But anyone who's read any of their cruddy books should know why I don't like them. Have *you* read any of their books?"

"Two of them. Have *you* read any of them?"

"You can't catch me that way," Betsy said amiably. "I have read, not two, but two hundred. I may never recover my wits, such as they are. For Christ's sake, Jake, you used to be a liberal. How can you stand that stuff?"

"What makes you suppose . . ." Jacqueline broke off. She was tired of fencing; she wondered if she would ever again be able to make a simple statement. She gave it a try. Gesturing at the woman standing beside the booth, she said, "This is Dubretta Duberstein. Dubretta, this is Betsy Markham. Betsy, Dubretta. Dubretta, are you— No, scratch that. I'm not asking any more questions."

"Can't find a table," Dubretta explained. "Mind if I join you?"

She might have been telling the truth. The bar was filling up and she had been standing in the doorway for some time. How long, Jacqueline was not sure. Perhaps she had not seen Jean, AKA Valerie Vanderbilt. Betsy was a reasonable quarry for a journalist, and Dubretta's notebook was ready in her hand.

"You one of the pickets?" she asked.

"Brilliant deduction," said Jacqueline, eyeing Betsy's oversized army fatigues and chestful of slogan-imprinted buttons.

"What's your gripe, Betsy?" Dubretta asked.

Betsy told her, eyes shining; free publicity was a boon to a protester. "Romantic novelists perpetuate an image of women that is archaic, sexist, and harmful," she recited. "It's the old 'women love to be raped' myth. Men still believe it; for a woman to encourage their disgusting delusion is not only degrading, it's treacherous."

Dubretta scribbled. ". . . degrading but treacherous," she repeated.

"Men are still hung up on the old *Lustful Turk* image," Betsy said. "They . . . Jake? What's the matter?"

"Nothing," Jacqueline said.

"You remember that book, don't you? We all read it. What was the name of that girl, the English major—"

"There is certainly a great deal of *The Lustful Turk* in contemporary romance fiction," Jacqueline said hastily. "You're right, Betsy; the fact that the heroine is overpowered by a sexy, handsome hero, who eventually falls in love with her, doesn't compensate for the damaging implications."

"Right on!" Betsy cried.

Jacqueline relaxed. Her diversionary tactics had succeeded, for the moment.

Betsy went on heatedly. "A great deal of contemporary fiction specializes in the victimization of women. In the horror stories and suspense thrillers, who gets shafted? Who is terrorized and chased and brutalized? A beautiful young girl, that's who."

Dubretta tossed her pen onto the table. "Is that it?"

"Hell, no," Betsy said indignantly. "I can go on at length."

"More of the same? Oh, it's fine as far as it goes, kiddo, but I can't repeat myself for a whole column. Haven't you got anything good on these people?"

"Got anything? Like what?"

Jacqueline smothered a smile, and Dubretta snorted explosively. "That's what bugs me about you do-gooders. You're so goddammed naive! You march up and down yelling slogans about justice and fair play and equality, and hitting a cop over the head now and then—yes, honey, I saw you slug poor old Jackson Billings—and what does it accomplish? Not a damned thing. Don't you understand that if you want to nail these people you have to fight dirty—the same way they fight?"

Betsy, who would not have blushed at any four-letter

word in any language, turned brilliant scarlet at the accusation of naiveté. Sensing a potential ally, she leaned forward. "Is that what you're trying to do, nail them?"

"You've got to go after the people at the top," Dubretta said. "Most of the writers are poor honest slobs like you and me; they're just trying to make a buck. They're the real victims of exploitation—forced to write crap they hate, and getting screwed out of their paltry returns by publishers and agents."

"Paltry?" Betsy exclaimed "Do you happen to know how much money Von Damm and Valentine and Vanderbilt make?"

"So go after them," Dubretta said. "But you're missing the one behind the whole thing—the spider in the middle of her sticky web. Harriet Foster. Good old Aunt Hattie. Twenty-five-percent Hattie, she's known as. Most agents take ten, maybe fifteen. And God knows how much she rakes in on the side. What I wouldn't give to expose that sugary, smiling bitch. If I could only . . ."

Her voice had become increasingly hoarse. Now she broke off, breathing harshly. Betsy raised her hand to administer a therapeutic slap on the back. "No," Jacqueline said quickly. "Don't. Dubretta?"

After a time the columnist relaxed. She took a small plastic bottle from her purse and swallowed one of the pills it contained. "I keep forgetting to take the damned things," she said sheepishly.

"Are you all right?" Jacqueline asked.

"Sure. Three pills a day, and the old ticker stays in tempo. Now listen, Betsy, let me give you a few tips. Forget your cutesy signs and your generalized wrath.

What you've gotta do is target particular people. The strongest weapon in the world is ridicule. If you could make these jerks look silly, expose their pretensions and their lies . . ."

"Go on," Betsy said eagerly.

The two graying heads bent toward one another, ignoring Jacqueline. She listened for a while, but since Dubretta's lecture avoided personalities and confined itself to the basic principles of muckraking, she soon lost interest.

Dubretta's antagonism toward Hattie Foster had all the passion of a personal vendetta. The antics of Hattie and her stable—particularly their taste in interior decoration—were deliciously funny, and left the history-romance group wide open to satire of the kind Dubretta specialized in. But silliness wasn't scandalous. Jacqueline wondered whether the lies Dubretta wanted to expose had any connection with the hints Joe and Jean had thrown at her. There was a distinct odor of blackmail in the air; but what hold could Hattie Foster have over a carefree, harmless ham like Joe?

She was aroused from her meditations by the realization that Dubretta and Betsy had stopped talking and were staring accusingly at her.

"Jake, we are trying to have a dialogue," Betsy said.

"So who's stopping you? I haven't said a word."

"You were singing."

"I was?"

"I hoped you had gotten over it." Betsy explained to Dubretta, "She used to do that all the time. When she was bored."

"What was I singing?" Jacqueline asked interestedly.

Betsy sighed. "You started out with 'Love in Bloom.' Then you went on to 'Love's Old Sweet Song,' and 'As Time Goes By.' "

"Well, well." Jacqueline picked up her purse and got up. "Since I seem to be interfering with the intellectual tenor of the discussion, I will take my leave. Goodbye."

Crooning under her breath, she collected her room key and headed for the elevator. "Moonlight and love songs, Never out of date; Hearts full of passion . . ."

She was no stranger to hearts full of passion, jealousy and hate. There is no more fertile breeding ground for those emotions than the damp and shady groves of academe. Yet, though she had been an unwilling participant in several cases of violent death, she had never encountered an ambience so fraught with potential violence as this one. Everybody hated everybody else, for one reason or another.

Which only went to prove, she supposed, that writers of love stories were no better and no worse than any other cross section of humanity. It was the contrast, between lace-paper valentines on the one hand and verbal mayhem on the other, that made this situation so bizarre.

The occupants of the elevator were relieved when she got out, still singing.

Her room was unoccupied, but Sue had been there; her shabby suitcase was tucked humbly away in a corner and her clothes occupied a bare one quarter of the closet. There was a note on the table between the beds. Jacqueline picked it up.

"Have gone out with Victor! Thank you so much—I'll see you soon—can't tell you how much I appreciate your kindness! Sue."

"Bah," said Jacqueline.

Also on the bedside table was a stack of paperback books. The cover of the topmost showed an exquisitely beautiful young girl crushed in the arms of a tall handsome Indian (American variety). Her off-the-shoulder blouse was about to give way and she was bent back at an angle impossible to a human spine. Jacqueline's dour expression lightened a trifle. She kicked off her shoes, settled down on the bed, and reached for *Winds of Passion*.

Chapter 3

"Long Arrow shrugged the quiver and bow from his brawny shoulders. The muscles in his bronzed chest rippled. 'I will call you Windflower,' he said in his guttural English. 'It is the flower of love in my tribe, for it bends to the winds of passion.'

" 'No,' Flame whispered. She shrank back, her hands fluttering as she attempted to draw the rags of her blouse across the swelling whiteness of her breasts. The young warrior's eyes kindled.

" 'Come to me, Windflower.' He cast aside his breechclout of tanned leather. Hypnotized, Flame stared at . . ."

"Jacqueline?"

"Damn," Jacqueline said. She had not heard the sound of the key in the lock. Sue smiled uncertainly.

"I didn't mean to disturb you."

"That's all right." Jacqueline marked her place and closed the book. After all, she had a pretty good idea of what had hypnotized Flame. No reader of *The Lustful Turk* could entertain any doubts on that subject.

"I thought you were having dinner with Victor," she said.

"I changed my mind." Jacqueline was treated to the spectacle of a kitten trying to look like a lion. The result was so intriguing she forgot her resolutions about detachment. "What happened?" she asked greedily.

Sue crossed to the window and stood in contemplation of Central Park. "Nothing, really," she said, with an artificial laugh. "I mean—I knew the kind of man he was. That corny way he dresses, and he just adores being fawned on by those silly women . . . . Well, I mean, I knew he was a conceited ham; I only went out with him because I thought he was so funny. . . ." Her voice broke.

Jacqueline's maternal instincts were further developed than she liked to admit, but patting and cooing and getting her blouse soaked with tears was not her idea of therapy. She studied Sue's shaking shoulders and said briskly, "While you're on your feet, could you get me a glass of water?"

Sue shuffled sideways to the bathroom, her face averted. When she emerged with the water the curls framing her forehead were damp, but she was smiling doggedly.

Jacqueline accepted the water. "Thanks. I hope you don't mind that I borrowed one of your books."

"Oh, please—I only wish I could do more. I can't tell you how much I appreciate—"

"Not at all. I'm grateful for the chance to broaden my reading. Paperbacks are so expensive these days."

Sue flung herself across the bed. "I appreciate your

tact. But you needn't avoid the subject. I'm not upset. I don't mind talking about it."

Seeing that she was about to become a confidante whether she wanted to or not, Jacqueline leaned back against the pillows and resigned herself. "Did he make a pass?" she asked. "Excuse the old-fashioned terminology; I haven't read enough romance novels to learn the 'in' phrases."

"Oh, goodness, that wouldn't have bothered me." Sue produced another forced laugh. "I can handle that sort of thing."

"I'm sure you can," Jacqueline murmured. So Joe had not made a pass, and Sue had been disappointed.

After a moment the girl burst out, "He was so nice at first. We had a drink, at a little place he knows, and we talked. . . . He's only twenty-nine, did you know that? I said it was wonderful that he was so successful, but he said he didn't care about the money; he's tired of the adulation and the artificiality; he wants to give it up and return to a simpler, more genuine way of life. I told him about Finn's Crossing, and he said it sounded wonderful. . . ."

Her chin showed signs of instability, and Jacqueline said, "So what happened to shatter this romantic aura?"

Her voice was like a dash of icy water. The chin froze, and Sue gave her a rather resentful look before proceeding. "What happened was that he didn't mean a word he said. We were sitting there when that woman—Hattie—showed up. She'd been looking for him. 'Ah jes' knew Ah'd find you-all in your favorite little pub, Victor,' she said. 'Did you-all forget that appointment with Barton and Reed?' "

"Publishers?" Jacqueline asked.

"Yes. Victor glared at her in the rudest way. Then she looked at me and said—very nicely—'Ah do hope you-all will excuse me, honey; Ah can see why Victor forgot his boring old business appointment. Why don't you-all come along? I see you're a writer from that cute little red heart of yours, and it sure enough wouldn't do your career any harm to meet Mr. Barton.' "

"It sure enough wouldn't," Jacqueline said. "Frankly, I'm surprised Hattie offered. She isn't known for philanthropy."

"And that was when Mr. Victor von Damm showed his true colors! He jumped up like he'd sat on a pin, grabbed Hattie's arm, and left. He didn't even apologize, just muttered something like, 'See you around.' Hattie was embarrassed. He dragged her out before she could say anything, but I could see she was."

"Extraordinary," Jacqueline murmured.

"No, it isn't. He's just a conceited, selfish jerk, that's all. I mean, what the woman said is true—Hattie is the biggest agent in the business, and there was my chance to get her interested in me. But precious Victor can't stand even my kind of competition."

"That's one interpretation," Jacqueline said.

"Well, I've learned my lesson. I won't fall for that again. . . . Have you had dinner, Jacqueline? If not, perhaps you'd let me take you."

"Thanks, but I'm supposed to dine with friends this evening. Good heavens, what's the time? I'm going to be late."

As she was leaving the room a little later, the telephone rang. "It's probably for you," Sue said.

"I can't stop, I haven't the time. Maybe," Jacqueline added, "it's Victor, wanting to apologize."

"Ha," said Sue. But before Jacqueline closed the door she saw the girl reach eagerly for the phone.

As Jacqueline hastened through the lobby she heard someone call her name, but did not pause or look around. She believed in being on time when a friend proposed to cook a meal, and she was sick unto death of the love writers and their problems. She had looked forward to enjoying the absurdity of the proceedings and, if possible, adding to it; conducting a group-therapy program was not her idea of fun.

It was late when she got back but Sue was still awake. Jacqueline glanced at the cover of the book the girl was reading. "*Anne of Green Gables*? Don't tell me; it's a new version, where the sexy young doctor, Gilbert, seduces Anne in a field of violets."

"I found it in a bookstore this evening when I went out for a hamburger," Sue said. "I needed something to steady my stomach after all this romance. Have you been shopping?"

Jacqueline put the suitbox on her bed and stretched aching arms. "It isn't heavy, it's just bulky. I haven't been shopping. I borrowed a few things from my friend. My wardrobe wasn't quite the thing for this event."

She removed the cover of the box and lifted out a dress. Folds of lavender voile flapped and fluttered Sue gasped. "It's gorgeous. Is that real Brussels lace?"

"I guess so." Jacqueline frowned. "The dress is a little out of date. Joan wore it to the Queen's garden party two years ago. But the matching hat is rather divine."

"It's pretty large," Sue said doubtfully, eyeing the flower-bedecked cartwheel.

"We added a few more bows and flowers." Jacqueline put the hat on her head. Sue let out a gasp of laughter, and then clapped her hand over her mouth. "I'm sorry—I didn't mean—"

Jacqueline looked pleased. "That's just the effect I'm aiming for, my dear. Wait till you see the whole ensemble. There's a frilly little parasol, and long white gloves, among other things."

"What else did you borrow?" Sue asked.

"My gown for the ball day after tomorrow." Jacqueline put the top back on the box and simpered coquettishly. "I think I'll save it for a surprise. Joan has the most money, and the most appalling taste, of anyone I know. Lucky me, to have such friends."

"You're crazy," Sue said admiringly.

"Thank you. I'm going to hit the sack now. I want to be bright and shining for the breakfast tomorrow."

She hung the dresses tenderly in the closet and started for the bathroom. "That telephone call was for you," Sue said.

"Who was it?" Jacqueline didn't pause.

"He wouldn't leave a name. He called again about an hour ago. . . ." Jacqueline vanished into the bathroom. Sue raised her voice. "When I said you weren't back, he growled at me."

Jacqueline's head appeared. She was wearing a white plastic shower cap with "Coldwater College Swim Team" printed on it. "Growled?"

"Literally. I asked if he wanted to leave a message, and he yelled, 'Tell her she can't avoid me forever,' and hung up."

The white plastic shower cap tilted. "Tenor or baritone?"

"Rather deep."

"Ah." Jacqueline's head vanished "Damn," said Jacqueline's voice.

"Do you know who it was?"

Water gurgled and splashed. Sue returned to *Anne of Green Gables*.

Jacqueline turned from the mirror. "Well?"

"It's marvelous," Sue said. "The parasol is the final touch. But I thought you'd save it for the cocktail party tonight."

"I expect there will be a few equally tacky garments at the cocktail party. They will lessen the effect. I should stand out like a sore thumb at the breakfast. Hurry up; I want to sit close to the head table."

She rammed two hatpins as long as sabers through the crown of the cartwheel, picked up her purse, and beckoned to Sue, who followed with a bemused grin.

Heads turned as they marched through the lobby, and a taxi driver on Sixth Avenue yelled, "Hey, lady, where'd you get that hat?" Jacqueline waved at him.

They were very early, but a few guests had already taken their places. Jacqueline pre-empted two chairs at a table in the first rank below the platform and arranged herself. A gaping young woman sidled up and asked for her autograph. Jacqueline signed with a flourish: Valerie von Hentzau.

"That's awful," Sue exclaimed, as the autograph seeker backed away, her eyes fixed on the hat. "You aren't—"

"As of this moment, I am." Jacqueline opened her purse. From it she took a stenographer's notebook, a ballpoint pen, and a small thermos bottle. Taking the cap off the thermos, she filled her cup and Sue's. "I'm going to write a historical romance novel. Had I but known what riches lie buried in the fields of schlock, I'd have done it long ago. Excuse me for a while. I may as well get my first chapter finished during this lull."

She began scribbling furiously. Sue tried to see what she was writing, but was foiled by the hat.

Jacqueline had filled half a dozen pages with her big, sprawling script before her literary aspirations were interrupted by a gasp from Sue. It was not her first gasp; as the flame of inspiration waxed hot, Jacqueline had shoved the hat back from her brow, thus enabling Sue to read what she was writing. But this gasp had a more poignant quality. Jacqueline looked up from her work to find Victor von Damm looming, and doing it very well.

His costume helped—high polished boots, trousers that clung to the muscles of his thighs, gold braid, gold stripes, gold buttons, and a "slung" pelisse trimmed with fur. Jacqueline considered him in silence for a moment before remarking to Sue, "Tacky is not the word for that outfit, is it? My generation would call it corny, but I'm sure yours has more forceful terms."

Victor stopped looming. "I have to talk to you," he said to Sue. "I have to explain—"

"No explanations are necessary. I quite understand.

I wouldn't want you to put yourself out for me. I can't do your career any good, can I? Excuse me, Jacqueline, I'm going to the ladies' room. All that coffee . . ."

She was out of her seat and away with a celerity that left Victor gaping. He turned. Jacqueline said, "You can't follow her into the ladies' room."

"Then you explain. Tell her I . . ." His voice died away. The other seats at the table were now occupied, except for the one on Jacqueline's right; the purse and the outer extremities of the hat filled that space, and no one had had the courage to suggest Jacqueline remove either. However, Victor's presence had been noted, and the other guests were staring. One elderly woman, her eyes soft with passion, extended a quivering hand.

"Excuse me—Victor—"

Without taking his eyes off Jacqueline, Victor grabbed the hand and planted an emphatic kiss on the air above it.

"Your technique is slipping," said Jacqueline. "And so is your pelisse. That strap is supposed to go—"

"Oh, hell." Victor hoisted the dangling jacket back into place. "I better split before . . . Tell Sue. She doesn't understand. I couldn't let her . . . Oh, hell."

He gave the palpitating matrons a hunted look. Several had risen and were edging toward him, right hands raised. "VV gave me a message for you," he said rapidly. "Call her—room 1215—after the breakfast. Oh God, here they come!" He bolted, his pelisse again at half-mast.

"Humph," said Jacqueline. She poured herself another cup of coffee and returned to her writing.

Before long she was interrupted again. A hand removed the purse from the empty seat and a voice said, "Thanks for saving me a place."

Jacqueline scowled. "Hello, Betsy. I was—"

"Don't tell me you were saving it for someone else. I know that purse, and that trick."

Jacqueline closed her notebook. "What's this, infiltration of the enemy camp?"

"Dubretta suggested it. Should have thought of it myself."

"Spies," Jacqueline suggested, "pass undiscovered longer when they assume the enemy uniform."

Betsy was wearing the same khaki shirt and pants she had worn the day before. With her broad shoulders, muscular forearms, and short hair she looked like a boy—or, more accurately, a middle-aged man in excellent physical condition, for her skin showed the wear and tear of innumerable sit-ins and marches.

"I took off my buttons," Betsy said. She inspected Jacqueline, from her hat to her voluminous skirt, and shook her head. "You have a lot of gall criticizing me. That's the tackiest dress I ever saw."

"Thanks. Why don't you go protest something?"

"That's what I'm doing." Betsy leaned back and folded her arms. "Oh, don't worry, I'm not going to say a word. I'm just going to look. Where'd you get the coffee?"

"I brought it with me." Betsy reached for the purse. Jacqueline said, "There isn't any left. We should be starting soon; there's Hattie."

"Ah." Betsy sat up.

Sue slid into her chair. She looked curiously at Betsy, and Jacqueline introduced them. "So you're one of the piglets," Betsy said, seeing Sue's red name tag. "How'd you get into this racket, Sue? You look reasonably intelligent."

Jacqueline sighed. "I love the way you infiltrate," she said. "Like a bulldozer."

"Were you in the protest march yesterday?" Sue asked.

"I organized it," Betsy said proudly. "Here—have a button." She produced one from the pocket of her shirt. Bright-grccn letters on a daffodil-yellow background proclaimed, STOP RAPE.

"Go on, take it," Betsy urged. "Or are you in favor of rape?"

"Of course not!"

"I'll take it." Jacqueline affixed the button to the bosom of the lavender gown and studied the effect approvingly. The button was the perfect touch. "I should have brought my ERA NOW button," she remarked. "One on one side and one on the other. . . ."

Sue and Betsy ignored her. Sue had decidcd that the radical was just another of Jacqueline's eccentric friends, and Betsy had decided that Sue was a potential convert. "I'll bet you just started writing this slime," she said winningly. "Think what you're doing. It's not too late to quit."

"And find salvation in the arms of the movement," Jacqueline chanted. "Glory, glory, hallelujah—"

"Shut up," Betsy said. "We'll talk later, Sue. The old bag is about to open the proceedings, and I want to take notes."

Hattie breathed into the microphone. "One, two, testing . . ." The head table was less flamboyantly furnished with authors that morning; only Victor von Damm and Emerald Fitzroy were present. As Hattie prepared to address the room, Victor leaned across the empty seat that separated him from Hattie. Her hand quickly covered the open mike, but not before the assembled throng heard, "I'm getting the hell out of here. I won't—"

Hattie's fixed smile tightened. Her reply was inaudible. After a moment Victor subsided and Hattie began speaking.

Betsy earnestly wrote down every word Hattie said in her obviously brand-new stenographer's notebook. Jacqueline was reminded of the old academic joke that describes note-taking as the transfer of words from the notes of the professor to the books of the students, without passing through the brain of either. The speech consisted solely of reiterated greetings plus a rundown of the day's activities. Hattie then picked up her fork and the waiters served breakfast.

Jacqueline, whose appetite was hearty, devoured her leathery scrambled eggs and chilly sausage and toast before polishing off the cheese Danish she had had the foresight to bring with her.

"Where are the rest of them?" Betsy asked.

"I only brought one."

"Not the Danish, damn it; the authors. The ones I particularly wanted to observe aren't here—the Valeries."

"Valentine wasn't supposed to be here," Sue informed her. "She's the big star; I understand she only agreed to make one appearance a day. She'll probably be at the cocktail party."

"What about the other one?"

"Maybe she's sick."

Jacqueline suspected this suggestion was correct, though not in the sense Sue meant. Jean's nerve had finally broken under the strain. Or—more interesting idea—was a rebellion brewing? Jacqueline was sure Jean had been forced to attend the conference, probably by Hattie. Jean would do anything to avoid exposure; she was the perfect blackmail victim.

That didn't necessarily mean that the other writers had been subjected to the same duress. Most of them positively cried out to be exploited. However, the change in Victor's attitude suggested another recruit to the ranks of the rebellion. The day before he had reveled in the absurd pageant. Now, after his protest, he had relapsed into sullen silence, never raising his eyes from his plate.

Jacqueline considered raising this intriguing point with Betsy, but decided against it. Why should she do Betsy's work for her? Speeches by two of the guests— a reviewer of romance novels, and an editor who praised his writers for helping to make him a lot of money—wound up the breakfast. Victor started for Jacqueline's table, but Hattie collared him and marched him away.

"Do you know him?" asked Betsy, who had not missed the byplay.

"Who?"

"The gorgeous hunk in the Merry Widow costume. I don't know why it is," Betsy went on mournfully, "but the most gorgeous men are all chauvinist pigs."

"Thank God for Alan Alda," Jacqueline said.

Betsy brightened. "Right."

Jacqueline made her escape. Sue trailed after her. "Which of the workshops are you going to?" she asked.

Jacqueline consulted her program, which was, of course, printed on pink paper. "I can't decide between 'How to Write the Erotic Romantic Historical Novel,' and 'The Leading Men of Love.' Victor will be at that one, I suppose."

"Then I'm going to the other one." Sue's lips set tightly.

"They aren't the only choices. How about 'Romantic Costumes for Heroines and Authors'? Or 'Setting the Mood: Moonlight, Powdered Wigs, and Swordplay.' Swordplay?"

"Your friend is right," Sue snapped. "It's disgusting. Exploitive, leering, prurient. . . . I'm going for a walk. I need fresh air."

She walked off before Jacqueline could point out that fresh air was not a commodity easily obtained in Manhattan. Jacqueline returned to her program. "Setting the Mood" sounded like the most imbecilic, i.e., entertaining, of the workshops, but, on the other hand, writing an erotic romantic historical novel was her new goal. Though she had every confidence in her ability to produce a best-seller without any assistance whatever, the workshop might give her some useful ideas.

She wafted her lavender way along the hall, picking up promotional literature from the publishers' booths as she went. Before long she was accosted by Dubretta. "I couldn't believe it was you," the columnist said. "Do you mind if I get a picture?"

"Not at all."

Jacqueline posed obligingly for the photographer Hattie waved to the fore. Parasol over her shoulder, hat shading her face, she simpered and twirled and looked sentimental until Dubretta said, "That should do it. The satire will be wasted on most of my readers, but a few of them might catch it. 'One of the writers at the—' "

"I refuse to be anonymous," Jacqueline protested. "My pen name is Valerie von Hentzau."

"Right." Dubretta scribbled. Jacqueline looked shamelessly over her shoulder, and Dubretta said maliciously, "You'll have to wait till it comes out in print. Nobody can read my private shorthand but me. Did you see my column this morning?"

"Yes, I did. How do you keep your pens from melting in all that vitriol?"

"Just wait. I think I'm on the trail of something big. It ought to blow this whole . . . What is it with you, hypnotism? Am I the only sucker who pours out her soul to you?"

"No. Are you feeling better this morning?"

"I feel fine. Why do you— Oh, that. No problem. It's a congenital condition, but it's under control."

Jacqueline wondered. In her gray linen suit, with her iron-gray hair, Dubretta was all gray that morning, including her face.

"Don't confide in me," she said lightly. "I'm not interested."

"I think I should warn you," Dubretta said slowly, "that I'm on to that friend of yours. Oh, don't look so bland. I'm talking about Valerie Vanderbilt, whose noble family has disowned her because of her wild and woolly sex life. And who is in reality Jean Frascatti, mild-mannered English prof, who probably hasn't even kissed a man in thirty years."

"How did you find out?"

"It was damned ingenious, as a matter of fact." Dubretta smiled smugly. "You two are about the same age. I had a hunch you might have gone to school together. Your friend Betsy told me where; I tracked down an old grad who has all her college yearbooks, and—*voilà*."

"Not bad," Jacqueline admitted.

"That makes two," Dubretta gloated. "Jean and Joe—both frauds set up by dear old Hattie. But they're small-fry. Hattie's the big fish, and I think . . . Damn it, there I go again. I'd better leave before I spill my guts."

Jacqueline did not detain her. She started toward Suite C, having decided to attend the seminar that promised training in the writing of erotica; but before she had gone far, a hand caught her arm and spun her around.

"I told you to stay away from that bitch! What are you, one of her stooges?"

Laurie's pustulant countenance was only inches from hers, and Laurie's voice held the high, whining note that betokened incipient hysteria.

Jacqueline replied instantly: "Why, Laurie, what a gorgeous dress. It's even prettier than the one you wore yesterday. Where did you get it?"

Laurie's mouth remained open, but instead of continuing her tirade she swallowed and stuttered before muttering, "I made it."

Jacqueline's unexpected response had caught the

girl off guard and calmed her—for the moment. However, Jacqueline's compliment had been sincere. The dress, a frothy concoction of lace-edged frills and ruffled petticoats, was unsuited to Laurie's large frame, but it was beautifully made, even though the dainty rosebud print was sweat-stained and soiled, and smears of chocolate marked the bodice.

"Did you really?" Jacqueline exclaimed. "You are clever. Where did you get the pattern?"

"I copied it from a picture in the museum," Laurie mumbled.

"Without a pattern? That's really impressive."

The look of gratified pride on Laurie's face roused an unwilling pity in Jacqueline, though the girl's heavy hand still held her hostage. She knew her advantage might be only temporary; she had seen the signs of drug addiction often enough to know that the user's changes of mood could be violent and unpredictable. The hallway had emptied. The seminars must have started.

"I make all my clothes," Laurie boasted. "I made a gown for Valentine, too. . . ."

Her idol's name brought on the change Jacqueline had feared. Rage darkened her face. Her hand tightened its grip.

"Oh, the hell with it," Jacqueline said. She swung her purse, heavily laden as usual, into the pit of Laurie's stomach.

Laurie howled like a banshee. Clutching her middle, she leaned forward, squashing Jacqueline against the wall. Tears streamed down her face.

Jacqueline could have escaped then, but it was impossible to abandon someone in such voluble distress. Squeezing out from under Laurie's weight, she patted the girl's heaving shoulders. "Control yourself. I didn't hit you that hard."

Laurie's uninhibited wails had attracted attention. Curious faces appeared in open doorways, and people sidled cautiously toward the scene. Among them was Hattie herself. She took over the job of shoulder-patting, and glared at Jacqueline.

"What have you done to this pore chile? There, there, honey, just quiet down."

"What have I done to her? If you have any influence over this perturbed person, try to persuade her to see a doctor. The girl's goofy."

"She hit me," Laurie wailed. "All I was doing was talking to her, and she hit me!" She clutched Hattie in a feverish grip.

"There, there." Pat, pat. "There, there. You just go and wash your face, honey, and calm yourself. Aunt Hattie will take care of the mean woman."

Laurie departed, snuffling and wiping her nose on the back of her hand.

Jacqueline's lip curled. "The girl is goofy," she repeated. "She's rowing with only one oar. There ain't no top rung on her ladder. She is, to put it another way, in need of help."

"I know," Hattie murmured. "You must have done something to upset her—"

"Don't try those tactics on me," Jacqueline said sharply. "The girl virtually attacked me. I feel sorry for her, but I'm not taking any guilt trips."

"I'm not her guardian," Hattie said. "If you've got

any complaints . . . Wait a minute. I've seen you before. Talking to Dubretta Duberstein."

"I know her slightly," Jacqueline said warily.

A broad, remarkably unconvincing smile stretched Hattie's jaws. "Honey, I am so sorry about all this. You just must forgive me for bein' so sharp, I was a teeny bit upset. I expect you're all shook up too. Why don't you come to my suite and let me give you a nice cup of tea?"

Jacqueline needed no urging. This promised to be even more entertaining than the workshop on moonlight and swordplay.

Hattie chatted non-stop, in her phony southern accent. "My, what a pretty gown. I noticed you at the breakfast, and thought, my, what a gorgeous gown that is. I just can't tell you how sorry I am you were upset. That pore chile has so many problems. I try to help her, but what can I do? She's from quite a nice family, you know. Pots and pots of money. But it's one of those nasty modern situations—drinking, neglect, you know what I mean. Well, here we are. You sit down over there, in that nice comfy chair, and I'll put the kettle on."

She trotted out.

If Jacqueline had doubted Dubretta's statement that Hattie was making a good living out of love, the luxurious surroundings would have supported the columnist's claim. Living room with balcony, bedroom and bath, kitchen— If single rooms commanded a price of over one hundred dollars a day, this suite must be setting Hattie back a pretty penny.

Hattie bustled in with a tray.

"I shouldn't be keeping you from your workshops," Jacqueline said, figuring she had better speak first or she might not get a chance to speak at all.

"Oh, honey, don't you-all worry about that. I'm not responsible for Laurie—not in the least—but she's turned to me as a sort of mother substitute. I feel people ought to help others when they can."

The image was so incongruous, Jacqueline almost laughed aloud. Hattie cultivated the kindly-old-aunt technique rather badly; her eyes were as empty as the windows of an abandoned house, and her motherly instincts, if any, resembled those of the black widow spider. Or did spiders eat their offspring? While Jacqueline was considering this point of natural history, Hattie rambled on.

"She does seem more disturbed lately. Of course, seeing Valentine has shaken the pore thing. She absolutely idolizes Valentine. I'll talk to her and tell her to behave herself."

This was not the solution Jacqueline had had in mind, but she knew it would be a waste of time to suggest that Hattie take any decisive action. She wondered when Hattie would get to the point. Subtle she was not.

"Have you known Dubretta long?" Hattie asked casually.

Jacqueline smiled. "Not long."

"Such an intellectual woman. Almost too intelligent, don't you think? Really almost masculine. I suppose I should resent all the cruel things she says about me and my friends, but I just can't hate her, honey; she's too pathetic. It's envy, that's what it is. She's never known the rapture of love, and she resents those who have."

"Have you known her long?" Jacqueline asked.

It was a random shot, designed to cut off the nauseating flow of hypocrisy, but she struck a nerve. The sandy, graying lashes flickered, and Hattie said brusquely, "No."

"Something she said made me think you were old acquaintances," Jacqueline murmured. She sipped her tea. It was terrible—teabag-cheap, and very weak. Hattie had probably used only one teabag for the whole pot.

"What else did she say?" Hattie replaced her cup in the saucer with a decisive thump and abandoned her fake accent. "What's she up to? Look here, Miss— Mrs.—what's your name, anyhow?"

Jacqueline indicated her tag with a fingertip. She had painted her nails to match her dress; her hands looked like those of a corpse in the first stage of decomposition.

"Kirby," Hattie said. "Should I know you?"

"Not yet. I," said Jacqueline modestly, "am writing my first romantic historical novel. If you'd like me to send you the manuscript when I've finished—"

"Oh, I get it." Hattie smiled cynically. "Well, you might make it at that. You've got the feeling for the— the—"

"Hype," Jacqueline supplied.

"Background," Hattie corrected. "Okay, I'll read your manuscript—if you'll do me a teeny tiny favor in return."

"I can't tell you anything about Dubretta. She dislikes you—but I don't suppose that's news to you."

"It sure isn't."

"And she would like to—I believe she used the

phrase 'get something on you.' But that isn't news to you either. And," Jacqueline said, "it can't worry you, since you have nothing to hide."

"Good gracious no." Hattie laughed heartily. "I suppose she's been saying all sorts of mean, slanderous things about me and my writers?"

"Oh, yes." Jacqueline laughed heartily.

Silence followed. Seeing that her not-too-covert hints had failed, Hattie abandoned subterfuge. "What?"

"I beg your pardon?"

"What did she say? I'm entitled to know."

"But you aren't entitled to hear it from me. I am only a bystander," Jacqueline explained. "An onlooker, if you will. I do not interfere in other people's business."

She had, of course, already taken sides. Hattie was a predatory, nosy old crook. The woman couldn't even make a decent cup of tea.

"Laurie claims Dubretta is after Valentine," Hattie said. "Of course the girl is crazy, but . . ."

"I must be going," Jacqueline said. "Thank you for the lovely tea."

Hattie stared at her from under her heavy brows and said slowly, "I'd like to look at your manuscript, honey, but I'm pretty busy. I may find I don't have time to read it."

"I see."

"I knew you'd understand."

It would have been difficult to misunderstand. Hattie could hardly have stated the proposition more crudely: Find out what Dubretta is doing and I'll push your book. Jacqueline wasn't surprised at Hattie's bla-

tant attempt at bribery; what surprised her was that
Hattie should be desperate enough to proposition a
stranger. Perhaps Hattie hadn't believed her when she
said her acquaintance with Dubretta was of the slightest. From Hattie's point of view it was worth a try; she
wouldn't keep her side of the bargain even if she got
the information she wanted.

Jacqueline smiled her sweetest smile. "Perhaps I'll
see you again before long," she said meaningfully.

"I do hope so." Hattie's smile was equally saccha-
rine and equally significant. She rose ponderously to
her feet. The audience was over.

But before she could escort her visitor to the door,
another door burst open and an agitated voice cried, "I
tell you, I won't stand for it any more. I've got to talk
to Hattie. . . . Hattie?"

Valerie Valentine—for it was indeed (Jacqueline assured herself) the Queen of Love—came to a halt. She
looked like the heroine of one of her books, her tumbled red-gold hair held back by a white satin ribbon
and her slender body wrapped in an opulent negligee
that contained enough yards of white chiffon to drape
a king-sized bed. Seeing Jacqueline, the girl's violet
eyes opened wide.

"Valentine, my dear . . ." A man appeared behind her
and put his hands on her shoulders. He was not as ugly
as Valentine was beautiful, but there was a distinct
suggestion of the classic fairy tale in the juxtaposition
of the two faces.

The newcomer, whom Jacqueline had last seen in
the car with Valentine and Hattie, was the first to
speak. "I'm sorry, Hattie. You have a guest?"

"As you see," Hattie snapped. "It was nice of you to come, Mrs. Kirk."

"Kirby," Jacqueline said. She braced herself against Hattie's nudges, and stood like a rock. "I know you all have things to discuss, but I just can't tear myself away till I tell Valentine how much I admire her. This is such a thrill—you can't imagine!"

Valentine started, as if she had been poked from behind. "And it's a pleasure for me to meet my readers," she said, in a breathless monotone. "You inspire me to do better. I always feel . . . Did you say Kirby?" Shaking off the hands that tried to hold her back, she started toward Jacqueline.

Grudgingly Hattie introduced them. The chubby little man was Max Hollenstein, Valentine's business manager. He took Jacqueline's hand, and as their eyes met, Jacqueline realized that here was an adversary as dangerous in his way as Hattie was in hers. His luminous, weary brown eyes were frighteningly intelligent, and there was humor as well as self-deprecation in the curve of his thin lips. Or was he an adversary? At any rate, he knew she was not simply one of Valentine's fans. Fans were not invited to take tea with the great Hattie.

"Which of Valentine's books is your favorite, Mrs. Kirby?" he asked, with a skeptical smile.

"I love them all," Jacqueline said.

The little man's smile broadened. Before he could continue his delicate inquisition, Hattie explained, "Mrs. Kirky has had a little encounter with pore Laurie. I really am worried about that chile."

"Worried? Encounter?" Max's lips twisted. "Your

euphemisms enchant me, Hattie. I hope, Mrs. Kirby, that you aren't in need of more than casual first aid."

"No damage done, Mr. Hollenstein."

"I can't stand that girl," Valentine said vehemently. "She's disgusting. She makes me nauseous. I told you before, Hattie, you've got to keep her away from me."

"And I told you . . ." Hattie's teeth snapped together. "Well, honey, I'll see what I can do. Now I must run. An appointment with a publisher."

"It's been a pleasure meeting you, Mrs. Kirby," Max added.

Jacqueline had no choice but to take her departure. She turned to Valentine. "It's been such a thrill."

". . . pleasure . . ." Valentine murmured. She gave Jacqueline a look that, on a face less virginally innocent, might have been considered sly. "Let me give you one of my books."

"Oh, how wonderful," Jacqueline cried.

"It's just a paperback, but . . . Wait here." Valentine flowed out the door through which she had entered. The suite was obviously more extensive than Jacqueline had imagined; beyond the door she saw, not another room, but a hallway leading to unknown regions. Hattie had her top writer and the latter's manager literally in her stable.

Before long Valentine came back, carrying a book. The cover painting was similar in style and content to most of the others Jacqueline had seen. In this case the brawny hero was wearing part of a uniform—boots and tight blue trousers with a stripe down the side. As Valentine held it out to Jacqueline, Max reached for it.

"Have you written something charming, my dear?"

Valentine's face froze. Before Max could take the book, Jacqueline grabbed it. Opening it, she glanced at the inscription.

"Oh, Valentine, how sweet! I'll always treasure it and never allow anyone else to see it—my own private, personal message. And now I must let you busy people get back to work."

Hattie escorted her to the door. Jacqueline glanced back. Valentine had dropped into a chair, but Max stood watching, a faint enigmatic smile on his lips.

Jacqueline tucked the book carefully into her purse. The message had indeed been private and personal. It read, "Help me—please help me." And then, incongruously and rather pathetically—"With best wishes, Valerie Valentine."

Chapter 4

Jacqueline wandered into the erotic-novel seminar in time to catch the last lecture—"The Act of Love: Be Original." She paid scant attention to the speaker's examples. None was original, at least not to a reader of *The Lustful Turk*.

She had called Jean's room before going to the seminar, but there had been no answer. Perhaps Jean had grown tired of waiting and had gone out—or else she was hiding in the closet, biting her nails and muttering, "Oh God," at regular intervals. Jacqueline shook her head disgustedly. Jean was as limp and wet as a soggy mop. She had walked straight into the web in whose center Hattie squatted like a cannibalistic spider. . . .

Surely it was their mates black widow spiders devoured, not their children? No matter; the figure of speech still applied. " 'Come into my parlor,' said the spider to the fly. . . ." Jean had walked right in, and had handed Hattie the weapon with which to blackmail her. Jacqueline only hoped fear of exposure to the university was the only weapon Hattie had. Most people wouldn't have cared about that, but Jean had always been timid as a rabbit.

Jacqueline's eyes crinkled with amusement as she remembered the night their dormitory head had almost caught Jean with *The Lustful Turk*—or was it one of the other masterpieces of Victorian pornography they had smuggled from room to room, swathed in brown paper? It had taken two hours, and half a bottle of the cheap red wine they kept hidden in the bookcase, to restore Jean. They had shared a lot of things—long solemn conversations about Life and Men and Sex, orgies of eating followed by fanatical diets. . . .

"Strawberry jam and whipped cream," said the lecturer. The phrase caught Jacqueline's attention, but after listening to the rest of the sentence she decided the procedure was messy, not sexy. She returned to her meditations.

She had better take steps to extract Jean from Hattie's clutches without delay. There was something rotten in the History-Romance business, or at least that part of it under Hattie's influence. Everything pointed to that conclusion—Victor's dire hints, Hattie's clumsy attempt at bribery, Valentine's plea for help, Laurie's strange behavior. The girl was obviously suffering from some variety of mental illness, possibly exacerbated by drugs, but the particular form her delusion had taken might be affected by the underlying malaise. Even if she didn't know the secret, the uncanny perception of the slightly goofy made her aware of her idol's fear. Valentine must be a little goofy herself to resort to such a hackneyed device as scribbling a message in a book. Presumably she had learned of Jacqueline's reputed detective talents from Jean. Were all Hattie's top writers involved in the plot? And what was the role of the smiling, enigmatic little man named Max Hollenstein?

Jacqueline was happy. Old loyalties and old friendships demanded action on her part, but she would have been the first to admit that her predominant motive was resentment. Hattie had not only served her weak tea, she had had the effrontery to offer her, Jacqueline Kirby, a bribe. It would be a pleasure to step on Hattie and squash her flat. A dark and evil miasma followed the woman, like the slime of a snail's track. . . . Not bad, Jacqueline thought, reaching for her notebook. I can use that to describe Sir Wilfred Blackthorn, the villain.

Sue slammed the door. "You didn't go to the awards ceremony."

Jacqueline did not look up from her book. "Was I supposed to?"

"You want to know who won?"

"Not particularly."

"Valerie Valentine!" Sue kicked the foot of the bed. "Valerie Valentine, Valerie Valentine. Three awards in three different categories. And you—you're reading one of her books!"

"Had I but known, I would not have transgressed," Jacqueline said sarcastically. "Actually, I was writing my book, but the font of inspiration dried up. I'm priming the pump."

"Disgusting," Sue muttered.

Reaching the end of a chapter, Jacqueline closed *A Willow in Her Hand.*

"No," she said. "It isn't. It's good. It's better than good. In terms of characterization, style, pace, all other literary criteria, it is far above every other romance I've read. It shouldn't even be put in that category. And this sleazy cover is a complete misrepresentation of the action, the setting, and the mood."

"I know," Sue admitted, in a small voice. "It was her books that inspired me to write. Damn, damn! It just isn't fair. She's got everything—looks, talent, fame, wealth. . . ."

"But not love," Jacqueline said. "The Earl of Whatever is obviously a publicity stunt; the only man in poor Valentine's life seems to be that middle-aged manager of hers."

"If she hasn't got it, it's because she doesn't want it." Sue kicked the table. "She could have any man she wanted. They're all crazy about her."

Enlightenment dawned on Jacqueline. "Victor is not in love with Valentine," she said.

"You wouldn't say that if you had seen them today." Jean kicked the bureau. "He was all over her, bowing and kissing her hand, and . . . Hattie kept throwing out hints about a royal love affair—the King and Queen of Romance. . . ."

"So that's Hattie's latest scheme," Jacqueline mused. "The Earl must have turned out to be a dud."

Her suggestion did not convince Sue. "I hate that girl," she muttered. "Valentine, Valentine . . . Everything just falls into her lap. I could kill her."

"Don't say that," Jacqueline said sharply.

Sue's shoulders sagged. She sat down on the edge of the bed. "I didn't mean it."

"I know. But don't say it. How did the other awards go?"

"Valerie won the top three—Historical Romance, Historical Novel, and Classic Historical Romance."

"The categories seem to overlap somewhat," Jacqueline said. "Didn't anyone else win anything?"

"Victor won the Love's Leading Man award." Sue laughed cynically. "And Valerie Vanderbilt took Historical Saga. All Hattie's writers, by a strange coincidence."

"That reminds me." Jacqueline reached for the phone. "Excuse me a minute. . . . Jean? Where the hell have you been? I've been calling all day. . . . Well, most of the day. I lost track of . . . What? I thought you wanted . . . I know it's late. I tried to . . . Yes, I'll be there. I want to talk to you too. Afterwards? . . . Fine. See you then."

She hung up. "We'd better get ready for the cocktail party. I didn't realize how late it is."

"I'm not going."

"Oh yes, you are. Sulking is childish."

"I am not sulking!"

"Besides, I need a foil—someone who looks normal. Don't desert me; I'll buy you a drink or two, and then we'll have dinner and talk about everybody."

A faint gleam of interest showed on Sue's face. "Big deal," she murmured. "The drinks are free."

"You poor innocent." Jacqueline swung her feet off the bed and stood up. "I've attended similar affairs; your exorbitantly priced ticket entitles you to one cocktail. After that you're on your own, with Hattie getting her cut of every drop you imbibe."

"Well . . . What are you going to wear?"

"The same thing I wore this morning. But I've added a few touches."

The hat now boasted a ruffle of lace five inches wide. It hung down over Jacqueline's eyebrows in front. Amid the flowers and bows on the crown perched a stuffed cockatoo, its molting wings spread. It had one red glass eye. The other was missing. A cascade of glaringly fake amethysts dribbled from Jacqueline's ears to her shoulders. Her sheer gray stockings had clocks of tiny hearts running halfway up the calf.

She applied makeup with a lavish hand. Her cheekbones were not inconspicuous even when unadorned; following the advice of the expert at the lecture she had attended, she "sculptured" them so enthusiastically that they stood out like snow-covered islands in a muddy sea. Heavy black false lashes dragged her eyelids down to half-mast.

Squinting between the lace fringe and the eyelashes, Jacqueline outlined her mouth with frosty plum lipstick and then turned from the mirror. "How's that?"

"You aren't going like that!"

"Am I not? Hurry up and get dressed. Or are you going in your petticoat? You know," Jacqueline said musingly, "that might not be a bad idea."

Sue snatched her dress off the hanger and backed away, as if she feared Jacqueline might bustle her out the door in her underwear. "You're kidding. Aren't you?"

"On second thought, it would be more effective at the ball tomorrow night. It is a costume ball, you know; the others will be dripping with ruffles and encased in crinolines. We'll slash that lacy camisole and rip the petticoat in a few strategic places, and you can go as Blaze, heroine of *Slave of Lust*, trying to veil her snowy charms from the lascivious eyes of the Sultan. We could bleach a lock of your hair, too. Blaze had a silver streak rippling through the midnight glory of—"

"Stop that!" Sue put on her dress and attacked the zipper so forcefully that it jammed.

"Turn around," Jacqueline said. As she dealt efficiently with the zipper she said, "The trouble with you is, you have no sense of humor."

"I do, too!"

"Now—let's have a look at you."

Sue tugged her skirt straight and posed, looking self-conscious.

"Humph," Jacqueline said.

"You don't like my dress?"

Jacqueline shook her head. "Sexy doesn't suit you. Black is not your color. The neckline is too high. The skirt is too long. Other than that . . ."

Sue glared at her and Jacqueline said approvingly, "Good. When someone is rude to you, don't cry— swear. All I'm saying is that you are one of the few writers present who should wear what Hattie seems to think of as romantic clothes. Ruffles and lace and organdy look ridiculous on elderly ingenues like Valerie Vanderbilt and Emerald What's-Her-Name. You could get away with that image. And take off your glasses."

"I can't see without them."

"Obviously you did not attend the lecture on how to promote yourself. Don't you want to be a successful romance writer?"

"I'm beginning to think I don't."

"Indeed? Well, we'll discuss it later. It's time to go."

As Jacqueline had predicted, some of the ensembles worn by the guests at the cocktail party were almost as remarkable as hers. Emerald Fitzroy exposed her brittle collarbones in an off-the-shoulder gown of crimson taffeta whose vivid color wrought havoc with her sallow complexion. Another writer, whom Jacqueline did not know, had obviously made her dress. It was pink muslin with pink, red, and purple hearts appliqued at random. She had forgotten to remove the basting threads. However, Jacqueline's cockatoo rescued her from anonymity; it rose over the heads of the crowd, squinting malevolently out of its single red glass eye.

At the door Jacqueline and Sue exchanged their tickets of admission for other tickets entitling them to one cocktail apiece. "Told you so," Jacqueline remarked, as they got in line at a table where bartenders were sloshing various liquids into small pink plastic cups.

Having settled this first and most important matter, Jacqueline inspected the gathering. A string quartet was sawing away at one end of the room; the results of its labors were inaudible except at close range, since all the people in the crowded room were talking to one another, or in a few cases to themselves. The latter appeared to be fans, nervously rehearsing the graceful speeches they hoped to address to their favorite writers as soon as they got up the courage to approach them. The classification of colored name tags was unnecessary; it was possible to distinguish editors from authors, fans from publicists by the clothes they were wearing. The older fans had donned the standard "afternoon" or "cocktail" dresses of their youth—linen, silk, and linen- or silk-look polyester. A few perspired gently in fur jackets.

For the most part, the writers doggedly tried to live up to the romantic image. There were even a few picture hats—though none, Jacqueline observed complacently, was of the dimensions of her own. The editors, publicists, and agents had made token concessions to the mood, in the form of pink shirts and dresses, but most wore the usual New York business attire, which is one of the drabbest in the universe.

It was on these individuals that Jacqueline's mercenary attention focused. She had not yet decided which publishing house to favor with her completed manuscript when she completed it. In the course of the past few days she had identified the big names. The pretty blonde, who resembled the heroines of the contemporary romances she peddled so successfully, was an assistant editor of one of the big lines—Lost Love Romances. The tall, broad-shouldered woman in the pinstripe suit was Margo Barrister, editor-in-chief of Windblown Romances; her companion, a graceful young man with shoulder-length blond curls, was Robin Bernstein, who represented the rival Wax Candle line. It was rumored that Wax Candle had lost its shirt on Regencies and was now focusing on earlier historic periods, specifically the Late Stone Age.

From the fixed smiles on the faces of the two editors Jacqueline deduced that they were being poisonously polite to one another, and she wondered if their antagonism had anything to do with the fact that Wind-blown's most recent hit had featured a Neanderthal hero and a Cro-Magnon heroine. ("From our joining, Fleet Gazelle, will come a new people.") Maybe, Jacqueline mused, I can change my setting from fifteenth-century France to the Middle Paleolithic. It shouldn't be too difficult. Stone axes instead of swords, a lake village on stilts instead of a castle. The villain could be a wicked medicine man. . . .

"I want another drink," Sue announced, jogging Jacqueline's elbow. "How do I get it?"

Annoyed at having her literary plotting interrupted, Jacqueline was brusque. "You buy a ticket. Get one for me if you will." She took a twenty-dollar bill from the mauve satin envelope with which she had reluctantly replaced her usual huge purse. She felt undressed and incapable without the purse. But Art must be served, and the purse had not matched her ensemble.

"Thanks." Sue took the money and vanished into the mob. Under the lace fringe Jacqueline's brow furrowed. Then she dismissed Sue with a shrug. She was tired of dewy-eyed innocents who had to be protected from themselves and everyone else.

Along one side of the room was a row of tables draped in white with the usual decorations, where the promotional gimcracks of the publisher sponsoring the cocktail party were prominently displayed. Among the litter was an enormous reproduction of the cover of Valentine's latest book—the one Jacqueline was reading. Not far away was Valentine herself, and as she studied the arrangement, Jacqueline's painted lips cracked in an appreciative grin.

It was a masterpiece of romantic kitsch, but it had the practical purpose of isolating the Queen of Love from the admirers who—Hattie hoped—might otherwise have trampled her. White picket fences twined with artificial vines and roses enclosed a space that was meant to suggest a lovely garden. The floor was covered with imitation grass of the variety used in football stadiums. Wrought-iron patio furniture and potted plants were scattered about. In this enclosure Hattie and her stable had taken their picturesque places. A wobbly arch of plastic greenery framed the baroque bench where Valentine sat, with the "Earl of Devonbrook" beside her, stiff as a wax dummy. Victor von Damm, once again wearing his Prisoner of Zenda garb of black trousers and flowing white shirt, leaned over the back of the bench. Hattie, in gray satin with a huge corsage of sweetheart roses dangling from the shelf of her bosom, was seated at a nearby table. Her eyes never left Valentine. At first Jacqueline thought VV had found an excuse not to attend. Then she made out a rigid form trying to hide behind a skimpy screen of fake roses and a potted rubber plant.

Having located the stars of the evening, Jacqueline turned her eagle eye (critics were inclined to substitute the name of another, less socially acceptable bird) upon the assemblage at large, and was gratified to see many familiar faces. The genteel lady from Boston, heading purposefully in the direction of the bower and Victor von Damm; Emerald, scowling in the direction of the bower—she had not been asked to join the elite; the haggard woman agent, looking for clients; the bald head and cherubic countenance of Max Hollenstein, buttering up the editor-in-chief of Moonlight Love Romances. And surely that was Betsy, almost unrecognizable in flowered silk, gold sandals, and a brassy wig that was the identical twin of Jean's. It must be the most popular model this year.

Betsy's eyes moved shiftily around the room. She saw Jacqueline, and twisted her face in a violent grimace before she disappeared behind a large publisher.

Another familiar face made Jacqueline wish she had a portly publisher to use as a screen. Laurie was wearing a flowing pink caftan, ornately embroidered in gold thread. When her black-rimmed eyes found Jacqueline, the latter conquered a cowardly impulse to retreat. But Laurie's greeting was more than amiable, it was positively friendly.

"Hi, Mrs. Kirsky. Listen, I'm really sorry about what happened. I didn't feel too good. I was sick at my stomach. Afterwards I threw up."

"I'm sorry to hear that," Jacqueline said sincerely.

"Oh, I'm okay now. I get sick at my stomach a lot, but it doesn't last. As soon as I throw up—"

"Maybe you shouldn't be drinking," Jacqueline said, glancing at Laurie's pink plastic glass. (Anything to change the subject.)

"It's just diet ginger ale. I'm on a diet. I haven't had anything to eat all day except a candy bar and some cottage cheese."

"Good for you."

"So Hattie said I should apologize. She says you're a friend of Valentine's. I guess you were just sucking up to that woman to find out what she wants so you can tell Valentine."

Curiosity overcame the repugnance Laurie's proximity inevitably induced. Jacqueline said, "Can I ask you a question, Laurie?"

"Sure."

"What is Dubretta Duberstein trying to do to Valentine?"

"She writes lies about her," Laurie said. "You know that notebook she carries, the one she's always writing in? It's full of lies about Valentine. Like, she's a Lesbian, or she's frigid, or she's an ex-hooker. Like that."

"But what possible difference . . . Would it bother you to learn that one or all of those things were true?"

"They aren't true!"

"Of course not. So why worry about lies people tell?"

Laurie's eyes turned toward the enclosure where Valentine sat enthroned. "She's the most beautiful thing in the world," the girl murmured. "Like an angel. Throwing mud on somebody like that is like—is like . . ."

"Blasphemy?"

"Yeah. Yeah, that's it." Laurie nodded emphatically. "You do understand."

"Yes, I understand."

Laurie smiled at her. "Valentine was right. You are a nice person. So I'm glad I talked to you. I've got to get back to Valentine now. Good-bye, Mrs. Kirby."

Jacqueline's face was very sober as she watched the girl billow off in a cloud of pink. The peculiar combination of loathing and pity Laurie inspired was not a comfortable feeling.

"You sure know how to stand out in a crowd," said a

voice at her elbow. "Where did you get the dead pigeon?"

"It's a cockatoo," Jacqueline said, turning to find Dubretta beside her. "You're in costume too, I see."

Dubretta tugged at the enormous corsage of sweetheart roses that covered one entire side of her suit jacket. "It's just like Hattie's, but twice the size. I don't know why I try to be funny; you're only the second person who's caught the joke."

She began to rummage in her shoulder bag, which was almost as big as the one Jacqueline usually carried. The liquid in her glass sloshed wildly, and Jacqueline said, "What are you looking for? Maybe I can—"

"Oh no." Dubretta pressed the purse tightly against her side. "Nobody, but nobody, puts a hand in this. It's full of goodies tonight. You can hold my drink, if you will."

Jacqueline obliged. Dubretta dug into the purse with both hands and finally extracted a cigarette. She lit it and then retrieved her drink. Jacqueline looked hungrily at the cigarette. There had not been room in the mauve envelope for the pack she had guiltily purchased, and she had decided it was time to quit smoking again. Her nostrils flared as she tried to inhale the smoke Dubretta blew out.

"You seem very merry this evening," she said.

"I'm not drunk, if that's what you mean. This is only my third. I may tie one on, though. I've got things to celebrate, and my mama taught me never to pass up a free drink."

"Free, my eye."

"Never having to buy a drink is one of the perks of my profession," Dubretta said with a grin. "My victims have been trying to get me liquored up in the hope of loosening my tongue."

"Did it work?"

"What do you think?" Dubretta gestured at the inadequately hidden form of Valerie Vanderbilt. "Have you said hi to your friend yet?"

"Why don't you leave her alone?" Jacqueline demanded.

"She's a pusher," Dubretta said. "The crap she peddles stupefies the brain just as dope rots the body. In a way she's the worst of the lot. They're doing the best they can. Their best is pretty cruddy, but they don't know the difference. She knows."

The brutal accuracy of the analysis silenced Jacqueline. She found it hard to believe that Dubretta was as noble and disinterested as she pretended, but the columnist had unerringly pinpointed the cause of Jean's present agony. She did know better. She suffered from the painful self-loathing of a patriot who has betrayed the Cause.

"Bah," said Jacqueline.

"Bah? I thought you'd agree with me. Whose side are you on?"

"I'm not on anybody's side. I dislike the quality of these books as much as I dislike anything that smacks of censorship. Who are you to tell people what they should or shouldn't read? Besides, not all of it is bad. Have you read Valentine's books?"

"Valentine." Dubretta's eyes rested on the slender, gold-crowned figure. "She's really something, isn't she? Beautiful, successful, brilliant . . . Oh yes, I've read everything she ever wrote. She's good. If Hattie hadn't lassoed her and labeled her as the Queen of Love, she could have made a name as a serious writer."

There was a curious, almost gloating note in her voice. She lifted her purse to her breast and closed her arms over it, as if she were holding a baby. "Just look at her," she said softly. "Beauty like that is unreal. She's like a woman of legend—Guinevere and fair Rosamund, Helen of Troy. . . ."

Jacqueline shivered. Was it only a coincidence that all the fabled women Dubretta had mentioned were doomed by their own loveliness to death or disgrace? The columnist might not have had too much to drink, but she was behaving very oddly.

Sue joined them. She handed Jacqueline a glass and sipped at her own with such primness that Jacqueline suspected she had had an extra on the side.

"Who're you?" Dubretta asked. "One of Hattie's stable?"

"No such luck," Sue said bitterly.

"I wouldn't be so sure, dear. Before this night is over, you'll be thanking God you aren't mixed up with that bunch."

Victor bent down to speak to Valentine, who looked up at him with a smile. Sue snorted. "What a ham," she said distinctly.

"Victor? He sure is," Dubretta agreed. "Better not fall for him, honey; he's all sham, including that pretty face of his. Too pretty, if you ask me. . . . Now there—there is a good-looking guy. And he's been staring at you."

"He's too old," said Sue, looking at the man Dubretta indicated.

"His white hair is premature," Jacqueline said. "But he is definitely too old for you."

"Friend of yours?" Dubretta asked curiously.

"Not any more." Jacqueline raised her glass in an ironic salute. From across the room, Professor James Whittier saluted her with even greater irony. Jacqueline beckoned. James shook his head. Jacqueline shrugged. James started toward them.

Amused at the exchange, Dubretta watched his approach. "Just my type," she announced. "What a gorgeous head of hair! A few wrinkles add character to a man's face. He looks intelligent, too."

"I am," said James, who had heard most of the speech. "And I have a terrific sense of humor. Who are you, you perceptive woman?"

"This is Dubretta Duberstein," said Jacqueline. "Don't pretend you don't know who she is; you read her column every day. Dubretta, may I present Professor James Whittier, chairman of the English Department at Coldwater College, Nebraska. He is a distinguished scholar and a rotten sneak."

Dubretta shifted her shoulder bag so she could shake hands. The strap caught on her corsage and pulled it from its moorings. James bent to pick it up. Their hands met among the blossoms, poetically but confusingly; James pricked his thumb on a loose bit of wire, and Dubretta gave the battered flowers a rueful look before dropping them into her bag.

"You her boyfriend?" she asked.

"No," Jacqueline and James said in chorus.

"He just happens to be in New York at the same time I'm here," Jacqueline added. "It was a spur-of-the-moment decision, no doubt."

"Since when am I obliged to tell you of my intentions?"

"I told *you*."

"And you made it plain that my company was not welcome. I can take a hint," James said loftily. "You wanted to be alone; I have left you alone. It is indeed pure coincidence that we happen to be—"

"You didn't try to catch my attention in the lobby yesterday?" Jacqueline demanded. "You didn't telephone two—no, three—times?"

James's face took on a look of righteous indignation. "I meant from the first to attend this debacle. It promised to be an event worth the attention of a connoisseur in schlock. So far it has lived up to my expectations, and I hope . . . Where the hell did you get that hat?"

"I hurt your feelings," Jacqueline said gently. "I wasn't deliberately ignoring you, James."

"You weren't?"

The two gazed soulfully at one another. "Shall we leave you two alone?" Dubretta asked.

"No," Jacqueline said. James's face fell. Jacqueline added, "But perhaps he deserves some compensation for my inadvertent rudeness. Let's introduce him to Hattie and the gang."

"Good idea. I have a few things I want to say to Hattie."

As they passed the podium, the ensemble began "Some Enchanted Evening." James nudged Jacqueline. "Don't do it. Don't sing."

" 'Once you have found him, Never let him go. . . .'
Oh, all right. What a killjoy you are, James."

"How did you like the books I gave you?"

"You have opened vast new vistas of enjoyment,
James," Jacqueline said fervently.

The audience outside the picket fence had diminished as the professionals, having paid their respects,
turned to the real purposes of the evening—drinking
and dealing. Only a few shy matrons stood by, ogling
Victor von Damm, and a woman with the desperate
look of a competing agent sought to attract Valentine's
attention. Hattie, ever alert, moved to block the attempt.

As they approached, James let out a profane exclamation. "What in God's name is that?" he demanded,
indicating the lumpy object squatting on the floor outside the gate.

Laurie was sitting cross-legged, the folds of her pink
caftan spread around her like a puddle of melted strawberry ice cream. Her head turned toward them with the
alert suspicion of a sentry's. Then she smiled. "Hi,
Mrs. Kirsky."

"Hi," Jacqueline said.

"Friend of yours?" James inquired.

Hattie saw the procession bearing down on her. Dis-
missing her defeated rival, she squared her shoulders
and prepared to deal with this new threat.

"Well, just look who's here. Dubretta darling, how
nice of you to mingle with us despicable characters!
And Victor's cute little friend! And Mrs. Kirk!"

"Her name is Kirby," Dubretta said. "Same as Joe."

Hattie ignored this. "Who is Joe?" James demanded

of Sue. She shrugged helplessly. "I never know what's going on," she admitted.

"And who's this ha-a-andsome man?" Hattie asked coquettishly. "I'll just bet he's a big important publisher or investor."

"He's a teacher," Dubretta said, as James self-consciously fingered his tie. "An English teacher, Hattie. If he has any money to invest, I'd advise him to look elsewhere."

"Dubretta just doesn't like us, Professor." Hattie showed all her teeth. "Ours is the fastest-growing segment of the publishing industry; we control over forty percent of the paperback market, and I myself—"

"That's today, Hattie," Dubretta interrupted, cradling her purse. "Today. Better wait till tomorrow before you invest, Professor."

"You're planning to write some more mean things about us." Hattie's fixed smile did not change. "You just go right ahead, Dubretta honey. You know the old rule of publicity—"

" 'Mention my name, I don't care how.' But you may not like the way your name will be mentioned in my next column, Hattie. I told you," Dubretta said, unsmiling, "that one day I'd get even. It was a long time ago; but I haven't forgotten."

For a moment Hattie's features reflected the deadly malice of Dubretta's. Before she could reply to the columnist's threat, a soft voice called, "Mrs. Kirby. Hello, Mrs. Kirby."

Valentine rose, with such ineffable grace that all eyes were drawn to her slender white figure. James gulped audibly. Jacqueline scowled at him.

"Come in, won't you?" Valentine said. "Join us."

Hattie looked as if she were choking, but got a grip on herself. "What a charmin' idea. We'll all have a friendly little chat."

Dubretta was the first to pass through the gate Hattie opened. James followed, stepping heavily on Jacqueline's foot as he stared bemusedly at the smiling Queen of Love. The fans let out a sigh of envy and admiration as Victor bent over Jacqueline's hand.

"Where've you been?" he muttered. "VV was looking for you."

"She can't have looked very hard," Jacqueline retorted. The stuffed cockatoo wobbled, as if nodding agreement.

Victor did not reply, but turned hopefully to Sue. The girl ignored his outstretched hand and walked past him, her nose in the air. She followed James, who had homed in on Valentine; Victor followed Sue, leaving Jacqueline alone with the cockatoo.

Her lip curled as she watched James go into his act. It was a performance with which she was only too familiar, consisting of an intense, burning stare, a deep reverberant voice, and quotations from the Elizabethan poets. " 'Was this the face that launched a thousand ships?' " he inquired, taking Valentine's hand in his. " 'And burnt the topless towers of Ilium?' "

Valentine stared—as well she might, Jacqueline thought sourly. Sue continued to ignore Victor with an ostentation that verged on caricature. No one paid the slightest attention to the "Earl," nor did he seem to be aware of their presence. One could not help but wonder what thoughts, if any, were passing through his handsome head.

Jacqueline had not been unmoved by Valentine's plea for help; she simply couldn't figure out how to respond to it. Valentine was a virtual prisoner in Hattie's suite. There was no way Jacqueline could reach her without endangering the secrecy Valentine obviously wanted. Even if Val answered the telephone herself, she couldn't speak freely without the risk of being overheard. Jacqueline had decided she would have to wait for the girl to get in touch with her. If this was the best Valentine could do, it wasn't very good. There were too many people standing around. Though Hattie was deep in conversation with Dubretta—not a cordial conversation, to judge by their grim faces—she kept a close watch on Valentine.

Jacqueline decided she might as well take advantage of the concentration of the others on the Queen of Love to have the long-delayed conversation with Jean. But when she turned to the corner where her friend was trying to imitate a potted plant, she met the quizzical gaze of Max Hollenstein.

"How nice to see you again, Mrs. Kirby. Perhaps you can persuade VV to come out and face her admirers."

The rubber plant shook violently and a thin voice squeaked, "He knows me! I met him at the MLA meetings two years ago."

"James? He couldn't possibly recognize you, Jean. He has a terrible memory for faces anyhow, and you look—"

With an agile bound Jean cleared the fence and

melted into the crowd. Max let out a low whistle of amused admiration, and Jacqueline said, "She used to be standing-jump champion of our dorm."

"Ah, so that's where you two met. You know the hideous truth about our VV."

"I don't know anything," Jacqueline said. "Presumably you do. Would you care to enlighten me as to the cause of the air of imminent eclipse that shadows this bright assembly? What the hell is the matter with everyone?"

Max's eyes widened in simulated horror. " 'Clouds and eclipses stain both moon and sun. . . .' "

" 'And loathsome canker lives in sweetest bud.' But you wouldn't call Hattie a sweet bud, would you?"

The expression on Hattie's face as she spoke to Dubretta was anything but sweet. Max chuckled. "She does look angry. Perhaps she's caught on to Dubretta's little joke. I don't know why she lets Dubretta get under her skin."

"You don't resent Dubretta's attacks?" Jacqueline asked.

"I shouldn't admit it," Max murmured, pretending to glance guiltily at Hattie, "but I enjoy Dubretta's pungent comments. She has a pretty wit and a forceful personality. Her attacks, as you call them, aren't damaging; they are merely entertaining."

"Then why are Hattie and Jean so uptight?"

"Dear Mrs. Kirby," Max said earnestly, "you've been infected by VV's peculiar moods. I've tried to convince her that she's worrying needlessly; even if the academic world does learn of her second profession, the worst she has to fear is a little ridicule."

"That's threat enough to Jean."

Max's eyebrows rose. "Has she always been so—er—" He paused delicately.

"Neurotic? No. Shy, self-conscious, conventional, yes. But I've never seen her as bad as this."

"But this is her first public appearance," Max argued. "Even experienced actors suffer from stage fright. And, of course, there is Laurie. Valentine isn't the only one whose nerves are affected by the poor creature. 'Fandom,' as I believe it is called, attracts some unbalanced persons—not as commonly in our profession as in certain others, notably films and television, but . . ."

"But Hattie has added a show-business element to her profession," Jacqueline said. "That's one of the reasons for her success as an agent."

"True. It has contributed to her success, but, as is so often the case, it has certain drawbacks. Laurie is one of the drawbacks."

"I see. Everything is A-OK except for a few loonies."

"How well you put it." Max laughed. "But I'm forgetting my manners, and dear Hattie, of course, has never had any. Let me get you a glass of wine." He indicated a table behind him, where bottles and glasses had been set out.

Hattie had not forgotten her manners, or perhaps she had decided the best way of dealing with Dubretta was to get her drunk. She and Max collided on their way to the refreshment table, to Max's disadvantage. Recovering himself, the little man said breathlessly, "I was about to offer Mrs. Kirby a glass of wine."

"We'll all have a glass," Hattie said. She and Max exchanged glances. Then Hattie reached for a bottle, and Max said casually, "I'll do it, Hattie."

Afterwards, when it became critically important to recall the exact train of events, Jacqueline could not decide how much of the confusion was planned and how much was accidental. The others wandered toward the table, except for Valentine, who remained in her seat. Even the "Earl" got up, to Jacqueline's relief; she had begun to wonder if he was dead.

The pink lump on the floor beyond the fence made a slow heaving motion, like lava lifting over the rim of a volcano. "You said I could give her the wine."

"Now, Laurie," Hattie began.

"You said I could."

"Oh, very well. But you must be careful."

"I'll be careful." Laurie fumbled at the fastening of the gate.

"I don't want any wine," Valentine said quickly. "Really I don't."

"I'll be careful," Laurie crooned, with a look of canine adoration. She lumbered toward the table.

James skipped out of her path as she bore down on him and sought refuge at Jacqueline's side. "The kid is bombed out of her skull," he said under his breath. "What kind of witches' Sabbat is this?"

Trust James to pronounce the word correctly, even when he was perturbed. Jacqueline said, "She was all right—for her—when I talked to her half an hour ago."

"I'm sorry we haven't anything to offer except wine," said Max, trying to preserve the social amenities, while Laurie hovered over him, breathing heavily.

"This is Valentine's favorite. It's a rather pleasant Bordeaux, and of course red wine suits the theme of the conference."

"I'd have expected a rosé," Jacqueline said. Max smiled; Hattie explained seriously, "That's what I wanted, but Val doesn't like any of the pink wines, and Max backed her up. He's got no feeling for setting the right mood."

The bottle Max had selected contained just enough wine to fill one glass. He set it aside. "There seems to be some sediment in this one. I'll open another bottle. No, Laurie, don't take that. Valentine doesn't want that one."

Laurie stared, uncomprehending. Again she reached for the glass Max had placed on the table. He started to open a new bottle, repeating patiently, "Not that one, Laurie. Here's another glass. Take this one. It's better."

Laurie didn't seem to hear him. Her hand remained poised over the first glass he had filled. Max poured wine into several other glasses. They were not the cheap plastic throwaways the bartenders had been using, but crystal goblets, which set off the ruby-red glow of the wine.

"Take this one," Max said, in the same slow, patient voice. He selected a glass he had filled only half full, perhaps because he had no great confidence in Laurie's steadiness of hand.

Laurie was obsessed by the first glass. She made no move to take the one Max was offering her. Before she could decide, Valentine glided toward the table. "I'll take this one," she said, selecting a glass at random. "I don't want anyone to wait on me. I'll get it myself."

Laurie's face puckered, and tears made havoc of her makeup. "You said I could give it to her! You promised!"

"Oh, for God's sake!" Hattie snatched the glass from Valentine's hand and put it back on the table. "Give it to her, then. Take one—any one—that one, Laurie. Go on, give it to her."

The transfer was made, though Valentine's lovely face was rigid with disgust, and she was so reluctant to touch Laurie's hand that she almost dropped the goblet. At a gesture from Hattie, Laurie trundled back to her post, and the others, who had been prey to various uncomfortable emotions, took their wine.

Jacqueline was never certain what happened in the next critical seconds. James and Max had their heads together, discussing wine; Sue and Victor-Joe withdrew to a corner where they could speak privately. Valentine stared at her untouched goblet as if it bore the visible marks of Laurie's hand. Dubretta and Hattie stood side by side, unspeaking, sipping their wine. The "Earl"—she had not the faintest recollection of what he was doing, or where he was.

The goblet fell from Dubretta's hand. It bounced undamaged on the rubbery artificial floor surface. Dubretta doubled over, clutching her middle. Hattie, who was closest to her, instantly backed away. Dubretta crumpled to the floor.

Her falling body, or the rush of the others to assist her, overturned the table, which was one of the small tottery variety. Wine poured out in a bloody stream, staining the artificial turf. Glasses bounded and rebounded in macabre playfulness.

Jacqueline was the first to reach the recumbent woman. Dubretta's breath came in ragged gasps. She tried to speak. "Forgot . . . pills. . . ."

Jacqueline disentangled the straps of Dubretta's purse from her arm and turned the bag upside down. An assortment of coins and other small, loose objects bounced down and up. One was the plastic bottle of pills. Jacqueline caught it in midair and wrestled with the cap, cursing the well-intentioned regulations of the pharmaceutical industry. Removing the cap at last, she took out one of the pills and got it into Dubretta's distorted mouth. Someone handed her a glass. Wine. Probably not advisable, but it was the only liquid immediately available. She held Dubretta's head and helped her swallow.

"Get a doctor, quick," she ordered.

"I'll make an announcement." The speaker—Max Hollenstein—started for the gate. Hattie got in his way. "Like hell you will. People are staring already. Pick her up, take her away from here."

"Hurry," Jacqueline said, her hand on Dubretta's wrist. The pulse was faint and irregular. Dubretta's eyes stared blankly. Then an expression of surprise spread over her face. "Blue," she gasped. "It's . . . blue."

The erratic beat under Jacqueline's fingers flickered and faded out.

Chapter 5

Jacqueline snatched up Dubretta's compact, wiped the mirror on her sleeve, and held it before Dubretta's lips. "Where's that damned doctor?" she exclaimed.

"Victor's gone to find one." Pale but composed, Sue knelt on the columnist's other side. "Anything?"

"No." Jacqueline threw the mirror aside and ripped Dubretta's suit jacket open. Placing the flat of one hand over the motionless breast, she struck it with her clenched fist, waited a moment, and repeated the gesture.

"No good," she muttered. "Sue—do you know CPR?"

The girl nodded mutely. Jacqueline cupped one hand over the other in the center of Dubretta's chest. Sue turned Dubretta's head to the side and bent over, her lips covering those of the fallen woman, her hand pinching her nostrils shut. Jacqueline began pumping. ". . . four—five—now, Sue . . ."

It seemed to both of them that they repeated the movements a thousand times before Victor returned, towing a tall man wearing glasses and a bright-red tartan waistcoat. They had to force their way through a whispering, staring crowd, and when the doctor took in the scene he scratched his head and asked, "Which is the patient?" His confusion was understandable. Valentine had fainted, and was being supported by Max and the Earl. Laurie was struggling to reach her fallen idol, and was being forcibly restrained by Hattie and James.

"Here." Jacqueline stood up. "I think it's her heart."

"It usually is," was the dry response. The doctor fussily adjusted his trousers and knelt. After a brief examination he said, "Well, you seem to be correct, madam. Did she have a heart condition?"

"Never mind that now." Abandoning James to struggle with Laurie, Hattie bent over the doctor. "Is she dead or isn't she?"

"She is," the doctor said brusquely. He rose and dusted off the knees of his trousers. He patted Sue on the arm and his voice softened as he went on, "It's no use, child. I'm sorry."

"She didn't even know the woman," Hattie said. "I don't know what she's bawling about. Look, Doc, I have to get this—this thing out of here. It's ruining the party."

Realizing that he was the focus of myriad curious stares, the doctor stepped back. "I'm not a cardiac specialist," he said quickly. "I'm a dermatologist, and I don't . . . There's nothing I can do. I didn't actually *do* anything—you saw I didn't. . . . You had better call the—er—the authorities. Excuse me, please."

He removed himself with more speed than dignity.

He was replaced by one of the hotel staff, whose chief concern, like Hattie's, was to clear away the mess as quickly as possible. The body, discreetly draped in a sheet, was removed via a service door. Then Hattie took a deep breath and considered what to do next.

Valentine, conscious but pale and shaken, leaned against Max's arm. James and Laurie were locked in motionless combat, reminding Jacqueline of two equally matched wrestlers. Sue, weeping beautifully, had taken refuge in the embrace of Joe-Victor, on whose face gratification struggled with a seemly sobriety. Through a gap in the screen of roses Jacqueline saw the gleam of a brassy blond wig. She began edging toward it, but when Hattie cleared her throat, the wig eclipsed itself.

"First things first," Hattie announced. "Professor— what the hell are you doing? I told you to get that girl out of here."

James rolled his eyes, but was too hard-pressed to reply. Hattie went on, "Victor, stop whatever you're doing with that girl and help Max take Val to her room. You . . ." She eyed Jacqueline, but before she could express her feelings, Jacqueline said, "I'm going to call the police. Unless someone has already done so?"

She turned an ironically inquiring gaze upon the hotel official. He nodded glumly. "Yes, madam, I'll attend to that."

"But—" Hattie began.

"It must be done, madam. The regulations are clear. In cases of sudden death—"

"She died of a heart attack," Hattie insisted. "The doc said so."

"A mere formality . . . unpleasant but necessary . . . follow the proper procedure . . ."

"Son of a—" Hattie began. She caught herself in the nick of time and, after a struggle, recaptured her misplaced image. "Ah just don't know what Ah'm sayin', Ah'm so upset," she explained to the audience outside the fence. "Valentine, honey, you go lie down. Aunt Hattie will be with you as soon as she explains to the nice people."

She climbed nimbly over the fence and headed for the platform, where the musicians, with admirable dedication to duty, were rendering a spirited version of "It's Love, Love, Love." Max led Valentine away. Joe, in flagrant disregard of the general's orders, tenderly escorted Sue through the mob. Laurie released her stranglehold on James and set off in pursuit of Valentine. James reeled backwards into a chair, where he sat breathing raggedly. And Jacqueline was appalled to find herself crooning the obscure lyrics of the song the quartet was playing. "When your heart goes bumpity-bump . . ."

She stopped singing. Once again a gleam of gold nylon hair showed behind the lattice of roses, and this time it did not disappear when she approached. Peering through the screen she asked, "How long have you been there?"

"I saw the whole thing." Jean's teeth chattered. "Oh God, oh God. What will happen now?"

"How should I know? If I were you, I'd get out of here."

"Come with me." A quivering hand reached for her through a gap in the lattice.

"Not now. I'll talk to you later."

The sound of the strings was replaced by Hattie's voice, her accent firmly in place. "Deah friends, Ah hate to cast a shadow over this happy gatherin'. . . ."

Jean disappeared and Jacqueline turned to see that a squad of waiters had begun restoring order. The table had been set back on its legs, the unopened bottles of wine had been replaced on its top, and the used wineglasses had been removed. A waiter knelt, blotting up puddles of wine, while another brushed shards of broken glass into a dustpan. Someone must have stepped on one or more of the goblets; Jacqueline had a vivid memory of the way they had bounced, undamaged, when they fell.

Speed was of the essence. Swooping, she snatched a gleaming fragment from the path of the whisk broom, holding it carefully to prevent the few drops of liquid cupped in its curve from spilling. Then she pounced on the man who was wiping the floor. "I'll take that," she announced. Too surprised to protest, he let her whisk the stained cloth from his fingers.

With both hands occupied and her elbow holding her lavender bag against her side, she looked around for help. She might have known she would need her usual purse.

Everyone had left except for James. Jacqueline advanced on him and he looked up from his gloomy inspection of a ripped seam in the shoulder of his jacket.

"Take this," she ordered. "No, not that. This. No, not that! How dull you are, James. What's the matter with you?"

His tie under his left ear, his snowy mane in wild

disorder, James was too enraged to speak even if Jacqueline had given him the chance. "Take my purse," she said. "Slide it out from under my arm. Open it. Take out my handkerchief. Hold it out. . . . That's right. Splendid work, James."

A powerful stench of eau des violettes wafting from the handkerchief made James's nose twitch like a rabbit's. "I'm not going to ask what you think you're doing," he mumbled. "I'm not going to ask."

Jacqueline laid the fragment of glass on the handkerchief, which was lace-trimmed and embroidered with purple violets. The wine-stained cloth went into a plastic trash bag commandeered from the supplies on the cleaning cart. Then Jacqueline wrapped the handkerchief carefully around the piece of glass and the small spot of scarlet surrounding it.

"Thank you, James."

"I am not going to ask what you think you're doing," James repeated.

"You shouldn't have to ask. A man of your superior intelligence—"

"Are you ready to leave now, or do you want some more garbage?"

"James, we can't leave. The police should be here soon."

"The police? Good Lord, that's all I need. Let's go."

"It is every citizen's duty to assist the police, James."

One of the waiters approached. "Excuse me, ma'am, does this belong to you?"

Jacqueline murmured an abstracted thanks, slung the purse over her shoulder, and went on with her lecture. "We shouldn't leave the scene. The police will want to question the witnesses."

"Everyone else has gone," James pointed out.

"All the more reason why we should do our duty."

"God, you're revolting when you're being self-righteous. Are you coming with me or not?"

"Not."

James stalked away. Jacqueline shifted her shoulder bag into a more comfortable position. Then the truth hit her. She had not carried her shoulder bag. This one must belong to Dubretta.

Jacqueline made a quick and—she hoped—unobtrusive exit, mingling with the departing guests. Finding an unoccupied couch in a corner of the lobby, she sat down and emptied the purse onto the seat beside her.

Whether the waiter had found all the scattered contents she did not know, but she assumed he had; the cleaning process had appeared to be quick and thorough. Dubretta's purse contained almost as much junk as her own. The untidy heap was copiously sprinkled with tobacco. Fastidiously, Jacqueline brushed each article before returning it to the bag. Tissues, comb, lipstick, compact, keys, cigarettes, matches, wallet, coin purse, letters and bills, checkbook, the corsage, crushed and wilting, a tube of toothpaste . . .

"Hmm," Jacqueline said.

She put most of the things back in the purse, leaving aside a few that required more detailed examination. The wallet contained some bills, which she didn't bother to count, and several credit cards, plus a black-and-white snapshot of a pretty young girl. It was an old photograph; the girl's dark hair was arranged in the

long page-boy coiffure popular in Jacqueline's youth.
She wondered if it could be a picture of Dubretta; for
the setting of the eyes and the shape of the nose resembled the columnist. Remembering her last view of
Dubretta's dead, time-scored face, she shivered, and
closed the wallet.

The vial of pills was half full of small yellow tablets.
The label bore a brand name, followed by the generic
designation and the dosage. Jacqueline borrowed
Dubretta's pen and a scrap of paper—the register tape
from a grocery store—and carefully copied the information before she restored the bottle to Dubretta's bag.

There was only one personal letter. It was addressed
to "Dubretta," in care of the newspaper in which her
column appeared, and began, "You muckraking old
bitch."

One of Dubretta's fans, evidently. Jacqueline put the
letter in the purse.

One item remained. Jacqueline riffled through the
pages of the stenographer's notebook. It was the same
one in which she had seen the columnist writing over
the past few days. About eighteen or twenty pages
were filled with Dubretta's peculiar and, to Jacqueline,
unintelligible shorthand.

With some difficulty Jacqueline squeezed the notebook into her lavender satin evening bag. It made a no-
ticeable bulge, but that could not be helped. She stood
up, shaking the tobacco crumbs from her skirt.

"Disgusting," said a woman sitting nearby.

Jacqueline looked at the mess on the carpet. "I
couldn't agree more," she said, and caught her glasses
as they were about to fall off the tip of her nose.

Restoring them to their place, she set off in search of someone who could be bullied into giving her the information she wanted.

His directions led her to an office in the service area of the hotel. Assuming that if she knocked she would be told to go away, she turned the knob and walked in.

Four pairs of eyes stared at her. Dubretta's head had fallen to one side. The transparent film of secretion had not yet dried on her eyeballs; they glistened in the light, as if she were about to welcome the newcomer.

One of the three men said, "Hey!" Another began, "Who the hell—"

Jacqueline put out her hand and pressed Dubretta's eyelids shut.

"Which of you is in charge?" she asked briskly.

The man who had said, "Hey," scowled and pulled the sheet back over the dead woman's face. The second speaker had started to his feet when Jacqueline entered. He was scowling too. The third man remained seated. From the cigarette he held between his fingers a thin stream of smoke rose smoothly toward the ceiling.

He was neatly, almost foppishly dressed, though to Jacqueline it was obvious that his suit had come off a rack in a discount men's store. The deep wine of his tie matched the stripe on the handkerchief in his breast pocket and the socks exposed by his extended legs. A fringe of piebald hair—part gray, part black, liberally sprinkled with white—framed his high forehead. His heavy eyebrows were straight and black; they formed an emphatic parallel to the lines creasing his brow. Only two incongruous notes marred the elegance of his appearance: a seamed white scar bisecting his left cheek from jawline to eyelid, and a pink plastic rose in his buttonhole.

"I'm O'Brien," he said. "And who might you be, lady?"

Jacqueline frowned critically. "The rose jars with your ensemble, Mr. O'Brien."

"Not in the best of taste, in any sense," O'Brien agreed. "Found it stuck to Dubretta's sleeve. Where'd you get her purse?" He added, with a grimace that produced a slash in his right cheek, balancing the scar, "It jars with your ensemble."

Jacqueline sat down in the chair the other man had vacated. His eyes widened indignantly, but before he could protest O'Brien said, "On your way, Kelly. Nothing more to do here."

"I'm leaving too," the third man grunted. "Waste of time, of which I have not enough as it is. Nobody but you would have had the gall to drag me down here to tell you Dubretta's ticker finally gave out on her."

When the others had left, O'Brien turned cool gray eyes to Jacqueline, who had settled back with the air of one who plans a long stay. He held out his hand. Jacqueline gave him the purse. "Thanks. Where'd you get it?"

"The waiter thought it was mine."

"You a relative?"

"No. I felt I ought to bring the purse to you at once."

"So you have. I really can't see," said O'Brien meditatively, "why you are still here."

"Don't you want to ask me any questions?"

The deeply creased cheeks were evidently O'Brien's

version of a smile, and the only visible indications thereof. Jacqueline smiled back at him. "There are pills in her purse. A variety of digitalis."

"Everybody knew about Dubretta's wonky heart."

"So you believe it was a natural death?"

"I don't believe in anything," O'Brien said plaintively. "Not Santa Claus or Tinker Bell or justice or truth. When I have received the official medical report, I will have an informed opinion as to how she died. At the present time I know nothing to contradict my uninformed opinion that she had a heart attack. Can you give me one good reason why I should sit here discussing it with you?"

"No," Jacqueline admitted.

"Oh, come on. Think of a reason. Compared to what lies in store for me the rest of the night, this is a restful interlude. I'd like to prolong it."

Jacqueline muttered under her breath. O'Brien cocked his head. "What did you say?"

"Nothing."

"It sounded like 'smart . . .' "

"Just your vulgar imagination," Jacqueline said primly. She took her wallet out of the bulging satin evening bag, taking care to keep O'Brien from seeing what else it contained. Extracting a card from the wallet, she handed it to O'Brien. "How's that for a reason?"

The card was a trifle frayed around the edges, but the look of age only added to its baroque elegance. Hand-engraved in an ornate antique script and bordered in gilt, it was one of Jacqueline's favorite souvenirs. O'Brien held it at arm's length and translated effortlessly.

" 'The bearer, Mrs. Jacqueline Kirby, is an honorary member of the Carabinieri of Rome, with the rank of sub-lieutenant.' All stamped and sealed and signed, by Guido di Cavallo."

"Do you know him?"

"He spoke at a police conference I attended. Quite the rising star."

"So I understand."

"An honorary carabiniere," O'Brien mused. "And are you also a writer of historical romances?"

He was looking, not at her name tag, but at her hat. Jacqueline straightened it. "I'm a librarian. From Coldwater College in Nebraska."

"Holy shit!" O'Brien let out a roar of laughter, which he cut off as abruptly as it had begun. "Sorry, Mrs. Kirby."

"I've heard the word before," Jacqueline said gently.

Unaware of the implications of that deceptive mildness, O'Brien went on, "You're an entertaining woman and I have enjoyed this little encounter, but I fear I must move on. You know, of course, that this card entitles you to a polite 'Hello' from the NYPD but nothing else." He handed it back to her.

"I am well aware of that," Jacqueline said. "I thought it might get your attention."

"You already had my attention," O'Brien assured her. "I regret the necessity that forces me to turn it in another direction."

Jacqueline bowed her head meekly and rose, the green plastic trash bag tucked under her arm. The meekness was also an ominous sign; perhaps O'Brien suspected as much, for he reached the door before Jacqueline and took hold of the knob.

"Was there anything else you wanted to tell me, Mrs. Kirby?"

Jacqueline blinked at him from under the lace fringe. "Not a thing, O'Brien. Not a blessed little old thing."

"I figured you for one of these writer types, looking for publicity," O'Brien explained, resisting her attempt to turn the knob. "I don't need a self-appointed private eye to tell me Dubretta wasn't popular. But if you have any solid evidence, I'll listen."

"If I discover anything of that sort I'll be sure to tell you," Jacqueline said earnestly.

O'Brien opened the door and Jacqueline went out, clutching her trash bag. She turned and wriggled her fingers coyly at him in farewell. O'Brien took the rose from his lapel and flourished it in response.

Jacqueline was not at all surprised to find James lying in wait for her when she walked into the lobby of her hotel.

"I've decided to overlook your outrageous behavior," he announced.

"Your magnanimity overwhelms me. Excuse me, James. I want to change. This dress is making me bilious."

"I'll come up with you."

"No, you won't."

"I'll wait for you down here," James said, less enthusiastically.

"Don't bother."

"I made a reservation at Le Perigord."

Jacqueline hesitated. James played his trump card. "I'll pay."

"Well . . ."

James had to admit that only Jacqueline could have walked into an elegant French restaurant carrying a green plastic trash bag and wearing a lavender picture hat two and a half feet in diameter. She was persuaded to check the hat, but refused to part with the trash bag. James bided his time until after she had selected the most expensive items on the menu. Then he indicated the trash bag, upon which one of Jacqueline's elegant purple shoes was firmly planted.

"What do you think you're doing?"

"You said you weren't going to ask me that."

"And you said, correctly, that it should be self-evident. I know what you're doing, as a matter of fact. Playing detective."

Jacqueline's eyes shone like green garnets, in a look of delicate mockery James found enchanting—when it was directed at someone else. "Dear James. You want to play too."

"I intended to offer you the benefit of my considerable experience. . . ." It sounded so pompous, even James couldn't keep a straight face. He gave Jacqueline his famous crooked smile. "Right. I want to play too. But I'll be damned if I'll play Watson to your Sherlock Holmes, if that's what you had in mind."

"I fully intended to ask your advice, James."

"That would be a first. . . . Never mind. Ask. I'm all ears."

While she prodded snails out of their retreats, Jacqueline gave James a synopsis of the situation up to the death of Dubretta. "The atmosphere was positively poisonous with passion, James," she finished. "I had no idea writers were so greedy and selfish. They're as bad as academicians."

"No doubt. But we don't often murder one another."

"I don't suppose writers do either," Jacqueline admitted. "And of course I'm discounting the usual verbal exaggeration—you know what I mean—'I'd like to kill that woman,' 'I wish she were dead,' and so on. We all say things like that. But in this case several people had good reason to wish Dubretta would drop dead. She'd been after Hattie Foster for years; she said so, tonight. She also said she had found evidence that would destroy Hattie or damage her badly. The hints she dropped were as broad as Hattie's hips, and she kept hugging her purse like a bag of gold. I'm convinced the evidence is in this book."

She extracted the notebook from her evening bag and gave it to James. When he realized what it was, the timid, law-abiding professor replaced the amateur detective. He stuttered, "Did you steal this from Dubretta? Holy God, Jacqueline, you can't do that!"

"I didn't steal it. It was in her purse. The waiter gave it to me by mistake."

"But—but— You've got to give it to the police!"

Jacqueline's teeth snapped viciously on the last of the unfortunate gastropods. "O'Brien believes Dubretta died from natural causes. He patronized me, James. He practically patted me on the fanny and told me to go home and tend to my knitting."

"Did he? That explains a lot. . . . Well, but look here, Jacqueline, maybe he's right. All you've talked about so far is motive. As we both know, that's the weakest part of a case. What about means and—uh—opportunity?"

He looked so pleased with himself, Jacqueline didn't have the heart to sneer. "What about them, James?"

"I was so busy wrestling with that monstrous young woman, I didn't follow all the action," James said. "But if Dubretta was murdered, the method had to be poison, administered in her glass of wine. The wine— Why are you looking at me like that?"

"I agree with your first conclusion, but isn't your second a bit sweeping? We don't know what else she had to eat or drink that evening. Some poisons don't take effect immediately."

James didn't appreciate her interruption or her logic. "If you don't believe the wine was poisoned, why did you take samples of it?"

"I didn't say it wasn't poisoned. I only said it wasn't the only possibility. Certainly any proper investigation of Dubretta's death would include testing the remains of the wine. Unfortunately, I wasn't able to collect the used glasses. The waiter had removed them by the time I got my wits together, and I couldn't quite see myself chasing him down the corridor and grabbing the tray out of his hands. However," Jacqueline went on more cheerfully, "the broken wineglass is the important one. The rest of us were holding our glasses when the table fell over, so the broken glass must have been Dubretta's. The others that fell with the table had no wine in them. What's more, Dubretta's glass didn't break when she dropped it. I remember seeing it bounce."

"Someone must have smashed it deliberately," James exclaimed.

"It is certainly possible. The wine the waiter was mopping up came from the bottle. We should have that tested too."

"I know a chemist at Columbia," James offered eagerly.

Jacqueline was about to say, "So do I," when she had second thoughts. It might be a trifle awkward, in view of certain events in her past, if her chemist and James's turned out to be the same person. Besides, James would be flattered if she left this job to him. He might even be deluded into believing they were equal partners in what Jacqueline had come to think of as her investigation.

She took her foot off the trash bag and nudged it toward James. "Try to talk him into doing it first thing tomorrow," she urged.

"I will. Jacqueline, I don't see why we have to consider other means of administering the poison; the party began at five, so she couldn't have had dinner before she came. Anything she ingested at lunch would have taken effect before then."

Jacqueline realized he had fallen in love with his theory, and with the macabre thrill of having actually witnessed a murder, so she didn't raise any further objections. To consider other hypotheses was nonproductive anyway; for all she and James knew, half the population of New York might have wanted to exter-

minate Dubretta Duberstein; and half of that select
group might have had a chance to do so during the afternoon. Actually, it wasn't particularly productive to
speculate at all until they had received the results of the
chemist's tests, but that consideration had no effect on
either of them.

"The big problem is not means but opportunity,"
Jacqueline said. "How did the poison get in Dubretta's
glass?"

After a somewhat acrimonious discussion they managed to agree on a few facts. There had been a single
glassful of wine left in the first bottle. The second bottle had been corked and sealed; they had both watched
Max open it. That a foreign substance could have been
added to the bottle thereafter was unlikely, verging on
impossible. Also impractical—why poison a whole
bottle unless the killer's goal was a general massacre?

Where they disagreed was on the disposal of the
glasses of wine Max had poured. James insisted that
someone—he couldn't remember who—had taken the
glass Max had set aside, claiming it was full of sediment. Jacqueline felt sure that glass had not been
touched. They couldn't even agree on their own
glasses. James claimed he had passed the glass Max
gave him to Jacqueline. She distinctly remembered
taking hers from Max himself. Valentine had selected
a glass, apparently at random, had had it snatched
away by Hattie, and had received a second glass from
Laurie, via Hattie. Laurie had touched not only the
first, sediment-filled glass, but several of the others.
The glasses filled by Max had stood on the table during Laurie's tantrum, during which time someone

could have added poison to a particular glass without being observed. The only other thing the two amateur sleuths agreed on was that neither had the faintest idea where and how Dubretta had obtained her glass.

"I've always been suspicious of those detective stories where every person at the party knows exactly where his or her drink was at any given moment," James grumbled. "Anyhow, we agree it could have been done. Now let's make a list of the suspects."

Hattie obviously headed the list. There was no question about that. She was the one threatened by Dubretta's discoveries—whatever they may have been—and she had fussed over the glasses of wine. By forcing the issue between Valentine and Laurie, she had created a distraction that might have provided her with an opportunity to tamper with Dubretta's glass.

"Besides, she makes a rotten cup of tea," Jacqueline said.

James was not deceived by her flippancy, but he wasn't sure what she meant. Out of loyalty to Jean, Jacqueline had glossed over the peculiarities of Hattie's relationships with her authors, mentioning only the agent's reputation for squeezing them financially. He gave her a questioning look, shrugged, and went to the next suspect.

His favorite candidate for chief suspect was Laurie. Jacqueline agreed that she was unstable and antagonistic to Dubretta, whom she had actually threatened. She did not voice aloud her feeling that James's partiality for Laurie was prompted in part by personal vindictiveness, and in part by his literary tendency to dismiss the most obvious suspect—Hattie.

They agreed that Max had had the best opportunity to poison one of the glasses. He had acted as host and had handed glasses to several people. If Dubretta had unearthed some scandal involving Valentine, the latter's business manager might have had solid mercenary reasons for silencing the columnist.

Valentine's name was the next to be mentioned, by Jacqueline. James summarily dismissed her from consideration. "She has the same motive as Max," Jacqueline argued. "Ridiculous," said James.

Victor and Sue were the last to be considered. James thought Victor might be a dark horse, for reasons he refused to specify, but insisted Sue was obviously innocent. Jacqueline callously added both to her list.

"That's all the suspects, then," James said, summoning the waiter to refill his coffee cup. "Let's talk about the motive."

There was another suspect, though Jacqueline didn't feel obliged to tell James that. Jean was not a very likely suspect. As she had demonstrated, the gaps in the lattice were wide enough to admit an arm, and the table had been within her reach; but although Jean could have poisoned the open bottle, or even one of the glasses, she couldn't have made sure the deadly liquid reached the right person. Nevertheless, Jacqueline added Jean to her private list. Something was rotten in the romance-book biz, and until she knew what secrets lurked in the hearts of VV and Victor von Damm, she couldn't be certain Jean was in the clear. It was imperative that she talk to her friend at once.

"Check, please," she said to the waiter, and to

James, "The motive is in this notebook, somewhere. I'll get to work on it right away."

James looked sulky. He picked up the check, which had been placed discreetly on the table, and his expression changed to one of abject consternation. Swallowing, he handed over a credit card and then returned to his grievance. "Since when are you a cryptographer? I want—"

"The word, I believe, is cryptanalyst. And since when are you?"

But she agreed to James's suggestion that they walk instead of taking a cab. It was a fine night, for Manhattan. Now and then a genuine breeze struggled into the canyoned streets, and a full moon hung low over Rockefeller Center. Jacqueline had every intention of calling Jean as soon as she got in; conscience as well as detective fever demanded that she do so. However, when the desk clerk handed her her key he also gave her a message slip, and Jacqueline realized her obligation to Jean would have to be postponed again.

Frustrated by the hat, James rested his chin on her shoulder, trying to read the note. Jacqueline held it up. "Valentine wants to see me."

"Are you going?"

"It's rather late. . . ."

"Not really. A lot has happened since five o'clock, that's why it seems later than it is. Besides, she says, 'As soon as you get in, no matter what time.' "

"I can read." Jacqueline shrugged her shoulders, dislodging James's chin.

"I think we ought to go."

"We?"

James dodged the hat brim as she turned to face him. "This is an equal partnership, isn't it?"

Jacqueline neglected to answer the question. "That's not why you want to go with me. Valentine is not for you, James. She's a remote, glimmering star, far beyond the grasp of mortal men."

Recognizing Jacqueline's peculiar version of agreement, James took her arm as she walked toward the revolving doors. "Swinburne? Keats—in his corny youth?"

"Kirby. I'm practicing romantic clichés." She didn't say why, and James wisely didn't ask.

Jacqueline had scarcely touched the bell before the door of Hattie's suite was flung open. When he saw her, Max's tired brown eyes lit up. "It was good of you to come, Mrs. Kirby. Valentine is very distressed. She has some notion—"

"Is it her? Max, is it Mrs. Kirby?" Valentine ran toward them. Her flying draperies fell like dying moths as he stopped her and put a protective arm around her. "Val, my dear, let Mrs. Kirby catch her breath. Shall we go in and sit down?"

As she entered the living room of the suite, Jacqueline had an uncomfortable sensation of déjà vu. The fat cabbage roses printed on the draperies and slipcovers irresistibly recalled the dreadful plastic flowers of the bower, and the same faces confronted her. Valentine and Max, Hattie and Victor von Damm, the Earl, looking more than ever like a waxwork escaped from Madame Tussaud's, Jean, hunched miserably in a chair. Only Sue was missing. Apparently Hattie had tightened the lasso and dragged Victor back to the stable.

Hattie was the first to speak. The sugary sweetness of her voice aroused Jacqueline's darkest forebodings.

"Honey, I sure do appreciate you helping us. Why didn't you tell me you were a famous detective?"

Jacqueline cleared her throat. "Who told you that?" she inquired gently.

The huddled form of Valerie Vanderbilt quivered. Hattie glanced betrayingly at her and said, "Why, sure 'nuff, everybody knows that. Now, Mrs. Kirby, you've just got to help. That policeman is on his way here right this minute—"

"O'Brien?"

"I think that's his name. He'll be here any second, and Valentine has this idea—"

"It's not an idea, it's the truth." Like a cloud bathed in the rosy hues of dawn, Valentine pulled away from Max and approached Jacqueline. "You've got to help me, Mrs. Kirby. Someone is trying to kill me!"

Jacqueline took the girl's fluttering hands in hers. "Sit down," she said quietly. "Here, on the sofa. You're confused, Valentine. It was Dubretta who died."

"It was a mistake." Clinging to Jacqueline's hands, Val drew a long shuddering breath. "The poison was meant for me."

"Poison?" Jacqueline's eyebrows disappeared under the lace fringe of the hat. "Dubretta died of a heart attack, Valentine. At least that's what the police believe. Why would anyone want to harm you?"

Before the girl could answer, Hattie exclaimed stridently, "Why, honey, that's a stupid question, if you'll pardon me. A girl like Valentine attracts enemies just by being what she is. Every other writer in the business is green with envy, and there must be hundreds of men who—"

"Every other writer?" Jacqueline repeated.

"Oh, I didn't mean you, VV." With a deliberation that verged on insult, Hattie glanced at Jean, who had risen shakily to her feet. "You're a good writer, but you aren't in Val's class, and you're smart enough to know it."

"I beg your pardon." James had been feeling left out. He looked at Jean. "Haven't we met? Of course— you're Dr. Jean Frascatti. We met at the MLA meeting in LA two years ago. I thought your paper on Richard the Second was . . . Dr. Frascatti?"

He hastened to support Jean as she swayed, one hand pressed to her brow. "It's too late," she muttered hysterically. "The die is cast, the battle lost. . . . Where's the cup? There's yet some poison left. . . ."

James shook his head sympathetically as he helped her into a chair. "You mustn't be morbid. This has been a trying day for everyone, but . . . VV? Did I hear Mrs. Foster call you VV? Are you the author of *Slave of Lust?*"

Jean shuddered violently. Her eyes, glazed with despair, remained fixed on James.

"How marvelous," the latter exclaimed. "Clever woman! I'll wager you're the only member of our underpaid profession who is solvent these days."

"Marvelous," Jean repeated dully. "Marvelous? Clever?"

"How many of us have the intelligence to augment our paltry incomes by making use of the neglected masterpieces of literature?" James perched on the arm of Jean's chair and smiled his crooked smile. Jean's pale cheeks regained their color, and she looked at James with dawning adoration.

Seeing that that particular situation was under control, Jacqueline turned back to Valentine. "I'm sure a lot of people envy your beauty and your success, Valentine; but people don't kill other people because of envy."

"Normal people don't," Valentine said. Her voice had a harsh, grating quality.

"Laurie!" Hattie clapped a theatrical hand to her forehead. "What about Laurie?"

"What about her?" Jacqueline asked.

"I sure do pity the creature, but we all know she isn't right in the head. I blame myself," Hattie said nobly. "Yes, I really do. I should have seen it coming."

"Don't be silly, Hattie," Valentine snapped. "I can't stand the girl—she gives me the creeps—but she wouldn't hurt me. She adores me."

"Love turned to hate," Hattie murmured vaguely. "I'm not sayin' it had to be Laurie. What about that girl—the little schoolteacher—"

"That's a crock of crap, and you know it!" Victor's black cloak flared as he strode toward Hattie. She didn't flinch, even when he shook his fist at her.

"Oh, I'd hate to think it was little Sue. But you haven't been nice to her, Victor—now, have you? Leading her on and then dropping her . . . She knows how you feel about Val, of course."

Victor's look of horrified bewilderment transformed him back into Joe Kirby. "Me—Val—since when have we—I don't—she never . . ."

"In heaven's name, Hattie, control yourself," Max exclaimed. "What you say is nonsense. We are all talking foolishly tonight—and small wonder, after what has happened. I'm sure we will find that by morning things will look quite different."

"But that policeman is on his way here now," Hattie said. "Mrs. Kirby, I want you—"

The doorbell rang. Jacqueline said, "You don't want me. I don't know what the devil you do want. A lawyer?"

"Good gracious, no." Hattie's nostrils flared and she drew a deep, sensuous breath. "Why would I want a lawyer? I'm going to appeal to the police to protect pore little Valentine."

She went to answer the door.

It wasn't difficult for Jacqueline to understand Hattie's sudden change of attitude toward Dubretta's death in general and Jacqueline in particular. The great god publicity beckoned, and Hattie was sharp enough to sense the delicious possibilities. Jacqueline pictured the headlines: "Queen of Love threatened. Who tried to kill Valerie Valentine? Famed private detective on the case. . . ." And her picture, smirking under the brim of the lavender hat.

Jacqueline had no objection to appearing in the newspapers, but she was damned if she was going to be manipulated by Hattie. It is one thing to make a fool of oneself, deliberately and cheerfully; quite another to be made a fool of by someone else.

Before she could decide what to do about it, O'Brien was among them.

His eyes went straight to Jacqueline. "Well, if it isn't Mrs. Kirby. Nice to see you again, ma'am. And Miss Valentine—Mr. von Damm—Miss Vanderbilt—your Grace . . . ." The barely concealed amusement in his voice as he pronounced the names rose to the surface when he addressed the Earl, who looked as blank as he always did. O'Brien glanced at James. "And Mr.—"

James drew himself to his full height. "Professor James B. Whittier. I am chairman of the English Department at Coldwater College."

"Right." O'Brien's gaze lingered on the trash bag James was holding under his arm, but he didn't comment on it. He went on, "I'm sorry to bother you at this hour, Mrs. Foster. I have a little problem I hoped you could help me with."

"Thank God you are here, Inspector." Hattie grabbed his hand.

"Lieutenant," O'Brien corrected gravely.

"What does it matter? You're a police officer, and it's your duty to protect us innocent citizens. Look at that pore chile—" The pore chile was Valentine, who started nervously as Hattie jabbed a finger at her. "Inspector, you must protect her from the assassin who tried to kill her. He will certainly try again, and—"

"Just a minute, ma'am," O'Brien interrupted. "This is the first I've heard of an attempt on Miss Valentine's life. When did it happen?"

"Why, tonight, of course. Dubretta's death was a mistake. The poison was meant for Valentine."

O'Brien looked at Jacqueline. She shook her head.

"I'm not taking the rap for this, O'Brien. Did I ever mention the word 'poison'?"

"It was implicit in—"

"All I did," said Jacqueline, in the high, penetrating voice she adopted when she wished to control a conversation, "was ask whether you were satisfied that Dubretta died a natural death. This was Valentine's idea."

O'Brien's gaze shifted to Valentine. Though his countenance was as impenetrable as a boulder, the girl's beauty had its effect; when he addressed her his voice was unusually gentle. "Tell me about it, Miss Valentine."

Like many writers, Valentine was not a fluent speaker. "Well—uh—there was a mix-up about the glasses of wine. I was supposed to have a certain one, then I took another one, and the one I finally got wasn't either of them. Dubretta took the one I was supposed to have."

O'Brien blinked. "You want to go over that again, miss?"

Valentine looked frightened. She had explained the situation as well as she could, and was apparently incapable of clarifying it. Max came to her rescue. "The fact is, Lieutenant, no one can be certain who got a particular glass of wine."

"I didn't notice you," O'Brien said, in chagrin. "Who are you?"

Max smiled. "Most people overlook my presence, Lieutenant. I am not a conspicuous person. I am Max Hollenstein, Miss Valentine's business manager. I was pouring the wine, and I think I know as much about it

as anyone—which isn't much." He went on to tell
O'Brien what had happened, glossing tactfully over
Hattie's insistence that Laurie be allowed to hand
Valentine her glass, and ended, "Honestly, I don't see
how anyone could have tampered with a specific glass,
if that is what you are wondering. They were being
passed back and forth like damp babies."

"But she took my glass," Valentine insisted. "The
one Hattie grabbed away from me. Hattie put it on the
table and Dubretta took it. She only drank about half of
it and then she just crumpled up."

The implications of this passionate and ingenuous
declaration escaped Hattie; she returned O'Brien's inquiring look with a puzzled frown.

"Well, Miss Valentine," O'Brien said, "I haven't re-
ceived the coroner's report yet, but it looks as if
Dubretta had a heart attack. That should reassure you.
Unless you have an enemy."

"Not one but a hundred," Hattie cried. She expanded
on the theme, in more or less the same terms she had
used before, but when O'Brien invited her to be specific, she rolled her eyes and looked coy. "Dubretta
was one of the ones who hated Valentine," she suggested.

"Hoisted by her own petard?" O'Brien's lip curled.
"Not Dubretta. She was too smart to make a dumb mistake like that. The fact is, Miss Valentine—and the rest
of you—there's no indication that murder was intended or committed. Do any of you know anything
that would contradict that conclusion?"

No one spoke. "Oh, come on," O'Brien said. "No
threatening letters, no . . . Yes, Mrs. Kirby?"

"It's probably irrelevant," Jacqueline began.

Instead of following up this tantalizing remark, O'Brien agreed. "Probably. Well, ladies and gentlemen, I'll leave you in peace. Oh—I almost forgot the reason I came. One of Dubretta's possessions has been misplaced. Did any of you see her notebook this evening?"

The faces of the listeners did not change. O'Brien elaborated. "She always carried a stenographer's notebook. With a red cover. She said the bright color made it easier for her to keep track of it."

"That's right," Jacqueline said. "She was taking notes yesterday, at the lecture."

Silence followed this disingenuous comment. No one seemed anxious to add anything until Joe said tentatively, "Maybe it was in her purse. I remember her hugging it in both arms like she was afraid somebody was going to steal it."

"That's right," Max agreed. "Didn't you find her handbag, Lieutenant?"

"We have it," O'Brien said. "The notebook wasn't in it."

"But that's—" Hattie stopped.

"Yes, Mrs. Foster?"

"That's strange. Maybe she didn't bring it with her today. The notebook, I mean."

"Dubretta's notebook was part of her," O'Brien said. "She'd no more leave it behind than she'd go out without her clothes."

"Oh, who cares about a silly notebook?" Hattie snapped. "Lieutenant, I demand police protection for pore little Valentine."

"If I thought she needed protection, she'd get it," O'Brien replied shortly. "No one has anything more to tell me about Dubretta's notebook? All right, then. Mrs. Kirby, I'd like a word with you. In private."

All eyes turned toward Jacqueline. James took a step forward. "What are you implying, Lieutenant? If you have anything to say to Mrs. Kirby, I insist on being present."

"Don't be silly, James." Jacqueline rose, tucking her evening bag firmly under her arm. "The lieutenant and I spoke earlier today; no doubt he wishes me to elaborate on certain points I raised at that time."

She fixed James with an icy stare. Jean put a timid hand on his arm. "Please don't go, Professor Whittier."

Bookended between two women, one who plainly didn't want his company and the other pleading for him to remain, James did not find the decision difficult.

"But, Mrs. Kirby . . ." Valentine began.

"Don't worry about a thing, my dear," Jacqueline said. "You're perfectly safe. I have decided to take the case."

O'Brien opened the door for her and she swept superbly out. "What case?" he inquired, the creases in his thin cheeks deepening.

"If there is no case, why are you so determined to find Dubretta's notebook?"

"You believe in taking the war into the enemy's camp, don't you? Why don't you give me the notebook, Mrs. Kirby?"

They stepped into the elevator. "What makes you think I have it? This is an absurd conversation," Jacqueline went on acrimoniously. "Five questions in a row and not one answer."

"You asked two of the five. All right, I'll give you an answer. That suitcase of Dubretta's had been searched. She was a smoker and she never used a cigarette case; the bottom of her bag and every object in it should have been covered with tobacco. It was too clean."

"Very good," Jacqueline said admiringly. "There are a few flaws in your reasoning, however."

"Don't try to pin it on the waiter," O'Brien warned. "She had over a hundred in cash. A thief wouldn't have left that much."

"She might have cleaned it herself," Jacqueline said. "Before she came to the party. Is that all you had on your mind, O'Brien?"

"As a matter of fact, I have a favor to ask. If you aren't too tired, there's someone I'd like you to meet."

"All right."

"It isn't far from here and it shouldn't take . . . Did you say, all right?"

"Yes."

"No questions, no hedging, no cries of alarm?"

"I'm not at all alarmed. And I presume you'll tell me who it is in your own good time."

"You are a damned annoying woman," O'Brien said.

"So I've been told."

O'Brien's car was unmarked, but its position, in a clearly defined "No Parking" zone, gave away its official status. Once they were under way O'Brien said, "I'm taking you to see Dubretta's sister. She wants to talk to the person who last saw her sister alive."

"You have a literal mind, I must say. And a lot of information I didn't expect you to have."

"I spoke with a number of the witnesses earlier. It's just routine, Mrs. Kirby; just routine." O'Brien turned right onto Fifty-fourth. This move resulted in a screech of brakes and a scream from the driver of the car that had barely missed him, and he said, with visible restraint, "Would you mind taking off your hat, Mrs. Kirby? I can't see a damned thing on my right."

"Sorry." Jacqueline reached up. O'Brien glanced apprehensively at the pair of long steel hatpins she removed from the crown of the cartwheel.

"Put those away, will you?"

Jacqueline stuck them through the hat and tossed it onto the backseat. O'Brien ducked reflexively. It may have been embarrassment that made him rude. "You sure you didn't run one of those lethal weapons into Dubretta's windpipe?"

Jacqueline did not reply.

The late night joggers and dog-walkers were out in full force, the latter armed with the implements required by the city's most recent and most stringent "Curb Your Dog" regulations. It had always been a source of wonder to Jacqueline that New Yorkers, whose living space probably cost them more per square foot than anyone in the world, favored large dogs—retrievers, Dobermans, Saint Bernards. An elderly couple passed, towing, or being towed by, matched Irish wolfhounds.

Before long O'Brien pulled up in front of a block of apartments that dated from the period when architects could afford to dabble in whimsy. Turreted towers and crenellated battlements topped a facade of timber and brick in the Tudor manner. The defenses were feudal; O'Brien's ring at the outer door was answered by a doorman who peered suspiciously at him until he produced his identification.

The woman who admitted them to Dubretta's apartment was stout and white-haired. She tried to smile at them, though her lips trembled and her eyes showed signs of recent tears.

"I'm sorry to be so late, Anne," O'Brien said.

"Night and day are the same to us, Patrick. You ought to know that."

"How is she?" O'Brien asked in a low voice.

The woman shrugged fatalistically. "For once I thank God she's the way she is. Mercifully she doesn't . . . Sssh."

"Who is it, Anne?" The light, youthful voice came from a room at the end of the hallway. Then the speaker appeared in the open doorway. The face was that of the girl in the photo in Dubretta's wallet, but if Jacqueline had not been expecting to see those features she would never have recognized them, distorted as they were by rolls and lumps of fat. Dubretta's sister was only five feet tall, and enormously overweight. Yet her skin was fresh and unlined, and the smile with which she welcomed them was radiant with goodwill.

O'Brien bent to kiss her cheek. "This is the lady I was telling you about," he said. "Mrs. Kirby, I'd like you to meet Dubretta's sister, Prudence."

"Come into the living room, Mrs. Kirby. Would you like a cup of coffee, or something else to drink?"

"No, thank you." Jacqueline followed her into a

pleasant though shabby room. It served as a study as well as a living room; bookcases lined the walls, and two desks stood side by side.

"Please sit down, Mrs. Kirby," Prudence said.

"Call me Jacqueline. I only met your sister a few days ago, but I liked and admired her very much. I'm so very, very sorry."

Prudence sat down on a sofa whose sagging cushions marked it as her favorite seat. Tears overflowed her eyes. "You tried to help her. I wanted to thank you, and ask you if—if she—"

"It was very sudden," Jacqueline said gently. "She felt no pain; there was only a moment of . . . surprise."

"She would be surprised," Prudence murmured. "She never believed anything could happen to her. Did she say anything? I hoped she might ask for me."

"She did say something—one word, actually, repeated twice. It meant nothing to me at the time, but . . . It must have been your name—your nickname. Prue."

Prudence nodded. After the hints the housekeeper had dropped, Jacqueline had expected to find Dubretta's sister handicapped in one way or another; but except for her weight problem she appeared to have no disabilities, mental or physical.

A stifled sob burst from the housekeeper. "What are you crying about, Anne?" Prudence asked.

"I'm sorry, Prue . . . ."

"I can't imagine why you should be crying." Prudence's voice rose in pitch. She began to talk in a rapid, breathless monotone. "Here's one of my fans come to visit and you stand there crying. Would you

like to see where I work, Mrs. Kirby? That's my desk
there, beside Dubretta's. I'm working on a book right
now. My latest. My publisher keeps nagging me, he
wants it on the fall list. It will be his big book. He's
budgeted half a million for promotion."

Through the horrified paralysis that gripped her
Jacqueline was aware of O'Brien, eyes intent, body
poised like a tiger's. Prudence's long speech gave her
time to recover her wits. When Prudence rose, with
surprising lightness and quickness, and beckoned her
to the desk, Jacqueline followed without delay or comment.

"These are all my books," Prudence said, with a
sweeping gesture. The bookcase she indicated was
filled with paperbacks. Jacqueline recognized several
of the authors' names. "I write under several different
noms de plume, of course," Prudence went on quickly.
"The demand for my work is so great. It takes up a
great deal of my time. Not just the writing, but the public appearances and autographings, dining with publishers, and so on. And fan mail! I feel obliged to
answer each and every letter. Dubretta helps me with
that. She is a great help to me. That's her desk, next to
mine. She should be here soon. She's late. It's really
most inconsiderate of her to be late. I have a lot of letters to answer. Anne, have you made coffee? You know
Dubretta always wants her coffee when she comes in.
We'll have to work late tonight. I have a lot of fan mail
to answer."

"Then I mustn't keep you any longer," Jacqueline
said. "Thank you so much. I'm so grateful to you for
letting me come."

"I'm always happy to see one of my fans." An uncertain smile flickered across Prudence's face. "I wish Dubretta would come. She's late. She knows I worry. And I have so many things to do. . . ." Turning her back on Jacqueline, she began shifting the papers on her desk.

The housekeeper accompanied them into the hall. "Will you be all right?" O'Brien asked softly.

"Oh yes. This is . . ." The housekeeper smiled wryly. "This is normal. She's like this whenever Dubretta is late. Don't worry, Patrick. I'm used to dealing with her."

"Call me if you need anything."

Neither of them spoke until they were in the car and O'Brien had started the engine.

"How long have you known Dubretta?" Jacqueline asked.

"Almost twenty years. She was a cub reporter on the old New York *Post* when I was a rookie cop. She drove me crazy. Whenever there was a brawl or a murder or a drug bust, Dubretta was in the thick of it, waving that damned notebook and asking questions in that strident voice of hers." O'Brien was silent for a moment. "Quite a woman," he said.

"You became friends."

"Yeah," said O'Brien.

"And Prudence?"

"She was the prettiest thing you ever saw. Little and light on her feet, and always laughing. An honor student at CCNY. She had a lot of boyfriends, but Dubretta guarded her like a dragon."

"You might have warned me. For her sake, if not for mine."

"I wouldn't have let you say anything to upset her." The whites of his eyes glinted as he glanced at her.

"Brrr," said Jacqueline, shuddering affectedly.

"You handled it well," O'Brien admitted with a grudging air.

They glided to a stop at Forty-fourth, as the light turned red. Park Avenue lay quiet and at peace under the streetlights, in a deceptive serenity.

The light changed. O'Brien put his foot down on the gas. "It happened during the sixties—the height of the drug culture, if you remember. I was on the desk the night the call came in—some kid overdosed on a combination of heroin and PCP. Only one of hundreds. . . . But I knew the name.

"It could have been an accident—a mistake in the dosage. But she never touched the stuff. 'I'm too chicken,' she used to say. A little pot, maybe, for recreational purposes, but never the hard stuff. What made her do it? She couldn't or wouldn't say. But she had been trying to get a book published. You saw, tonight, the form her delusion has taken."

"I also see what you're getting at," Jacqueline said. "But even if she had suffered a cruel disappointment, or had been victimized by—let's say some anonymous member of the publishing profession—that would be insufficient cause for suicide."

"You know better than that, Mrs. Kirby. Christ, they slash their wrists over rock stars, and starve themselves into anorexia for some sick dream of beauty. And Prue had—call them emotional problems—before. There's a background—Dubretta hinted at it once, when she got tight—neglect, child abuse, God knows what. The overdose may have set off an illness that would have appeared sooner or later anyway."

"That seems likely." Neither of them voiced the corollary: whatever the real cause of Prudence's illness, Dubretta had fixed on Hattie as the scapegoat. She needed to blame someone, and perhaps the real villain was beyond her reach.

O'Brien stopped in front of the hotel. He left the engine running. "What about the threatening letters, Mrs. Kirby?"

Jacqueline had been expecting the question. Her acquaintance with Patrick O'Brien had been brief, but she had already learned to respect his abilities and his brains. She turned to retrieve her hat from the backseat. "Dubretta got several of them. They were just notes, incoherent and scrawled. She said they came from the girl who is the president of Valentine's fan club."

"Name?"

"Laurie Schellhammer," Jacqueline said, rather reluctantly. "But the notes don't mean anything, O'Brien. Laurie is seventeen, and not quite—er—"

"I get the picture."

"She couldn't have poisoned Dubretta's wine."

"Are you still harping on poison, Mrs. Kirby?"

"Good night, O'Brien."

"Good night, Mrs. Kirby."

Jacqueline got herself, her billowing skirts, and her hat out of the car unaided. After one quick identifying look, the doorman had left them strictly alone. She was

so preoccupied that she gave short shrift to the man
who tried to accost her as soon as she entered the
lobby. Jacqueline looked through him and darted past
before he could speak.

He caught up with her at the desk, where they were
joined by two women. A single glance told Jacqueline
what she should have realized immediately, even before they all spoke at once. "Mrs. Kirby, I represent the
Daily Bugle—" "Mrs. Kirby, I wonder if I might—"
And from the third, obviously a neophyte, "Are you
Mrs. Jacqueline Kirby?"

"No," Jacqueline said.

She snatched her key from the clerk and headed for
the elevators. The trio of reporters followed, spouting
questions. Jacqueline broke into a run. With all three in
pursuit, she pounded across the lobby and squeezed
herself into an elevator whose doors had begun to
close.

She knew they would be hot on the trail, via the next
elevator, so she bolted down the hall, her key in her
hand. She was mentally braced for a tussle at the door
of her room, but none of them had thought to stake it
out—or else none of them had had enough money for
a respectable bribe. She opened the door and slammed
it shut behind her. The room was pitch-dark. Cursing
Sue's midwest awareness of economy, she fumbled for
the light switch.

For several seconds she stood perfectly still.

The room was a shambles. Every article of clothing
had been torn from the hangers and thrown onto the
floor. Her suitcase and Sue's had been upended. The
mattresses of both beds were askew, sheets and blan-

kets trailing; every drawer in every piece of furniture stood open.

Jacqueline shifted her lavender evening bag from one hand to the other. Until that moment she had actually forgotten Dubretta's notebook.

Chapter 6

"Rigid with horror, Blaze gazed upon the rape of her chamber. That was how she felt it—as a violation, a ravishment. Rough, cruel hands fumbling among her treasures, touching her silken . . ."

Jacqueline shook her head. She had been reading too many romantic novels.

Her first act was to pick up the gown she meant to wear to the ball. Murmuring maledictions, she restored it to a hanger and smoothed the crumpled flounces. Turning to the next most pressing matter, she made a quick search of the room. She did not find the burglar. She had not expected she would; but she was half afraid she might find Sue, unconscious or worse. Sue wasn't under the bed or in the bathtub, and Jacqueline felt sure she would have noticed if there had been a body in the closet.

After exchanging the loathsome lavender gown for a robe and restoring the room to relative order, Jacqueline propped herself up in bed with all four pillows and (after a guilty look around the empty room) lit a cigarette.

None of her belongings was missing except for a few pieces of costume jewelry. She hoped Sue had not been foolish enough to leave cash or expensive jewelry in her suitcase. They would probably be gone as well.

Taking the costume jewelry had been an error though. No professional thief, even a beginner, could have mistaken her *faux perles* earrings and vermeil chain for the real thing, despite the misleading terms the jewelry industry had invented for those frauds. And only a professional thief could have gotten into the room without leaving any trace of his entry or exit.

Blissfully inhaling, Jacqueline glanced at the door, which was now bolted and chained. The thief had to have come in that way. There were no balconies or fire escapes within reach of her window. The lock had not been broken, nor was there any sign of tampering. The old credit-card technique, known to all readers of thrillers and all viewers of TV detective series, would not have worked on this lock. Probably there was no such thing as a burglar-proof lock, but in this case the most likely explanation . . . Jacqueline reached for the telephone.

The assistant night manager's first reaction was alarm, but when Jacqueline assured him she was not reporting a robbery, he became indignant. It was impossible that her key could have been given to the wrong person. The hotel personnel were trained to observe . . .

Jacqueline thanked him and hung up. If any of the desk clerks had given a stranger her key, he wouldn't admit it. She had always had her doubts about the system. No clerk had ever asked her for identification, he had simply handed over the key she requested. With guests checking in and out daily, it was impossible for anyone to remember which face went with which room.

She reached for Dubretta's notebook. It was lucky she hadn't had time to change clothes that evening, for she would probably have decided to leave the notebook in her room. Lucky, too, that she had spent the evening in the company of a police officer. If she had gone window-shopping or walking alone . . .

The notebook would have to go to O'Brien in the morning. Jacqueline had never had any sympathy with heroines of thrillers who clung doggedly and feeble-mindedly to the clue that *(a)* would have solved the case on page 50 if the police had had it, and *(b)* rendered said heroine vulnerable to kidnapping, assault, and mayhem. However, the hour was late; O'Brien (poor man) had had a long hard day; it would be cruel to disturb him now.

Conscience thus speciously assuaged, Jacqueline lit another cigarette and went to work.

Her knowledge of codes and ciphers came from such standard works as Dorothy Sayers' *Have His Carcase* and the Friedmans' pleasant book about the reputed Shakespeare ciphers. That, she considered, should be sufficient.

And indeed, a quick survey of the contents of the notebook confirmed what she had assumed from the beginning. Dubretta's was not a conventional code, but, as she herself had described it, an arbitrary and personal form of shorthand. Having been educated in the era when women were advised to learn secretarial skills as the best means of breaking into one of the professions, Jacqueline had wrestled briefly with shorthand before deciding she would rather scrub floors. She recognized some of the conventional symbols in Dubretta's book, but no longer remembered what any of them meant, except for the slash and comma that signified "Dear Sir" in the Gregg system. Instead of cheering her, this discovery cast her into deeper gloom. Not only was it unlikely that Dubretta would write rough drafts of letters in her scandal book, but the symbol appeared in the middle of a page, surrounded by others. Obviously it did not mean "Dear Sir." If Dubretta had used this common symbol for something other than its original meaning, she had probably done the same thing with other symbols. An expert knowledge of shorthand would not be of much help in decipherment.

Modesty was not one of Jacqueline's more conspicuous attributes, but she knew when she was licked. She felt sure she could decode the book if she had enough time. One simply listed groups of symbols and compared the frequency, and . . . Something along those lines. But if she could do it, an expert, assisted by a computer, could do it much more quickly.

Was that why O'Brien wanted the notebook, or was he just tidying up loose ends? Everything he had said gave the impression that the police were satisfied that Dubretta had died from natural causes. Jacqueline felt sure that O'Brien himself was not satisfied. He could deny it all he wanted to, but he had his suspicions. Not that he would ever admit she was right. Shaking her head in sorrow over the unaccountable egotism of the male sex in general, and O'Brien in particular, Jacque-

line put the notebook under her pillow and reached for
A Willow in Her Hand.

It was after two when she turned out the light. Sue
had not returned. Jacqueline hoped she was enjoying
whatever she was doing. She slept the sweet sleep of
the innocent, and dreamed she had been carried off
into the desert by Patrick O'Brien, riding an ostrich
and dressed in a flowing burnoose, uniform trousers
with a stripe down the side, and the lavender hat, complete with cockatoo.

"Have you seen the papers?"

"How can you speak of newspapers at a time like
this?" Jacqueline murmured, twining her arms around
O'Brien's bronzed shoulders. "And would you mind
taking off that hat?"

"Oh, I'm sorry. Were you asleep?"

Jacqueline opened one eye. Sunlight assaulted her
naked eyeball. She closed the eye.

"Brilliant deduction," she muttered.

"Your picture is on page three," Sue exclaimed. She
rattled the paper under Jacqueline's nose.

Jacqueline sat up. She had neglected to braid her
hair the night before, and the tumbled bronze mass fell
over her face, tickling her nose and getting in her
mouth. She pawed irritably at it. Sue laughed.

"You look like one of Valentine's heroines," she said.
"Beautifully disheveled, and drowsy with loving."

"Drowsy with five hours' sleep, you mean. How
dare you speak to me at this hour in that cheerful tone
of voice."

"I brought you some coffee." Sue sat down on the

other bed and proffered a plastic container. "My mother's like that in the morning too. I figured—"

Too outraged to speak, Jacqueline seized the coffee and drank.

"I've been with Joe," Sue said. Flushed and dewy-eyed, she stared dreamily at the ceiling. "He's wonderful, Jacqueline. Do you know what his real ambition is? To find a nice little town, somewhere in the Midwest, and settle down. He wants me—"

"I know what he wants," Jacqueline growled. "And I don't want to hear about it."

"Oh no, you're wrong! Joe isn't like that. We didn't—we were talking."

"All night?"

"In an all-night coffee bar. That's where I got your coffee."

"It was a kindly thought," Jacqueline admitted, the caffeine finally having reached her brain. "Let me see that newspaper."

There were two newspapers, the *Times* and the less reputable periodical in which Dubretta's column appeared. The *Times* had treated *l'affaire des* romance writers with the contempt it deserved; but the *Daily Blank,* never known for reticence, had pulled out all the stops. Hattie must be rolling on the floor in fits of rapture, Jacqueline thought. Never had so much publicity been attained for so little expenditure.

They hadn't made the headlines, but a box on page 1 referred readers to the story. It used the precise phrases Jacqueline had imagined. "Who tried to kill Valerie Valentine? Queen of Love threatened. Famous detective on the case."

Turning to page 3, Jacqueline was about to remark, "Who is that blowsy-looking frump in the . . ." when she recognized herself. The picture was the one Dubretta's cameraman had taken the day before. Parasol over her shoulder, hat over her brow, Jacqueline leered at the reader. The caption read, "Famous private detective?" She could not blame the editor for adding the question mark.

There were also photographs of Valentine and Victor von Damm. The story was a masterpiece of innuendos and non sequiturs; its style leaned heavily upon the meaningful question: "Who handed Dubretta the fatal glass?" "Was the wine poisoned?" "Is there in the past of this exquisite and talented young writer a man driven mad by jealousy and tormented passion?"

"And why, and wherefore, and if not, why not?" Jacqueline murmured.

"What did you say?"

"Nothing."

The story went on to misspell Jacqueline's name and describe her as a professor of astrophysics at a well-known eastern university, and a writer whose "best-selling novels have appeared under a pseudonym. She shuns publicity, preferring to allow the local police to take credit for the cases she solves." Picturing O'Brien's reaction to that, Jacqueline grinned broadly.

The reporter had made the most of his non-interview. "When questioned by this reporter, Ms. Kirky replied in her low, throaty voice that she was unable to discuss the case at the present time. It is rumored that she is working closely with the New York Police Department. When asked about Ms. Kirsky's relationship with the department, Lieutenant Patrick O'Brien refused to comment."

Jacqueline laughed aloud.

"What's so funny?"

"Everything. There isn't a sentence in this story that isn't mirth-provoking."

"Are you a professor of astrophysics?" Sue asked, wide-eyed.

For once Jacqueline was not tempted to embellish a handsome lie. "My dear girl, you know who and what I am. I told you the day we met."

"I thought you might have been under cover," Sue explained.

"Under . . . You don't believe that guff about my being a detective, do you? Didn't they teach you in college that the printed word is not sacrosanct? In other words, don't believe everything you read in the paper."

"Joe said you were a detective. He said Valerie Vanderbilt said—"

"Never mind that. What else did Joe say?"

"About what?"

"He told you his real name was Joe Kirby."

"Yes. Are you sure you two aren't—"

"I'm sure. He also told you that Victor von Damm's books are ghost-written, by a couple of Brooklyn housewives?"

"Well . . ."

"Does that bother you?"

"Joe explained how it happened," Sue said, avoiding Jacqueline's eyes. "It was Hattie Foster's idea, all of it. A lot of books are ghost-written. You know, the ones by famous Hollywood stars, and politicians, and . . .

The real author's name doesn't appear, but everyone knows . . . It's done all the time. There's nothing wrong with—"

"It's a form of fraud, though," Jacqueline said soberly. "Not in the legal sense, perhaps, but morally and ethically. Besides, the examples you mentioned aren't comparable. People don't buy a memoir because it is written by Famous Actress, they buy it because it is about Famous Actress. There's no actual misrepresentation. But Victor von Damm's fame and reputation rest on his writing. And Victor von Damm is nobody. He doesn't exist."

"He hates it," Sue said in a low voice. "He wants to quit."

"Why doesn't he?"

"He's going to quit. But it will take a little time to set things straight. He can't just walk out."

"Why not? Oh, forget it," Jacqueline said, as Sue looked at her tearfully. "I gather he didn't tell you anything that—"

The telephone rang. Jacqueline stared at it in consternation. "Who the hell could be calling at this hour?"

"It's eight-thirty," Sue said.

"My God." The instrument buzzed again. Jacqueline snatched it up. "Yes?"

Sue retreated tactfully into the bathroom, leaving Jacqueline free to express her emotions. "No, James, you didn't wake me up. Sorry to disappoint you. That does not mean I am in any mood to talk to you at the crack of dawn."

"What do you mean, crack of dawn," James demanded. "It's eight-thirty."

"When I am on vacation, eight-thirty is the crack of dawn."

"When did you go to bed?"

"None of your business."

"I was not inquiring into your social activities, Jacqueline. I was exercising my prerogative as duly appointed co-sleuth, to ask what information you elicited from O'Brien."

"I don't feel like discussing it at the crack of—"

"Meet me for breakfast, then."

"What an obscene suggestion."

"Lunch, then."

"Where?"

"The Algonquin. Noon."

"Well . . ."

"I thought that would get you, you greedy snob."

Jacqueline hung up. Scarcely had she done so when the telephone rang again. Jacqueline snatched it up. "What do you want now?" she shouted.

"Sue," said a meek, surprised voice. "Is she—"

"You just left her half an hour ago."

"So? Is that any reason why I can't—"

"Why didn't you tell her the truth?"

Silence followed. Then the voice of Victor von Damm, stiff with aristocratic hauteur, said, "I don't know what you're referring to."

"Neither do I," Jacqueline admitted. She rubbed her forehead. "Sue is busy now. Call later." She hung up.

She expected Joe to protest this brusque dismissal, and was not surprised when the telephone shrieked an immediate summons. Before she could pronounce the devastating comment she had prepared, a voice cooed,

"Good morning, Mrs. Kirby. I do hope I didn't waken you."

"You damned well—" Jacqueline began.

"Oh, good," Hattie said. "I figured you'd be up and busy with your detecting. Did you see our publicity this morning?"

"Yes, I did, and I thought it was the most—"

"Those boys and girls on the New York papers are really efficient, aren't they? The reason I'm telephoning, Mrs. Kirby, is to tell you I've called a press conference for eleven A.M. I think that's the easiest way of dealing with this sort of thing; I mean, reporters can just drive you crazy if you don't cooperate. They're just doin' their job, after all. Room 415 at my hotel— eleven sharp. Don't be late."

"No."

"What did you say?" Hattie asked doubtfully.

"No. Meaning, I won't be there."

"But—but—you have to come. I told the man from the *Times*—"

"Aunt Hattie—if I may call you that—get one thing straight. I don't know what you're holding over the heads of your terrorized authors, but you've got no hold over me. They may jump when you crack your whip. I don't."

From the other end of the line came sounds of struggle and alarm. Then another voice said breathlessly, "Mrs. Kirby."

"Mr. Hollenstein?"

"Max—please. I couldn't help overhearing Hattie's side of your conversation, and I don't blame you for refusing her invitation—"

"You usually have a keener ear for the appropriate word, Mr.—Max."

The manager chuckled. "Don't take it personally. She talks that way to everyone. But I wish you would join us, for your own sake, if not for Valentine's. Heaven only knows what Hattie will say if you aren't there to defend yourself."

Jacqueline heard Hattie's indignant rebuttal: "Why, Max, you ought to be ashamed!"—and Max's reply. "Be quiet, Hattie. Mrs. Kirby?"

"I have a lot to do this morning," Jacqueline said.

"I think you should come."

"Has something happened?"

"I'd rather not discuss it over the telephone."

"All right. I'll be there. Do tell Hattie 'Go to hell' for me, won't you?"

She slammed the telephone into its cradle. The bathroom door opened and Sue's head appeared. "Is anything wrong?"

"Why do you ask?"

"You were yelling."

"So I was." Jacqueline smiled and stretched. "My, that felt good. Is there any more coffee?"

"I'm sorry—"

"That's all right. Hurry up in there, will you?"

Sue's head vanished. Jacqueline swallowed the dregs of her coffee and studied the empty cup regretfully. This was beginning to look like a three-, or even four-cup morning. She transferred her gaze to the telephone, but it remained silent. Throwing the covers back, she got out of bed and cautiously opened the door.

The hallway was empty. So much for Hattie's belief that the press was hot on the trail of the Big Story. In a world reeling with war and corruption and famine and imminent nuclear holocaust, the death of one columnist was an extremely minor story. It would probably be forgotten in a day if Hattie left it alone. Which Hattie had no intention of doing.

Jacqueline reached the telephone just as it rang for the fourth time. "Now what?" she asked resignedly.

"Is that you, Jake?"

"Who else? That's all I do, answer telephones."

"It's me. Betsy."

"I know."

This response constituted a conversational dead end. There was no reply from Betsy. After a moment Jacqueline said, "Well?"

"Have you seen the newspapers?"

"I have."

"Is it true?"

"Is what . . . Betsy, what the hell do you want?"

"I was there," Betsy said.

"I know. I saw you. For God's sake, get to the point."

"Was it really . . . Did somebody try to . . ."

"So far as I know, the official view is that nobody tried to do anything to anybody. Dubretta died of a heart attack."

"But the paper says—"

"Another example of our inadequate educational system."

"What?"

"I thought you were a rough, tough radical. Do I detect a yellow streak?"

Unlike Sue, Betsy was well acquainted with Jacqueline's peculiar conversational style. She replied irritably, "I wish to God you could talk like a normal person. I know perfectly well that all this crap about somebody trying to kill Valentine is probably just another publicity stunt. But if it isn't . . . I was there, Jake—slinking around in that ghastly wig and revolting dress, as if I had something to hide. That was your idea, you know! An evil-minded cop might interpret the things I've been saying about the Queen of Schlock as threats."

"That's pretty farfetched, Betsy."

"Oh yeah? Have you read Dubretta's column this morning?"

"I haven't had time. I've been on the phone for hours," Jacqueline added pointedly.

"She quoted a couple of the things I said. Taken out of context. . . . Call me a coward if you like, but I prefer to anticipate trouble instead of being ambushed. Can I count on you, Jake?"

"I'll be happy to testify as a character witness," Jacqueline said. "I'll say you're all talk and no do. That you're basically chicken. That—"

"God damn it, Jake!"

"All right, calm yourself. You're making a mountain out of a molehill and brewing a tempest in a teapot and also crossing your bridges before you come to them. I'll keep an eye on the situation and let you know if anything interesting develops."

Betsy thanked her effusively and Jacqueline hung up, reflecting on the unaccountable tendency of people to be reassured by a series of meaningless aphorisms.

Betsy had gone off half-cocked (she had forgotten that one). Yet Betsy had a point. An evil-minded investigator might consider that she had a motive. Jacqueline whipped out her notebook and added Betsy's name to the list she and James had compiled. Not that she really believed Betsy had poisoned the wine. But a detective had to be impartial.

She heard the sound of rushing water from the shower in the bathroom, and decided Sue would be out of the way for a few more minutes. From under her pillow she took Dubretta's notebook, and opened it. She had had a couple of ideas during the night.

One was a promising lead. She was so deeply engrossed that she failed to respond quickly enough when the bathroom door opened and Sue, fetchingly draped in a towel, darted into the bedroom.

"Son of a gun," said Jacqueline, trying to sit on the notebook.

"Why, that's—isn't that the book the detective was looking for last night?"

"No."

"Joe told me about it. He said it had a red cover—"

"I picked it up by mistake," Jacqueline said.

This explanation was so weak even Sue refused to buy it. Head on one side, she looked quizzically at Jacqueline, who said sullenly, "I'm going to give it to the police this morning. As soon as you get out of the bathroom and give me a chance to shower."

"I forgot my toothpaste," Sue said, retreating with the tube.

"Humph."

When Jacqueline went back to her research the

promising lead had evaporated. Sue had broken her train of thought—and had made it necessary for her to carry out her promise of returning the notebook. She had intended to do that anyhow, but now prompt action was imperative. Sue would probably mention the notebook to Joe; she was in that state of imbecilic infatuation where not even a promise of silence would keep her from confiding in her beloved. She might tell other people, and Joe certainly would, and before long the omnipotent O'Brien would know for certain what he already suspected.

Jacqueline had considered various methods of handing over Dubretta's property. The easiest way out was to put it in an envelope with no return address and drop it in the mail. However, she had no great confidence in the United States Postal Service; the book might take two days or two weeks to reach the police, or it might disappear altogether. Besides, that was a coward's way out. She was not intimidated by Lieutenant O'Brien.

The safest and surest method was to deliver it herself. She reached for the phone. The operator gave her the number of the local precinct station, and a telephone call elicited the information that Lieutenant O'Brien was indeed at that location. "Do you want to talk to him, ma'am?" the sergeant inquired.

"No," Jacqueline said hastily.

She hadn't expected O'Brien would be on the job so bright and early. He had implied he was on night duty. Apparently the visit to Prudence Duberstein had been made on his own time.

Sue was still in the bathroom, so Jacqueline returned to the newspaper. Dubretta's column appeared in its usual place. It contained no revelations. Jacqueline had not expected any; Dubretta hadn't had time to write up the new information she had collected. Instead the column featured a sardonic review of the previous day's proceedings, including a description of the protest march and an interview with Betsy, "Chairperson of the Women's United Front Against Sexism."

Jacqueline, who had a penchant for acronyms, performed a mental operation on the initial letters of this organization, and decided Betsy should have chosen a different name.

Her eyebrows lifted as she read. Betsy and Dubretta must have gotten smashed after she left them. But smashed or sober, Betsy had a habit of shooting her mouth off. Statements like "Verminous leeches who ought to be exterminated," and "Mindless creeps who belong on the list of people who never would be missed" could indeed be taken the wrong way.

She was about to bang on the bathroom door when Sue finally emerged, wearing a lacy nightgown. She fixed wide, nearsighted blue eyes on Jacqueline and said humbly, "I'm sorry."

"Stop apologizing for everything," Jacqueline grumbled. "Are you going to bed now?"

"Just for a few hours. Then I'm meeting Joe. Do you know if Hattie has canceled today's workshops?"

"I can't imagine that she would. And in all fairness to her, I don't see why she should."

"Are you going to the conference this morning?"

The red notebook lay on the bed in plain sight. Sue carefully avoided looking at it. Jacqueline picked it up and brandished it. "I am returning this—*taking* this—

to the police station. Then I am having lunch with a friend—at the Algonquin, if anybody wants to know. But first I am going to have two, possibly three, cups of coffee, downstairs, in the coffee shop of this hotel. I'll call later and let you know what I plan to do this afternoon."

"I wasn't trying to pry. I just wondered."

"Okay, okay."

After Jacqueline had closed the bathroom door she heard the telephone ring. Shamelessly she eased the door open and listened. She couldn't make out the words—Sue must have retreated under the bedcovers with the phone—but the soft, intimate murmur of the girl's voice brought a reluctant smile to Jacqueline's lips. It had been so long since she felt that way that the memory was as remote as ancient history, but it had been marvelous while it lasted. She hoped this affair would be longer-lived. Joe might or might not be serious about Sue. He was so soured by romance writers that anyone outside the trade would look good to him, and Sue was so credulous she'd believe anything he told her. He had not been honest with her. Hattie was unquestionably blackmailing him, as she was Jean, but unless she had evidence of something more serious than the Von Damm masquerade, there was nothing to stop Joe from thumbing his nose and walking away clean. He wasn't a timid rabbit like Jean, and there was nothing illegal about what he had done. Unless . . .

Jacqueline closed the door and began brushing her teeth. She felt sure she could get the truth out of Joe. She had successfully intimidated stronger characters than he. If she only had more time! Things were happening so fast she couldn't keep up with them, and in the meantime her own book was suffering.

So much to do—and she loved every bit of it. The face that looked back at her from the mirror wore an expression of bright anticipation. She thought complacently, Not bad, considering that I only had five hours' sleep. I think I'll make my heroine a little older—mid-forties, perhaps. Those fans at the conference—a lot of them are middle-aged, I'll bet they would really identify with a heroine closer to their own age, instead of some nubile chit in her twenties. The wise woman of the tribe, priestess of the Goddess. . . . (Which Goddess? Never mind, I'll figure that out later.) Desired by all men, but sacred. "Her lissome figure in its scanty covering of deerskins moved gracefully along the path to the shrine. Watching from behind the bushes, Lurgh the hunter wet his lips. To possess this woman he would risk the wrath of the Goddess. . . ."

As she drank her coffee Jacqueline wrote busily in not one but two notebooks. First Oona the priestess dealt with Lurgh the hunter, eluding his sweating hands and striking him down with the sacred staff of the Goddess before he had done more than remove the deerskin from strategic portions of her anatomy. "She pointed a quivering finger at the gasping, panting hulk sprawled across the path. 'The wrath of the Goddess be upon you, profaner of the sacred virgin,' she cried."

The second notebook contained Jacqueline's thoughts on the case. She was grateful to Max Hollenstein for wrestling the telephone from Hattie, for she had been dying to attend the press conference. It was a matter of principle not to yield to Hattie, and if Max hadn't apologized and cajoled, she would have had to think of an excuse. However, that appointment meant that she would have to postpone some of the other plans she had made for the morning. Thoughtfully she considered the list she had made earlier.

It was a pity she couldn't wait until after the press conference before running her other errands. She was meeting James at twelve. The Algonquin was on West Forty-fourth, only three blocks from the library and four blocks from the police station. If she delivered the notebook first, she would have to go to Forty-first, then back to Fifty-third, then back to Forty-fourth. However, it couldn't be helped. To carry Dubretta's notebook with her to the press conference would be asking for trouble. The person who had searched her room must have been looking for the notebook. Not only had O'Brien stressed its importance, but he had practically accused her, Jacqueline, of having it. The group of people who had been informed of those facts at ten P.M. the night before would be at the press conference, or at the hotel, and she had no reason to suppose that interest in the notebook had diminished in the meantime. The notebook must go to the police at once, there was no question about that.

Well . . . Almost at once. Jacqueline's eyes glinted as she considered what she meant to do.

Avoiding the temptations of the shops on Fifth Avenue, she walked along Sixth to Forty-second and then went to Fifth and climbed the stairs between the noble stone lions. The copying machines on the third floor were all in use; she had to wait. When a machine became available she methodically reproduced the pages upon which Dubretta had written. Tucking the sheaf of papers into her purse, she yielded the machine to the impatient Indian student, turbaned and bearded, who was next in line.

Forty-second Street is one of the main cross-streets in midtown Manhattan, with traffic going in both directions. Even hardened New Yorkers are wary of running the lights on Forty-second, though they do it all the time on other, one-way streets. However, they jostle and jockey for position at the curb, so as not to lose even a second when the vehicular traffic stops. Jacqueline wormed her way to the brink and stood poised. It was after ten-thirty, and she had to drop off the envelope containing Dubretta's notebook and get back to Fifty-third before eleven.

The shove that sent her tumbling forward did not come until after the light had changed. It was hard enough to mash her midriff against the fender of a taxi that had screeched to a stop, and knock the breath out of her. She fell, ungracefully and emphatically, and was stepped on by a dozen feet.

New Yorkers are not, however, the callous robots they are reputed to be. A dozen other feet avoided her, by agile quicksteps, and several hands reached out to help her up. "Don't do that," several voices objected. "Hey, lady, are you okay? She might have a concussion or a broken leg. Hey, lady, don't move till you're sure you're okay."

Dazed though she was, Jacqueline had no trouble deciding it was safer to move out of the street rather than stay where she was, under the fender of one taxi and in the path of a number of others. Supported by a pair of Good Samaritans, she limped back to the curb and propped herself against a lamppost to survey the damage.

Most of it was cosmetic—a broad smear of dust and oil across the middle of her pale-green dress, scraped and bleeding knees, and the total destruction of a pair of pantyhose.

One of the Samaritans, a heavy-set black woman, tried to dust off her dress. "You okay, dearie? Maybe you better sit down."

"My purse," Jacqueline said. "About two feet square, white, shoulder strap . . ." Traffic was in motion again. There was no handbag visible between the rolling wheels. She had not expected to see it.

The other woman shook her head. "Honest to God, what some people will do. Practically kill a person just so's they can grab her purse. You want me to—"

"No, thanks. I really appreciate your help." Jacqueline gave her an abstracted smile. As soon as the light changed, she dashed across the street.

The open, parklike area surrounding the library offered few places for concealment. It was more likely that the thief had scooped up her purse as she fell, and proceeded on across Forty-second, mingling with the majority of the pedestrians who had not stopped to assist her. Office buildings and stores lined the opposite side of the street. If she was quick enough . . .

She found the purse in the third doorway she investigated, that of an office building. She had expected the thief would discard it as soon as possible—it was large enough to be conspicuous and therefore dangerous—

but she was both relieved and surprised that she had found it before a second, more mercenary thief had picked it up. Nothing had been taken except the notebook and the bundle of copies.

Jacqueline glanced uneasily over her shoulder. The thief must have been on her trail from the time she left the hotel. Unless he had actually watched her reproduce the pages he wouldn't have recognized them, for they had been folded so that only the blank side showed.

Limping and ruminating, and glancing nervously from side to side, she made her way back to her hotel. Unaccustomed as she was to self-recrimination, she wasn't particularly proud of her performance that morning. Not only had she lost what might have proved to be a valuable clue, but she was going to have a hard time explaining to O'Brien how she had lost it. If Sue hadn't seen the damned notebook that morning— and, in all probability, broadcast the news to the world, via Joe—she could simply deny that she had ever had it. Maybe, she thought cravenly, I can buy another notebook, scribble some nonsense in it, and pretend that was the one Sue saw.

She might or might not have yielded to this ignoble impulse, but she was not given the chance to decide. By the time she reached her hotel her scraped knees were aching, and the look on the doorman's face, as he leaped to perform his duty, told her that she looked even worse than she felt. She went as rapidly as she could toward the elevator, but somehow she was not surprised to see a familiar figure waiting there.

O'Brien was wearing a light-gray suit. His tie, his socks, and the stripe on the handkerchief in his breast pocket were of deep forest green. The controlled fa-cade of his face cracked for an instant when he saw Jacqueline, but he said only, "Don't tell me. The bad guys got it."

"No comment," Jacqueline said.

O'Brien followed her into the elevator. He remained discreetly silent, in the presence of the other occu-pants, but got off with Jacqueline at her floor.

"Get lost, O'Brien," Jacqueline said.

"You've always wanted to say that, haven't you?"

"Don't you have any other business?"

"My business is with you."

"Later. As you can see, I have to change."

"I'm coming in with you." O'Brien whipped the key from her fingers. Before Jacqueline could object, he added, "I think it would be better if I went in first."

Jacqueline shrugged. "It's not necessary. The room was searched last night. And this morning . . ."

"Yes?"

"Later."

O'Brien opened the door. Sue had drawn the draperies, and the room was dusky with shadows. Jacqueline reached past O'Brien and switched on the light. "See? All quiet. That's Sue. She's asleep."

O'Brien looked at the motionless hump in the bed. "Sure she isn't dead?"

"Get lost, O'Brien," Jacqueline said, out of the cor-ner of her mouth. It sounded even better that way.

O'Brien's face creased in his sinister smile. He leaned against the wall and folded his arms. "I'll wait out here, Mrs. Kirby. Just scream if somebody jumps out of the closet with an ax."

Jacqueline slammed the door in his face. Sue stirred. "What?" she asked sleepily.

"Go back to sleep," Jacqueline snarled.

Ten minutes later she emerged from her room wearing a navy-blue suit, a row of Band-Aids across her knees, and a sour expression.

"That was quick," O'Brien said. "May I offer you my arm?"

"You may not." Tucking her purse close to her side, Jacqueline walked away. O'Brien fell in step with her.

"On your way to the press conference?"

"I'm late. So if you'll excuse me—"

"Those things never start on time. Don't you want to know why I was waiting for you at the critical and dramatic moment?"

"You wanted to see me," Jacqueline said. "I wasn't in my room. You knew I would be at the press conference at eleven—you seem to know everything—so you hung around, hoping I'd come here to change before attending. Don't you have any other responsibilities?"

"You're a smooth-talking lady, Mrs. Kirby, but you can't get me off the track that easily. Your deductions are correct, as far as they go, but you've omitted one major item. The notebook. Now please don't waste my time by denying you had it. I know you did, and so do a lot of other people."

"Thanks to you," Jacqueline said venomously. The elevator reached the lobby. She stepped out, with OBrien close on her heels.

"I owe you one for that," he said seriously. Jacqueline glanced at him in surprise. "It's your own fault, in a way," O'Brien insisted. "I figured you for one of those romance crackpots, playing out some private fantasy. I didn't think the notebook was important, but it irked the hell out of me that you would have the gall to make off with it the way you did. Later I got to thinking. . . ."

"That Dubretta's death might have been murder?"

O'Brien grabbed Jacqueline's arm and spun her around to face him. "Wait a minute. Just one minute."

"Oooh." Jacqueline shivered. "Golly-gee-whiz, Lieutenant, you really scare me. I do believe this is police brutality. Hey, everybody, look at the—"

"Mrs. Kirby." O'Brien's grip relaxed. It took another twenty seconds or so for him to get his voice under control. "Give me a break, will you? Just let me say what I came here to say, and you can go."

"Okay."

"All I want is . . . Okay?"

"Okay."

The encounter had not gone unobserved. People were looking at them, and one very large man had begun walking slowly in their direction. O'Brien smiled. Jacqueline smiled. Neither smile was convincing, but the big man stopped, gave O'Brien a thoughtful look, and allowed himself to be removed by a woman who appeared to be his wife.

O'Brien fingered his tie. "One of these days," he said under his breath, still doggedly smiling, "somebody is going to wring your neck, Mrs. Kirby."

"Spit it out, Lieutenant. I'm late."

"Where was I? Oh. I got to thinking. Not that Dubretta's death was murder, no, ma'am. But that notebook of hers could be dangerous, for reasons that have nothing to do with murder. She collected dirt, and she was looking for scandal about the romance writers. It occurred to me in the dark reaches of the night that maybe I had put you on the spot when I fingered you as the one who stole Dubretta's notebook. I stopped by this morning because I thought maybe . . . And," O'Brien concluded, staring at Jacqueline's bandaged knees, "I was right. Wasn't I?"

Jacqueline glanced ostentatiously at her watch. "Much as I enjoy these verbal sparring matches, I must be on my way. So I will be brief. I did find, to my utter astonishment, that somehow Dubretta's notebook had found its way into my purse."

"You didn't notice it until you got back to the hotel last night," O'Brien suggested politely.

"How did you know? Someone had entered my room while I was absent and had turned the place upside down. I assumed it was a casual thief—"

"Like hell you did."

"—and, since nothing of value was missing, I decided to forget the whole thing. It was late when I realized I had the notebook. I didn't want to disturb you at such an hour, but as my roommate will tell you—if she hasn't already told you—I had every intention of giving it to you this morning. In fact, I was on my way to the station house—"

"The check is in the mail," O'Brien murmured.

With an effort Jacqueline kept her face straight. "Precisely. I was about to cross Forty-second Street when someone shoved me. Luckily for me, traffic had stopped, but I careened off a taxicab and fell flat on my . . . knees. By the time I got my wits together, my purse had disappeared. I found it shortly afterwards, in a doorway where the thief had left it. The notebook was gone."

She saw no reason whatever to mention the loss of the pages she had reproduced. They were gone, along with the notebook, so why bring them up?

"Traffic had stopped," O'Brien repeated.

"You do have a logical mind, Lieutenant. That thought occurred to me too. One can never be certain, of course, but unless there was an error in timing I might suppose that the miscreant didn't intend to do me serious harm. Just dent me a little, so he could make off with the evidence in the confusion."

Somewhat to Jacqueline's annoyance O'Brien waved this consideration aside. He might not care whether she was demolished or merely dented, but the distinction was of some concern to her.

"Did you read . . . Of course you did. What was in the notebook?"

"I couldn't read it. Believe it or not, O'Brien."

"I believe it. Dubretta's private shorthand was one of her trademarks. You realize, Mrs. Kirby, that if we had had that notebook we might have deciphered her code?"

"But why would you bother?" Jacqueline asked innocently. "This isn't a murder case. Is it?"

O'Brien stepped back a pace. "Get lost, Mrs. Kirby."

"Right." Jacqueline started for the door, then paused. "Lieutenant."

"Yes, Mrs. Kirby?"

"I want to report an assault. Forty-second and Fifth

Avenue. Someone pushed me in front of a taxi and stole my—"

"Get lost, Mrs. Kirby," O'Brien said out of the corner of his mouth.

It sounded even better that way.

The press conference was a fiasco. There were only three reporters present, and not a single photographer. Jacqueline was no help. In her prim navy-blue suit, with her glasses perched insecurely midway down her nose and an expression of bovine perplexity on her face, she was ignored by the reporters, including one of the young women who had tried to interview her the night before. When Hattie pointed her out as the famous detective who was investigating the attempt on Valentine's life, she looked so horrified that the same reporter burst out laughing, and the others smothered skeptical smiles. A few pointed questions made it clear that Hattie had no evidence whatever of murder or attempted murder, and the reporters closed their notebooks and wandered off in search of new sensations. This one hadn't been worth much to begin with.

Hattie fastened a malignant look on Jacqueline. "You let me down, Mrs. Kirsky."

At least one was never in doubt as to how one stood in Hattie's estimation. Unlike some of the other characters with whom Jacqueline was involved, enigmatic she was not. One of the more engaging demonstrations of her animosity was her inability to remember Jacqueline's name. When they were on good terms, it flowed trippingly from her tongue.

"I couldn't let you down," Jacqueline replied crisply.

"You're already down so far, there's no place lower to go. What did you hope to accomplish by this inane performance? And where is your stable? You'd have made a stronger impression if you had produced Valentine, sighing and wringing her lily-white hands."

"She's too upset," Hattie said. "If you think this is just a publicity stunt—"

"I know it's just a publicity stunt. Where is Max?"

"With Val. She can't be left alone. She—"

"You didn't get here until a quarter past eleven. Where were you?"

"Shopping. I ran out of—"

"Anyone see you?"

Hattie's bosom swelled to alarming proportions. "What the hell is this, a third degree?"

"Where's Laurie?"

"How should I know? She hangs around the lobby near the registration table, until Val—"

"I want to talk to her."

"So who's stopping you?"

Jacqueline started for the door. Hattie said, "Max wants to see you."

"I haven't time now. I have a lunch date."

If Hattie had expostulated, Jacqueline would have walked out. Hattie's silence worried her. "Has something happened?" she asked.

Hattie's square jaw sagged. "Oh hell," she muttered. "What's the use? You try to help these kids, you give 'em everything you've got, and what do they do? They stab you in the back. You can't depend on 'em for a damned thing."

Her tone invited commiseration, from one aging P.

to another, and was as phony as her southern-lady act;
but Jacqueline sensed a genuine grievance.

"Don't tell me, let me guess," she said. "Valentine
has decided no one wanted to kill her after all. That's
what Max wanted to tell me."

"When I think what I could have done with that,"
Hattie muttered, a far-off look in her eyes. "Sometimes
I'd like to strangle that little jerk."

"Really."

"Just a figure of speech," Hattie said quickly. "Ah
love that little girl like my own chile."

"Cheer up," Jacqueline said. "Your publicity ploy
has fallen flat for the moment, but I'm sure you'll be
tickled to know that I'm on your side. Dubretta was
murdered. You know it and I know it, and I'm going to
find out who did it."

It was a good exit line, and Jacqueline decided she
had better take advantage of it before Hattie could
voice her reaction. She was very much afraid Hattie
didn't appreciate her offer of alliance.

The food at the Algonquin was excellent, but that
wasn't why Jaqueline liked the place. As James had
implied, she was a literary snob; the old hotel might be
a little shabby around the edges now, but it retained the
glamour of the old *New Yorker* days, when Dorothy
Parker and Thurber and Ross met over lunch and scandal. Another cat had replaced the famous Hamlet, but
he had the same conscious look of superiority as he sat
in front of the newsstand with his paws tucked under
his snowy breast.

The lobby cocktail lounge was a favorite meeting

place for literary and theatrical celebrities, and those who considered themselves to be celebrities. Jacqueline was pleased to see that James had secured a table. He was not alone. At first she didn't recognize the woman with him. Her graying hair hung lank and limp around her face, which was innocent of makeup except for a touch of pale pink lipstick. She wore a severely cut dark suit and a white shirtwaist blouse, buttoned up to the neck.

James seemed engrossed by the conversation of this drab female, and Jacqueline frowned as she made her way toward them. It was not until the woman looked up and smiled that she recognized Jean.

After somewhat stilted greetings had been exchanged, James said, "I'm trying to persuade Jean to join us for lunch."

"I wouldn't dream of intruding," Jean said. "But this seemed like a good opportunity to explain . . . Why are you looking at me like that, Jake?"

"Is that the way you normally dress?" Jacqueline asked.

"Why yes. What's wrong with it?"

"I think I prefer Valerie Vanderbilt. At least she has some pizzazz."

Jean flushed angrily, and James said, "For God's sake, Jacqueline, control that trivial mind of yours. I persuaded Jean to come out of the closet, so to speak. She's agreed to tell us about her deal with Hattie."

"It's high time," Jacqueline said. "Excuse me a minute." Extending a long arm, she intercepted a passing waiter and ordered a martini. Then she leaned back and looked expectantly at Jean. "Go ahead."

"I've been behaving very stupidly," Jean began. "James has helped straighten me out. As he says, it's really a trivial problem. I followed his advice; I talked to Hattie, and just as he predicted everything is all right now."

She turned an adoring smile on James, who cleared his throat and tried without conspicuous success to look modest. Jacqueline was sorely tempted to point out that James's advice was not only self-evident to anyone with an ounce of sense, but it was precisely what she had told Jean herself. Jean was apparently one of those dim females who only heeded advice when it came from a man. Fearing, however, that criticism would halt the flow of information, Jacqueline simply coughed pointedly and said nothing.

"Tell her about your talk with Hattie," James prompted.

"Oh. Well, I just told Hattie I was tired of writing. I didn't want to be Valerie Vanderbilt any more. And do you know what? She said fine, if that was what I wanted. She was sorry to lose me, but the most important thing was that I should be happy. And she won't tell anybody that I was Valerie Vanderbilt!"

From the delight in her voice Jean might have been announcing that she had won the Irish Sweepstakes. The waiter brought Jacqueline's drink, and just in time; she felt the need of a restorative.

"Wait a minute," she said. "Let me get this straight. Hattie is releasing you. In exchange for what?"

"Why, nothing." Jean blinked. "Oh well, I told her she could use the Vanderbilt name. She'll get someone else to write under that pseudonym. It's done all the

time in the book business. Like Alexandre Dumas, and
the Nancy Drew books."

Jacqueline reflected that Hattie had a miraculous talent for making questionable deals sound reasonable.
She ought to have been a politician.

Jean rambled on, in an orgy of self-congratulation,
until Jacqueline interrupted her again. "How big a percentage is she giving you?"

"Percentage?"

"For the use of the Vanderbilt name. You created it."

"Not really. Hattie—"

"And I thought the academic world was a bog of
hypocrisy," Jacqueline muttered, half to herself. "Start
at the beginning, Jean. How did you get into the romance business?"

It was a long, rambling story, made even more discursive by Jean's reluctance to discuss Hattie's questionable tactics and her own stupidity at being taken in
by them. Jean had been reading historical romances on
the sly for some time before she decided to try her
hand at one. She insisted she had done it as a joke, but
when pressed by Jacqueline, she admitted that money
had been a consideration. There was also the implicit
challenge, to which most students of literature are susceptible: this stuff is so bad, surely I can do better.

After completing the manuscript, with the help of
several obscure Victorian masterpieces of pornography, Jean had decided to send the book to Hattie. Hattie had responded promptly and flatteringly. She
adored the book. It was sensational. She would be honored to handle it and was sure she could sell it.

She had no trouble persuading Jean to use a pen

name. Somewhat appalled at the accomplishment of
what had been only an idle daydream, but seduced by
the opportunity to make money, Jean had signed a contract with Hattie.

Since she was afraid to risk her anonymity by getting in touch with other writers, Jean didn't realize for
some time that the contract she had signed was a disaster. When a dim inkling began to dawn, she fought
the realization. It was a normal reaction; people will
submit to almost anything rather than admit they have
committed a stupid blunder. Even now Jean tried to
deny Jacqueline's criticisms. Written contracts between authors and agents were not the rule in the publishing business, but some agents insisted on them;
twenty-five percent was admittedly a little higher than
the average commission. . . . All right, it was more than
twice the average. No, Hattie never forwarded royalty
statements from the publisher, but the checks were
larger every time, and there was no reason to suspect . . .

Jacqueline dropped the subject. Hattie had taken
Jean to the cleaners, and there was very little Jean
could do about it. The twenty-five percent commission
was outrageous, but Jean had agreed to it, in writing.
Hattie's additional rake-offs from the royalties were
probably covered by creative accounting. (Office expenses had gone up, and everyone knew postage was
sky-high these days.) By comparing the publishers'
copies of the royalty reports with the checks she had
received, Jean might be able to prove fraud, but it
would involve a long, costly, acrimonious court battle—the last thing a wimp like Jean would want to en-

gage in, especially if it meant admitting she was Valerie Vanderbilt.

Jacqueline didn't doubt that Hattie owned the name Valerie Vanderbilt, and God only knew what else. She would have given a good deal to read the contract Jean had signed; there might be a clause, in very small print, committing Jean to a year in a brothel of Hattie's choice if she reneged on her agreement to write sixteen more books on Hattie's terms. Jean had obviously never even read the damned thing. This did not surprise Jacqueline; intellectuals were no smarter about business than the average high school graduate, and their touching assumption that they were smarter made them even more vulnerable.

Jean hadn't found her situation too unpleasant until Hattie had decided it was necessary for her to attend the Historical Romance Conference. Jean had been aghast when Hattie first made the suggestion. When she refused, Hattie turned her reason for refusing into a weapon against her. She'd lose her job if the truth were known? Nonsense. Her colleagues would think more highly of her if they knew of her success as a writer. She was too modest, that was her trouble. What a pity she didn't have a friend who would tell the world how wonderful she was!

"That sounds like Hattie, all right," Jacqueline said. "You really are hopeless, Jean. Why didn't you tell her to take her contract and stick it in her ear?"

"Jean doesn't resort to vulgarity," said James, who was tired of being excluded from the conversation. He patted Jean's hand. A gentle ripple of rapture ran across her plain face.

"Anyway, it's all right now," she murmured. "Thanks to James—and," she added hastily, glancing at Jacqueline's darkening brow, "and you, Jake. I let myself get all worked up about nothing. It's always been one of my weaknesses. Once I faced the problem, it solved itself, and Hattie couldn't have been nicer."

Jacqueline grunted. She felt sure she knew the reason for the change in Hattie; it had nothing to do with nice. When Jean had first joined the stable, Hattie had just begun her nefarious career; it had taken her several years to develop her ingenious approach to the promotion of romance writers. The new and lucrative angle was glamour, and of that commodity Jean had none. She was a liability instead of an asset; the new VV would undoubtedly be a breathtakingly gorgeous actress or model, who could posture and perform in public.

"I really must run now," Jean said. "I've taken too much of your time."

"Wait a minute. What about the other writers, particularly Valentine and Von Damm. Does Hattie have similar contracts with them?"

"Honestly, Jake, I don't know anything about their arrangements with Hattie—aside from what everyone knows, like Joe pretending to be Victor. He says he wants to break off with Hattie; he's very bitter about her. But he never went into detail."

"And Valentine?"

Jean's face twisted unpleasantly. "Nobody talks to Valentine, Jake. Hattie watches her every second."

"You must have spoken with her at least once," Jacqueline said pointedly.

Jean blushed. "Oh—the detective thing . . . I'm sorry about that. I was so upset I didn't know what I was saying. It happened a couple of days ago. Hattie was talking to some publisher, and Valentine got away from her. She saw I was—well, upset—and asked me what was wrong. Not that she cared," Jean added vindictively. "She was just bored and inquisitive. I don't remember exactly what I said, I was too distraught; but I may have used the word 'blackmail,' and explained that I intended to consult you, and . . . That was the only time I've ever talked to her. Honestly."

The headwaiter informed James that their table was ready. Jean left, visibly relieved to escape Jacqueline's inquisitorial questions.

Scarcely had James and Jacqueline seated themselves, however, when they were approached by a waiter. "Excuse me, but I believe you were sitting with the lady in the gray suit—at the second table from the door? I'm afraid there has been an accident."

James struggled to rise from the banquette, endangering the glassware on the table. The waiter said quickly, "She doesn't appear to be injured, sir, only shaken up. I thought you might wish—"

"Yes, yes, of course." James extricated himself. "Where is she?"

Jacqueline followed at a more leisurely pace. "Save our table," she instructed the headwaiter. "We'll be right back."

Jean was sprawled in a chair. She did not lack for attention; the doorman was patting her, a waiter offered her a glass of water, and James stood by wringing his hands. Jacqueline arrived in time to hear him demand a doctor, the manager, the police, and a drink, in that order.

"I don't want a drink," Jean stammered, fumbling with her disheveled hair.

"I do," James said. "Are you all right? What happened? Why doesn't someone fetch a doctor?"

Jacqueline saw at a glance that the waiter's diagnosis appeared to be correct. Jean was rumpled and scratched, and her skirt bore traces of contact with the filthy sidewalk, but there was nothing else wrong with her. Jacqueline sent James back to hold their table—never losing sight of the essentials—and removed her friend to the ladies' lounge.

"My stockings are ruined," Jean wailed.

"And your purse is gone," Jacqueline said.

"Oh my God." Jean stared wildly around the room. "It is. It is! It had all my credit cards and my makeup . . ."

"Any family jewels? Wads of cash?"

"I never carry much cash in New York. I—"

"Then it's more of a nuisance than a disaster. Did you see the person who took it?"

"See her? Of course I saw her. She's hard to miss. It was that awful girl, Laurie."

Chapter 7

Jacqueline returned to the Oak Room and picked up the menu. "I'm starved. Let's order as soon as he brings our drinks. I wonder if they have snails?"

"How can you talk about food at a time like this?" James demanded. "Where's Jean? Where are the police? What have you done about—"

"I put Jean in a cab. She's gone back to her hotel; she'd rather be robbed of every penny she possesses than appear in public with torn hose. She'll call the police and report the incident. . . . Oh, good, *escargots à l'arlésienne*."

"You had snails last night."

"I plan to have them again tonight. I can't get snails in Coldwater."

"And a damned good thing, if you ask me." James raised a hand to his brow. "Why am I talking about snails? What happened to Jean? Why don't you tell me what the hell is going on?"

"I will, I will. Just a minute." Having given her order and nagged James into doing the same, Jacqueline settled back against the padded leather banquette and gave James a brief, well-organized account of recent events. It was an ill wind that blew no one good, she thought piously; Jean's misadventure allowed her to gloss over her own, and cut short James's sarcastic comments about her loss of the notebook.

"That is so typical of you," he remarked. "If you had given O'Brien the notebook last night, or let me take charge of it—"

"You're missing the point, James. As of ten-thirty this morning, the thief had Dubretta's notebook. Why attack Jean?"

This proved an effective distraction. James ate pâté and pondered. "Two possibilities," he said finally. "Either two, or more, people are after the notebook, or no one is after the notebook."

"It was the only thing stolen from my purse," Jacqueline argued. "It and the copies I had made of it. I had two stenographer's notebooks of my own, and they weren't taken."

"The thief thought the notebook might contain what he wanted. He found it did not contain what he wanted. He's still looking for what—"

"She, not he. Jean was certain the person who knocked her down and grabbed her purse was Laurie."

"How about you? You didn't see your assailant?"

"No. And I think I would have spotted Laurie if she had been following me this morning. As Jean said, she's hard to miss."

"So you incline toward my first theory."

Jacqueline prodded the last snail out of its shell. "I incline toward it, but I'm not certain. What if the notebook is a red herring? Granted, there are a number of people who might want to suppress Dubretta's notes, but suppose there's some other object someone wants even more?"

"Such as?"

"The possibilities are endless. Maybe she had microfilm concealed in her tube of toothpaste. Maybe—"

"Toothpaste? Why would Dubretta have a tube of toothpaste in her purse?"

"I don't know. But she did. She may have been fanatical about brushing after meals. James, you're getting off the subject."

"I don't even know what the subject is," James said.

"Murder," Jacqueline said, as the waiter removed her plate. He didn't give her a second look. The Algonquin is a favorite haunt of mystery writers.

"Murder in the plural," Jacqueline went on. She put her notebook on the table and took out a pen.

"But there's only been one murder. If it was murder."

"What I mean is that Dubretta may not have been the intended victim. Valentine thought the poison—"

"What poison?"

"James, you seem determined to be disagreeable today. 'What poison' is your department. Did you see your chemist friend?"

"Yes, I did. And a damned humiliating interview it was," James added resentfully. "First I had to listen to a lot of stupid jokes about my love life."

"What does your love life have to do with . . . Oh, I see."

"I put up with it." James looked martyred. "I thought it was better to have him assume one of my ladies was trying to do me in rather than explain the true facts."

"That was very wise, James."

"Yes, it was. He also pointed out, at some length and with considerable sarcasm, that there are several hundred poisonous substances known to man—and woman—and that without some idea of what to look for—"

"James, please don't go on and on about things I already know. Be brief. Is he going to do the job?"

"Yes."

"And don't sulk. When?"

"It will take a little time," James recited.

"Well, keep after him. Where was I? Oh, yes. Valentine seems to have changed her mind about being murdered, but the point is worth considering. If there was an error, several people are potential victims. Hattie is a logical murderee if ever I met one, and there have been moments when I myself have contemplated removing Laurie to a higher sphere."

"Really, Jacqueline!"

"So what we'll do is this." Jacqueline shifted the notepad to one side so that the waiter could put her *rognons de veau* in front of her. She continued to write while using her fork with her left hand. "We'll write down the suspects and consider their motives for all the potential victims."

"That is the most illogical—"

"Hattie. Dubretta was threatening her. We agree Hattie had a motive for killing Dubretta? Good. She might also have wanted to get rid of Laurie. She may

use the girl for various illicit purposes—stealing people's purses, for instance, or poisoning drinks. Laurie
has been increasingly unstable and may constitute a
danger if she tells what she knows. Now Valentine. Actually, I can't see why Hattie would want her dead.
She's Hattie's biggest moneymaker. But one never
knows. Valentine is afraid of something. Maybe she
knows about Hattie's scam and was threatening to go
to the police."

"What scam?"

"Never mind that now. Dubretta. She hated Hattie's
guts. But I agree with O'Brien—for once—that
Dubretta wouldn't make a stupid mistake like drinking
the poison she had prepared for Hattie. Besides, she
had her weapon of revenge in her hand. Exposure,
ridicule, criminal prosecution perhaps—far more satis-
fying than a quick death."

Seeing that James's mouth was full, she paused to
swallow, and resumed before he could speak. "The
same basic objection applies to the possibility of
Dubretta trying to murder anyone else. She wouldn't
drink her own lethal brew.

"Valentine. She was one of Dubretta's targets.
She—"

"That's outrageous," James exclaimed. "That girl is
as innocent as a lamb."

"I'm sure Laurie would be delighted to enroll you in
Valentine's fan club," Jacqueline said. "As I was saying
—Valentine had an excellent opportunity to poison the
wine."

"How? I can't see how anyone could have poisoned
the wine."

"Never mind that now. Valentine is repelled by Laurie. Laurie is the type that's faithful unto death; the only way Val could get the girl off her back was to kill her. Laurie was only drinking ginger ale that night, but she'd toss down a glass of green slime if Valentine told her to. And by claiming she was the one in danger, Valentine disarms suspicion."

James shook his head in dumb disbelief. Jacqueline turned a page.

"Max. Same motive as Valentine's for poisoning Dubretta. If Dubretta threatened his client, who is probably his chief source of income . . . Neither he nor Valentine had reason to kill Hattie—unless they figure they can do without her now that Val is established. I wonder how much commission Hattie collects from Valentine? Twenty-five percent can amount to a lot.

"Joe, AKA Victor von Damm. Dubretta knew his real identity, and it didn't worry him. But I suspect Hattie has some other hold over him. Maybe Indiana wants him. Maybe he's an escaped ax murderer. He'd kill to keep Dubretta from sending him back to the Big House. Or he'd kill Hattie to get out from under her thumb. He's been increasingly restive, and she's been pushing even harder lately. No particular motive for killing Laurie, outside of her general loathsomeness. Poor kid . . ."

"Poor kid?" James roused himself from the stupor of disbelief into which Jacqueline's wild theories had sent him. "She's the hottest suspect of all. She had her pudgy paws all over those wineglasses, and she hated Dubretta."

"Oh, she's on the list," Jacqueline agreed. "But only

if Dubretta was the intended victim. I don't believe Laurie would want to kill Hattie or Valentine. Now Sue . . . Were you about to speak, James?"

"What's the use?" James said mournfully.

"She's an unlikely suspect, but I don't know her well; she may have a few buttons undone in her brain. She's jealous of Valentine for professional and personal reasons. Then there's Jean. Even a soggy rabbit will bite if it's cornered. Dubretta knew of Jean's true identity. Hattie was blackmailing her. Valentine is Hattie's top author, overshadowing Jean—"

"But those are contradictory motives," James groaned. "Either Jean wants out of the romance business or she wants to be number one—you can't have it both ways."

"It all depends on the identity of the victim," Jacqueline said, in the tone of a parent admonishing a dull child. "Jean could be putting on an act, pretending she wants out, when she really wants to be the Queen of Love. Mere theorizing, of course . . ."

Her thoughtful gaze rested on James. He squirmed. "If you put me on that list," he began.

"A sudden passion for Valentine. A noble desire to defend her against all traducers." Jacqueline's face was rapt. "I love it, James."

"We are not amused," James said.

"There's one person we've forgotten."

"The mayor of New York? Frank Sinatra? Bella Abzug?"

"The Earl of Devonbrook."

"You're out of your mind, my girl. The man is an android. Hattie probably winds him up every morning."

"He's a dark horse," Jacqueline murmured.

"Very dark."

"I must talk to him. Tell you what we'll do, James. We'll divide up the suspects. You take the women, I'll take the men."

James's face brightened, then as quickly fell. "Not if I have to include Laurie."

"If you want Valentine, you'll have to take Laurie."

"I don't think she likes me," James said.

"Coward."

"Right. I'm not going to play any more."

"I'm not playing, James."

Her eyes were downcast and her lashes shadowed her elegantly modeled cheekbones. The hollows under those structures seemed more pronounced than usual, and her mouth had taken on a soft, pensive curve. She didn't often look like that, for her green eyes held a hint of mockery even in her tenderest moments. James found himself short of breath. But he was a man of iron control—he told himself—and this did not seem an appropriate time to express the proposition that had entered his mind.

Instead he said, "You really believe it was murder."

"Don't you?"

"It's awfully tenuous, Jacqueline—surmises and hypotheses and ifs and maybes. . . . As an intellectual game it is entertaining, if somewhat tasteless, but . . ." He shrugged.

"It was murder, James."

"How was it done?"

"I have a couple of ideas, but they're so far-out, I'll have to do some research before I can be sure." She looked up at him, and her green eyes gleamed with the familiar amusement. "The real reason Holmes never told Watson what he was thinking is because he didn't have the solution figured out yet."

Before James departed he had grudgingly agreed to meet Jacqueline later at the romance conference. "The Love Lottery is at four," she explained. "The winner gets a date with Victor von Damm. You wouldn't want to miss that, would you?"

James's response was repetitively profane. However, when Jacqueline reminded him that most of Victor's fans were old enough to be his mother, and so infatuated that the few brains they possessed turned to mush in the presence of their idol, he agreed that it might be amusing to watch Victor cope with an elderly, inarticulate admirer. They parted on reasonably amicable terms, and Jacqueline hastened back to Fifty-third Street. The Romance Editors' Forum was due to begin at two-thirty, and she wanted to look them over before selecting a publisher for her book.

All the major publishers were represented. A dozen or more chairs had been arranged behind a long table. Hattie was on the platform, heckling the attendants who were setting out glasses and carafes of water, notepads, pencils, and microphones. She pretended not to notice Jacqueline until the latter tapped her on the shoulder.

"Oh, hello, Mrs. Kirsky. Are you attending the forum? You'd better find a seat, dear, this will be one of our most popular events."

"I thought you'd like my report on Dubretta's murder," Jacqueline said.

"Ssssh." Hattie drew her to one side. "I don't want talk like that disrupting the meeting. This is a professional association, you know. We can't allow a tragedy, however sad, to interfere with our work."

"Oh dear." Jacqueline's mouth drooped. "You mean I can't be the famous detective any more?"

Hattie looked at her suspiciously, and then decided she was making a joke. She tittered in a genteel fashion. "Now you know I pushed you into that. It wasn't nice of me, was it? But it wasn't all my fault. Valentine really was in a state. Pore chile, she's such a sensitive, high-strung creature—the artistic temperament, you know. She's all over that now."

"Everything is fine? No more worries?"

"Not a one." Hattie tugged her drooping corsage of white orchids back into place.

"You must have neglected to mention your new peace of mind to Laurie."

"What on earth do you mean, honey?"

"A little while ago she knocked Jean down and stole her purse."

"What?" Hattie's surprise was genuine. The hairs on her upper lip quivered. "That stupid little . . . Are you sure?"

"Jean recognized her. What was she after, Hattie?"

"How the hell should I know what's in that chile's vacant mind?" Hattie shook her head. "I can't imagine what's wrong with her."

"How about drugs?"

"They all take 'em," Hattie said, with chilling indifference. "Well, it's only a couple more days. The conference ends tomorrow night, and that will be the end of Laurie. You'll excuse me, Mrs. Kirk, I must open the forum."

Jacqueline found a chair. Keeping up with Hattie's changes of mood was a full-time activity, but just now it was Valentine, not Hattie, she wondered about. Hattie was a pragmatic soul; the publicity stunt had backfired, so it had been abandoned. But why had Valentine changed her mind? Or had she?

Jacqueline dismissed the problem and concentrated on the discussion. This particular forum had been designed for authors and would-be authors rather than readers. There were over a hundred people present. Apparently everybody thought she could write a romantic novel. (Or perhaps everybody already had.) The editors were refreshingly candid about their requirements, and so specific Jacqueline wondered why they didn't feed the plot into a computer and program it to change the names next time around.

Heroines had to be beautiful, voluptuous, and "feisty." Sweet Sixteen wanted them unawakened but capable of sensual passion. Last Love wanted them capable of sensual passion, period. Heroes could have dark, auburn, or fair hair, so long as they had hair. Gray hair was okay for Last Love, but the editor warned it was risky; a streak of white at each temple went over better. Some lines accepted chubby heroines, so long as the baby fat was voluptuous fat, and providing the heroine sweated off the excess before the end of the book.

Jacqueline took copious notes. She was particularly struck by the fluffy-haired young editor who warned, "Your heroine must not be promiscuous. She can tumble into bed with someone every forty pages or so, but she has to be in love with him. Or raped, of course."

Jacqueline raised her hand. "What about *Forever Amber*?" she asked seriously.

Half the audience laughed, the other half looked blank. The editor looked blank. "There are always exceptions to every rule, but only if you really know what you're doing," she said. Jacqueline did not write down this piece of advice.

By the time the forum ended, her brain was teeming with ideas and with an uneasy feeling that Betsy and the Woofasses might be right after all. Several editors had warned that their heroines must be "liberated," independent women, proud of their own sensuality. So far, so good; Jacqueline had no quarrel with that. But the same editors had warned against promiscuity. Was it more liberated to be overpowered against one's will than to seek amorous adventures (the phrase had been used by one of the more old-fashioned editors) for the sheer fun of it? The word "love" kept cropping up. The heroines were all monogamous, in intent if not in actuality, and the happy ending consisted of capturing the hero and making him monogamous too. The books *were* anti-feminist, and anti-female, not only because of their prurient interest in rape but because they voiced the tired old moral view (invented and enthusiastically supported by most men) that a woman's only legitimate goal in life was to devote all her time, energy, and sexual abilities to one man. So far as Jacqueline could see, the only difference between the new romances and the old love stories was that "love" had replaced marriage as a prerequisite for sex.

In a mildly disgruntled mood she made her way toward the Washington Room, where Victor von Damm was to be handed over to the winner of the Love Lottery. But this was a spectacle she was destined never to enjoy.

James was waiting for her. His famous crooked smile was no longer crooked, it was lopsided. His lower lip was swollen to twice its normal size. A reddening bruise on his temple matched a scraped patch on his jaw. As Jacqueline approached, slowly and delicately, he held out his arms. Both wrists were ringed in red.

"Oh, James," Jacqueline breathed.

"Is that all you can say?"

"When did it happen?"

"Just now."

"Don't tell me it was—"

"It was."

"James, darling, you're hyperventilating." Jacqueline took a paper bag from her purse, shook out the contents, and offered it to her afflicted friend. "Breathe into this."

James snatched the paper bag and crushed it in his fists.

"This is serious, James," Jacqueline exclaimed. "Tell me—"

"You're damned right it's serious! That girl ought to be locked up. She was waiting for me when I came out of my room, on my way over here. She shoved me back into the room and—and—"

"Hit you on the head?"

"No, that happened when I fell," James admitted,

more calmly. "She caught me off balance, damn it. The fall stunned me for a minute. Then she—she—she sat on me. If you laugh, I'll kill you."

"I'm not laughing." And indeed, after a momentary spasm, Jacqueline's face remained grave. "She actually tied you up?"

James nodded. "With my own necktie. Half choked me getting it off. While I was lying there trying to catch my breath, she tore the room apart. Threw everything onto the floor, pulled out all the drawers—"

"Did she look under the mattress?"

"What difference does it make? The damned notebook wasn't there anyway."

"I just wondered. Go on, James."

"No, she did not look under the mattress. It wasn't what you would call a carefully organized search." James sounded more relaxed now that he had confessed the worst. "It only took her a couple of minutes. She looked in my jacket pockets too. Then she bolted out, leaving the door open."

"Someone saw you and came to the rescue?"

"No, I got loose without any help. I tell you, Jacqueline, the girl has flipped her lid. I'm going to call the police."

"Yes, you had better do that." Jacqueline's expression changed from serious to grim. "Try to get O'Brien if you can. I'll meet you here—in the bar—in an hour or so."

"I'll be plastered in an hour or so. Where are you going?"

"I'll be back as soon as I can."

Jacqueline found Hattie behind the makeshift stage

applying more glue to the false hair on Victor's chest. "You again?" the agent demanded. "Are you trying to drive me crazy?"

"I'm looking for Laurie."

"I don't know where she is, and I don't care. Stand still, Victor."

"It itches," Victor complained. "Hey, Mrs. Kirby. When you see Sue, will you tell her—"

"Shut up, Joe. Hattie, this is serious. Laurie just attacked a friend of mine and ransacked his room. I've got to find her."

"Wow." Victor whistled softly. "I told you that kid was flaky, Hattie."

"I'm not responsible for what she does," Hattie said. "Don't try to involve me, Mrs. Kirsky. She's crazy as a loon. You can't believe anything she says."

"I don't give a good goddamn about you," Jacqueline snapped. "I want that girl. I've got to find her before she hurts someone or herself. Where does she hang out? What's her address? Phone number? Who are her friends?"

"I don't know her address. Her last name is Schellhammer, and she lives on Park or Fifth, in the upper eighties. Joe—I mean, Victor—will you stop squirming?"

"Her friends," Jacqueline insisted. "She's president of Valentine's fan club, isn't she? Where are the rest of them?"

"Probably hanging around outside," Hattie said disinterestedly. "They usually are."

Realizing she had obtained all she could from Hattie, Jacqueline left. A group of fans were waiting outside the door. Among them were several of the girls

who had been clustered around the Valentine Lovers
booth on the opening day. Jacqueline pounced on the
nearest, a vacant-faced child with protuberant blue
eyes. "I'm looking for Laurie."

The girl's eyes bulged till they looked as if they
were about to pop out of her head. "I don't know . . ."

"You're choking her," said another girl, bespecta-
cled and plain.

"Sorry." Jacqueline released her grip. The pop-eyed
child scuttled behind a friend. "Does your club have a
vice-president?"

"That's me," said the plain one. She stood her
ground as Jacqueline turned to her. "Are you a friend
of Laurie's?"

"I guess you could say that," was the cautious reply.
"What's she done now?"

Jacqueline nodded, satisfied. "You're the one I want
to talk to." She drew the girl aside. "What's your
name?"

"Meredith. Meredith Katz. Who are you?"

"My name is Jacqueline Kirby."

Meredith's lips parted in a sardonic smile. Light
flashed blindingly from her braces. "The famous
sleuth?"

Jacqueline grinned back at her. "What are you doing
in this bunch of—er—fans?"

Meredith gave further proof of the intelligence
Jacqueline had acknowledged by recognizing this as a
compliment. "They're okay. I happen to admire Valentine's writing."

"So do I. Listen, Meredith . . . I don't suppose anyone calls you Merry."

"You're damned right they don't."

"Laurie is in deep trouble, Meredith. I want to help her."

"What kind of trouble?"

"Assault."

"Wow." Meredith pondered for a moment, but Jacqueline noticed she did not appear to be surprised. Finally the girl said slowly, "I guess you could call Laurie a friend of mine, mainly on account of she hasn't got any other friends, just the fan club. She's always been pretty weird, but lately she's gotten a lot worse. I mean, really weird. I wouldn't mind giving her a hand, but . . . How do I know you want to help her?"

"You'll have to take my word for it," Jacqueline said flatly. "It's a gamble. Like everything else in life."

"Let me think about it."

Meredith duly thought about it. While she was thinking, Jacqueline glanced at the door of the Washington Room, where an usher was taking tickets. The group of teenage fans stood to one side.

"Why don't they go in?" Jacqueline asked. "Are they waiting for you?"

"Are you kidding?" Meredith laughed scornfully. "Tickets for this conference cost three hundred bucks. Most of us don't have that kind of bread. We pooled our dues so Laurie could get in."

"Laurie had to buy a ticket?" Jacqueline repeated.

"There's a free reception for fans tomorrow afternoon," Meredith said in an expressionless voice. "Tea and cookies and a talk from Aunt Hattie."

"Don't tell me, let me guess," Jacqueline said. "Part of your dues goes to Hattie."

"Half. They go to the national organization, to be precise. You can also guess who's executive secretary."

"I might have known," Jacqueline muttered. "That old bat doesn't miss a trick."

Meredith said abruptly, "If I see Laurie I'll tell her you want to talk to her. She stays at my house sometimes. I don't know where she is right now. Usually she's hanging around waiting for Valentine to make an appearance, if she isn't running errands for Aunt Hattie."

The word "aunt" was obviously meant to be ironic, and Jacqueline acknowledged it with a wry smile. "Errands," she repeated. "What kind of errands, Meredith?"

"Oh, you know—going for coffee, taking Hattie's clothes to the cleaners. I wouldn't be surprised if she polishes her shoes and washes her undies."

"Neither would I." Intriguing as the conversation was, Jacqueline knew time was running out. "Could Laurie be at home, do you think?"

Meredith's thin lips curled. "There's nobody home but the maid. Her folks are in Europe. They usually are in Europe. She could be there, but I doubt it."

"I get the picture." Jacqueline tore a page from her notebook and wrote quickly. "Here's my room number and the telephone number of the hotel. Meredith, this is serious. Try to convince her I'm on her side."

"Okay." Meredith took the slip of paper. Jacqueline delved in her purse again. "I won't be using my ticket for this affair. Do you want it?"

"You mean it?"

Jacqueline gave her the ticket. Meredith gloated over it for a moment and then said nobly, "We'll draw straws. Thanks."

"Have fun," Jacqueline said.

Laurie was not in any of the public rooms of the hotel. Jacqueline used a house phone to call Hattie's suite. Max answered. When Jacqueline explained why she was calling, his voice mirrored her concern.

"I was afraid something like this would happen. I tried to persuade Hattie only yesterday that she ought to warn the girl's parents she was unwell, but . . ."

"You know Hattie," Jacqueline finished the sentence for him. "I understand her parents are out of town anyway, so it wouldn't have done any good. You haven't seen her today?"

"No. Wait, I'll ask Valentine."

Jacqueline heard Valentine's emphatic negative, but Max duly repeated it. "Not since last night, she says. What can I do?"

"Nothing, at the moment. Just hang on to her if she comes to you, and call me immediately."

After she had hung up, Jacqueline moved to a public telephone and looked in the book. There was only one Schellhammer on Fifth Avenue in the upper eighties. Jacqueline dialed the number.

The phone rang for several minutes before she gave up. She stood for a moment in a rare state of indecision before making up her mind. It was essential that she cover all the places to which Laurie might go, especially since there were so few known to her. Much as she hated to take the time, she would have to go to the girl's home.

She accomplished the remarkable feat of finding a taxi by going to the head of the line waiting outside the hotel and announcing, "Official business," as she flashed her Rome police card at the couple who had been about to get into the cab. Whenever the taxi stopped for a traffic light she wrote in her notebook. She didn't expect to find Laurie at home, but at least she could leave a message. And that message had to be as persuasive and reassuring as she could make it.

The building facing Central Park confirmed Hattie's claim that Laurie's parents were wealthy. Some of the apartments in the beautiful old structure had been handed down in the same family for generations. Rented or owned, they cost astronomical sums per month. The security arrangements were correspondingly stringent, but Jacqueline's respectable appearance and glib lies got her past the guard and into the elevator before he remembered to ask the name of the school at which she claimed to be a teacher.

The maid was at home. She simply hadn't bothered to answer the telephone. Despite the guard in the lobby, the apartment had the usual multiple locks and bars. Again Jacqueline's announcement that she was one of Laurie's teachers won her admission.

The maid was a woman in her forties. Her coarse black hair was wound around her head in a heavy braid and she wore a neat print housedress, but she had taken advantage of her employers' absence to replace her shoes with loose slippers. "Laurie ees not 'ere," she announced. "Meester an' Mees' Schellhammer ees not 'ere. They come back soon."

This was obviously a memorized speech, including the precautionary refusal to admit the owners were out of town. As soon as Jacqueline began questioning the

woman, her supply of English dried up. She shook her
head and repeated her prepared statement.

Jacqueline switched to fluent if ungrammatical
Spanish. "Where is the Laurie? I have the need to
speak at her. It is of an important much urgent."

"You are a teacher of Spanish, señora?" the maid
asked doubtfully.

"I am the teacher of the English," Jacqueline replied.
"The young woman is not in the school for today and
the week. At what hour is it the possibility that she returning to the house is?"

The maid replied with an expressive gesture, eyes
rolling, shoulders raised. "Who can say? It is very
strange, here in America. There is no respect for the father and the mother, no discipline for the child. It is
very different in my country."

On the grand piano in the living room Jacqueline
saw a large studio portrait of a man and woman in formal evening dress. Their faces might have been
stamped out of the same mold, not because they really
resembled one another, but because they had been
groomed and exercised and dressed by the same fash-
ionable firms.

She gave the maid the note, impressing on her the
urgency of giving it to Laurie immediately if the fugi-
tive turned up.

The visit had been useful, if only to give her a
clearer insight into Laurie's problems. It appeared to
be a classic case of an Ugly Duckling despised and ignored by her beautiful parents. The more they nagged
her about her weight and her looks, the more Laurie
would eat.

Knowing the futility of looking for a cab at rush hour, Jacqueline started walking. It was after six when she entered the cocktail lounge where James was waiting for her.

"I can't stay," she announced. "Did you reach O'Brien?"

"He wasn't there."

"Damn it, James—"

"What message was I supposed to leave? You didn't tell me where you were going or when you'd be back."

"You didn't report the attack, did you?"

James's eyes fell. "I don't want to get the kid in trouble."

"Like hell. You were embarrassed. You didn't want to admit you were mugged by a seventeen-year-old girl. Of all the curses with which I have been afflicted in the course of a long hard life, male ego is the worst. Get up from there."

She hauled him out of his chair and led him out of the hotel, lecturing all the way. "Get over to the precinct house right away. It's on West Forty-first, just off Broadway. You'd better walk, it will be faster. If O'Brien isn't there, leave a message asking him to call me. But whether he is there or not, report the assault and swear out a complaint."

"I thought you felt sorry for the kid. This will mean a criminal record for her. Isn't there a less drastic method of locating her?"

"Not in a hurry, no. Even if I reported her as missing, which I haven't the authority to do, it would be several days before the police would take action—and they don't take much action in cases of missing juveniles. They'll be forced to act on a complaint of assault and battery."

"Why is it so important to—"

"James, will you go? If you don't understand the urgency of the matter I'll explain it to you later."

"Where and when?"

Jacqueline rolled her eyes heavenward. "Come to my room after you've been to the police, then."

"That's better," James said. "What are we going to do in your room?"

"I will be waiting. I don't care what you do, so long as you don't expect me to do it with you."

A cunning expression spread over James's countenance. "I'll go if you promise to buy me dinner afterwards. It's your turn."

"I'm not planning to go out for dinner."

"That's okay with me," James said.

"All right, I'll buy you dinner. Get going."

"See you later." With a jaunty flip of the hand, he started off. Jacqueline watched him for a moment, with a faint ambiguous smile on her lips. Then she plunged into the traffic and made her way across the street.

She was relieved to see Sue unbruised, unmarked, and unmolested. The girl was getting dressed to go out; slim and dainty in a white petticoat and lacy bra, she turned from the mirror to greet Jacqueline.

"Are you feeling better?"

"Better than what?" Jacqueline realized she was referring to her pre-coffee morning grumpiness. "No," she said, after thinking it over.

"What's the matter?"

Jacqueline almost hated to tell her. She made a charming picture of Young Love—radiant face, shining eyes, that indefinable glow that comes from the heart to illumine the body. . . . Jacqueline pulled out her notebook and wrote the sentence down.

Sue put on her dress and pirouetted. "How do you like it?"

"You just bought it, didn't you?"

"How did you know?"

Jacqueline took a pair of shears from her purse and cut off the tags dangling from the wisp of eyelet framing the neckline of the dress. It was a copy of one of the "antique dresses" in vogue that year. The skimpy, low-cut bodice was modeled after a Victorian chemise. The skirt had three layers of ruffles, tucks, and lace inserts with narrow blue ribbons running hither and yon. "Is this what you had in mind?" Sue asked with a smile.

"It's perfect—for you." Jacqueline sighed. "I always wanted to be cute," she said wistfully.

"But I'm sure you were—I mean, you still are—"

"I was never cute. Gorgeous, yes. Cute, no. Ah, well." Jacqueline sighed a second time and then became practical. "Whom are you going out with?"

"Joe, of course." Sue turned for an anxious inspection of an already flawless face.

"I thought he had a date this evening."

"Oh, he's just buying the winner of the Love Lottery a drink," Sue said callously. "He'll dump her as soon as he can."

"Hmph. Do me a favor before you go?"

"Of course."

Jacqueline handed her the plastic bucket from the bureau. "Get me some ice. I'm expecting a call, and I don't want to leave the room."

Sue lingered, bucket in hand, watching Jacqueline as the latter took a bottle of Scotch from her suitcase and attacked the seal. "Are you going to drink all that?" Sue asked, laughing.

"No such luck."

When Sue returned, Jacqueline had assumed the peacock-blue robe. Her skirt and blouse were on a hanger, ready to be put on at a moment's notice. Her shoes were on the floor under her clothes. The top of the bureau was littered with packets of food—chips, peanuts, crackers, cheese straws. Jacqueline extracted a jar of mixed munchies and another bag of nuts from her purse and added them to the collection.

"Thanks," she said, taking the ice bucket.

"You're having a party," Sue deduced, seeing that the glasses from the bathroom had been added to the display.

"In a way. Before you go, I must warn you about something. Have you seen Laurie today?"

"Laurie? Oh—that girl."

"That girl. Have you seen her?"

"No. Should I have?"

"It's probably lucky for you you haven't." Jacqueline told Sue what had happened, and was pleased to see that Sue's reaction was proof of kindliness of heart, if not of quick perception. "Poor girl. I hope you find her."

"You may find her before I do," Jacqueline said grimly. "Both the people she has—er—contacted are friends of mine. I'm not sure there is any pattern in her behavior, so I can't be certain what she'll do next, but you might be a target. Be careful."

"Oh my goodness." Sue's eyes widened. "Do you really think—"

"I don't know. Where are you meeting Joe?"

"Downstairs in the lobby."

"Good. Don't leave the hotel. I don't believe she'd venture inside, but on the street you're fair game. Warn Joe. Tell him—and this is very important, Sue—tell him that if he spots Laurie he is to hold on to her. Sock her in the jaw, do whatever he has to do, but don't let her get away. Is that clear?"

After Sue had gone, Jacqueline settled down with the Scotch on one side and the telephone on the other. She suspected her vigil would probably prove fruitless, but she was afraid to take any chances. Her sense of uneasiness increased with each passing minute. There was some logical cause for concern, considering Laurie's behavior, but the real cause was harder to define. Danger, danger . . . The word kept echoing in Jacqueline's brain.

By the time James arrived she had eaten half the nuts and a packet of potato chips. She admitted him and returned to her chair.

"Well?" she said.

James took off his jacket and loosened his tie before turning to the impromptu bar. "Cutty Sark? I thought you were economizing."

"There are basic standards below which I refuse to sink. Help yourself," she added sarcastically, as James filled his glass.

He pulled up a chair next to hers and sank into it. "This is nice. Much better than going out to dinner."

"Did you see O'Brien?" Jacqueline removed his hand from her shoulder and returned it to him.

"He wasn't there."

"James—"

"I left a message," James said quickly. "And I filled out a complaint. They said they'd get right on it."

"Hah."

"What more could I do?"

"You could keep your hands to yourself. I am in no mood for dalliance, James. You still don't get the picture."

"No, I don't. What are you so uptight about? I'm the one who should be shaken to the core." James touched the lump on his intellectual brow. "I need sympathy and TLC," he said sulkily.

"That bump on the head must have scrambled your brains," Jacqueline said. "But then you haven't seen as much of Laurie as I have. Over the past few days she has exhibited violent changes of mood, from aggressive to amiable to lachrymose. She's taking a drug of some kind—"

"Maybe she's just psychotic," James said, putting his feet up on the foot of the bed.

"Just? The point is that she's getting worse. The violence is becoming more violent. She's after something and she'll go to any length to get it. If you had been a fragile old man with a bad heart; if your head had hit the corner of the dresser instead of the floor . . ."

"I see what you mean." James looked pained. "What's she after, do you suppose?"

"Maybe nothing. A figment of her own disturbed imagination. What really worries me is the possibility that someone put the idea into her head."

"Hattie?"

"She's the most likely person, certainly. But anyone could manipulate Laurie by telling her Valentine was in danger. Suppose, for instance, that the unknown killer got Laurie on the trail of Dubretta's notebook. Mr. or Mrs. X has it now, but he's been unable to reach Laurie to tell her to quit looking. Or else she is so far gone she can't be stopped. Not only is she a danger to others, she may be in danger herself, from the person who is using her. If we can find her, she may tell us who put her on the trail of the notebook."

"You haven't the slightest evidence to support that theory," James said.

"No."

"But your other point is well taken," James admitted magnanimously. "Have you warned the other people she's likely to attack?"

"I hope so. Since I've no idea what criterion she is using to select her victims, I can't be sure I've covered everyone; but I did warn Sue, who will warn Victor. Hattie and Max know what has happened. I also called Betsy. She wasn't at home, but I left a message telling her it was vitally important that she get in touch with me."

"Betsy?"

"I forgot, you haven't met her." Jacqueline explained Betsy. "Her involvement is only peripheral, but to a mind obsessed she might seem the logical person to have Dubretta's notebook. She knew Dubretta, she doesn't like Valentine, and she's a friend of mine."

"You've done all you can, then," James said reassuringly. "Relax, why don't you?"

A scuffle ensued. It was interrupted by a knock on the door, which distracted James and allowed Jacqueline to extract herself without the necessity of the physical violence she had been contemplating. Smoothing her hair, she went to the door and admitted O'Brien.

"Why, Lieutenant, how very dedicated of you to come by. Won't you join us?"

"Thank you." O'Brien nodded politely to James, who had regained his chair and was trying to look as if he had never left it. "I hear you were looking for me, Professor."

"I wasn't looking for you," James said. "I went to the station to file a report."

"I know. Sorry to hear about that. Sure you're okay?"

There was not the slightest trace of amusement in his voice or in his face, but James flushed angrily. "Certainly I'm sure. She caught me off balance."

"Crazy people can have astonishing strength," O'Brien said gravely. James did not reply. With the air of a man who has extracted all the entertainment he decently can from a situation, O'Brien turned to Jacqueline.

"You wanted to see me, Mrs. Kirby?"

"Sit down," Jacqueline said. "Have a drink."

"Thanks." O'Brien poured a discreet amount of Scotch into a glass and added ice cubes.

James said, "I thought you weren't supposed to drink on duty."

"I'm not on duty," O'Brien said calmly. He sat down on the foot of the bed. "Was there anything special you wanted to talk to me about, Mrs. Kirby?"

"That depends. Need I explain to you why it is imperative that we locate Laurie without delay?"

"No. At least," O'Brien added, "I have my own reasons for wanting to find her. I don't know that they are the same as yours. You have a free-wheeling imagination, Mrs. K."

"What are your reasons?"

"They're pretty obvious, aren't they? The girl has physically attacked two people in the last twelve hours. Or should I say three people?"

His eyebrows rose fractionally. Jacqueline was learning to read O'Brien's eyebrows. The degree of interrogation implied by this movement was minimal.

"No, I don't think it was Laurie who took my purse," she said.

"I figured you'd have mentioned it if you had thought so," said O'Brien. "In your expert opinion, is she liable to go after anybody else?"

"Possibly."

"That's a big help. If you could give me a name, I might be able to arrange protection."

"With your manpower shortage?" Jacqueline asked sarcastically. "I've warned, or tried to warn, the potential victims."

"Then what did you want to see me about?"

Jacqueline looked exasperated. "A number of things. For example, the autopsy on Dubretta."

O'Brien sipped daintily. "There won't be an autopsy."

"But—"

"Her symptoms were consistent with death from congestive heart failure. She's been under treatment for that complaint for years. According to her doctors she was stabilized, but it was a serious condition, and . . . One never knows. Sometimes she'd forget her medication, and she didn't take good care of herself." O'Brien studied Jacqueline's outthrust lip and contemptuous eyes and said defensively, "Mrs. Kirby, to say we have a manpower shortage is a laughable understatement. The coroner's office is piled high with stiffs. We aren't about to go digging up work when there's no reason for it."

James stared ostentatiously at his watch. "Well, that's that. Right, Jacqueline? It was nice of you to stop by, Lieutenant."

"No trouble at all," O'Brien said. "I haven't got anything else to do tonight. This is excellent Scotch, Mrs. Kirby."

"Have another."

"I don't mind if I do."

In a voice thick with annoyance James growled, "Hadn't we better order, Jacqueline? Room service always takes forever at this hour."

"Good heavens, James, can't you ever think of anything except your stomach?" Jacqueline demanded. The barefaced injustice of the charge left James speechless. Jacqueline went on, "There's a deli across the street. I'll have a pastrami on rye and one of those big kosher pickles. And coffee. How about you, Lieutenant?"

"Sammy makes a good shrimp-salad sandwich," O'Brien said. "Coffee for me, too."

"But you—" James sputtered. "You said you were taking me to dinner."

"I am." Jacqueline took money from her purse. "Get whatever you want, James."

After James had gone, O'Brien took the chair he had vacated, and crossed his ankles. "You're a vicious woman, Mrs. Kirby," he remarked.

"I assumed you wouldn't talk freely while he was here."

"You assumed right. But I'm not sure I'm anxious to talk freely now that he's gone."

"Let's not waste time. He'll be back soon. You also believe Dubretta was murdered."

O'Brien met her intent gaze with a face as blank as a stone wall. "Ah," Jacqueline said, in a satisfied voice, "you do believe it. Have you anything to go on, or is it your detective's sixth sense?"

The creases in O'Brien's cheeks deepened, in his version of a smile. "There ain't no such animal, Mrs. Kirby, except in the type of fiction you obviously read too much of. My suspicion—and it's even less solid than that—stems from something Dubretta said to me four or five days ago—the last time I saw her alive."

"Well?" Jacqueline leaned forward.

"I had stopped by to see Prudence. Dubretta came in as I was leaving. We talked for a couple of minutes and I asked her what she was working on. It was one of our standard conversational exchanges; sometimes she'd give me a hint, sometimes she'd just laugh and tell me to read her next column. This time she laughed. But she said . . ." O'Brien's eyes grew remote. " 'It's no big deal, O'Brien. No government scandal or corruption.

This is a grudge case. If I can pull it off it'll give me the greatest satisfaction I've had since I started in this business.' Then she laughed again. 'If I drop dead in the next week or so, O'Brien, it won't be heart failure.' "

"Aha!"

"Aha, hell. It's not evidence, Mrs. Kirby."

"Maybe not. But it fits my theories about the case."

"I figured you were going to tell me your theories sooner or later, whether I wanted to hear them or not." O'Brien's voice hardened. "Get this straight, Mrs. Kirby. I'm not playing Sherlock Holmes with you. So far as the department is concerned, the case is not only closed, there never was a case to start with. I'm screwing around in my spare time because—well, just for the hell of it. I'm talking to you because you have an in with that bunch of fruitcakes across the street. I am not going to confer with you or exchange information with you or defer to your opinion. If you want to give me what you've got, I'll think about it. And that's as far as I'll go."

"Why, of course, Lieutenant. I have better things to do with my time than play Sherlock Holmes. And," Jacqueline added, outrage getting the better of her, "if I did play, it wouldn't be with you."

"Spit it out, then. Your boyfriend will be back soon."

Jacqueline's eyes narrowed to malachite slits, but she kept her temper. "Hattie Foster is the agent for the three top-selling authors in historical-romance fiction, plus several of the lesser lights. As one of her jealous rivals said to me, she has a corner on the market. And that market means a lot of money. Romance editors claim to control forty percent of—"

"I know the stats."

"Good for you. Hattie is making an excellent living out of the writers she handles, not only because they command top prices, but because she is skimming off more than her share of their royalties. Her commission is more than twice the normal rate, and although I can't prove it, I'm pretty sure she is also chiseling money on the side. It's easy to cheat writers; they are very naive.

"I'm not familiar with Hattie's arrangements with Valerie Valentine. The girl was her first important client; handling Valentine gave Hattie her start. Valentine is as important to her as she is to Val, and Max, Valentine's business manager, is a shrewd man; so I rather doubt that Hattie is getting away with much there. The others are in a different category. Victor von Damm is Hattie's Frankenstein monster. She created him, out of two bored housewife-writers and an unemployed actor. She could legitimately claim she's entitled to more than the usual agent's fees because, without that combination, Victor von Damm wouldn't be making the money he does. It was a rather original idea, actually. The romance business is dominated by women authors. The few men who write use women's names. Victor von Damm is a unique phenomenon—a kind of literary glamour boy.

"Victor is played—literally—by Joe Kirby. He's getting fed up. He wants to quit and Hattie won't let him. What hold she has over him I don't know. If I had access to police files," Jacqueline said pointedly, "I'd check up on Joe."

"Checking on all the writers' backgrounds would

certainly be a reasonable starting point," O'Brien agreed blandly. "Including that of Valerie Vanderbilt."

"Valerie Vanderbilt is Jean Frascatti, an English professor," Jacqueline said. "Hattie was blackmailing her too, but in a different way." She went on to explain Jean's dilemma.

O'Brien's eyebrows soared. "That's crazy," he said. "Your friend sounds like a nut."

"The threat was real to her."

"Real enough to kill for? No, it won't work, Mrs. Kirby. Motive is the least important consideration in a murder investigation, for the simple reason that some people kill for reasons you and I would consider absurdly inadequate. But in this case there isn't a motive. So Dubretta found out Victor von Damm was an actor and Valerie Vanderbilt was an embarrassed English prof. So what? She could broadcast those facts to the world and the world wouldn't so much as blink. Even the readers of this romance tripe don't care. The disclosure wouldn't lop five bucks off Hattie's income, and her hide is so thick she's incapable of shame. She didn't like Dubretta's jeers, but she'd shrug them off the way you'd shrug off a mosquito."

"What about Dubretta's grudge against Hattie? She told you it was a grudge case—"

"Hattie was the one who turned down Prudence's first book, years ago," O'Brien said, his face taking on the shuttered, defensive look it assumed whenever Dubretta's sister was mentioned. "She was an editor at one of the publishing houses then, and she was notorious for her vicious rejection letters. She's done nothing since to lessen Dubretta's contempt for her. But again, so what? I'm telling you, Mrs. K., there's no motive."

Jacqueline started to speak. O'Brien waved her to silence. "I need to know two things. First, Dubretta's symptoms. Was there anything—anything she said or did, anything in the way she looked—that was inconsistent with death from heart failure?"

"That's a stupid question, O'Brien. Heart failure isn't a medical term. There are different kinds of heart disease, and they can exhibit an infinite variety of symptoms."

"That's what I thought you'd say. What about opportunity? Did you see anyone drop anything into one of those glasses? Did anyone hand Dubretta her glass? Was it possible for anyone to ensure that she got a particular glass?"

"Well . . ."

"Right. You can amuse yourself with motive from now till doomsday, Mrs. Kirby, but unless you can tell me how it could have been done, you're talking to yourself."

"I have an idea," Jacqueline said haughtily. "Unfortunately I have been so busy with other matters I haven't had time to check it out." A frown replaced her lofty look; she struck her hands together. "Damn. Why doesn't that girl call?"

Realizing that genuine worry underlay her attempt to change the subject, O'Brien did not pursue it. "What makes you think she'd call you?" he asked.

"It's a far-out chance." Jacqueline ran a distracted hand through her hair. "But we had a kind of rapport going yesterday. I left messages with her best friend, the maid at her apartment, and with Max and Hattie. The only reason she might turn to me is that she hasn't got anybody else. Now that she's in trouble, Hattie will dump her, and Valentine has always loathed her." Jacqueline paused. Then she said again, "She hasn't got anybody else."

"I see."

The silence was broken by a peremptory pounding on the door. "Damn," Jacqueline said. "I didn't think he'd be back so soon."

"Sammy's Deli closes at five. As you probably know."

"Certainly I knew. I also knew that James wouldn't quit until he spent the money I gave him. He's a petty man in some ways. I figured it would take him at least half an hour to find a place that was still . . ." A second, more emphatic thud sounded on the door. "I guess I'd better let him in," Jacqueline said resignedly.

But when she opened the door she found herself confronting Betsy Markham. Jacqueline's eyes opened wide. Before she could speak, Betsy pushed her out of the way and slammed the door.

"I think the fuzz is after me," she gasped. "You took your time about . . ." Seeing O'Brien, she came to an abrupt halt, physically and verbally. "Oh, damnation."

"Good evening, Ms. Markham," said O'Brien, rising.

"Hi, O'Brien." Betsy collapsed onto the bed, propping her shaggy gray head on one hand. "Sit down, sit down. I can't stand you when you're polite."

"I take it you two know each other," said Jacqueline from the doorway.

"Yeah," said Betsy.

"Ms. Markham is a frequent performer in my precinct," O'Brien said. "By the way, Ms. Markham, Jack Billings says next time don't hit so hard. He's got a lump the size of Plymouth Rock."

"I'm sorry. The damned sign slipped," Betsy explained.

As the eyes of the other two focused on her, a harsh flood of color moved up her weather-beaten throat till it blended unprettily with the purple-and-green bruise under her left eye. After a moment her sense of humor triumphed over her embarrassment. "Your message came too late," she said throatily, indicating the eye. "At least I presume your call referred to the large young person who clobbered me this afternoon."

"When?" Jacqueline demanded.

"Three, four hours ago. I was on my way to a meeting of the executive committee of WUFAS. No sooner did I walk out of the house than the kid jumped me. She was trying to get my knapsack." Betsy indicated the lumpy khaki pack beside her on the bed. "So I gave her a karate move—you know—" She came up off the bed with an ear-splitting shriek, hands lifted. Jacqueline and O'Brien jumped. "Like that," Betsy said, subsiding. "I hit her on the shoulder and then she hauled back her fist and socked me in the eye."

"Don't do that," Jacqueline protested.

"Just demonstrating." Betsy grinned "How about pouring me a drink? In view of the fact that your message came too late."

Jacqueline complied. "She didn't get your knapsack, I see."

"Apparently she changed her mind," Betsy said equably. "She dumped the contents out while I was squirming around on the pavement with her on top of me. I was yelling my head off, too. You can't ever get a cop in this town when you need one."

"So that makes three," Jacqueline said to O'Brien, who had taken no notice of Betsy's criticism.

"Your arithmetic is faultless," was the courteous reply.

"I found your message on my answering machine when I got back from the meeting," Betsy rattled on. "So I thought I'd come on over and tell you what I think of your friends. What's Hattie Foster doing, using the girl as a hit person?"

Jacqueline and O'Brien exchanged glances. "It was her idea," Jacqueline said cryptically.

"Hmmm," said O'Brien, even more cryptically.

The arrival of James ended the discussion. "I had to go clear down to Broadway and Forty-second," he complained, placing a leaking brown paper bag on the bureau.

"I don't suppose it occurred to you to get another bottle of Scotch," Jacqueline said, looking sadly at the depleted remains of that beverage.

"Luckily I got an extra sandwich." James stared at Betsy.

"Oh, I couldn't intrude," said Betsy. The contrast between her New England boarding-school accent and her sixties protest costume made James stare even more.

Jacqueline introduced them. "How do you do," James said. He looked at Betsy's shiner, she studied his lumps and bruises, then they said in chorus, "Laurie?"

A bond having been established, James formalized his invitation and Betsy was persuaded to accept an egg-salad sandwich. He and Betsy exchanged lies about their encounters with Laurie, both claiming she had caught them off guard. Betsy demonstrated her karate move, and James explained what he would have done if he hadn't slipped and hit his head.

"Of course I had an additional handicap," he explained, having thought up this excuse during his search for sandwiches. "My mother drilled it into me from childhood—don't hit a girl."

"That's sexist," said Betsy.

"You're damned right," said James. "Most of the girls in my grade school were bigger than I was."

Jacqueline and O'Brien ate in silence. Jacqueline's eyes kept turning to the telephone.

It was not quite eight o'clock when the first call came. Jacqueline's hand shot out like a rattlesnake striking, but her expression changed when she heard the voice on the other end of the line. "Max?" she repeated, glancing at O'Brien. "You did? When? What did she say?"

She listened for a few minutes, then said, "Thanks," and hung up. Again it was to O'Brien that she spoke. "Laurie just called. Max said she was pretty incoherent. She kept saying someone was trying to kidnap her, and asking if Valentine was all right. He tried to find out where she was, but couldn't make much sense out of her. He thought she said something about the Village."

Betsy jumped up. "Let's go look for her."

"A lot of people are already looking for her," said O'Brien, not moving. "That's not much of a lead."

"Anyway, this is a job for the police," James said, looking alarmed. "You can't go wandering around the alleys of Manhattan at this hour. If Laurie doesn't clobber you, someone else will."

They were still arguing when the telephone rang again. This time Jacqueline did not address the caller by name. After a brief and obviously unsatisfactory conversation she hung up and pushed her glasses back up to the bridge of her nose. They immediately began slipping again.

"Well?" said James.

"That was Meredith, Laurie's best friend. Laurie must have called her right after she talked to Max. She kept giggling and saying she was like Midas; everything she touched turned to gold."

"My God," Betsy muttered.

"Did she say where she was?" O'Brien asked.

Before Jacqueline could answer, James said pedantically, "None of you seems to have thought of the most obvious place. Maybe the girl has gone home."

O'Brien did not move or speak, but Jacqueline turned on him. "You staked out the apartment, didn't you? I thought you had a manpower shortage. I don't suppose it occurred to you that the sight of a police car would keep her away?"

A shade of vexation crossed O'Brien's face. "If she spotted us it was a blunder on someone's part. She hasn't gone home. I'd have heard."

"She told Meredith she was at the museum," Jacqueline said.

"Is there a museum in the Village?" Betsy asked, with the normal ignorance of a native of New York.

"There are a hundred museums in Manhattan." O'Brien eyed Jacqueline's glasses, which hovered on the brink of catastrophe. "But they're all closed now."

"She might be lurking outside one of them," Betsy insisted. "Check the museums, O'Brien. She shouldn't be hard to spot—big as she is, and wearing what looks like an antique nightgown. Even in Manhattan that getup—"

"What?" Jacqueline whirled, just as O'Brien, unable to control himself any longer, reached for her glasses. "What was she wearing?"

"You know, dirty white with lace and ruffles. Like an old-fashioned costume."

O'Brien made another stab at the glasses, missing by a foot as Jacqueline turned and began scrabbling among the objects on the top of the bureau. Finally she found what she was looking for—a booklet describing sights and shops (especially shops) for visitors to the city. She thumbed through the pages; stopped; stared; threw the booklet on the floor; ripped off her robe and threw it on top of the booklet.

James let out a wordless bleat of disapproval, and O'Brien's eyes popped. Jacqueline grabbed her skirt and blouse and got into them.

O'Brien rose slowly to his feet and brushed a crumb off his lapel. "Where?"

"The Metropolitan Museum. I should have known. . . . The Costume Institute is having a Romantic Images show. That must be where she got the idea for the dress she wore the other day. She said she made it herself. We talked about clothes . . . sewing. . . . She's making a dress for Valentine. A copy of an antique gown."

"But the museum is closed," James objected.

"Not tonight. It's open till nine."

Betsy grabbed her knapsack. "Let's go," she cried.

"No." Jacqueline paused. "You stay here. I don't think she'll call—Meredith said she mouthed obscenities when my name was mentioned, so apparently I'm back on her hate list. But we can't all go barreling into the place, we'll scare her off."

"I can get you there in ten minutes," O'Brien said coolly. "It's eight-fifteen."

"I'll stay," James said.

Jacqueline wasted no more time. She headed for the door, with Betsy and O'Brien close behind her. James reached for the bottle. Not until the door had closed after the hunters did he see Jacqueline's neat blue pumps on the floor. She had gone out in her bedroom slippers.

O'Brien brought the car to a strictly illegal stop in front of the museum. Jacqueline was out before the wheels stopped turning. She went up the monumental staircase at a pace that left the others far behind.

By the time O'Brien and Betsy reached the door, Jacqueline was out of sight. They were further delayed by a guard who informed them that the museum was about to close, and by another guard who wanted Betsy to check her knapsack. Having peremptorily disposed of these persons, O'Brien gazed helplessly at the huge hall, with galleries leading off in all directions.

"Where's the costume place?"

"You're asking me?" Betsy indicated her droopy army fatigues. O'Brien turned to one of the guards.

They made their way through the Egyptian halls against the stream of exiting visitors and took an escalator going down. Here they were again informed that the museum was closing, and O'Brien identified himself. After a bewildered glance at the artistically shadowed exhibit hall beyond, where life-sized mannequins postured and posed in a variety of extravagant costumes, he looked at the girl behind the desk where souvenirs and postcards were sold. "Did a woman just come in here?"

At any other time of day this question would have been received with amusement. Instead the young woman replied, "Tall, red-haired? She ran down the escalator and went past me before I could stop her. Is she a policewoman? What's going on?"

Instead of answering, O'Brien beckoned to Betsy. "Stay here. Stop her if she tries to go out this way."

"Right." Betsy assumed her kung-fu stance.

O'Brien plunged into the gloom. Guards tactfully shepherded visitors toward the exit. O'Brien waved them away when they attempted to intercept him, but as he penetrated farther and farther into the shadowy hall he began to exhibit signs of nervousness. The life-sized mannequins stood or sat in various poses, separated from the spectator only by inconspicuous rope barriers. Their elaborate and extravagant costumes had the unnerving authenticity that derives only from actual use; all the garments had been worn, by the beauties and worthies of other times. The contrast between the realistic clothing and the blank, eyeless faces, which were covered with coarse fabric in shades of beige and brown, had an uncanny effect that was increased by the lighting—soft but sharp spotlights on the figures themselves, shadowy spaces between the exhibits. The insistent beat of a Viennese waltz in the background, pouring from concealed speakers, lost its gaiety in that ambience and took on the macabre suggestion of a dance of the dead.

Rounding a corner, O'Brien shied back as he found himself confronted by a figure clothed entirely in black, from the sable plumes atop its bonnet to the tip of the black parasol lifted in a menacing gesture. A transparent black veil hung from the bonnet; behind it, the featureless head, swathed in black fabric, seemed to stare inquiringly at him from empty eyesockets.

Jacqueline's face peered round the figure. "She isn't here."

O'Brien took the handkerchief from his breast pocket and mopped his brow. "How can you tell? This is worse than the chamber of horrors at a wax museum."

Jacqueline glanced at the grisly figure looming over them. "This is how widows were supposed to dress a hundred years ago. Cute, isn't it? Laurie couldn't disguise herself as one of the mannequins, if that's what you're thinking, not even if she put a stocking over her head. She's too big. These clothes were made for women wearing corsets so tight they couldn't take a deep breath. It's no wonder they swooned all the time."

"I didn't come here for a lecture on fashions," O'Brien said between his teeth. "I don't know why I came here, period. This was a far-out idea, Mrs. Kirby. If the girl was here, she's long gone."

"She was here. One of the guards remembered her.

I'm going back to the main door. Maybe I can catch her on the way out."

She was gone before O'Brien could stop her. Avoiding the embrace of an elaborately ruffled blue tea gown, and the flirtatious gesture of a white, pin-tucked morning dress, O'Brien retreated to the desk, where Betsy was waiting. She had abandoned her karate stance and was studying the nearby exhibits with somewhat sheepish interest.

Interrogation of the guards persuaded O'Brien that the costume galleries had been swept clean of visitors, but when one of them asked if he wanted to speak with the director, O'Brien caved in. He had no reason to suggest, much less insist upon, a thorough search of the museum—a laborious process that would have necessitated the approval of various high officials. Several of the guards remembered seeing Laurie. No one had seen her leave, but as they all pointed out, there were several possible exits.

O'Brien climbed the stairs, swearing under his breath. "This is ridiculous," he informed Betsy. "I don't know why I let that woman talk me into coming here."

"It was rather interesting," Betsy said. "Did you notice that pleated coral silk evening dress with crystal beads? Of course clothes like that are symbols of the oppression of women, but they are rather—"

With a wordless snarl O'Brien broke into a trot and pulled away.

Jacqueline was not in the lobby. The last of the visitors were being urged out the great front doors; she was not among them. O'Brien and Betsy went out.

Standing at the top of the staircase, O'Brien scanned the area, which was brightly lighted by streetlamps and by the lights on the facade of the museum itself. He caught a glimpse of a distinctive mop of auburn hair behind the balustrade on the left, at the bottom of the stairs, and started toward it.

When Jacqueline saw him she made a violent and peremptory gesture. O'Brien understood its meaning but went on anyway. Looking over the balustrade, he demanded, "What are you doing?"

"Will you get away from here?" Jacqueline hissed. "I thought I saw her—at least I saw something large and white in those bushes. If she thinks I'm alone she might—"

"Throw a rock at you," O'Brien said. "Where was she—it—whatever you saw?"

"There." Jacqueline pointed.

"Stay here." O'Brien added, "Both of you," and glared at Betsy, who had joined them. He sauntered toward the path that led alongside the museum.

"Arrogant bastard," Jacqueline said.

"He's not so bad," Betsy said cheerfully. "In fact, he's rather attractive—if you like the strong, sardonic type. Maybe I'd better go with him, in case he gets into trouble."

"Yes, why don't you?"

No sooner had Betsy set out in pursuit of O'Brien than Jacqueline headed in the opposite direction. She went as fast as she could without actually running, but the facade of the Metropolitan covers two city blocks. After an extremely cursory investigation of the area she had indicated, O'Brien returned in time to see her turn into the path that led into the park on the south side of the museum.

"Damn it, I told her to stay here," he exclaimed.

"I guess she was trying to get rid of us," Betsy said. "That's Jake for you. She never lets—"

O'Brien began to run. Betsy kept pace with him, talking as she went. "She never lets anybody interfere with her. She can drive you crazy, but she's efficient, in her own peculiar way. Maybe she really did see the girl."

The pedestrian path on the south side of the museum parallels Seventy-ninth Street for a short distance and then divides. Without hesitating, O'Brien took the right-hand path. It was not entirely deserted; a few joggers and dog-walkers had braved the fringes of the park, but as O'Brien and Betsy went deeper into the night-darkened regions, the lights shone on empty paths and benches. Finally they spotted their quarry ahead. Jacqueline was walking slowly, swinging her purse. Her disheveled hair shone ruddy in the lamplight.

"Mrs. Kirby!" O'Brien's shout shattered the silence.

Jacqueline looked back. The concentrated venom of her expression could almost be felt. She turned and plunged into the darkness beside the path.

O'Brien put on a burst of speed. By the time Betsy caught up he had found and retrieved Jacqueline. She was rigid with fury, but she did not resist, and when O'Brien demanded, "If I let go of you, will you stand still?" she nodded curtly.

"It's too late now. She's gotten away."

O'Brien released his grip. Jacqueline rubbed her

arm and then began tucking up loosened strands of hair. Her hands were unsteady.

"Did you really see her?" Betsy asked.

"I think so. There was someone following me, in the shadows."

"Probably a mugger," O'Brien growled. "Mrs. Kirby, are you out of your mind? Haven't you heard about the park at night?"

"I am well aware—"

"You wouldn't last ten minutes in some parts of this place," O'Brien went on heatedly. "Come out of here."

Without replying Jacqueline turned back toward Fifth Avenue. The others followed. After an interval O'Brien said, "I'll call in and report she was seen. Though God knows I didn't see her . . . Maybe some-one will spot her when she comes out of the park."

But it was not until dawn the following morning that Laurie was found. The jogger who saw her thought at first she was sleeping, for she lay neatly disposed, with her skirt pulled down over her knees and her arms folded. It was not until he bent over for a closer look that he realized the back of her head had been smashed in.

Chapter 8

O'Brien was at Jacqueline's door at eight-thirty, shortly after the report reached him. The promptness with which she responded to his knock, and the lines of strain on her face, told him she had not slept. He was not inclined to be sympathetic; he hadn't been to bed either. One look told her the truth before he could speak. Every muscle in her face gave way, and for a moment she looked her full age.

"I'm sorry," O'Brien said. "We tried."

"B.S.," Jacqueline said clearly. She tightened the sash of the peacock-blue robe and stepped back. "You'd better come in."

O'Brien glanced at the huddled lump in one of the beds. "I wouldn't want to disturb . . . her?"

"Your humor is particularly out of place this morning," Jacqueline remarked. "That, as you know, is Sue Moberley, and I don't give a damn whether we disturb her or not. Sit down and tell me."

"I'll stand, thank you. I shouldn't even be here. Her

death is being put down as a mugging. Her skull was fractured and her purse was taken."

"Where was she found?"

"Not far north of the museum." O'Brien made this admission without visible signs of chagrin or guilt. "You know the playground, around Eighty-sixth? She was near there, under some bushes. She was found around seven this morning. The coroner thinks she'd been dead six or seven hours."

"Anything unusual? Oh, don't be cute, O'Brien; you wouldn't be here if you were satisfied she had been mugged."

"There was nothing to indicate that was not the case. Only . . ." O'Brien hesitated. "She'd been laid out. Stretched out with her hands folded and her clothing arranged. Her eyes were closed. She looked . . . peaceful."

"There is that," Jacqueline said. "Well. Anything else?"

"Your hypothetical murderer did not leave a scrap of his tie in her clenched fist, if that's what you mean."

"The murder weapon?"

"A rock. Picked up from the ground. It had blood and hair on it. Yes," O'Brien went on, anticipating Jacqueline's next question, "it's being tested for fingerprints. But a rough surface like that won't have taken prints."

"What are you going to do now?"

"I'm going back to work. There's plenty of it. Two burglaries, six assaults, a couple of rapes, three drunk and disorderlies. And the day is young. Good-bye, Mrs. Kirby."

"O'Brien."

"Yes?" O'Brien was already at the door.

"This is the last day of the conference. Tonight is the Grand Ball."

O'Brien turned and looked at her. Her unbound hair streamed down her back in a torrent of molten bronze. She was still wearing the shabby bedroom slippers in which she had led the hunt for Laurie.

The corners of his mouth lifted briefly. "Are you inviting me to be your escort, Mrs. Kirby?"

The evil expression on Jacqueline's face made O'Brien sorry he'd made the suggestion. "Never mind," he said quickly.

"It's a costume ball," Jacqueline murmured. "James won't like it, but . . . I'd be honored, Lieutenant, if you would agree to go with me. I'll even find you a costume."

"I'll bet you'd enjoy that. I'll find my own costume, thanks. What time?"

"Nine. Unless you'd like me to take you to dinner first."

"No, thanks. I'm not in the mood for pastrami on rye tonight. See you at nine."

After he had gone the blanketed lump on the bed reared up, and a pair of sleepy blue eyes blinked at Jacqueline. "I had the most peculiar dream," Sue mumbled. "I dreamed that policeman came in and said he was going to take you to the ball."

"It wasn't a dream." Index finger on the bridge of her glasses, Jacqueline stood deep in thought. "He meant to attend all along," she said, as much to herself as to Sue. "By tomorrow morning the suspects will be scattered to the four corners of the globe. This is his last chance to catch the killer. He has no authority to hold them. Laurie's death hasn't changed the official view of the case. So he—"

"Laurie?" Caught in the middle of a yawn, Sue choked. "Dead?"

Jacqueline explained as she got dressed.

James didn't like it.

"You said I could go with you. Are you planning to seduce O'Brien, or employ him as a bodyguard?"

"I might point out that I did not say you could go with me; that I never invited you to come to New York in the first place; and that your references to O'Brien are childish, libelous, and uncalled-for. Instead I will simply remark that in view of the recent tragedy your reaction is tasteless in the extreme."

James added another spoonful of sugar to his coffee and sought a change of subject.

They were having breakfast in a coffee shop down the street from his hotel. Jacqueline had arrived first; the book she had been reading lay on the table. "I see," James said, "that you're reading Valentine's latest."

The distraction worked better than he had hoped, for reasons he had not anticipated. "Just getting an idea of what is selling," Jacqueline explained. "For my book, you know."

"I didn't know. At least—I thought you were joking. Are you joking?"

"Certainly not."

"Interesting title. What's it about?" His nod indicated Valentine's book, and his casual dismissal of

Jacqueline's big news about her own venture into literature didn't please her. Her eyes narrowed.

"The heroine loses her lover to another woman, so she turns to satanism and black magic in the hope of getting him back."

"Sounds corny."

"It isn't corny. Valentine has researched Aleister Crowley and his crowd—a particularly nasty bunch of sickies, if you recall—and has created a similar cult. Poor Magdalen doesn't realize what she's getting into until it's almost too late. There are some very powerful descriptions of her struggle with evil, in the cult and in her own soul. Of course," Jacqueline said smoothly, "you recognize the source of the title."

James said promptly, " 'In such a night stood Dido with a willow in her hand upon the wild sea-banks, and waft her love to come again to Carthage.' *Merchant of Venice,* Act V, Scene—er."

Jacqueline waited. James smiled, smugly pleased. Jacqueline smiled back at him. "If you've finished your literary commentary," she said, with suspicious mildness, "perhaps we could return to the reason why I woke you from your slumbers. The death of a seventeen-year-old girl."

"I'm sorry about the girl," James said sulkily. "But I hardly knew her. If you expect me to go into mourning over every victim of our current crime wave, I'd have to wear a black armband for the rest of my life."

"She was murdered." Jacqueline's eyes were cold and opaque as jade.

"Of course she was. Anybody who wanders around Central Park at midnight—"

"James, don't be obtuse. She was killed by the same person who murdered Dubretta."

James would have objected if she had given him time. She didn't. "The ball tonight is our last chance to catch the killer before the delegates to the conference leave New York. Are you going to help me or aren't you?"

"Since when have you needed my help?" But two of the four lines on James's forehead smoothed out, and Jacqueline fanned the feeble flame of interest with the wind of flattery.

"Why do you think I asked you to be Jean's escort tonight?"

"To get me out of your hair so you can work on O'Brien," was the prompt reply.

"I need O'Brien to make the arrest once I've exposed the killer. I've read about citizen's arrests, but I'm not sure I could get away with—"

"You're serious." James stared at her. "You really think . . . Who is it?"

Jacqueline met his look with one of crystalline candor. "It's one of three people, James. I'm certain of that. If you'll help me, we can eliminate two of the suspects before tonight."

"Oh no." James shook his head vigorously. "I'm tired of sitting around listening to you utter veiled hints like the classic detectives of fiction. That's your idea of helping, but it isn't mine. Tell me whom you suspect and why—especially why—and I might cooperate. Might."

"You force my hand, James." Jacqueline looked pensively at her egg-stained plate, giving James a breathtaking view of her long curling lashes. "I didn't want to put my cards on the table in case I was wrong. But I need you. If that's the only way I can get your help . . ."

"You're damned right it is." James squared his shoulders and spoke in a gruff voice.

"All right. The three suspects are Hattie, Max—and Jean."

The last name broke James's calm. "Jean? Of all the unlikely people . . . Do you really think . . . Is that why you want me to be her escort?"

"Yes." Jacqueline put both elbows on the table and leaned forward, holding James's eyes with her own. "So far two people have been killed. I think a third person is in danger. The killer must dispose of that person tonight, before the delegates disperse. If we can't eliminate the other suspects we must watch all three, and watch them closely. It won't be easy. Our aim will be to prevent another murder—but not prevent an attempt at murder."

"In other words, you propose to set some poor innocent up as a decoy," James said slowly. "That's pretty cold-blooded, Jacqueline."

"It's the only way I can think of. The third victim will be in danger anyhow."

"You could at least warn . . . Who is it?"

Jacqueline's breath caught in a tremulous gasp. "Me," she murmured modestly.

They separated at the corner of Fifth and Forty-third. James headed purposefully toward Sixth Avenue, where he could catch an uptown bus. "Sit on that chemist buddy of yours until he gets results," Jacqueline had instructed. "I don't care what you tell him, just make sure he knows every minute counts."

As soon as James was out of sight, Jacqueline headed for the library. She felt bad about deceiving James, but she comforted herself with the assurance that she had told him part of the truth. Only one statement had been a flat-out lie. It wasn't her fault if he had leaped to erroneous conclusions.

She spent an hour in the main reading room, but when she emerged her brow was furrowed. She was sure she was on the right track, yet she had failed to find substantiating evidence. Weaving a path around the students and tourists and derelicts sunning themselves on the stairs between the stone lions, she pondered alternatives, and decided it was unlikely that the experts she might consult would have anything useful to add. Most of them derived their expertise from the books she had been reading.

With a fatalistic shrug she took out her notebook and considered her next move. Maybe something would occur to her during the course of the day.

Since the demise of the late lamented Brentano's there are only five major bookstores on Fifth Avenue between Forty-second and Fifty-ninth. Jacqueline visited all of them. She did not buy a single book, but by the time she finished she had a good idea of what was selling in the romance trade. Valerie Valentine's position as Queen of Love was unchallenged. No fewer than six of her books were in print, and they occupied the choicest places on the racks. Heaps of them filled the heavy cardboard display boxes known (appropriately, in Jacqueline's opinion) as dumps. VV ran a distant second—three books in print, one dump to every five of Valentine's—with Victor von Damm not far behind VV. Together the three took almost half the shelf space allotted to historical-romance fiction. If Hattie had not cornered the market, she controlled a sizable share of it.

One of the bookstores had a window display keyed to the conference (paper hearts and cupids) and featuring Valentine's latest book. It had appeared in two formats—a hardcover edition and a trade paperback, larger than the usual softcover, and printed on better paper. As Jacqueline had learned from her assiduous study of the trade, this was a departure, and a testimonial to Valentine's selling power. Only the top few romance writers had achieved the status symbol of hardcover publication, and that only in recent years. Most of the books were produced as cheap, original paperbacks. Apparently Valentine's publishers believed her readers would shell out four times the paperback price for a longer-lasting format. And apparently they were correct.

By the time Jacqueline finished her survey it was almost time for lunch, so she consumed fettuccine Alfredo and strawberry pie smothered in whipped cream, assuring herself that food was essential if one lacked sleep. An afternoon nap would have been nice, but she knew she wouldn't have time for that luxury.

The inner woman having been satisfied, she started on the next stage of her investigation. The first stop found her on the mezzanine of the hotel where the romance conference was in progress. Workshops and

lectures were in full swing, and it was evident that the
news of Laurie's death had not affected the partici-
pants. The only exception was the little group that huddled around the booth, with its ill-made sign.

Jacqueline approached them reluctantly. Her feeling
that she was in some way responsible for the tragedy
was unreasonable, but apparently it was shared by
some of the Valentine Lovers. Most of the girls turned
or stepped back without looking at her. Meredith
stepped forward instead and faced her. The girl's
square, unattractive face was expressionless but her
brown eyes, magnified by her thick glasses, were hard
and accusing.

"I tried," Jacqueline said. It wasn't what she had
meant to say. The words came out of some deep inner
pool of guilt.

"Swell," said Meredith. Jacqueline reflected wryly
that it was a less pejorative response than the one she
had given O'Brien when he made the same disclaimer.

"How did you find out?" she asked.

"That cop told us," Meredith said. "O'Brien?"

"Right. Meredith, can I talk to you for a minute?"

Meredith shrugged and allowed Jacqueline to draw
her away from the others. Jacqueline chose her words
carefully. It was essential that she find out whether
Laurie had confided in Meredith, but the last thing she
wanted was to involve the girl in a matter that had already snuffed out two lives.

"Did Laurie say anything to you about what she was
doing yesterday?"

"You mean that business about a notebook? No.
O'Brien told us about it. Laurie never said a word."

"But you knew she was angry at Dubretta Duberstein."

"A lot of them were." Meredith glanced at the group of whispering, sober-faced girls. "Dubretta wrote some nasty things about the conference and about us fans. She said she'd think we had been brainwashed by pink goo except that none of us had any brains to start with."

"She can't have talked to you if she said that."

This time flattery had no effect. Meredith said coolly, "I'm smart enough to wonder what you and O'Brien have on your tiny minds. Why all the questions?"

"I can't tell you."

"At least you're honest," Meredith said grudgingly.

"I can't even ask pertinent questions," Jacqueline mumbled, half to herself. "Just one more, Meredith. Was Laurie the only one of the group who had close associations with Valentine and Hattie and the other writers?"

"She was. We were allowed to worship from a distance. And pay our dues, of course."

"None of you ran errands for Aunt Hattie or Val?"

"No. That's two questions." But instead of turning away, Meredith hesitated. Finally she said, "You've got some pull with that crowd."

"Not much. What is it you want me to do?"

"Make them—make them . . ." Meredith groped for words. Then she burst out, "It's like Laurie was just a—a thing. She was here and now she's not here, and nobody gives a damn either way."

"I think I understand what you mean. You want Hattie to acknowledge the fact of her existence."

"Well—yes."

"I'll buy that. What did you have in mind? Some sort of tribute?"

"Laurie would've liked that," Meredith said. "She was making a dress for Valentine, you know. I saw it. It's gorgeous. She worked her tail off on that dress. If Valentine wore it tonight and Hattie said something . . ." Her voice broke. One huge, magnified tear formed in the corner of her eye.

"I'll see what I can do," Jacqueline said.

"Okay." Meredith pressed her lips tightly together. "Thanks," she added.

"Don't thank me." After a moment Jacqueline turned away, leaving Meredith in command of the field.

Either the newspapers had not yet made the connection between Laurie's death and the romance writers, or—which Jacqueline considered more likely—they didn't care. The hallway outside Hattie's suite was deserted. From Hattie's behavior, however, one would have supposed that the place was under siege. She took her time about answering the door, and then peered warily out through a crack, leaving the chain in place. The sight of Jacqueline did not relieve her anxieties. "What do you want?" she demanded. "I'm busy."

"So am I," Jacqueline said. "I won't take much of your time, but I'd rather not yell my questions through the door."

The not-so-veiled threat had the desired effect. Hattie opened the door and switched on the southern accent. "I'm sorry if I sounded rude, honey. We are in such a state you can't imagine. That pore chile—"

"I know. How did you find out?"

"That nice policeman—Kelly, or whatever his name is—came by a few hours ago to tell us. Well, you can just imagine, honey. Valentine is so upset. . . ."

The cries coming from Valentine's room certainly bore out this claim, but after listening to them Jacqueline began to doubt that Laurie's death was the cause of Valentine's woe. She kept repeating, "No, I won't. I tell you, I won't do it!"

"Won't do what?" Jacqueline asked.

Hattie's smile grew fixed. "Don't you worry your head about that, dear. It's none of your business, is it?"

Jacqueline slid neatly through the other woman's attempt at a block and sat down. "I want to talk to Valentine and Max anyway. Maybe I can help. I always think we should help others when we can, don't you?"

Hattie didn't miss the reference, but before she could reply, Max appeared in the doorway: "Did I hear—ah, it is you, Jacqueline. I'm glad to see you. Perhaps you can help me talk some sense into Val."

"I'll be glad to." With a smug smile at Hattie, Jacqueline settled back in the chair. "What seems to be the trouble?"

Max ran his hand over his scanty hair. "She's a very high-strung, sensitive creature. The news about that unfortunate child hit her hard. She—but if you wouldn't mind, you had better come and see for yourself."

"I don't mind." Jacqueline rose with alacrity.

"Max," Hattie began ominously.

"Something has to be done, Hattie. She can't go on like this. And she does admire Jacqueline. . . . If you'll just wait a minute Jacqueline, I'll tell her you're here."

He disappeared. Jacqueline and Hattie stood smiling fixedly at one another like matching gargoyles until he returned and reported that Valentine would be happy to see Mrs. Kirby.

The other part of the suite consisted of a second, smaller apartment that could be rented separately or made part of a larger ensemble by unlocking a door. It had its own entrance. There were three other doors, two of which were closed. The third led to Valentine's bedroom.

It was a pleasant but not particularly luxurious room, with wide windows giving a view of the park. It did not share the balcony outside Hattie's sitting room. Not, Jacqueline thought, an appropriate setting for the Queen of Love and her manager. Hattie had the lion's share of the living quarters.

Jacqueline turned her attention to the girl who lay across one of the twin beds. Valentine's chin was propped on her hands and her mouth was mutinous, but she looked almost as enchanting in anger and disarray as when she was dressed in her formal smile. Her pouting lips might have inspired a poet to babble about rosebuds, and the hair tumbling over her slim shoulders foamed like molten gold.

On the other bed lay an evening dress of pink damask patterned with chrysanthemum petals, its tiered skirt festooned with a triple garland of pearls and beads. Hand-embroidered lace trimmed the flounces and the wide band of fabric atop the bodice, which was caught by glittering pins at either side to form tiny cap sleeves. The long smooth waistline and draped skirt belonged to another time, and Jacqueline thought she could even name the designer. The dress was an exact copy of a gown by the great Worth, which she had seen at the Costume Institute the night before.

"I'm not going to wear it," Valentine said. "So don't try to talk me into it. Hattie and Max have been nagging me all morning and I'm sick of being lectured. I won't wear it, and that's final."

"Is that the dress Laurie made for you?" Jacqueline asked. She knew it must be, but found it hard to believe, even though she had noted Laurie's skill as a needlewoman. The dress was a masterpiece.

"That is correct," Max said. "The girl had been working on it for weeks—"

"Months," Jacqueline corrected, contemplating the delicate hand embroidery and the painstaking perfection of the beaded garlands. "She must have started it as soon as the exhibit opened in April."

"Naturally, Valentine was flattered and pleased," Max went on, glancing at Valentine, who looked nothing of the kind. "Hattie had given the girl Val's measurements, and we had a fitting last week when we arrived in New York. Val had planned to wear it to the ball tonight. It suits the theme of her last book, which as you know is set in late Victorian times. There is even a scene in which Magdalen goes to a ball wearing a Worth creation."

"I remember the scene," Jacqueline said. "It's a magnificent gown, Valentine. Why don't you want to wear it?"

Valentine dropped her head onto the bed and covered it with her arms. From the tangle of red-gold came a muffled voice. "She's dead, that's why. It's sick. Like—like grave clothes."

Hattie burst out, "Now that's just silly, Val. It's all the more important that you wear the dress. It's like a tribute, don't you see? That fan club can drive you crazy, but you don't want to alienate them. You can't afford—"

Jacqueline was about to administer an admonitory kick in the shins when Valentine interrupted the tirade. Lifting herself with both hands, she screamed. It was an exquisitely musical scream, like a fanfare from a golden trumpet, and just as piercing. Having caught Hattie's attention, Valentine went on, "You've said all that a dozen times, Hattie, and I'm sick of hearing it. I'm not going to wear that damned dress! I swear to God, when I put it on I can feel her hands all over me, touching me—cold, dead hands, like lumps of frozen lard."

The simile lacked the elegance of Valentine's written prose, but it had a certain power. Max winced, and Jacqueline fought a sudden desire to slap the lovely, petulant face. She decided that, come hell or high water, Valentine was going to wear the dress.

"I understand perfectly," she said, sitting down on the bed beside the distraught Queen of Love. "And I admire your sensitivity. You think it would be tasteless and unfeeling to wear a dress that will undoubtedly be the most beautiful gown at the ball. Everyone will be envying you. There's only one other gown like that in the world, and it's in a museum. Yes, you're quite right to refuse to flaunt it."

Valentine's face went absolutely blank. Jacqueline

patted one of her small, pink-nailed hands. "Yes, my
dear, I agree. Someone ought to wear it, though. Hattie
has a point. Laurie's friends would be pleased by such a
tribute. Especially if Hattie made a graceful little speech
about it. I was talking to the girls about that very thing
just before I came here. And the publicity value . . . I
wonder if it would fit Sue. She's about your size."

"Sue," Valentine repeated. "That girl Victor has
taken up with? The dumpy little schoolteacher?"

"Oh, I wouldn't call her dumpy," Jacqueline said seriously. "She has a nice little figure. Not as nice as
yours, of course. We may have to pad the bodice; that
gown requires a beautifully shaped bosom and shoulders to set it off. But I think I could fix it. Shall I take
it with me now?"

"No!" Valentine got up. "I don't know. . . ." Crossing to the other bed, she touched the lacy flounce with
a tentative finger.

"All hand-embroidered," Jacqueline crooned. "You
can't find work like that these days. Oh, I suppose a
French designer could reproduce it, but the cost! Thousands and thousands of dollars."

Valentine's five fingers and palm pressed against the
damask of the dress. Jacqueline wondered why she had
never noticed before what a predatory little hand it
was—like a delicate ivory crab.

"I'll think about it," Valentine said. "Maybe . . ."

"Well, let me know." Jacqueline got to her feet. "I'd
like to have it by five at the latest. It will take a while
to alter it to fit Sue."

Valentine didn't reply. Max was smiling; as his eyes
met Jacqueline's his eyelid dropped in a wink.

Jacqueline had hoped to talk to Valentine alone, but she realized there was no hope of that. "Maybe you can help me with something," she said. "I'd be so grateful for your advice."

"What?" Valentine looked up. "Me?"

"Yes. You see, I'm writing a book, and I need a title. I think titles are awfully important. And yours are particularly good."

"Thank you," Valentine said abstractedly. Her eyes returned to the dress.

"I came up with one I rather like, but I want to ask your opinion."

"Valentine," Max said sharply.

"What? Oh—I'm sorry, Mrs. Kirby. Were you—"

" 'Come Again to Carthage,' " Jacqueline said rapidly. "That's my title. It's a quotation, of course—"

"It won't sell." Hattie shook her head. "You need something with more—"

"Lust?" Jacqueline inquired. "Thanks, Hattie. Valentine, what do you think?"

"I agree with Hattie. It's kind of a boring title, Mrs. Kirby. If you'll excuse my saying so."

"No, you mustn't apologize. I appreciate your opinion. Turning to another, more important matter, I wonder if I might ask a few questions."

Max and Hattie converged on her, each taking one of her arms. "Val has to rest now," Hattie said.

Max added, "We'll be more comfortable in the sitting room, Jacqueline."

They left the Queen of Love contemplating the ball gown with a pensive frown.

"I assume you want to talk about—about the girl,"

Max said, closing the door. "I didn't want to destroy the good work you did by reminding Val. That was very clever, Jacqueline."

"Yes," Hattie admitted. "Thanks."

"I wasn't exaggerating," Jacqueline said. "If Valentine refuses to wear the dress, I'd like to have it. I wouldn't want it thrown in the trash."

"Oh, we'd never do that," Hattie said.

Jacqueline was willing to bet she wouldn't—not now that she had been made aware of the gown's monetary value. "I wanted to ask you about Laurie's telephone call last night," she said.

"I didn't talk to her," Hattie said. "I was out all evening."

"What time did you get back?"

"Around one, I guess. I was . . . Hey. What are you getting at?"

"Laurie was killed between midnight and one o'clock. Whom were you with last night?"

"God damn it to—" Hattie's voice rose in a roar. Max clapped his hand over her mouth. "You fool," he said softly and evenly. "Do you want Valentine to hear you?"

Hattie subsided, glowering. Jacqueline deduced that once again she had fallen from the heights of approval to the pits of Hattie's regard. It did not distress her unduly.

"The girl was a victim of the random violence that marks our society," Max said. "That is what Lieutenant O'Brien indicated to us."

"Did he? How interesting. Did he ask where you were last night, Max?"

"I went to bed early, as did Valentine. I didn't even hear Hattie come in."

"I see." Her opinion of the little man's intelligence rose another notch when he made no attempt to protest the implication. Instead he said soberly, "As for the telephone call, I think I told you the essentials. I called you immediately, Jacqueline."

"I appreciate that. Tell me exactly what she said."

But Max had little to add to what he had already told her. Laurie had asked for Hattie, and, on learning that her mentor was not available, for Valentine. "Val didn't want to talk to her," Max explained. "And I saw no point in persuading her to do so; the girl was literally babbling. I told her you had been trying to get in touch with her. Her response was—er—profane. Then she went off into a mumbled monologue about the dress she had made for Valentine; it would have been Greek to an ignorant male like myself even if she had been sensible—words like darts and tucks, and so on. I kept asking where she was. I thought she said the Village, but I may have been wrong."

Hattie stared pointedly at her watch. "I'm late for the workshop. You'll have to excuse me, Mrs. Kirsky."

"I was just leaving." Jacqueline sauntered toward the door while Max repeated his thanks. Her hand on the knob, she stopped as if struck by a sudden idea. (She had picked up the trick from a favorite TV detective, and had always wanted to try it.)

"By the way—what has become of the Earl of Devonbrook?"

Hattie looked blank. "Who?"

*   *   *

"You're going as what?"

"An Arab princess," Jean said "That was the setting of my latest—"

"Oh, yes—*Slave of Lust.*"

The costume laid out on Jean's bed was fashioned chiefly of pink chiffon, or a cheap imitation of that fabric. Dubiously Jacqueline studied the voluminous transparent trousers and the exiguous sequined wisp of the bodice and the yards and yards of pink veiling. She transferred her skeptical gaze to her friend's meager body.

Jean blushed. "Of course I'll wear a body stocking under it. And—do you think?—long tights, the kind with built-in panties."

Jacqueline tried to visualize this ensemble, perhaps with an added blouse, if Jean's feet got colder, and her imagination reeled.

"Oh, you're always criticizing my clothes," Jean said, reading her expression correctly. "What are you going to wear?"

"I haven't decided."

Jean turned to the bed and pretended to fluff up the veil. She glanced slyly at Jacqueline over her shoulder. "Do you have an escort, darling, or are you going alone?"

Jacqueline leaned against the wall and crossed her arms. (She had not been invited to sit down.) "James has been here?"

"Oh yes, some time ago. You don't mind, do you, Jake? I wouldn't want to steal your boyfriend."

The obvious response to this was a sarcastic "Oh, yeah?" but Jacqueline didn't make it. Remembering their college years, she decided that Jean owed her a few. Besides she certainly was not catty enough to tell Jean she had practically had to threaten James to force him to take her. Not unless Jean got off a few more digs like the last one . . .

"I'm going with O'Brien," she said.

"The policeman?" Jean's eyes opened wide. "Oh, well . . . He's rather attractive, in his way."

"He's about as attractive as a rattlesnake," said O'Brien's date. "And I doubt if he attends social functions of this sort for their own sake."

She expected this ominous hint would bring squeaks and twitches from the white rabbit, but something had stiffened Jean's spine. "Are you still harping on that murder theory? Really, Jake, you ought to grow up and stop playing games. O'Brien said the police were satisfied Dubretta died of a heart attack and Laurie was killed by a criminal—"

"O'Brien was here? This morning?"

"Yes. I thought it was most considerate of him to take the time to reassure me."

Jacqueline gritted her teeth. So far O'Brien had been ahead of her every step of the way. She wondered whether he was asking the same questions she was, or whether he was on another, parallel track. Both led to the same goal, and she had never doubted that O'Brien was as single-minded, and as tight-lipped, as she was.

"The police may be satisfied, but O'Brien isn't," she said. "He's tricky, Jean. Watch out for him."

"I've nothing to worry about." Jean lifted the veil and draped it across her nose, studying the effect in the mirror. "I need . . ." She spat out a fold of veiling and went on, "I need lots of eye makeup. Don't you think so?"

"Yes," Jacqueline said truthfully. Jean's lashes were even grayer than her hair, and the faded blue of her pupils blended into the whites of her eyes. She added, with a certain malice, "Is that why you chose that costume—to hide your face from inquisitive reporters?"

"Oh, no." Jean continued to admire her reflection, adjusting the veil in different positions. "I don't care about that any more."

"You don't?"

"Oh, no. Not any more." Jean's voice was soft and dreamy. "It's all settled. There's nothing to worry about any more."

Before she left, Jacqueline ascertained that Jean also claimed to have retired early the night before. Her hotel was one of the mammoth chains; if she had taken her key with her, she could have come in at any hour without being observed.

Jacqueline's next stop was the shabby brownstone where Betsy had lived all her life. Tall office buildings now towered over the house, which gave the impression of huddling earthward for fear of being squashed. The neighborhood was no longer what it had once been, but the property, Jacqueline surmised, was worth a tidy sum of money.

Her hope that for once she had anticipated O'Brien was dashed by Betsy as soon as she opened the door. "Well, well, the third musketeer. You just missed O'Brien."

"The three horsemen of the Apocalypse would be more like it."

"I thought there were four."

"Need I remind you who, or what, the fourth horseman was?" Jacqueline followed Betsy into the hall. Dust lay thick on lovely old furniture and a single bulb shone from one of the Limoges sconces. All the other bulbs were burned out.

"You want a beer or something?" Betsy asked hospitably.

"No, thanks. Just a brief chat."

"Come on upstairs then. I want to show you something."

"I'm surprised you still live here," Jacqueline said, removing her hand from the stair rail. It felt sticky. "Why don't you get yourself a pad in the Village or someplace equally chic?"

"Believe it or not, this is cheaper. The trust pays all the expenses. That means I can give most of my income to WUFAS and the other organizations I belong to. If I moved, I'd have to pay rent. Do you have any idea what apartments in Manhattan cost?"

"Then you don't own the house?" Jacqueline asked curiously.

"Oh yes, I own it. I just can't sell it." Betsy chuckled. "Mother and Dad didn't have a very high opinion of my good sense, let alone my political views. Everything's tied up in trusts. Just as well, I guess. Handling money is a bore, don't you think?"

"I wouldn't know," Jacqueline said glumly.

Betsy threw open a door and ushered Jacqueline into her bedroom. It represented her austerity stage, and the furniture had probably been taken from one of the little attic cubbyholes that had been occupied by a maid in long-gone days. An iron bedstead and a cheap pine bureau, two straight chairs and a table, bookcases made of boards and bricks, filled with paperbacks, made up the furnishings. The floor was bare. Jacqueline didn't know whether to feel pity or exasperation; Betsy's emotional development seemed to have gone into deep freeze during the sixties. It was time she grew up.

Then Betsy took something out of the closet and Jacqueline's mouth dropped open. For once she was taken completely by surprise.

Betsy held the garment up high so its skirt wouldn't touch the dusty floor.

In comparison to the elaborately embroidered and beaded gown Laurie had made for Valentine this dress was almost austere. Yet the infinitesimal pleats covering every inch of the silk tunic and straight skirt shouted the name of the designer as loudly as Worth's tailoring had proclaimed his work.

"Fortuny," Jacqueline breathed "There's one like it at the Costume Institute—it's coral instead of turquoise, but . . ."

"I know. I saw it last night. Then I remembered Mother had one like it. I dug it out of a trunk in the attic when I got home. It had been rolled up in a wad for forty years, but you'd think it had just been cleaned and pressed."

"Those magic pleats were one of Fortuny's trademarks."

Jacqueline's admiration for the Worth copy had been

simple artistic appreciation. The emotion she felt now could only be described as hunger—no, lust would be closer to the mark. The dress would look absolutely divine on her. She remembered Betsy's mother—a handsome woman of impeccable taste, whose daughter's slovenly clothes had driven her wild. Mrs. Markham had been about Jacqueline's height. And the color would be sensational with auburn hair. . . .

Jacqueline swallowed. "How much do you want for it?"

"I wouldn't sell Mother's clothes," Betsy said in a shocked voice. "I thought I'd wear it tonight. What do you think?"

She held the dress against her.

Jacqueline glanced at the heavy bronze bookend supporting a stack of historical romances, and wondered if anyone had ever committed murder over a dress. The Fortuny was three inches too long for Betsy; it trailed on the floor. Her spare boyish figure would suit the straight lines well enough, but that cropped gray hair and those bony, freckled arms . . .

With an effort she got her mind off frivolities and back onto the serious business for which she had come. "I didn't know you were planning to attend the ball."

"I thought I might as well. I haven't got a date, though. I asked O'Brien, but he said he was busy. How about that boyfriend of yours—the professor?"

"He's taking Jean." Jacqueline sat down on the bed. Both chairs were occupied, one by a pair of grubby jeans, the other by stacks of mimeographed literature announcing a march on Washington for purposes unspecified.

"Damn. Oh, well. How about if I go with you? We've done it before."

Jacqueline considered the advantages and disadvantages of this plan. Both involved O'Brien's reaction to having Betsy with them. After some deliberation she decided it would serve him right. "Fine," she said. "Come to the hotel about seven-thirty and we'll get dressed there. And, Betsy . . ."

"Huh?" Betsy was trying to get a look at herself in the small mirror over the bureau.

"Don't do anything to the dress till I see it on you," Jacqueline said desperately. "I'll take care of any necessary alterations. Don't even cut off a loose thread. Promise?"

"Okay."

Jacqueline breathed a sigh of relief. Betsy was a woman of her word. She was also capable of taking a pair of shears and whacking the priceless garment off at the knees if it got in her way. A shudder ran through Jacqueline's body at the thought.

Watching Betsy squat and bend in a vain attempt to see her entire figure in a mirror six inches square she said, "Never in all the years I knew you were you interested in clothes. In fact, I don't think I've ever seen you in a dress—except for that ghastly disguise at the cocktail party. Are you in love, or are you abandoning feminism?"

"Clothes don't have anything to do with feminism," Betsy said scornfully. "There's no conflict between women's rights and looking nice."

Since this obvious fact was one Jacqueline had known for twenty years, she could not disagree. Still, there had to be some reason for Betsy's volte-face. "So what brought it on at this particular moment? Romantic balls aren't your scene."

"It's my last chance to get some dirt on Aunt Hattie and the piglets." The answer was so glib Jacqueline suspected Betsy felt the need to rationalize her decision. "After all," Betsy went on, "Dubretta never found what she was looking for, did she? There's been nothing in the papers."

"If she found anything, it's gone for good." Jacqueline saw no reason to go into detail. It was typical of Betsy that she had never inquired into the reason for Laurie's attack on her. Crazy people do crazy things; that was enough for Betsy.

There was another reason for her lack of curiosity. Jacqueline wondered whether it had occurred to O'Brien. She felt sure it had; O'Brien didn't miss much. But she refused to take it seriously. Betsy was on her list of suspects, but only for the sake of detectival completeness. Betsy had no reason to purloin Dubretta's notebook. Betsy couldn't have been the unknown assailant who had pushed her into the street and escaped unseen. Her chief talent was hitting people over the head with signs.

Betsy continued to stare at her reflection. In a different, more serious voice she said, "I'd like to find out what she was after. Not only for the reasons you might think. I liked Dubretta."

"So did I," said Jacqueline.

Her last call of the day was on Victor von Damm. That harassed celebrity had just emerged from the final symposium, one in which the leading publishers of historical romances boasted about their past successes and described their future plans. Jacqueline cut him out from the herd and announced her intention of talking with him.

"Come up to my room," Victor said, running a hand through his waving black hair and giving the hovering ladies a malignant look. "It's the only place where I can get a minute's peace."

Jacqueline waved at the well-bred lady from Boston, who was still in devoted attendance, before following Victor. "They seem very well behaved," she remarked. "I don't see anybody trying to tear the buttons off your shirt or whack off a piece of your ambrosial locks. What are you complaining about, anyway? I thought adoring fans were part of the deal."

"They look at me all the time," Victor said hysterically. "They hover and they stare at me. If I go to the bar for a drink, there are always three or four of them at the next table. Looking."

"You have to expect people to stare if you walk around dressed like that." Victor's billowing white shirt was showing signs of wear. "Is that the only shirt you've got?" Jacqueline asked critically.

"Hattie's too cheap to supply unnecessary changes of costume," Victor said. "Here we are. Come in."

His room was an example of Hattie's penny-pinching habits; since he wasn't expected to entertain fans or publishers, it was an ordinary hotel bedroom, without sitting room or bar. Victor went straight to his suitcase and took out a bottle. "Want a drink?"

Jacqueline shook her head. Victor uncapped the bottle and raised it to his lips.

"Great," Jacqueline said. "Go on, turn yourself into an alcoholic. You are already a fraud and a hypocrite and a chiseler and—"

"You don't understand." Victor put the cap on the bottle and put the bottle down. "This is it. Tonight is the last public appearance of Victor von Damm. I'm through."

"Oh, yeah?"

"I mean it." Victor dropped into a chair. His saturnine features relaxed, and Joe Kirby made a tentative appearance. "It's funny," he said, in Joe's lighter, more diffident tones, "the closer I get to breaking out, the harder it is to hang on. You'd think that after two years of this crap I could handle a few more hours."

"Maybe," Jacqueline suggested, "you're suffering from a sense of impending doom."

Joe gazed sadly at her. "You don't like me, do you, Mrs. Kirby?"

"I don't trust you. You're weak, Victor-Joe; weak, vacillating, and undependable. You've got Sue on a string and you treat her like a yo-yo—up one minute, down the next. You don't have the guts to act on your resolution. Why should I assume you mean it this time?"

"Things have changed. Hattie's agreed to let me go."

"I see." Jacqueline's voice dripped sarcasm. "You've been struggling to free yourself from the web. You're the helpless fly and Hattie is the spider."

"Hattie has a contract," Joe said. "You ought to see that contract, Mrs. Kirby. It commits me for the rest of my life to anything Hattie wants."

"Why did you sign it?"

"I was broke." After a moment Joe added morosely, "I was also stupid."

"Contracts have that effect on some people," Jacqueline said. The slight softening of her voice made Joe look up hopefully.

"Mrs. Kirby, I really mean it, about getting out. Hattie owns the Von Damm name. I've never had anything to do with the writing end of it, I was just a hired front man. She can get somebody else before Victor's next public appearance."

"A look-alike?" Jacqueline appeared dubious. Then her eyes narrowed thoughtfully and her glasses began to slip. James would have recognized the look; Jacqueline's outrageous imagination was going into action.

"You know what might work," she said. "Victor von Damm could die. Heroically. Saving a girl from being raped or a child from being run over—"

Joe recoiled. "Hey," he protested.

"Oh, you wouldn't really die. It would be a fake. Then Hattie could discover a whole trunk of Victor von Damm manuscripts and publish one or two a year—in black covers with a tasteful 'In Memoriam' notice. Victor von Damm could become the idol of a cult. Look what happened to Valentino and James Dean and Elvis Presley. Grieving women swathed in mourning would visit your grave on the anniversary of your death. . . . Souvenir stands selling books and locks of hair—you could send a fresh supply of hair now and then—make sure she pays you for it—little bottles of the water in which your broken, bleeding body was bathed. . . ."

"Jesus Christ," Joe gasped. "Mrs. Kirby, you're

worse than Hattie. That's the sickest, most ghoulish thing I ever . . . I wonder if it would work."

"Work?" Jacqueline glowed with creative enthusiasm. "It would be the greatest publicity stunt of the century. I'm going to sell it to Hattie. And I'll make her pay through the nose."

"You'd have to have a body," Joe said uneasily. "You can't have a heroic death without a body."

Jacqueline waved this minor detail aside. "That's no problem. I can think of three or four ways around it already, and I haven't really put my mind to work on it yet. Maybe Victor could be kidnapped while rescuing a girl or a child. The body would never be found. Instead of a grave we'd build a cenotaph. Or he could fall overboard on a cruise or disappear while visiting some trouble spot—Hattie could identify a body. . . . Good heavens, Joe, the possibilities are endless."

"You terrify me," Joe said sincerely.

"Hattie would be a fool not to jump at the idea," Jacqueline assured him. "And that would get you off the hook—if you really want to get off it."

"I do. Sue and I are going to get married."

Jacqueline wrenched her mind away from the dazzling vision of Victor von Damm's heroic death. "I'll talk to Hattie then. On one condition. I can understand how you got into Hattie's clutches—though I think you're a wimp to have submitted so long. I can also understand why you didn't want Sue mixed up with her. What I don't understand is your vacillation. One minute you appear to defy the old witch, then she reels you back in. Was it only the contract that kept you subservient? And why has she changed her mind about releasing you?"

"You never know what Hattie is thinking," Joe said gloomily. "But I think her major concern was this conference. It turned out to be the breaking point for me. I'd made publicity appearances, on talk shows, autographings, book and author luncheons, that sort of thing. I didn't mind them. It was like putting on a performance—acting a part for a couple of hours and then taking off the makeup and going home. This was different. Hattie was on my back every damned minute. Then I met Sue. She's so honest, so innocent—there isn't an ounce of sham in her. She made the whole thing look so shabby and cheap. . . ."

Jacqueline could see why Joe had never been involved in the writing end of Victor von Damm. Even by the dubious standards of historical romance, his style was insipid. "All right, I'll see what I can do," she promised. "I came to ask you about something, Joe. Have you seen Lieutenant O'Brien today?"

"Yes, he was here a couple of hours ago. Is something wrong, Mrs. Kirby?"

Jacqueline unlocked her clenched teeth. "No, nothing. He told you about Laurie?"

Joe nodded. "I'm sorry. Poor kid must have been nuts to wander around the park late at night. But maybe she's better off. She never had much of a chance."

"Hmph," said Jacqueline. "Did O'Brien inquire into your whereabouts last night?"

"I was with Sue. You probably know better than I do what time she got in. We weren't watching clocks." Seeing the gravity of Jacqueline's expression, Joe's reminiscent smile faded. "O'Brien said it was just routine. Was it?"

"No. Laurie was killed by the same person who murdered Dubretta Duberstein."

Joe's face turned a sickly shade of gray. "You're kidding."

"I don't kid about things like murder."

"Yes, but . . . Oh my God." Joe buried his face in his hands. "You've just thrown me back to the spider," he muttered.

"What do you mean?"

"That was the other hold Hattie had over me." Joe raised his head. "You know how she tried to get publicity out of Dubretta's death. It backfired; the press wouldn't go for the idea that Valentine was the intended victim. So Hattie gave up the murder stunt. That's all I thought it was—a publicity stunt. But before that she told me Dubretta's dying words accused Sue."

"What?"

"She accused Sue," Joe insisted. "You heard her too. 'It's Sue.' That's what she said. Hattie threatened to tell the police if I didn't knuckle under."

"Oh, for . . ." Jacqueline saw the shadow of Victor von Damm, nobly risking worse than death to save the woman he loved. She didn't know whether to shriek with laughter or sneer. "That's the most idiotic thing I've ever heard, Joe. Even if Dubretta did mention Sue's name—and I, who was closest, am not certain what she said—Sue had no reason to harm her. No one with an ounce of sense would pay any attention to such an accusation."

"I guess you're right," said Joe, banishing the ghost of Victor von Damm. "But Sue did have a motive for wanting to kill Valentine—at least, some people would consider it a motive. I tell you, Mrs. Kirby, you don't know what it's like dealing with Hattie Foster. She kind of hypnotizes a person, you know? You get so you believe everything she says."

"Strange," Jacqueline said. "My reaction to Hattie is precisely the reverse. I get so I don't believe anything she says."

"I guess I was a jerk."

"I guess you were."

"Now you tell me Dubretta was murdered." Joe shook his head. "I don't know what to do."

"For starters, stop believing everything you hear." Jacqueline rose. "I must be going."

Joe stared at her. "You mean I shouldn't believe you?"

"Believe this." Jacqueline pointed a stern finger. "All sorts of things are going to happen tonight. Be on your guard. Watch Sue. And be ready to do exactly what I tell you to do."

She left Joe staring bemusedly at the spot where her index finger had pointed. He was certainly a good hypnotic subject. No wonder Hattie had found him so easy to push around. It augured well for his relationship with Sue, if the girl could learn she would have to wear the pants in that branch of the Kirby family. Joe was an outstanding example of the fact that people's personalities didn't match their looks. The macho face and figure of Victor von Damm clothed a malleable, naive man who only needed someone to lead him firmly and gently into the right path.

Jacqueline was pleased with her scheme for killing Victor. In fact, she thought it was nothing short of brilliant. If only she could get an equally brilliant inspiration about the murders! There was still one vital piece of the puzzle missing, and the most aggravating part of it was that she almost had the answer. Something tickled her subconscious, like a word well known but momentarily misplaced. Something she had heard or read. The harder she tried to capture it, the farther it retreated.

When she got back to her room she heard the shower running behind the closed bathroom door. Surmising that Sue would be primping for a good long time, Jacqueline made her own arrangements. After assuming the peacock-blue robe she arranged her pillows—and Sue's—against the headboard of her bed and then lined up on the table two cardboard cartons of coffee, a hamburger wrapped in greasy paper, mustard and catsup, two chocolate bars, an apple, a pack of cigarettes, and a lighter. From her purse she took her notebook and pen. She had fallen behind with her novel. Now that the other business was settled. . . . A shadow of uneasiness crossed Jacqueline's brow. She had it worked out—well, almost worked out. What worried her was not what she was going to do with the information but whether O'Brien would cooperate with her plan.

There was nothing more she could do at the moment. She took a bite of the hamburger, wiped mustard off her chin, and began writing.

When Sue emerged from the bathroom Jacqueline was eating a chocolate bar and scribbling industriously. "Oh," Sue said brightly. "You're back."

Jacqueline glanced up. Sue was wearing a robe and a coiffure of huge pink curlers. Her eyes peered out of a mask of thick brown glop. She looked like an aboriginal witch doctor.

Jacqueline returned to her writing without bothering to reply. Sue sidled toward her and read over her shoulder. After a while she said timidly, "I don't think mammoths and copper weapons existed at the same time."

"Oona has just discovered copper," Jacqueline said, without looking up.

"Oh, yes." Sue read aloud. " 'Oona discovers copper.' "

"I'll fill that in later," Jacqueline explained abstractedly. "Do you mind not talking? I want to finish this chapter."

She filled two more pages before planting an emphatic exclamation point at the end of the last sentence. Closing the notebook, she reached for a cigarette.

"You're looking very bright and cheerful," she said.

This was an accurate description of Sue's emotional state, though how Jacqueline reached it was anybody's guess. Sue's face was completely encased in brown plaster. She sat down on the other bed and squinted at Jacqueline through the mud.

"I haven't had a chance to tell you—you were out all day. Guess what?"

"You and Joe are getting married," Jacqueline said thoughtlessly.

"Oh. Did you see Joe today?"

"About an hour ago. I think we've figured out a way to detach Hattie's claws from his gizzard."

"Oh? But he said Hattie had agreed—"

"Hattie's word is not her bond. This should make it a sure thing. Sue, do you know what you're doing? You only met the man a few days ago."

"You sound like my mother," said Sue, smiling.

"Damn."

"Oh, I like it," Sue assured her.

"You mistake my meaning," said Jacqueline.

"I couldn't be more certain. Joe is wonderful. He's flying back with me, to meet my folks and find out about applying to grad school." Sue sighed ecstatically. "To think that only day before yesterday I was wishing I'd never come to the conference."

"What are you going to do about your book?"

"I'm glad you asked me that, because I'd like to get your opinion." The solemn voice and the intent blue eyes peering through the muddy mask were almost too much for Jacqueline's sobriety, but she politely refrained from laughing. Sue went on, "I'm going to use my own title. And I'm going to take out all the parts the editor made me put in. You know, the parts—"

"The dirty bits?" Jacqueline suggested.

"Yes. That was never part of my book. If I can't sell it on its own merits, then I won't pander to people's depraved tastes."

"That's very nice," Jacqueline said. Betsy would be pleased; she had made one convert.

"I'm glad you agree." Sue's glance strayed to the notebook in which Jacqueline had been writing, but she did not point out that Jacqueline was not living up to her own standards: The manuscript had a good many dirty bits.

On her part, Jacqueline refrained from telling Sue of the dire events she expected would occur that evening. Why spoil the girl's pleasure? It would be as bad as kicking a baby chick. Sue had never been a serious suspect in Jacqueline's estimation. Sue was the heroine, and Jacqueline had always resented mystery writers who pinned the crime on the heroine, thus depriving the reader of the happy ending he or she had every right to expect.

She crammed the rest of the candy bar into her mouth just as the telephone rang. "Hello," she mumbled into it.

"Who's this?"

Jacqueline swallowed. "Me, of course. James?"

"Of course."

"Well?"

"The tests were all negative."

"What?"

"The tests were all—"

"I heard you. What did he look for?"

"The usual. Strychnine, arsenic, prussic acid—"

"James, you silly man, it couldn't have been any of those. Didn't you observe Dubretta's symptoms?"

"No, I did not, as you are well aware. If you knew what poison wasn't used, why didn't you tell me? This is the most inept excuse for a criminal investigation I've ever seen."

Jacqueline had to admit there was some justice in his complaint. Nor did this seem the moment to tell him that everything he had done that day had been a waste of time.

"It was essential that we tidy up the loose ends," she

said vaguely, and then, before James could ask what the devil she meant, she went on, "Did you interview the suspects?"

"Nobody has an alibi."

"Is that all you can say?"

"That's what it comes down to. It took me the whole damned afternoon to learn that much. Nobody was home the first time I went round. I don't know why I couldn't simply telephone them."

"I told you why. It's very important to watch faces and judge the subtle nuances of voices when they answer significant questions."

"The nuances were too subtle for me," James grumbled. "I didn't track down that weird libber friend of yours till almost five. I asked her where she was last night between midnight and one A.M. and she laughed and suggested I dump Jean and escort her to the ball tonight."

"I guess you just can't help being irresistible, James. What did Betsy say?"

"She said she couldn't see any reason why I couldn't take her."

"No, no. Where was she last night?" Jacqueline wasn't really interested, but poor James needed to feel useful.

"She said she was at home, watching 'Kojak.' It's her favorite program."

"Did you ask her about the plot?"

"I did, as a matter of fact," James said smugly. "And what's more, I checked it in the television guide. Of course she could have done the same thing. Or seen it the first time around. It was a rerun."

"That's very clever, James. You did good. I'm proud of you. Good-bye."

"Wait a minute. You haven't told me—"

"I have to make another call, James. I'll see you later."

James's mention of Betsy had reminded her that she had forgotten something, and for reasons she would have hated to admit. Vanity, vanity, saith the sage, and he had saith right. She had been so fascinated by Betsy's fabulous gown she had neglected to pursue the purpose for which she had visited her friend. It would probably turn out to be another dead end, but she couldn't afford to overlook any possibilities. Reaching for the telephone, she dialed Betsy's number.

The phone rang for some time without result. Jacqueline was about to give up when she heard the receiver being picked up.

"Where the hell were you?" she demanded.

"In the attic. You know, there are lots of things in that trunk of Mother's. I found a fan and a pair of satin slippers—they're too small for me, but—"

"Never mind that," said Jacqueline, with a catch in her voice. Her feet were several sizes smaller than Betsy's. Vanity, vanity, all is vanity, she reminded herself. "I forgot to ask you, Betsy. When Laurie jumped you yesterday, you said she kept mumbling to herself while she was searching your knapsack. What did she say?"

"How do you expect me to remember?" Betsy said indignantly. "I tell you, Jake, your hearing doesn't function too well when you've just been socked in the eye and you've got three hundred pounds sitting on your backside."

"Try," Jacqueline urged.

"Well . . . She talked about Valentine—how sweet and angelic and beautiful she was, that sort of slosh. She said that right after she hit me. I started to get up, and she sat on me and started calling me names. One of them was yellow-bellied sapsucker."

"Good heavens."

"It's amazing how insulting some ornithological terms can be," Betsy mused. "You break that name down, and apply it to a human being. . . . I guess she had yellow on the brain. Yellow-bellied coward was another of her charming epithets."

"Yellow," Jacqueline repeated.

"Is that all? I've got a lot to do if I want to get to your place by seven-thirty. See you then, Jake."

Betsy hung up. Jacqueline sat holding the telephone until a mechanical voice began to drone, "Please hang up. You have left the instrument off the hook. Please hang up."

Sue took the telephone from her paralyzed hand and replaced it. "What's wrong?" she asked anxiously. "Was it bad news?"

"News," Jacqueline mumbled. "News . . . By God, that's it!" She leaped up and tore off her robe. She was dressed and halfway to the door before Sue recovered. "Where are you going? What's the matter? Can I do anything?"

Jacqueline stopped. "Time. What's the time?" She looked at her watch, as did Sue; they chanted in chorus, "Five twenty-five." "The library will probably be closed," Jacqueline went on. "Pray God some of the bookstores stay open later."

She stormed out the door, leaving Sue staring.

Forty-five minutes later she returned, transformed. Her smile could only be described as smug, and her eyes glowed.

"Is everything all right?" Sue asked.

Jacqueline looked surprised. "Yes, of course. Why do you ask?" She tossed her purse onto the bed and stretched like a contented cat. "I'd better get ready. It will soon be time for the ball! La da da da da da dadadada, la da da da . . ." To the strains of "Tales from the Vienna Woods" she waltzed into the bathroom and closed the door.

At precisely seven-thirty Betsy appeared with the Fortuny gown slung carelessly over her arm. The dress and the brown paper bag she carried made her look like an unusually healthy specimen of bag lady after a successful raid on a trash bin.

Jacqueline rescued the dress and hung it carefully on a hanger. From her shopping bag Betsy extracted her latest discoveries—a pair of beautifully cut satin slippers that had been dyed to match the dress, long white gloves (cracked and faded to a sickly tan), and an ostrich-feather fan, with half the feathers reduced to bare sticks. Jacqueline got rid of the fan and the gloves, over Betsy's vehement protests. Then she picked up one of the shoes.

"You weren't planning to wear these, were you?"

"I thought I could cut out the toes," Betsy explained,

removing a pair of wire-cutting shears from her knap-sack.

"You touch those shoes and I'll stab you to the heart," Jacqueline said sincerely. "Haven't you got anything else?"

Betsy extended a foot. She was wearing sneakers. Jacqueline groaned. "Sue!"

Sue emerged from the bathroom. She had removed the mask. One eye was made up, complete with liner, lid color, crease color, highlighter, false eyelashes and a partridge in a pear tree. "Hello," she said uncertainly.

"Hi," Betsy replied. "Do you know you've only got one set of eyelashes?"

"What size shoe do you wear?" Jacqueline de-manded.

It was a forlorn hope. Sue's feet were as small as the rest of her, and Betsy's had spread, from miles of marching.

"Go buy some," Jacqueline ordered.

"The stores are closed." Betsy reclined ungracefully on the bed. "I'll just wear my sneakers."

The intensity of Jacqueline's response got her off the bed in a hurry. "I have a pair of white sandals someplace," she offered. "If I can find them."

"Find them." Jacqueline shoved her toward the door.

Betsy left. "I don't know why I bother," Jacqueline exclaimed dramatically.

"You're a very kind, sweet person," Sue said. The look Jacqueline directed at her sent her trotting back into the bathroom.

The next time she came out she had the second set of eyelashes in place. Scissors in hand, Jacqueline was

working on her borrowed ball gown. Bows and artificial flowers went flying as she snipped them off and
tossed them away. By the time she finished, the dress
had been reduced to its essentials—a white satin-and-
silk net creation with a bouffant skirt and narrow
shoulder straps.

"It's very pretty," Sue said. "But now that you've
taken all those extra things off, it isn't funny any
more."

"Funny is not what I'm after," Jacqueline said.

Dainty and delectable in a Watteau-style shepherdess
gown, complete with crook and stuffed lamb, Sue left
to meet Joe while Jacqueline was still trying to make
Betsy look like something other than a transvestite
who had robbed a museum. Makeup only made her
look worse and the best that could be said for the white
plastic sandals was that they were a slight improve-
ment over the sneakers. By lifting the skirt at the waist,
where the resultant bulge was hidden by the tunic,
Jacqueline managed to conceal the sandals while
shortening the dress enough so Betsy wouldn't trip
over it. She contemplated the result without enthusiasm.

"It's your hair," she grumbled. "Who cut it, the local
barber?"

"I have that wig," Betsy said, entering into the spirit
of the thing. "You know, the one I wore to the cocktail
party."

"Don't be vulgar." Jacqueline pondered. "Wait a
minute. I saw something of Sue's that might help."

Betsy submitted to the curling iron with unexpected

docility, even though Jacqueline singed her neck twice. A couple of feathers plucked from the defunct fan were pinned onto a black velvet ribbon (also purloined from Sue), which was tied filletwise over the mass of short curls. Jacqueline's dour expression relaxed. "It's not bad," she said, in a congratulatory tone.

The congratulations were for herself, but Betsy didn't know that. She beamed at her reflection. "I look pretty good, don't I?"

"Go stand over there in the corner and keep quiet," Jacqueline ordered. "I've only got ten minutes to get dressed. If I know O'Brien, he'll be here on the dot."

"O'Brien? You're going with him? Why, that rat fink! Why didn't he say so?"

"We're both going with him." Jacqueline dropped her gown over her head.

"I wonder what he's going to wear."

"Can't you guess?" Jacqueline's hands moved quickly, braiding her hair into a thick club at the back of her head. Gleaming coils and flirtatious curls framed her face in a coiffure reminiscent of some past era Betsy could not immediately identify. Jacqueline fastened a wide blue ribbon across the bodice of the dress from one shoulder to the opposite hip and completed the ensemble by putting atop her head a rhinestone tiara she had bought at the dime store that morning. *"Voilà,"* she said.

"Empress Eugénie," Betsy exclaimed. "No—wait a minute—I think I've got it. . . . Alexandra! The queen of Edward the Seventh."

"Very good."

"Well, I was a history major, after all. It's the hair that does it. Alexandra had red hair too."

"Auburn," Jacqueline said firmly. "That's the best I can do at short notice. And," she added, as there was a knock at the door, "just in time. That must be O'Brien."

She went to answer it. Betsy trotted after her, chuckling and speculating. "Charles the Second? He's got the face for it—swarthy, cynical. . . . Or George Washington? I'd love to see him in a white wig."

"You're on the wrong track," Jacqueline said. She threw the door open and stood back.

O'Brien took the pipe out of his mouth, removed his hat, and bowed. The pipe was a meerschaum; the hat was a deerstalker; his heavy coat was caped and reached to mid-calf.

"What else?" Jacqueline asked rhetorically. She extended her hand in a gesture whose regality was not one whit lessened by the horn-rimmed glasses riding low on her nose. "Good evening, Mr. Holmes."

Chapter 9

O'Brien voiced no objection to Betsy's joining them, even when she repeated her inane reference to the Three Musketeers. Jacqueline had an explanation ready in case he did object: this was not a social occasion, as both of them were well aware. She was vexed at having no opportunity to explain this.

Their costumes won a few amused glances as they crossed the lobby, but as soon as they entered the other hotel they became part of an equally unusual throng. It was rumored that some genuine notables would be present, including fans of the genre who had hitherto concealed their deplorable addiction, and Jacqueline heard snatches of speculation mixed with the now familiar shoptalk.

"I thought you were contemporary," said one young woman to another, whose ancient Egyptian costume certainly justified her companion's doubts.

"I'm changing lines," was the response. "Contemp doesn't pay as well."

". . . the First Lady?" cried a stately matron, her

rhinestone parure glittering with the rapid rise and fall of her agitated bosom.

". . . great fan of Victor's," said her friend breathlessly.

Other guesses were bandied back and forth. The star of the latest nighttime soap hit, *Schenectady?* Visiting royalty? A Du Pont, a Kennedy, a Rockefeller?

The decorations of the ballroom represented the culminating triumph of bad taste. Everything that was not pink to begin with had been painted that color, including the grand piano. The dinner jackets of the orchestra flashed with pink sequins. Bowers of plastic greenery and artificial roses bulged out from the walls. There were pink bulbs in the chandeliers. They shed a flattering light over the ladies' complexions, but when O'Brien stood under one of them he looked as if he were about to have an apoplectic attack.

Happily unaware of this effect, he looked at Jacqueline. "Well, Mrs. K., here we are. Would you care to let me in on your plans?"

"First of all, I think you should call me Jacqueline. We're trying to create the impression that this is an ordinary date."

"Oh, is that what we're trying to create? Don't you think this rather spoils the effect?" He glanced at Betsy, who was clinging to his arm.

"It spoils something," Jacqueline agreed. "Betsy, get lost for a while."

"Where?"

"I don't care. Go sit in a bower and be a rosebud. Cruise. There's a nice-looking man over there who appears to be unattached—the one who's dressed as Julius Caesar."

"He's bald," said Betsy.

"So was Julius Caesar. So is Kojak. Go."

Betsy wandered off. "She looks different tonight," O'Brien said, mildly puzzled.

"I should hope so," said Jacqueline, with a vivid recollection of her labors. "Now. What has happened since I last talked to you?"

"Another rape, two murders, five breaking and entering—"

"You know what I mean."

"Ask me questions, Mrs.—Jacqueline."

"The autopsy on Laurie?"

"We have a very astute coroner. He deduced almost at once that her skull had been fractured."

"I don't suppose he bothered to test for drugs," said Jacqueline, with visible self-control.

"Oddly enough, he did. Negative. No hash, no pot, no heroin, no coke, no PCP—"

"Good."

"Good?"

"Did you find her purse?"

"Purses are annoyingly prominent in this affair," O'Brien complained. "By the way, that suitcase you're toting doesn't go with your costume."

"I need it. Well?"

"We found it. In a trash can several hundred yards away."

"What was in it?"

"No money, no drugs."

"No medication of any kind?"

"A small tin of aspirin and a roll of antacids," O'Brien said gravely. "Also two candy bars and a bag of peanuts."

"Hmm."

"Okay, I've done my part. Now it's your turn."

"Hmm?"

"What are your plans?"

"Oh, that. I'm going to identify the murderer of Dubretta and Laurie. You'll have to handle the arrest."

"Well, well. You know who it is?"

"Yes."

"Can you prove it, Mrs. Kirby—Jacqueline?"

"I know how it was done," Jacqueline said. "I can prove that part of it. Pinning it on the murderer could be just a wee bit tricky."

"Please," O'Brien said prayerfully. "Please don't tell me you're depending on the murderer's confession. All the suspects sitting around while you sum up the case and suddenly turn, pointing: 'It was you, Dangerous Dan. Confess!' Please don't tell me that."

"It won't be like that."

"Oh yes, it will. Why do you think I'm here, Jacqueline?"

"Because you think Dubretta was murdered."

"Because I had a hunch you were going to pull some dumb stunt. Despite the fact that you are the most exasperating female I've ever met, I don't want you to become corpse number three."

"Ah," Jacqueline crowed. "You do think Dubretta—"

"What I think doesn't matter. There is the little matter of evidence. It's only in detective stories that the murderer admits his guilt and politely takes poison, saving the cop in charge the trouble of gathering proof that will convince a grand jury he's got a case—much less a case that will result in a conviction. Your brilliant deductions don't include that little item, do they? And if you think you're going to needle the murderer into attacking you so I can catch him or her in the act, forget it. I'm going to stick to you like the paper on the wall."

"That's just what I had in mind," said Jacqueline, batting her eyelashes. "Sssh. The ball is about to begin."

A fanfare of trumpets (two) hushed the babble of conversation. The leader of the orchestra advanced to the microphone in a pink glimmer; not only the lapels of his jacket but its entire surface was covered with sequins. "Ladies and gentlemen," he began, glancing at the paper he held. "Uh—pray make way for the (What the hell is this word? Oh.) for the appearance of the Queen of Love, who will open the ball."

Turning, he lifted his baton. The orchestra burst into a march.

Heads turned and people milled about uncertainly as they tried to locate the doorway whence the Queen of Love would emerge. Hattie had planned a Grand March but, as was typical of her arrangements, she had neglected to make sure the floor would be cleared. The head of the procession was immediately swallowed up by confused spectators, until eventually people moved back, leaving the center of the room free. From the melee emerged Hattie, flushed and scowling, on the arm of Victor von Damm.

Living up to her self-proclaimed image of "For me

it's too late," Hattie was a miracle of frumpiness, from her disheveled gray hair to her limp satin gown in a dismal shade of ashes of roses. What the costume, if any, was meant to represent, Jacqueline could not imagine.

The gorgeousness of Victor compensated for Hattie's dowdiness. His high black boots and white pants were so tight, it seemed impossible he could bend his knees, and indeed his stride suggested that of a military funeral. His tunic was a more gilded version of the one he had worn the day before. Fur trimmed the jacket slung from one shoulder.

Behind them, at a discreet distance dictated by the sword that was part of Victor's costume, came Valentine and the Earl. White tie and tails, fake diamond studs, and the ribbon of some undoubtedly apocryphal order distinguished the latter. At the sight of him Jacqueline swore under her breath. When O'Brien glanced curiously at her she shook her head.

Valentine was wearing Laurie's dress. Her beauty would have shone through rags and dirt, but the gown set it off as a jeweler's creation sets off a fabulous gem. Among the other costumes, which were all hired or homemade, Laurie's loving creation stood supreme.

Across the room in the front row of spectators Jacqueline recognized Meredith. She was not in costume, unless her faded jeans and man's shirt could be considered an attempt at something of the sort. Jacqueline suspected it was a demonstration of Meredith's contempt for the whole affair. But there was a look of grudging satisfaction on the girl's face as she watched the shining loveliness glide past. Jacqueline nudged

O'Brien. She had to nudge twice; like that of every other man in the room, his expression was one of unconscious hunger as he looked at Valentine.

"There's Meredith," she whispered. "Laurie's—"

"I see her."

"I wonder how she got the money for the ticket."

O'Brien made no reply. "Did you by any chance find Laurie's ticket in her purse?" Jacqueline asked.

"I thought one of the kids might as well use it," O'Brien said. "They paid enough for it."

Hattie climbed laboriously onto the stage and grabbed the mike. Her audience lost interest after she had introduced the evening's mystery guests—the wife of a congressman no one had ever heard of ("a vote is a vote, honey, and at least these people can read") and a minor actor in a daytime soap opera. The restiveness of her listeners finally warned Hattie to bring her speech to a close. "The Queen of Love will open the ball," she cried.

The orchestra began "The Blue Danube," and Valentine and the Earl took the floor. Jacqueline shook her head. "Trite. And it's damned hard to dance to."

It was, especially at the funereal tempo set by the orchestra. However, here the Earl came into his own, and Jacqueline understood why he had been picked for the role. A pink spotlight wavered and finally found the pair; and as the shining figures circled and glided, there was a moment of sheer romance. Valentine's skirts swung out; her hair was like a nimbus. Then Hattie shouted, "Everybody dance," and the spell was broken.

Few people accepted the invitation. Women outnumbered men by at least ten to one. Jacqueline, who loved to waltz, looked hopefully at O'Brien. He shook his head, the slashes in his cheeks deepening.

"Sorry, your majesty. I'm afraid I can't oblige."

"So few men know how to waltz."

"I waltz divinely," said O'Brien. "But not in this out-fit."

"Why don't you take off your coat?"

"It's part of the costume."

Jacqueline's frustration was increased when she caught sight of Jean rapturously circling in James's arms. James was in the full regalia of a Scottish chief. He was deplorably vain about his legs, and his dips and whirls were designed to make his kilt flare out. The maneuver also had the unfortunate effect of winding Jean's voluminous pantaloons and veils around both of them, and finally James had to stop to unwind them from his body. It was no accident that he guided his partner toward the spot where Jacqueline was standing with O'Brien. He pretended not to see her but Jean, flushed with pleasure and pink light, looked straight into her friend's eyes and smirked.

"Would you like to sit down?" O'Brien asked cour-teously.

"If you won't dance, you could at least buy me a drink."

"Perhaps a ladylike glass of punch?"

"A ladylike glass of booze would be more like it. There's probably a cash bar. Hattie wouldn't pass up a chance to make a buck."

"The Blue Danube" was succeeded by one of the *Fledermaus* waltzes. A few more dancers ventured onto the floor. Jacqueline caught sight of Betsy in the reluctant grasp of Julius Caesar, and Sue, drifting dreamily in Victor's arms. Valentine was dancing with her manager. They made a surprisingly congruous couple, despite Max's bald head and paunch, and the fact that the two were almost the same height. On the dance floor Max was transformed. He lacked the Earl's professional correctness, but his waltzing had panache. He was not in costume, but in regulation evening dress.

Jean and James swung by again, both ostentatiously ignoring their wallflower friend. O'Brien asked again if Jacqueline wanted to sit down. She repeated her earlier suggestion. O'Brien conceded that it might not be a bad idea.

They found the bar without difficulty. Signs inappropriately adorned with pink paper hearts pointed the way. Business was brisk, and all the tables were occupied. At one, Jacqueline saw Emerald Fitzroy in a Marie Antoinette wig and panniered gown. With her was the woman agent Jacqueline had met at the luncheon. Their heads were close together.

O'Brien joined the line waiting to be served and Jacqueline stood aside. Before long she saw another familiar face. The Earl looked as if he were glued to the bar. He was drinking champagne, and by bribery or some other means he had captured the undivided attention of one of the bartenders. His glass was filled as soon as he drained it, which he did as soon as it was filled. Jacqueline couldn't decide what fascinated her more, the rapidity of his arm movements or the utter blankness of his face. Except for the opening and closing of his mouth, not a muscle moved, and it remained equally impassive when he fell forward, with the slow, inexorable movement of a felled tree, into the arms of Emerald Fitzroy. The table fell over. The agent jumped to her feet. Emerald sat gaping with the Earl draped peacefully across her lap. Someone screamed, "My God! He's dead!"

O'Brien reached the fallen man an instant before Jacqueline. Kicking the table out of the way, he lowered the Earl to the floor. Emerald began to shriek. Jacqueline shook her. "Stop that. He isn't dead."

"Drunk as a skunk," O'Brien agreed. "Boiled as a lobster. Come on, Pierre, open your baby blues." He slapped the Earl's cheeks. There was no response, except that the man's lips curved into a smile.

"You know him?" Jacqueline asked.

"Sure. He dances at one of those topless-bottomless bars on the East Side. The boys run him in every couple of months. Wake up, baby. That's it."

The Earl opened one eye, saw O'Brien bending over him, shuddered, and closed it again. "Go 'way," he mumbled. "I didn't do nothin'."

"Drunk and disorderly," said O'Brien amiably.

Both the Earl's eyes opened. They were wide and indignant. "Wasn't disorderly. See . . ." His hands moved feebly, presumably indicating that he was fully clothed.

Someone had notified Hattie of her protégé's collapse. She pushed through the ring of spectators, her lips set and her eyes black with fury. She made one game attempt to save the situation. "He's been taken ill. One of those hereditary weaknesses like you find in old families. . . . Let me help you to your room, your Grace."

The Earl giggled. "I'd rather have Victor. How 'bout it, you ugly old bag? Little extra bonus. You got me cheap enough."

"Get him out of here," Hattie snarled.

Two waiters moved in and removed the Earl. He wrapped an affectionate arm around the younger of the two and went unprotesting.

Hattie pushed wisps of hair from her perspiring face and glared at Jacqueline. "If one word of this reaches the press—"

"Act your age," Jacqueline said impatiently. "There are thirty witnesses here; you can't shut them all up. Really, Hattie, nobody gives a damn. However, I have a proposition to put to you that could be worth . . ." She glanced around. "Not here. When can I talk to you in private?"

Hattie hesitated. Her dislike of Jacqueline warred with curiosity and a certain respect. Finally she said, "The band takes a break about ten-thirty. I'll see you then."

She moved away, straightening her corsage. "That's one suspect off the list," Jacqueline said. "Why didn't you tell me you knew the Earl?"

"Why should I?"

"I never seriously considered him."

"You should have. He's undoubtedly the most unlikely suspect."

O'Brien righted the table and gestured at an empty chair. Emerald had tottered out as soon as she had been relieved of the Earl; a good many other patrons had also escaped, following the tried-and-true rule of avoiding involvement. "Sit down and I'll get you some champagne," O'Brien said. "By the way—I intend to join you when you have your meeting with Hattie."

"Of course," Jacqueline said.

After O'Brien returned with their wine they were joined by James and Jean. Seeing Jean at close range, Jacqueline realized that she was indeed wearing a long-sleeved high-necked white blouse under her be-jeweled bra. The effect was indescribable, but Jean appeared to be unaware of this; excitement and grati-fication flushed her face.

"Is it true?" she asked, gathering armfuls of pink veiling into her lap as she sat down. "Is he dead?"

"Just drunk," O'Brien said.

"Really? Well, if that isn't just like Hattie. She's so cheap! You get what you pay for, I always say."

"You knew he was a hired actor?" Jacqueline asked.

"Well, of course I knew he wasn't an earl. I'm not stupid. James, darling, I'd adore a glass of cham-pagne."

"Have mine," said Jacqueline, who had not re-quested that beverage in the first place. "I haven't touched it."

There was a dreadful pause. Jean's eyes opened so wide, the whites showed all around the dim blue pupils. O'Brien grinned.

"On the other hand," Jacqueline said deliberately, "perhaps you've had too much to drink already." She picked up the glass and drained it. "James, will you dance with me?"

"Uh—yes, of course."

As they walked toward the ballroom James took her arm. "What's going on? Did she really think—"

"I guess she was settling some old scores," Jacqueline said. So much for friendship and loyalty; perhaps Jean herself hadn't realized the depth of her long-buried resentment. She added, in a lighter voice, "Or else you plied her with liquor earlier."

"I took her to dinner. You told me to take her to dinner, so I did. And a damned boring dinner it was, too. She's no murderer. She's a dull, boring woman. And a terrible dancer."

The orchestra was playing "The Merry Widow Waltz." Jacqueline went into James's arms. "Poor James," she murmured.

They circled the room once in silence, except for Jacqueline's humming. For once James made no objection, even when she began crooning one of the more banal translations of the undistinguished lyrics. " 'Though I've heard no single word of lo-o-ove from you . . .' "

James's arm tightened. "You're a weird woman," he said fondly.

"We do dance well together, don't we?"

"We would, except for that purse." His arm pinned the straps to her body, but it kept thumping Jacqueline on the derriere. "Can't you check it or something?"

"No."

James twirled her in a flamboyant pirouette that made the purse bounce. "Still on the trail, eh?" he said.

"I have an appointment with Hattie at ten-thirty." Jacqueline grunted as the purse whacked her again. "I want everyone there, James. Especially you."

"Where?"

"Her suite. As soon as you see me leave with her, follow us. Bring Jean, and make sure Victor and Sue come too. I'll speak to them myself, but it's vital that they be there."

The music came to a languorous close. "I lo-o-ove you," Jacqueline sang.

"That's nice. Another time around?"

"Not now. I want you to—" Jacqueline broke off with a gasp, partly because she hadn't known what she was going to say next, and partly because she had seen something that demanded quick action. She started across the floor, towing James with her. "Dance with Valentine," she said rapidly. "Keep her away from the bar. It's important, James."

James's brow furrowed. "I thought you were—"

"Sssh. Please, James."

They intercepted Valentine and Max outside the bar. Jacqueline greeted them effusively. "I'm so glad you decided to wear the dress," she gushed. "It wouldn't look right on anyone else. You remember my friend, Professor Whittier, don't you? He's been admiring you from afar all evening. Would you give him a dance, Valentine?"

James glared, but could not think of any way of objecting to this high-handed act without sounding like a petulant schoolboy. "I'll dream of it through the long, cold Nebraska winter," he said, holding out his hand.

"That's a plea that would move a heart of stone," Max said, chuckling. "Go on, my dear. I know what Nebraska winters are like."

He handed Valentine over to James and turned to

Jacqueline. "We were about to stop for refreshment, Jacqueline. Will you join me instead?"

"I'd rather dance," said Jacqueline. "You waltz magnificently, Max."

"I would be honored." They moved onto the floor, Max apparently unconcerned by the fact that Jacqueline towered over him. "Very good," he said approvingly. "You also dance well, my dear. But I hope Hattie has arranged for something other than waltzes to be played. Fond as I am of them, I suspect they may pall before the end of the evening."

His eyes shifted from Jacqueline's face as Valentine drifted by, a rosy glimmer in James's hold. "She is lovely," Jacqueline said. "Have you known her long?"

His smooth step faltered as Jacqueline's purse thudded into his side. "I'm so sorry," Jacqueline said.

"My fault," Max said, gallantly. "I can't help wondering, however, why a woman of your obvious taste would carry an object that is so incongruous with your charming dress."

"Oh dear," Jacqueline said, as the purse pounded him a second time. "Perhaps we had better not dance. Let's sit the rest of this one out."

"If you like." Max led her toward one of the bowers along the wall. " 'Here will we sit and let the sounds of music creep in our ears.' "

Jacqueline gave him a long steady look. "You're fond of Shakespeare?"

"I sometimes think Europeans appreciate him more than his own countrymen do. May I get you something to drink?"

"The bar is awfully crowded."

"Not surprising. There's nothing else for most of the guests to do. The disparity between the sexes limits dancing. Hattie has grandiose ideas, but she is weak in tactical application."

"I have an idea I want to talk over with her. She's agreed to meet me during the intermission. I'd appreciate your joining us, Max. I know she values your advice."

"Only when Valentine is involved. I don't interfere in Hattie's other affairs."

The music ended. Max turned to watch James and Valentine. It seemed to Jacqueline that there was an increased intensity in his regard that evening. Concern, affection, fear? It was impossible to tell from Max's well-schooled face.

Hattie bustled up, fanning herself with her program. "I declare, everything is going wrong. The air-conditioning isn't working right and I can't get the manager to do anything about it. Where is Valentine? She has no business wandering off . . . Oh, there she is. Now where is Victor? He's got to take over as her escort. He hasn't danced with anybody except that little schoolteacher."

She gave an annoyed grunt as someone touched her on the shoulder. "What do you want? I'm busy."

Meredith stood with her feet apart and her fists on her hips. "When are you going to make the announcement?" she demanded.

"What announcement? Who the . . . Who are you?"

"Meredith is the vice-president of Valentine's fan club," Jacqueline said. "I told her you would say a few words about Laurie and the dress she made."

Meredith's quick, oblique glance at Jacqueline held little favor. She hated every adult in the world just then, with no exceptions. "Well?" she said.

"Announcement." Hattie looked thoughtful. "I suppose I could, dear. At the end of the ball. We don't want to spoil the festivities, do we?"

"There won't be anybody left by then," Meredith said. "A lot of people have left already. This is a damned boring party."

Max intervened to stop Hattie's hot retort. "You're right, Meredith. We'll be taking a break shortly to give the musicians a rest. Perhaps, Hattie, you could make the announcement at the beginning of the second half."

The compromise didn't please either combatant. Meredith shrugged and turned away, her lip curled. "Boring party," Hattie sputtered. "Of all the insolence!"

The group was joined by Jean, in pursuit of James, and O'Brien, whose motives were anybody's guess. The sight of him brought another martyred sigh from Hattie. "And you're the last straw," she informed him. "Hanging around like a skeleton at the feast."

"No one will recognize me," O'Brien said. "My disguise is impenetrable." He took his meerschaum from his pocket and clamped his teeth on the stem.

"I'm going to make this the last dance of the first half," Hattie grumbled. "Maybe by the time intermission is over, the damned air-conditioning will be fixed. Here, Valentine"—as James led the lady toward them—"I want you to dance with Victor. Where the hell is he?"

"I'm tired," Valentine protested. Her pearly skin shone with perspiration. "And I'm thirsty. I want to sit down and have something to drink."

"There aren't enough men," Hattie exclaimed, as if she had just observed this obvious fact. "You've all got to dance. All you men. Professor—"

"I'm bushed," James said, ducking behind Jacqueline to avoid Jean's outstretched hand. With an adept flick of the wrist, Jacqueline diverted the hand onto Max's arm. "Max is a wonderful dancer. And he doesn't seem a bit tired. We've been sitting down."

"I promised Valentine," Max began.

"I'll get her something to drink," said O'Brien. "I'm not dancing. What would you like, Miss Valentine?"

"Now for Victor," Hattie said briskly.

"I'll find him," Jacqueline said. "He owes me a dance."

As she had expected, she found Joe and Sue in the most remote and shadowy of the bowers, happily entwined. She had to clear her throat twice before they broke apart.

"I told Hattie I'd force you to dance with me," she said.

"You go ahead, Joe," Sue murmured, as her beloved gave her an anguished glance.

"Never mind. Just stay out of her way. I'll leave you in peace if you promise me something. This is the last dance of the first half. As soon as the musicians leave the podium, come up to Hattie's suite. Both of you."

"What for?" Joe asked.

"Don't ask questions, just do as I tell you. If you forget, I'll blow your cover to the University of Nebraska admissions office."

Departing, she heard Joe's incredulous question. "She wouldn't do that, would she?" Sue's answer was inaudible.

From one end of the room she made a final check of her suspects. Max, flickering in and out of a pink haze as Jean's veils swirled around him; Jean, blissfully unaware of his martyred look; O'Brien, bending over Valentine; Hattie on the prowl, looking for Victor; Betsy . . . Betsy wasn't dancing. Jacqueline went into the bar. Yes, Betsy was there. The gray curls had gone limp with heat and the feathered diadem had slipped over one ear.

After she had spoken to Betsy, Jacqueline took up a position near the door and waited for the music to stop. Her heart was beating a little faster than usual, and as she waited she shifted her purse into her arms, pressing it to her breast in the same gesture Dubretta had used the night she died.

Hattie gave O'Brien a hard stare when he joined the group, but did not protest until they had reached her suite and Jacqueline began to explain her scheme for disposing of Victor von Damm. Hattie stopped her with a yelp of anguish. "Are you crazy? Not here—not in front of him!"

O'Brien closed his mouth. "She's putting you on," he said weakly. "Aren't you, Mrs.—Jacqueline?"

"Of course."

"It's not a very nice joke," Hattie said. Her face quivered with greedy speculation as the idea took hold.

"Just suppose . . . Just suppose something did happen to Victor. One of those strange coincidences. The lieutenant would wonder . . ."

"I might wonder, but there wouldn't be anything I could do about it." O'Brien recovered his equanimity. "Especially if it happened out of my jurisdiction."

"Hmmm," said Hattie.

So entranced was she by her own thoughts, she didn't respond when the doorbell rang. "I'll get it," Max said.

Hattie drew Jacqueline into a corner. "I hope you'll keep in touch, dear," she murmured.

"Oh, I will—dear. I wouldn't want any of those strange coincidences happening—without me."

There was no need to say more. They understood one another perfectly.

The new arrivals were Sue and Joe. "I thought we'd drop in," Joe said unconvincingly. He looked at Jacqueline.

"Well, you can drop right out again," Hattie said. "I wasn't planning to entertain the whole damned crowd."

Still under Hattie's spell, Joe turned obediently. "No," Jacqueline said. "Sit down. Everyone sit down. This may take a while."

"What's going on?" Hattie demanded.

"Wait till the others arrive," Jacqueline said.

The doorbell rang again. O'Brien waved Max away and went to answer it. When he returned he was accompanied by Betsy, whose feathers now protruded at right angles from her left ear, and by a bewildered Roman. "Do we want Julius Caesar?" O'Brien asked.

"I don't. Do you?" Jacqueline inquired.

Caesar went willingly, once Betsy's fingers had been pried off his toga. "It's not fair," Betsy grumbled. "All the rest of you brought your friends. I don't see why I can't—"

"You're drunk," Jacqueline said critically.

"I am not. And I don't see why I can't—"

"Sit down, Betsy."

The last to arrive were Jean and James. The latter began, "I couldn't find—oh, there they are. Hello, Mrs. Foster. I hope you'll pardon the intrusion—"

"Do sit down and shut up, James," Jacqueline said sharply. "This is not a tea party."

James thrust his lady into a chair. She bounced up again. "What is this?" she demanded, her eyes darting suspiciously around the room. "James, you said Hattie asked us to come. I'm leaving."

"You're staying," Jacqueline corrected. Jean blinked and settled back.

Jacqueline took up her position beside a table near the French doors. She put her purse on the table. "The party is over," she said. "One of you won't be returning to the ball. I know who you are, and I know why you killed Dubretta and Laurie. If you would care to confess now, you'll save all of us a lot of time and trouble."

Max's chuckle broke the shocked silence. "What is that popular television game? 'Will the real killer please stand up?' "

No one else appeared to be amused. O'Brien, the only person other than Jacqueline who was still standing, looked off into space as if deep in thought. The others stared fixedly at Jacqueline.

"Oh, all right," she said. "I didn't expect you would, but I can never resist a dramatic gesture. From the beginning, then. . . ."

"On my first encounter with the historical-romance writers I was struck by the vast amount of ill will in the group. Jealousy, greed, revenge—the overabundance of motive was one of the big stumbling blocks in the case. Half the people I had met had excellent reasons for wanting to exterminate the other half.

"Dubretta was the one who died. If her hints had a basis in fact, many of the people present that evening might have wanted to silence her. Yet there were at least two other potential victims, and Valentine's hysterical claim that she was the one who was supposed to die wasn't as wild as it sounded.

"Too many motives. So the question became: How? It seemed apparent that Dubretta was poisoned. It was equally apparent that the murderer had not employed any of the conventional poisons. Arsenic, prussic acid, strychnine, morphine—none induces symptoms that could be mistaken, by a trained medical man, for those of heart failure. I therefore concluded that Dubretta *was* the intended victim. If Valentine, young and healthy, had died of what appeared to be a heart attack, an autopsy would have been performed. Only the fact that Dubretta's heart condition was common knowledge made it unlikely that there would be any questions raised about how she died. The murderer counted on this. He had to select a poison that would produce that effect.

"The answer was so evident," Jacqueline said slowly, "that in retrospect it seems incredible no one thought of it. Especially those of you who stood by and watched me help Dubretta swallow a little yellow pill. None of you seems to have realized that that tablet contained one of the deadliest of all poisonous substances."

Though she had stationed herself in a place that gave her a good overall view of the audience, Jacqueline couldn't gauge the immediate effect of her announcement on all of them simultaneously. The one face she was watching showed the reaction she had expected: a flash of comprehension and alarm, quickly masked. Most of the others gaped or gasped or started. Jean shivered. James half rose, his hands gripping the arms of his chair.

"You didn't think of that, did you?" Jacqueline asked him. "When we were making our list of suspects. You'll never be a good detective, James. Sentiment must not enter into an investigation. No one can be eliminated from suspicion."

James collapsed with a thud. "You didn't," he said, without conviction. "Did you?"

"No, of course I didn't. But that was one method you overlooked—substituting a poisoned tablet for one of Dubretta's pills."

O'Brien cleared his throat. "It wouldn't have been so easy, you know."

"Perhaps not. Dubretta guarded her purse carefully. 'Nobody puts a hand in here but me,' she told me. Still, someone might have managed it, when Dubretta was a little drunk and off her guard. . . ." Jacqueline glanced at Betsy, who stared back at her in tipsy bewilderment.

"Or when she was off guard because she was with people she trusted." Jacqueline's gaze shifted to O'Brien. He knew what she was thinking; he had been fighting the same far-out but horrifying suspicion for days. She shook her head. "Dubretta's medication was in the form of pills, not capsules, which could have been emptied and refilled. Only a professional chemist could have reproduced the exact form of the pills. There was nothing in her medication except what should have been there.

"One of the problems a poisoner faces is getting hold of the stuff. You can't pop into a drugstore and pick up a pound of arsenic. It isn't in the pharmacopoeia. In fact, you need a doctor's prescription for any potentially dangerous drug, and pharmacists are wary about filling such prescriptions. I understand it's possible to buy morphine and cocaine and the like on every street corner, but in addition to the fact I've already mentioned—that these substances produce symptoms incompatible with a diagnosis of heart failure—I doubted that my killer would risk using such a source. Drug pushers are suspicious of strangers, and they aren't reliable confederates. For a conventional middle-aged citizen—a category that included most of my suspects—it isn't easy to obtain illicit drugs.

"But there was one suspect who might well have access to such sources. Laurie belonged to an age group and a social class inclined to dabble in drugs. I did not believe that Laurie was the killer. But suppose the killer had obtained the poison from her? She was obviously taking something; her increasing disorientation and personality problems made that painfully clear. I thought of the obvious popular drugs—PCP, heroin, uppers and downers of all kinds. . . . And that," Jacqueline said expressionlessly, "that stupidity was partially responsible for Laurie's death. If I had realized sooner what was wrong with her, I might have been able to save her.

"I did realize that she could be in danger from the killer, not only because she was becoming unreliable but because she might actually have in her possession the poison that had killed Dubretta. This assumption was confirmed when her body was found. There was nothing on her or in her purse except aspirin. I felt sure her murderer had removed the poison; but it wasn't until this afternoon, when the truth finally dawned on me, that I knew what it was. Laurie wasn't on any of the standard drugs. She had been suffering from digitalis intoxication."

This time there was no betraying change of expression on the face Jacqueline watched, only the same look of disbelief that marked most of the others.

"Digitalis," Jacqueline said, "is the name given to a group of substances derived from *Digitalis purpurea*, the foxglove plant. They are used in the treatment of certain varieties of heart trouble, particularly atrial fibrillation and congestive heart failure. That was Dubretta's complaint. She was taking a form of digitalis whose generic name is digitoxin—the most poisonous of the digitalis group. Many medications are deadly poisons if the dosage isn't carefully controlled. In cases of congestive heart failure, the digitalis medication is given in two stages. The first stage is called digitalization; carefully monitored doses of the drug are given over a short period of time to get the heart functioning normally. Once this is achieved, the patient goes on a maintenance dosage. Dubretta was taking tablets three times a day, in doses of 0.15 milligrams per tablet. Tolerance for the drug varies widely. Death has been known to occur from one sixtieth of a grain, which is equivalent to—er—well, I won't bore you with arithmetic. Suffice it to say that in order to kill someone with Dubretta's pills, one would have to dump a handful of them into a glass. Not exactly inconspicuous.

"However, Dubretta was already taking almost .05 milligrams of digitalis a day. In the pharmacy manual I consulted"—Jacqueline took it from her purse and brandished it like a club—"there is a warning. 'Patients already taking digitalis preparations must not be given the rapidly digitalizing dose of digitoxin.' That dose is only .06 milligrams. The reason is obvious. On top of what she was already taking, three or four pills of a normally harmless size could kill Dubretta. As it did.

"The murderer did not get the tablets from Dubretta. He got them from Laurie—who was taking them for obesity."

"You're out of your mind," Hattie exclaimed. "I never heard—"

"It's in the book too. Digitalis is an effective diuretic, which leads to weight loss. Several people have died from taking it for that reason. And the symptoms of digitalis intoxication—a potentially dangerous overdose—are just the symptoms Laurie exhibited. Nausea and vomiting, apathy, mental confusion, delirium—

and the definitive symptom, a condition of blurred vision in which everything looks yellow." Jacqueline looked at Betsy. "You said she had yellow on the brain when she was insulting you. It was literally true. And her reference to Midas, turning everything to gold . . . She even told me she was trying to diet. I should have put the pieces together long before I did."

"I don't think he tested for digitalis," said James, to the mystification of most of his listeners. "But I still don't understand how it could have been added to the wine. Three or four pills—"

"It wasn't in the wine."

"What? I thought we agreed—"

"Not at all, James. In addition to the other objections, there wasn't time for the poison to work. Dubretta collapsed within minutes of drinking her wine. Even in her condition, it wouldn't have taken effect so quickly. The tablet I gave her didn't affect her either; digitalis takes some time to be absorbed, unlike nitroglycerin and other preparations which are put under the victim's tongue and which act almost immediately.

"The business of the sediment in the first glass of wine distracted me," Jacqueline went on. "It was so delightfully suggestive. But that's all it was—a suggestion, a distraction. Dubretta got the poison earlier in the evening, from a drink someone had bought for her. She had a glass in her hand when I met her, and she said it was her third. She also said she never had to buy her own drinks, implying that someone else had given her the one she had. You all know how the system worked. There were long lines at each of the temporary bar tables. If someone was buying Dubretta a drink, there would be no reason for her to stand in the line with the donor. Sue performed the same service for me; after she had bought the drinks she found me and gave me mine. She had plenty of time to tamper with it."

"Hey," Joe began.

"Just an example," Jacqueline said soothingly. "To show how easy it would have been for the buyer of the drink to add something to it before he or she handed it to Dubretta. Tip the pills in, mix with one of those plastic stirrers, and the job was done. Digitalis is not soluble in water, but it is soluble in alcohol."

"But that means anyone in the room could have done it," James said, still clinging doggedly to his pet theory.

"Not quite everyone. Valentine and Hattie didn't mingle with the guests. Victor was with them, in that ridiculous artificial garden, and so was the Earl. Jean was there too—but she was hiding, and it is conceivable that she could have left the garden and returned without her absence being noted. She demonstrated her ability to get over the fence."

Jean's face went pasty white. "I didn't," she squeaked. "I didn't do it. I never saw her till she . . . Oh my God!"

Jacqueline let her stew in her own terror for a few agonized seconds before relenting. "No, you didn't. Some people discount motive as unimportant in a case of this kind, but it can't be dismissed. You had no reason to kill Dubretta. She wasn't the only person who knew your true identity. And even though you act like a first-class twit at times, you aren't insane enough to kill to protect your anonymity."

"I was wearing a wig like Jean's," Betsy said. "And I was hanging around that corner of the garden. You saw me."

"Don't try to get in the spotlight," Jacqueline said rudely. "Haven't you been listening? The poison was not in the wine. You might have bought Dubretta a drink, but your motive was even less compelling than Jean's. You had none."

"How do you know?" Betsy tried to look sinister.

"Oh, shut up, Betsy." Jacqueline's eyes moved on. "Sue? She had the opportunity, but she had no reason to kill Dubretta. Victor? His motive was stronger than Jean's. Like hers, his true identity was no secret, but unlike her, he should not have been so easily intimidated by Hattie's threats. I speculated about a criminal past, but . . ."

"He's clean," said O'Brien. He had been silent so long that the brief announcement had the effect of a shout. The listeners' heads turned as if on a single pivot; and on the one face Jacqueline was watching another flash of uneasiness came and went.

O'Brien went on, "A couple of drug busts. Possession, not dealing. One drunk and disorderly, a DWI—five years ago, in Wisconsin. The usual."

"My God," Joe gasped. "Sue, that was a long time ago. I never—"

"It's all right, darling." Sue patted his hand. She glared at Jacqueline, a mother tiger protecting her cub. "You said Joe was in the clear. He never left the garden."

"Just bringing out a couple of other points that needed to be mentioned," Jacqueline said. "Hattie's hold over Joe was only a contract, plus a meaningless threat no one but an idiot would have taken seriously. Joe didn't commit this crime. It was carefully planned and brilliantly executed. He hasn't the brains."

Sue looked even more outraged. "What's all this about threats?" Hattie exclaimed. "I never threatened anybody."

"Hattie. Dear old Aunt Hattie." Jacqueline's voice was a throaty purr. She owed Hattie a few minutes of terror, and it wouldn't do any harm to establish, at the outset of the lucrative partnership she was contemplating, that she could play rough too. She went on, "Dubretta did not accuse Sue. She didn't mention a name. What she said was, 'Blue.' I don't blame myself for failing to spot that, because it is a rare and seldom-mentioned side effect of digitalis poisoning. The drug often affects the vision, but most people see everything as yellow. Occasionally they see blue instead.

"You had the most compelling motive of all to kill Dubretta. She hated you, not only for your low-down tricks, but for a more personal reason. You know what it is, and I know what it is." Jacqueline hesitated. O'Brien had returned to his rapt contemplation of the ceiling. Jacqueline said, "And there's no reason for anyone else to know what it is. She was out to get you, Hattie, and by God, she did."

"I didn't kill her," Hattie stammered. "You know damned well I didn't. I never left the garden."

"I know." Jacqueline sounded regretful. "And that

only leaves one person." Her gaze moved to the chubby little man who sat watching her with a faint smile on his lips. "Everybody overlooks you, don't they, Max? As you yourself once said, you are not a conspicuous person. It's a useful characteristic for a murderer."

Max's face did not change. "Is this the moment? Do I now rise and admit my guilt, before swallowing the cyanide pill I have in my pocket? I'm sorry, Mrs. Kirby. You have a first-rate imagination. I'm looking forward to reading your book."

"You were mingling," Jacqueline said. "I saw you among the other guests earlier in the evening. You could have bought Dubretta a drink, and she'd have taken it from you. She might have been suspicious of anything Hattie offered her."

"Might, could," Max repeated. "I and a hundred other people. If I had encountered Dubretta during my mingling, I might well have offered her something to drink. However, I didn't happen to see her until she joined us in the garden."

"You shouldn't have said that, Max. It's one of the few damaging admissions you've made. You did see Dubretta earlier that evening. Remember her corsage—the one that was a deliberate take-off on Hattie's? She told me I was only the second person who had caught the joke. You were the first. You'd not miss the humor of it. Dubretta lost the corsage before we went to the garden. It was knocked off, and stepped on, so she put it in her purse. She wasn't wearing it when we joined you, but she was holding her purse against her chest, so you didn't realize it was gone. During our conversation just before the wine was poured you mentioned it. So you must have seen it earlier."

Max's smile broadened. "I must have, mustn't I?"

He had spotted the weakness in the argument, as Jacqueline had feared he would; and having made one verbal slip, he was not about to make another by talking too much.

Jacqueline tried again. "I fixed on you as the killer early in my investigation, Max. Not only were you the only suspect who had both motive and opportunity, but you're the only one with the intelligence to have planned a crime with so many built-in safeguards. You hoped Dubretta's death would be written off as heart failure, which in fact it was. But if someone had suspected the truth and looked for traces of the drug, your second line of defense would have come into play—an accidental overdose. It was her own medication, after all, and she was notoriously careless about taking it. If that failed, you had a third line of defense in Laurie. She had given you the pills you used. She trusted you; in her eyes you were an extension of Valentine, and I think you were moved by genuine concern when you first saw her take the tablets and asked her what they were. You may even have warned her of the danger and advised her not to take them. Did you persuade her to give them to you, or did you just steal a few? It wouldn't have been difficult; she was in a fog a good deal of the time."

"Poor girl." Max shook his head sadly.

"Poor girl indeed. I don't know how she got the digitalis; she was a city girl born and bred and she knew all the tricks. But if the medication could be traced, it would be traced to her, and she had a strong, if irrational, motive for killing Dubretta. She had become so mentally confused, she may even have believed she did commit the crime.

"You didn't plan to kill Laurie," Jacqueline said; but there was no sympathy in her voice, only remorseless condemnation. "The original scheme went wrong on two counts. First, I became involved, and you knew I would not be easily dissuaded from my suspicions. Second, and more important, you and Hattie got your wires crossed over the problem of Dubretta's missing notebook. You both wanted it. You both realized it could be dangerous. But it was Hattie's idea to send Laurie out looking for it. Why not? She'd had the girl running her other errands. You wouldn't have done anything so foolish. You knew Laurie was unreliable and might run amok. She did; and the police were called in. If Laurie were found alive she'd receive medical attention, and it wouldn't be difficult for a doctor to diagnose what was wrong with her—especially if she had a digitalis preparation on her person. Once cured, she might talk. With me— and," Jacqueline added, nodding graciously at O'Brien, "the police on the trail, you couldn't take that chance."

Hattie jumped up. "You can't pin that on me. I never told that girl to attack people."

Jacqueline's self-control slipped. She rounded on Hattie. "You're responsible for Laurie's death too. You used her, without concern for her condition or her illness. Why did you want the notebook, Hattie? What did Dubretta find out?"

"I don't know." Hattie's eyes shifted. She sank back into her seat. "I never had the damned notebook."

"But I know." Jacqueline paused, not only for effect, but to take a deep, steadying breath. She was approaching a crucial point, the confrontation on which her hope of solving the case depended.

"Motive," she said. "Always motive, and always it seemed inadequate. Unless Dubretta had uncovered evidence of criminal activities, her discoveries didn't constitute a serious threat. It wouldn't hurt you, Hattie, if the word got out that two of your top writers were frauds—that Victor von Damm was a pretty paper doll and Valerie Vanderbilt a timid schoolteacher instead of a decadent aristocrat. A few people might laugh; some would refuse to believe it; most would shrug and go right on buying books. But suppose Dubretta learned that everything you did was a sham? That not a single one of your top writers was what you had represented them to be? That Valerie Valentine, Queen of Love, was an even bigger fake than the others? Not only would her readers resent it, but her publishers would be extremely upset. Publishers are very sensitive to ridicule. And this particular scam was more than ridiculous—it was the funniest joke of the year."

Hattie's face turned an alarming shade of purple. Max got up, quickly and quietly, and crossed to Valentine, who was slumped half asleep in her chair. "Don't worry, Val," he said. "It's all right."

"She's not Valerie Valentine," Jacqueline said. "You are. You, Max. You wrote those books. And that's what makes the joke so poisonously funny. If Hattie hadn't set up a figurehead who was so spectacularly beautiful—

if the novels weren't so sensitive and so brilliantly written . . . The contrast is just too much. Dubretta was a superb satirist; she could have had the whole world holding its sides."

"Sensitive and brilliant," Max murmured. "You give me too much credit, Mrs. Kirby."

"Anyone who talked to either of you for five minutes would know," Jacqueline said. "You and Hattie controlled Valentine's public appearances. She could memorize brief speeches and conventional responses. People always ask writers the same inane questions: 'How did you become a writer, Miss Valentine?' 'Where do you get your ideas, Miss Valentine?' Many authors write more fluently than they speak; many are inarticulate and retiring. But no writer could produce a book like *A Willow in Her Hand,* and fail to recognize a quotation from *the same speech in the same play.* I asked Valentine what she thought of 'Come Again to Carthage' as a title. She said it wouldn't sell."

"It wouldn't," Max said, still faintly smiling.

"Maybe not. But *A Willow in Her Hand* isn't your average romance title either. It wasn't selected by Valentine's publisher. As Jean and Sue and other unfortunate writers know, publishers want juicy references to love and lust, not literary quotations. *A Willow in Her Hand* is a perfect title for that book. It comes from a speech in *The Merchant of Venice,* which describes Dido trying to charm her wayward lover back again to Carthage. If Valentine had recognized my quote, she would have made some comment, some reference to her own book. She didn't. But you know the play well, Max. Were you challenging me when you quoted the passage about sitting on a bank and listening to sweet music?"

"You are very clever, Mrs. Kirby," Max said tranquilly. "But you cannot prove it."

"I don't have to prove it. Once you're arrested for murder, the literary fraud won't matter. Your motive was as strong as Hattie's—stronger, because your feelings for Valentine are as violent and perverse as Laurie's were. You've fallen in love with your Galatea, the image you and Hattie created to assume the role of Valerie Valentine, and if the truth came out you'd lose her. She's in it for the money. She's not going to stick her neck out for you. You're in trouble, Max, and when your little friend gets that fact through her beautiful thick skull, she'll walk out on you."

Max's smile didn't change. He stroked Valentine's hand. "Would you leave me, Val? You wouldn't desert old Max, would you?"

"No," Valentine said. "I don't understand, Max. She can't prove any of that stuff, can she?"

"Of course not, darling."

Valentine yawned. "This is boring. Even more boring than that stupid ball. I don't want to go back down there. I want to go to bed."

Jacqueline glanced uneasily at O'Brien. He shook his head. There was no way in which Max could have drugged the girl, at least not after the ball began. When O'Brien had moved to prevent Max from getting her something to drink, Jacqueline had known he shared her foreboding—that Valentine might be Max's third victim. They had both been carried away by the general aura of romantic balderdash. Val was in no danger.

Jacqueline's heart sank. She had counted on Valentine to turn on Max once she realized their secret was known; but the girl had been under Max's influence for so long that it was almost impossible for an outsider to override his authority. And Valentine's consummate stupidity rendered her incapable of understanding how her position could be threatened.

Seeing the derisive gleam in O'Brien's eyes, Jacqueline rallied and returned gamely to the attack. "You won't have to be Valerie Valentine any longer . . . what is your name?"

Max laughed aloud. "My dear Mrs. Kirby, you don't suppose anyone was really christened Valerie Valentine, do you? We've never tried to conceal Val's real name. But I think I'll let you track it down for yourself, since you're so determined to play detective."

The others sat watching like spectators at a Pinter play, half fascinated, half uncomprehending. Jacqueline glanced again at O'Brien. She expected to see that he was enjoying her discomfiture. Instead O'Brien nodded, almost imperceptibly, and said, "Her name is Marilyn Hicks. She was born in Monmouth, Oregon. Left home when she was fifteen. Was on the road for a few years; turned up in Jersey five years ago."

He paused, and Jacqueline took up the story. "Where Hattie found her when she was looking for someone to play Valerie Valentine. Hattie had received Max's manuscript and recognized its potential, but when she met Max she realized he'd never go over as a romance writer. It was the same technique she's always used; we should have suspected that Valentine was her first and most effective use of the glamour angle.

"The partnership worked well. Since it was necessary to keep Valentine in relative seclusion, for fear she'd open her mouth and betray the fact that she never could have written the books, she and Max kept pretty much to themselves. Val couldn't be trusted to be out on her own, and she didn't object to the arrangement. For the first time in her life she had enough money to buy beautiful clothes and all the luxuries she wanted. That was all she wanted. She isn't . . ." Jacqueline hesitated, not out of prudery, but because it wasn't easy to explain Valentine's problem. "She isn't . . . capable of feeling. It's not only sexual frigidity, it's an absence of any kind of warmth. I've noticed several times during this case the disparity between people's true natures and the false impressions created by their physical appearances. Joe looks like Victor von Damm, but their personalities aren't at all alike. Valentine is so beautiful people think of her as warm and loving and sensual. Yet over and over again she demonstrated her essential coldness. I have never heard her express interest in, or concern for, anyone but herself. For Max, however, she became everything he had ever dreamed of in a woman. Max is a romantic; his books prove that. He saw in Valentine only what he wanted to see, as foolish men have done through the ages.

"Valentine was content with the status quo until the conference began. Then the adulation and adoration went to her head. She decided to ask for a bigger cut of the profits. That is the explanation behind her seemingly inexplicable about-face after she claimed someone had tried to kill her. It was not a very intelli-

gent plan; but Valentine isn't very intelligent. She put
the screws on Max and Hattie, and Hattie blew up.
Hattie doesn't like being blackmailed; she prefers to
be on the other end of the process. Then Dubretta
died. I think," Jacqueline said, watching Valentine's
lovely vacuous face, "Valentine was genuinely frightened that night. She's not that good an actress. She
was afraid she had pushed Hattie too far. Having
heard from Jean of my reputed detective talents, she
demanded my help. She didn't want the police; she
only wanted an impartial outsider to think she had
been threatened."

"That's nonsense," Max said. "Isn't it, Val?"

"Yes, Max."

"So you came to terms," Jacqueline said. "You convinced Valentine her fears were groundless and you increased her wages. She retracted her accusations. How
much of a raise did you get, Valentine?"

"I don't know what you mean," Valentine said.

It wasn't working. Jacqueline could have shouted
with frustration. There was only one card left to play.
She took it from her purse—a worn stenographer's
notepad with a red cover.

The look on Max's face confirmed her last lingering
doubt—for in spite of her pronouncements she had
begun to wonder whether, after all, she had been mistaken. But before Max could speak, James blurted out,
"I thought it was stolen from you."

Jacqueline froze him with a look as devastating as
Medusa's glare. Max relaxed. "I thought so too."

"Did you?" Jacqueline pointed an accusing finger.
"How did you get that idea? I never told you."

"Why . . . Laurie mentioned it. When she called last night."

"Laurie never had it," O'Brien said.

Again his audience jumped nervously. Jacqueline took up the dialogue without a pause. "The one I was carrying the other day was a dummy. You don't suppose I would be stupid enough to risk the real notebook?"

Max's smile faded. Jacqueline's flagging hopes began to rise. But before she or O'Brien could continue the inquisition, Betsy said, "That can't be Dubretta's."

"Shut up, Betsy," Jacqueline said between her teeth.

"No, but it can't," Betsy insisted. "Was that what the poor crazy kid was after—Dubretta's notebook? You never told me."

"You never asked. Betsy, would you mind—"

"It's a good thing I didn't have it in my knapsack that day," Betsy went on obliviously. "It was upstairs in my desk drawer. Imagine that. I was going to tell Dubretta at the cocktail party that she'd forgotten it, but I never had the chance to talk to her, and after that I forgot about it, since I assumed nobody—"

For once in her life Jacqueline was incapable of speech. It was O'Brien who interrupted Betsy with a muffled roar. "Ms. Markham!"

"You don't have to yell," Betsy said, hurt.

"Where," said O'Brien in a slow tight voice, "where did you get Dubretta's notebook?"

"It was the night of the protest march. We were having a few drinks—you remember, Jake, you introduced us. You saw her taking notes."

"Urk," said Jacqueline feebly. She had just remembered something else and was mentally kicking herself.

"The notebook was almost filled," Betsy went on. "After you left, we talked some more and had a few more drinks and she took a few more notes—and filled the remaining blank pages. She had another notebook in her purse, so she took that out and wrote in it. And when she left she forgot the first one. It was on the seat between us, and you know how dark it was in there. And she was a little—well, you know."

"I know," Jacqueline muttered. The second notebook—the one she had found after Dubretta's death had had only a few used pages. She ought to know, she had copied them, at twenty cents a page. Why hadn't she realized that eighteen pages of notes might represent only one day's work for Dubretta? When the columnist realized the first book had been misplaced she had not been able to remember where she had left it.

"Where," said O'Brien, in the same measured voice, "where is the notebook now, Ms. Markham?"

"In my desk, I guess." The focus of two pairs of malevolent eyes, Betsy belatedly realized she was not popular. "Well, I didn't know," she exclaimed. "Why didn't you tell me?"

Jacqueline's rage was not mitigated by the realization that the prolonged nature of the disclosure had given Max time to recover from his initial dismay. Her only hope had been to get him rattled enough to make a damaging disclosure. It had been a forlorn hope, for he was not the man to lose his wits. And one of the weapons she had hoped to employ had failed—

Valentine. Or had it? She glanced at O'Brien and got another small but meaningful nod. Taking a deep breath,
she returned to the attack.

"The notebook contains the proof Dubretta had
found that Valerie Valentine is a fraud. The game is
over, Val. You'd better get out while you can."

"I don't know what you're talking about," Valentine
repeated.

"She's talking about a criminal charge," O'Brien said.
"As accessory to murder."

"What?" The charge, and its source, finally penetrated Valentine's stupor. "He said . . . He didn't kill
that woman. And if he did, I don't know anything
about—"

It was the first crack in her armored ignorance, and
Jacqueline pounded at it. "Not Dubretta's murder,
Valentine. Laurie's."

"The girl told you where she was, Mr. Hollenstein,"
O'Brien said. "You set up a date with her, for later that
night."

"That's a lie." Max didn't look at him. He was
watching Valentine.

"Your call to me gave an impression of candor and
helpfulness," Jacqueline continued "But you didn't tell
me what Laurie really said to you. Did Valentine over-
hear your end of that conversation? Perhaps she re-
members your telling Laurie when and where to meet
you."

"I don't—" Valentine began.

"Under interrogation your memory may improve,"
O'Brien said with a sinister sneer.

"You may also remember that Max went out later that night," Jacqueline said.

"Your failure to tell me that leaves you open to a charge of accessory after the fact," O'Brien said, his eyes on Valentine.

"But I didn't think it was important!" She spun up and away, eluding Max's grasp with the flowing elfin grace that marked her movements. She hesitated for only an instant before throwing herself at Jacqueline. "Don't let him touch me!"

"He's got a gun," Jacqueline yelled, reeling from the impact of Valentine's body. The purse she had been about to throw at Max fell from her hand.

"Thanks a lot," said O'Brien. Max's automatic was pointed at him. The little man stepped back so that he could also cover Valentine, who had gotten behind Jacqueline.

"It's nothing to do with me," she gasped. "I didn't know anything about it. He said he had to meet a friend. . . ."

"Get away from her, Mrs. Kirby," Max said. "I don't want to hurt you, even though you are responsible for bringing this about."

The significance of his formality had not escaped Jacqueline. She made an attempt to reestablish the rapport they had shared. "Don't do it, Max. There are ways of escape for you, and God knows you're intelligent enough and wealthy enough to take advantage of them. But if you shoot someone in plain sight of all these witnesses—"

"I thought you would understand," Max said reproachfully. "How can I betray the classic demands of romantic tragedy? 'For each man kills the thing he loves. . . .' I have to kill her now. If you don't get out of the way, I'll put a bullet through both of you."

Jacqueline felt the full weight of the girl's slight body pressing against hers. Valentine was whimpering. "Don't, don't let him—please—"

"Oh hell," she said. "Max, you know I can't do that. She's a worthless little tramp, but I have a reputation to maintain too. Besides, she's stuck to me like a tick on a dog."

"I'm sorry," Max said simply. His finger tightened on the trigger.

Jacqueline's eyes narrowed angrily. "Do something, somebody! Why are you all sitting there like a gaggle of geese?"

Joe shook off Sue's clinging hands and rose. "I don't know what to do," he said uncertainly, fingering the hilt of his ceremonial sword.

James removed Jean's clutching hands and rose. "We'll all advance on him simultaneously," he suggested.

Max seemed more amused than alarmed by these manifestations of uneasy bravado, but the movements of the men distracted him enough to enable O'Brien to reach the gun concealed in the folds of the coat in which he had been sweltering all evening.

"Now it's a standoff," he said coolly. "Suppose you just drop it, Hollenstein. I can fire before you can."

"I'm not sure about that," Max said. "I wonder if Mrs. Kirby wants to take the chance."

"Shoot him!" Jean shrieked suddenly. "Shoot him,

shoot him, shoot—" James clapped his hand over her mouth. Then Betsy, who had been brooding in resentful silence, decided to take a hand. She arose with her ear-splitting kung-fu yell. Max's gun went off. Jacqueline dropped to the floor, pulling Valentine with her. O'Brien's first shot hit Max in the thigh and dropped him, but he did not lose his grasp of the gun. A rattling barrage went off as he emptied the magazine.

The silence thereafter was deafening. Betsy was the first to raise a cautious head from behind the overstuffed chair where she had taken refuge. Victor lay flat, his body shielding Sue. Jean had tugged James down on top of her; he was sitting on her lap, pinned by her arms. For the first time in her life Hattie had behaved like a southern lady. She had fainted.

O'Brien pounced on Max's gun, checked to make sure it was empty, and threw it across the room. One of the random shots had plowed a path through his hair, and blood streamed down his cheek. He flung aside the table under whose inadequate shelter Jacqueline and Valentine were huddled in a confusing tangle of arms and legs. O'Brien had to pry the girl's hands from Jacqueline before he could lift the latter from the floor. Her eyes were closed and her knees buckled when he tried to set her on her feet. He shook her till her loosened hair flew out in a wild tangle.

"Are you all right? Why didn't you tell me he had a gun? Where did he hit you? God damn it, say something!"

Jacqueline's eyes opened. They were as soft and green as spring grass. "I will—if you stop—shaking me."

Mutely, O'Brien complied with her request. Jacqueline surveyed the scene and nodded. She reached for her purse. "Patrick, you're bleeding all over your costume. Here. Have a tissue."

Chapter 10

James sprawled across the bed watching Jacqueline pack.

"I don't see why you have to go to Connecticut," he said sulkily. "Now that the other business is settled, we could have a good time."

"I couldn't enjoy myself when a sick friend needs me." Jacqueline's voice dripped with sanctimonious virtue, but there was a not-so-virtuous gleam in her green eyes as she folded a roll of pleated turquoise silk into her suitcase. It aroused in James a vague, faintly unpleasant sense of familiarity, which he decided not to pursue.

He picked up one of the newspapers that lay scattered on the bed. "I wonder if the story will make the Coldwater *Chronicle*," he said uneasily.

"I hope—I mean, I imagine it will. What are you worried about? Your name is barely mentioned."

"The same can't be said about yours. And your picture is plastered all over the place. 'Mrs. Kirby with Hattie Foster—Mrs. Kirby with Valentine, AKA Mari-

lyn Hicks; Mrs. Kirby with Joe Kirby, AKA Victor von
Damm. . . .' And with O'Brien." James's frown deepened. "That's a disgusting picture, Jacqueline. Why did
you let him hug you?"

"Hug? Hug?" Jacqueline glared at him. "If you can't
tell a hug from a supporting arm, you ought to be
ashamed of yourself."

"You didn't need support."

"O'Brien did. That was a nasty wound."

"A mere scratch."

"You're just jealous because you didn't get to play
hero."

"Well, I would have if I'd been given the chance.
You lied to me, Jacqueline. If I had known what you
were planning—"

"You had all the necessary information, James.
Good heavens, I practically spoon-fed you the facts
about Valentine's impersonation of a writer. An English professor should have spotted that after two minutes' conversation with the little nitwit. But that's just
like a man. You all go goofy over a pretty face."

"I'm not referring to that aspect of the case," James
growled. "What about the digitalis?"

"I didn't figure that out myself until after your
chemist friend had tested for other substances."

"Oh. Well, but damn it, Jacqueline, if you didn't actually lie, you misled me about practically everything
else. All that nonsense about Jean being a suspect and
you being the third victim—"

"I almost was, wasn't I? I couldn't be completely
honest, James. It was touch and go up to the final seconds. I had no proof. Even when Betsy popped up with

her news about the notebook (really, I wonder about Betsy sometimes), we were no better off. There was nothing in Dubretta's notes except information we already knew."

"We?" James's voice was sarcastic.

"O'Brien got it from the same sources Dubretta had used—a former secretary of Hattie's who resented her ex-boss, the firm Valentine had worked for as a—er—model, and so on. I deduced the same facts by literary means."

"But you didn't bother informing me."

"James, the information was useless. It did suggest a possible motive, but as those of us who specialize in criminal investigation know, motive is the least important part of a case. And in this case the motive was extremely complex, involving the subtleties of Max's relationship with Valentine. I was sure Max had committed the murder, once I realized the poison could not have been in the wine. He did everything he could to strengthen that false assumption, and to confuse the issue. In fact, he was almost the only one of our suspects who could have poisoned Dubretta. But without proof I had to bludgeon him into confessing, and the only weapon I had was his fear that he would lose Valentine."

"What will become of her, I wonder," James mused.

"James, you sentimental idiot, Valerie Valentine is a millionaire. Max will probably go on managing her money from Sing Sing, or wherever he ends up. He may even get off with assault or attempted murder. A clever lawyer can make hash of O'Brien's case unless it is properly presented."

"And Hattie Foster is getting off scot-free," James said. "The way she used that girl was criminal, but she'll never be charged for it. She's lost Valentine, but she still has Valerie Vanderbilt, or a reasonable substitute, and Victor von Damm."

"I have a few ideas in mind for her." If Hattie had seen Jacqueline's expression, she would have felt a cold shudder run up her spine.

Jacqueline straightened. "I think that's everything."

"You forgot your robe."

"Oh, that." Jacqueline rolled it into a ball and slam-dunked it into the wastebasket.

"What are you doing? I'm very fond of that robe."

"I'm not. I bought a new one." She lifted it from the suitcase and held it up.

After an unsuccessful marriage and a series of more or less successful love affairs James knew enough about women's clothes to estimate the price of the gleaming amber satin. "I thought you were broke," he said.

"I'm expecting to come into a large sum of money very soon," Jacqueline said. Tenderly she folded the robe back into her suitcase.

"Oh, that reminds me." James's voice took on its Granny Jimmy tone. "Tom Blackstone has registered for classes this fall. Last May he told me he'd have to quit school now that student aid has been so drastically reduced."

"Oh, really."

"He's rather a pet of yours, isn't he?"

"He shelves books at the library."

"He's a bright kid. I'm glad he managed to find the money. I wonder where?"

Jacqueline did not reply. Satisfied that his deductions were correct, James attacked from another angle. "Has the sick friend made you her heir?"

"Really, James, you have a mind like a sink," Jacqueline said disapprovingly. "I do not expect to inherit money, I expect to earn it. Hattie Foster is going to handle my book. And," she added, with a snap of even white teeth, "there won't be any twenty-five percent commissions in that deal, either."

"You weren't kidding about the book!"

"There it is, doubting Thomas." Jacqueline indicated the notebook on the bedside table. "I've only finished six chapters, but I expect to receive a sizable advance."

"Mind if I look at it?"

"You know I always welcome constructive criticism, James."

James reflected that this was probably the biggest lie she had told yet. He reached for *Lust Among the Savages* (working title).

Jacqueline scanned the room. Closet, bathroom, under the bed . . . A stifled sound from James made her turn sharply. His chuckle developed into a hearty guffaw.

"James!" she cried indignantly.

Her colleague looked up from the pages of the notebook. He was smiling. "I hate to admit it, but this is great," he said. "Funniest damned thing I've read all year.".

"Funniest?"

"A devastating satire," James said admiringly. "I knew you had a vicious tongue, but this—this is literature. The part where Oona catches Lurgh sneaking up on her while she's bathing in the stream . . ." His eyes returned to the book. He let out another chuckle.

Jacqueline stood staring at him, her eyes shooting out green sparks, her body rigid with fury. The telephone rang. She reached for it. James paid no attention.

"Yes?" Jacqueline said. James chuckled. "Come on up," Jacqueline said. James chortled. "I know I did, but I've changed my mind. Come up." James shook with laughter.

"I'll leave my manuscript with you, since you seem to be relishing it," she said gently. "You won't forget to bring it back to Coldwater, will you?"

"No, no," James said abstractedly. He let out a gurgle of mirth.

There was a knock at the door. Jacqueline went to answer it. James went on reading and chuckling.

"You ready, Jackie?"

"Yes, I'm ready. My suitcase was heavier than I expected. If you don't mind . . ."

"I don't mind." What followed was not silence, only a cessation of speech. Certain sounds could be heard.

James's grin froze. He looked up from *Lust Among the Savages.* "Jackie?" he said incredulously.

O'Brien came in. He wore a charcoal-gray suit with a scarlet tie. His socks were black. Passing his handkerchief over his mouth, he said, "Hi, Professor."

"Hi," James said. "Jackie?"

"Yes, James?" Jacqueline smiled at him.

"I wasn't talking to you," James said.

O'Brien picked up Jacqueline's suitcase. "So long, Professor. It's been nice knowing you."

"Good-bye, James. Thanks for all your help."

The door closed, but not before James heard a soft murmur of laughter from Jacqueline—intimate, tender, mocking laughter.

He hurled *Lust Among the Savages* across the room. It hit the wall and fell fluttering to the floor like a wounded bird.

Jacqueline had never allowed him to call her Jackie. She hated nicknames.

"That two-faced, double-crossing, cheating . . ." James cried aloud.

He sat brooding for a time. Gradually his face cleared. His comments on Jacqueline's manuscript had apparently annoyed his beloved—and his beloved she still was, despite the fact that she was two-faced, double-crossing, and cheating. She was certainly the best Coldwater, Nebraska, had to offer. The book promised considerable scope for harassment over the months to come, and the new mystery of Jacqueline's sudden affluence was yet to be explored.

James smiled his famous crooked smile. He'd lost this round, but the war wasn't over. Rising, he retrieved *Lust Among the Savages*.

"The last thing Oona remembered was the great wave crashing down on her frail canoe. Luga the sea god had taken his revenge upon the puny mortal who had dared end his cruel and sadistic worship. But the Goddess must have intervened to save her priestess. Instead of the icy waters of Luga's cold domain, warm air stroked her voluptuous unclothed body. She heard the soft sound of waves lapping gently on a sandy shore. Her long, curling lashes were sticky with saltwater. Lifting a languid hand, she rubbed them and opened her eyes.

"Standing over her was a man—if he was a mere mortal, and not a god. Luga himself, come to complete his revenge upon her helpless nakedness? Water dripped from his shoulder-length golden hair and formed a shining film over his broad, muscled chest, tanned to a glowing bronze. His eyes were the deep gray-blue of the stormy sea. They moved slowly and deliberately over her, from her rounded white shoulders to the blue-veined globes of her heaving breasts, down to . . ."

James giggled.

Turn the page for a look inside the wonderful world of Elizabeth Peters . . .

THE CAMELOT CAPER

For Jessica Tregarth, an unexpected invitation to visit her grandfather in England is a wonderful surprise—an opportunity to open doors to a family past that has always been closed to her. But sinister acts greet her arrival. A stranger tries to steal her luggage and later accosts her in Salisbury Cathedral. Mysterious villains pursue her through Cornwall, their motive and intentions unknown. Jessica's only clue is an antique heirloom she possesses, an ancient ring that bears the Tregarth family crest. And her only ally is handsome gothic novelist David Randall—her self-proclaimed protector—who appears from seemingly out of nowhere to help her in her desperate attempt to solve a five-hundred-year-old puzzle. For something from out of the cloudy mists of Arthurian lore has come back to plague a frightened American abroad. And a remarkable truth about a fabled king and a medieval treasure could make Jessica Tregarth very rich . . . or very dead.

"Gothica in the irreverent trappings I like best."
New York Times Book Review

SUMMER OF THE DRAGON

———

A good salary and an all-expenses-paid summer spent on a sprawling Arizona ranch is too good a deal for fledgling anthropologist D.J. Abbott to turn down. What does it matter that her rich new employer/benefactor, Hank Hunnicutt, is a certified oddball who is presently funding all manner of offbeat projects, from alien conspiracy studies to a hunt for dragon bones? There's even talk of treasure buried in the nearby mountains, but D.J. isn't going to allow loose speculation—or the considerable charms of handsome professional treasure hunter Jesse Franklin—to sidetrack her. Until Hunnicutt suffers a mysterious accident and then vanishes, leaving the weirdos gathered at his spread to eye each other with frightened suspicion. But on a high desert search for the missing millionaire, D.J. is learning things that may not be healthy for her to know. For the game someone is playing here goes far beyond the rational universe— and it could leave D.J. legitimately dead.

———

"No one is better at juggling torches while dancing on a high wire than Elizabeth Peters."
Chicago Tribune

350

THE LOVE TALKER

Laurie has finally returned to Idlewood, the beloved family home deep in the Maryland woods where she found comfort and peace as a lonely young girl. But things are very different now. There is no peace in Idlewood. The haunting sound of distant piping breaks the stillness of a snowy winter's evening. Seemingly random events have begun to take on a sinister shape. And dotty old Great Aunt Lizzie is convinced that there are fairies about—and she has photographs to prove it. For Laurie, one fact is becoming disturbingly clear: there is definitely *something* out there in the woods—something fiendishly, cunningly, malevolently human—and the lives of her aging loved ones, as well as Laurie's own, are suddenly at risk.

"[Peters] keeps the reader coming back for more."
San Francisco Chronicle

THE DEAD SEA CIPHER

Opera singer Dinah van der Lyn is trying to soak up a little history between singing engagements on her tour of the Middle East. But when she hears cries for help through her hotel room wall—cries uttered in English despite the fact that there are few Americans at the Beirut hotel where she is staying—she knows that something sinister is afoot. The police are at first dubious of her suspicions of foul play. After all, as the granddaughter of a rabbi and the daughter of a minister, her politics may be questionable. But as she travels through the fabled cities of Sidon, Tyre, Damascus, and Jerusalem pursued by a handsome government agent and a mysterious Biblical scholar, she begins to fear that she may not be safe in this most holy of places—instead, she may be heading straight into a deadly trap.

"Danger and romance. Excellent."
San Francisco Chronicle

DEVIL MAY CARE

It is the beginning of the best of times for Ellie—she is young, happy, rich, and soon to be married. Ready to spend two weeks house-sitting her eccentric Aunt Kate's Virginia mansion, she is looking forward to a quiet vacation in the secluded, cat-filled home. But when a mysterious apparition pays a visit late one night, she knows her peaceful time away will be anything but. For Ellie fears that a book she found in an antiquarian shop—a book she intended to be a special gift for her aunt—has revealed some long-buried secrets of the town's upper class. And as mysterious visitors begin to pay visits to the home, Ellie starts to worry whether the town aristocracy wants to keep these secrets hidden . . .

"Elizabeth Peters is wickedly clever.
[Her] women are smart, strong, bold, cunning,
and highly educated, just like herself."
San Diego Reader

THE COPENHAGEN CONNECTION

Elizabeth Jones never expected to spot her idol, Nobel Prize-winning historian Margaret Rosenberg, at the Copenhagen Airport. And after the esteemed scholar's secretary is injured, Elizabeth is even more shocked to learn that Rosenberg wants to enlist her as her new assistant. Thrust into a foreign world of glamour and intrigue, Elizabeth rushes from Tivoli to the Little Mermaid in the eccentric historian's wake. But when kidnappers take Rosenberg, leaving only a mysterious ransom note, it's up to Elizabeth and her employer's rude and surly—yet devastatingly handsome—son to locate her. Through restaurants, down dark alleys, and deep into the cave-ridden countryside, the duo are caught in a deadly game of chase and they may be the kidnappers' next targets.

"Elizabeth Peters' many fans can count on her for romantic mysteries, full of action and suspense, and *The Copenhagen Connection* is no exception."
Publishers Weekly

THE JACKAL'S HEAD

Althea "Tommy" Tomlinson claimed she came to Egypt as just another tourist, traveling around the country in the company of her spoiled seventeen-year-old charge. But what really drove her was a burning desire to discover the truth behind her father's disgrace and subsequent death ten years before. She had known something was terribly wrong—but what? Finding out might clear her father's name, but it could also prove to be perilous. For the secrets buried deep in the sands of the desert were as old as the treasure of Nefertiti . . . and unearthing them could result in one of the greatest archaeological discoveries ever . . . or lead to her own death.

"Elizabeth Peters is truly great."
San Francisco Chronicle

LEGEND IN GREEN VELVET

From kilts to bagpipes to the windswept hills, archaeology student Susan loves all things Scottish. So when she is offered the opportunity to go to a dig in the Scottish Highlands for the summer, there is no question in her mind that it's a dream come true. But after a strange and sinister soap box orator slips her a cryptic message in Edinburgh, and when her room is looted immediately afterward, Susan suspects that she holds a secret that someone would stop at nothing to get their hands on. But who has set their sights on her? And when she and the handsome young laird Jamie Erskine are pursued by the police, who want to speak with them about a mysterious murder, it's up to the fledgling archaeologist to get to the bottom of the crime. Here's another kick-up-your-heels tale of mystery and suspense from one of the world's most beloved writers.

"This is Peters at the top of her form."
Austin American-Statesman

THE NIGHT OF
FOUR HUNDRED RABBITS

————

Christmas is supposed to be a time of family, presents under the tree, and fond memories. But for college student Carol Farley, her most surprising gift is contained in an envelope waiting in her room, an anonymously sent piece of mail containing a newspaper clipping. Blurred, but recognizable, it's a picture of her missing father, and for the first time in years, Carol senses that he may still be alive. And when several other anonymous letters provide clues that he may be living in Mexico, Carol decides that someone wants her to fly south to find him. As the pyramids of Mexico's Walk of the Dead tower above and around her, their beauty is shrouded in the terror they suddenly hold for the young American. For the person who sent her to look for her father may not be her only enemy . . .

————

"A thriller."
Fresno Bee

The Vicky Bliss Mysteries by
New York Times Bestselling Author

ELIZABETH PETERS

TROJAN GOLD
0-380-73123-1/$6.99 US/$9.99 Can
"Wit, charm, and romance in equal measures."
San Diego Union

SILHOUETTE IN SCARLET
0-380-73337-4/$6.99 US/$9.99 Can
"No one is better at juggling torches while dancing
on a high wire than Elizabeth Peters."
Chicago Tribune

STREET OF THE FIVE MOONS
0-380-73121-5/$6.99 US/$9.99 Can
"This author never fails to entertain."
Cleveland Plain Dealer

BORROWER OF THE NIGHT
0-380-73339-0/$6.99 US/$9.99 Can
"A writer so popular the public library
needs to keep her books under lock and key."
Washington Post Book World